Praise for *The Feasting Virgin*

"Whether you're Greek or otherwise, anyone who's been fed on cultural identity since birth will be totally enthralled by Georgia Kolias's funny-yet-heartfelt, timely, and deliciously sensual debut novel. You need to read it. It will make you hungry, in many unexpected ways."

—Patricia V. Davis, author of *The Secret Spice Trilogy* and *Harlot's Sauce*

"*The Feasting Virgin* is a sensuous love letter to Greek food that will surely make you hungry. Through sexy cooking scenes and authentic recipes, Georgia Kolias brings the magic of food to life, showing how the heat of the kitchen can bring even the unlikeliest of pairings together. This novel teaches us to respect the origins of our food, encourages us to be our true selves, and celebrates the ultimate power of love."

—Michele Ragussis, Celebrity Chef and *Food Network Star* finalist

"*The Feasting Virgin* is a miracle! I laughed and I cried! This is Greek womanish storytelling—gutsy, magical, wise, funny, passionate, and immersed in the irresistible smells and flavors of a good Greek kitchen. In the crucible of Kolias' imagination, tradition, and even the most painful memories, can become ingredients for something altogether wondrous and new."

—Helen Klonaris, author of *If I Had the Wings*

"*The Feasting Virgin* is wildly inventive, both moving and hilarious, and full of delicious surprise."

—Nina Schuyler, author of *The Translator*, *The Painting*, and *How to Write Stunning Sentences*

"*The Feasting Virgin* is fresh, sizzlingly comic and tender at the bone. Plumbing the kind of longing that tr͏ ͏ ͏ ͏ ͏Kolias serves up every earthly delight: Greek food, (Magical and deeply real, this is the b you didn't know you were missing."

—H

"A sensuous, delightful banquet of a book with characters as irresistible as a batch of warm, sweet *loukoumathes*, dripping with honey. Georgia Kolias serves up a slice of Greek-American culture, complete with companion recipes, that is a welcome antidote to a time of anxiety."

—Julie Christine Johnson author of *In Another Life* and *The Crows of Beara*

"A beautifully wrought story told through the gaze of a woman who lightly inhabits two worlds, fully belonging in neither. With hints of magical realism, the characters fight their way through thousands of years of patriarchal bonds to try and find the perfect recipe to realize their needs, their wants, and finally, their deepest desires."

—Susan X Meagher, Award-winning author

"*The Feasting Virgin* takes its characters on an unforgettably sensual journey through yearning for the unobtainable and learning to trust our deepest desires. With layered, unforgettable characters and a clever plot twist, Georgia Kolias has tenderly rewritten the traditional Greek Family."

—Jordan Rosenfeld, author of *Women in Red* and *How to Write a Page Turner*

"*The Feasting Virgin* is a novel for our time of pandemic, when we have returned to baking and breaking bread at home. Georgia Kolias shows us how ancient culture nourishes us, portraying the joys and dilemmas of third culture kids. Just as when my *yiayia* patiently taught me how to put together the ingredients of our cuisine, so *The Feasting Virgin* imparts the recipes of the motherland translated into love, a family breaking bread."

—Aliki Barnstone, Poet Laureate of Missouri, translator, critic, editor, and visual artist

THE
FEASTING
VIRGIN

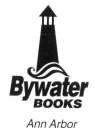

Ann Arbor

Print ISBN: 978-1-61294-173-8
eBook ISBN: 978-61294-174-5

Bywater Books First Edition: July 2020

Printed in the United States of America on acid-free paper.

Cover designer: Ann McMan, TreeHouse Studio

Bywater Books
PO Box 3671
Ann Arbor MI 48106-3671
www.bywaterbooks.com

This novel is a work of fiction.

For my three luminous miracles:

Skyler, Theoni, and Apollo.

Foreword

On November 7th, 2015, I lost my wife, Sandra Moran, and the world lost a talented writer and learned scholar. Sandra was a professor as well an author and shared her talents as an instructor and mentor at the Golden Crown Literary Society Writing Academy. Because Sandra gave so much to the Writing Academy, in 2016, the Golden Crown Literary Society established a scholarship in Sandra's name. The scholarship is given to a Writing Academy student who displays the potential to make a significant impact on lesbian fiction.

In April 2019, in addition to manuscript samples from other applicants, the scholarship committee read a sample from an early version of *The Feasting Virgin*. The committee unanimously selected Georgia Kolias as the 2019 Sandra Moran Writing Academy Scholarship recipient.

In July 2019, I was honored to present the scholarship to Georgia. And now it is my great honor to present this wonderful work of fiction to you.

After you read *The Feasting Virgin*, I know you will agree that Georgia was the perfect choice for this coveted scholarship. And, like me, you no doubt will be looking forward to her next novel.

Enjoy reading *The Feasting Virgin*!

Cheryl Pletcher
Ashville, NC
April 2020

MAY DAY

for Georgia

Spit on the ground; protect against the evil
eye. Sprinkle basil droplets from a bowl.
Bless home with amulets of blue glass. Mouth
prayers and spells and names of beloved people,
each name a breath, and save them from the lethal
germ. Bend to Earth. Weave Maia a wreathed crown
of olive branches, laurel, and wildflowers.
Picnic beneath the grape arbor. Fly gleeful
kites for the daughter's returned to her mother.
Forget your work. Love your ingredients
more than your guest's appetite. From air's wild
yeast, bread will rise. After winter, you'll touch her,
feed her tomatoes and cheese radiant
with oil, honey sweet as being with your child.

—Aliki Barnstone

The Virgin

I'm not asking for much. Some greedy people want money, cars, jets, or boob jobs. I just want a baby. It's a simple wish that comes naturally to so many women, who are then compelled by some biological imperative to bring forth life. It seems unfair that for some women the wish is so easily granted—or even an unwanted accident—when for others it's a struggle. Some of us are reduced to desperate measures, brought to the edges of our sanity and willing to try nearly anything to make our wish come true. I know what most people would say to me. You're thirty-eight years old and a virgin. You have to have sex to have a baby. But I'm not like other women, and I won't rely on a man to get pregnant. I would rather pray each day for a virgin birth.

How can I be thirty-eight already? Almost forty. What do I have to show for myself? Piles of baby clothes that I have bought, and even sewn myself, for a baby that hasn't come. I don't have my own home or a big job. I stay in a guest cottage, caretaking someone else's home while they travel the world. I teach bored housewives how to cook Greek food to please their husbands, and sometimes they let me watch their babies. Whatever odd jobs I can patch together to make enough money to live.

My joy comes from planting fruits and vegetables in the garden, watching the seedlings poke their heads up through the dirt and bloom into glorious produce that I transform into delicious meals for one. These hands that pray and search my body for signs of life

1

and come up empty are always full of ingredients: ripe tomatoes, verdant greens, sultry olive oil, salty anchovies, and magical yeast. Cooking is the only thing I do well. Even though I can't get the recipe right for baking babies, I can make any kind of dish you can think of. Just give me a request and I'll show you what I can do.

I was trained to be a good Greek wife from a very young age. That means that I can cook and clean. I know how to foster the religious life of my family, and I know how to be subservient. This last one is the most important trait of all—learning how to honor, serve, and obey my future husband. From the time I was a little girl my husband was already more important than I was, even though we didn't know who he was yet.

I remember being five years old at a Christmas party at my godparents' house in San Francisco. It was dark outside, and inside were lots of twinkly lights and a big, bushy, silver tree with round blue ornaments. There were piles of presents under the tree, and I wanted a Bozo the Clown punching bag for Christmas more than anything. The other children and I lurked around the tree, trying to see if our names were written on the biggest boxes. It seemed like everything was exciting and moving fast. The men smoked cigarettes and leaned forward, telling stories under their breath and slapping their knees as they laughed in the living room. My *nouno*, my godfather, would grab me as I walked by and put me on his lap and rub his bristly face against mine and bite my cheek. "*Tha se faw!*" he would say and take another bite. His lap was always hot, and I would squirm away feeling special and confused. My father never smoked, or grabbed me, or bit me, and when he drank he got mad. But the other men liked him because he told funny jokes and gave them free steaks at his butcher shop.

The women were in the kitchen in their skinny, shiny dresses and high heels getting the food ready. Their aprons were frilly and clean. They never seemed to get dirty. As each dish came out of the oven, the women complimented each other on the aroma of the lamb, or the nutty color of the béchamel sauce topping the moussaka. My favorite was the baklava, with chopped walnuts and cinnamon sugar tucked between crispy layers of filo and drenched in honey syrup.

My mother made the best baklava. She and my sister and I would sit in the kitchen and crack and shell a whole burlap bag full of walnuts over the course of a weekend. Our fingers would turn red and hurt from ripping open the sharp shells. But it was worth it for the freshest nuts, creamy tan and crunchy, free of any blemishes and handpicked to remove any little bugs. My mother always taught me to pick the best ingredients, using all of my senses so that I could make the best food. Picking produce by color, smell, and touch. Fish by firmness and clear eyes. Meat by bright color and bloodiness.

Young Greek wives are often picked by reputation, and being the best cook is second only to virginity and subservience in desired qualities. My mother told me to make myself useful and handed me a big silver tray. She told me to use both hands. As I walked to the living room the ice cubes clinked against the sides of the short glasses, and I could smell the 7-Up and whiskey. I served the men in the proper order, starting first with my *nouno* because it was his house and he was my godfather. He grabbed me and kissed me again, scratching my face with his bristly face and said, "*Bravo, Koukla!*" He almost made me drop the tray, but I was holding on tight with both hands and smiling because my mother trusted me with it. Then I went to the oldest male guest, and then the next oldest guest, and my father, and so on until I got to the youngest man old enough to drink. They smelled like cigarettes, alcohol, aftershave, sweat, and importance. As I was leaving the room, I noticed my *nouno* blowing air into something. I stopped long enough to see that it was a Bozo the Clown punching bag! He saw me standing there and grabbed me with his free arm, circled it around me tight, put his finger up to his lips—"shhh! It's our little secret"—and winked at me. I ran back into the kitchen so fast that I almost tripped, nearly dropping the tray.

Well, I probably don't have to tell you what happened next. Of course, it is so obvious. But it wasn't obvious to me back then. Little Greek girls don't get punching bags for Christmas. Punching is something that little boys do. They punch and grab and prod. Just as little Greek girls get taught how to be good wives, little Greek boys get taught how to be strong husbands. The boys learn how to push Bozo down, and the girls eventually learn how to try to get back up.

That was the same Christmas I got Doll. She had a bottle and diapers, and when I fed her, she peed her pants. Even though at first I thought the punching bag was cooler, I came to realize that a baby doll was the best. I could hug her and dress her and feed her and tell her what to do. When I was mad at everyone else, I still loved her. She always smiled at me and never yelled. Sometimes I tucked her into my pants like she was sitting in my kangaroo pouch and hopped around the house. But then my mother would scream at me to be quiet and Doll and I would go hide under the dining-room table and play house.

I have tried to take good care of her, but she is over thirty years old now. One of her eyes doesn't open anymore, but I like to think of her as winking at me. Her short yellow hair has gone bald in some patches from all the brushing, and no matter how hard I scrub I can't get some of the gray dirt off of her face. But she has all her arms and legs, ten fingers and ten toes.

I've never given these hands in marriage. I've kept them for myself. I could see why someone would want a Greek wife. She'd make you food, do your laundry, clean your house, serve you cold alcoholic drinks, and give you her virginity. But what does a Greek husband give his wife? He makes and spends the money, maybe throwing her a buck if she begs. He orders her around in every room of the house. He burps after dinner and doesn't even notice all the care she put into picking the freshest dandelion greens or cooking the pork chops just right so that they stay juicy and tender.

The older I got, the wiser I got. So, I thought to myself, why would I get married to some guy who'd make my life a living hell? Praying for a virgin birth seemed like a better bet to me than surviving the experience of being a good Greek wife. After all, the greatest miracles can happen when you are pure of heart.

The Dilemma of Birth

The spiraling sensation worked its way up from Callie's vulva, through the small of her back, and up her spine. She swayed in small circles, following the energy flow while releasing full breaths from between her lips. Her body was submerged in a bright blue plastic tub filled with warm water. Her red hair dripped with herb-scented water and sweat. Her only cover was her freckles. Surrounding the thick inflated walls of the tub were lit candles with undulating flames and petals from roses, pansies, and freesia. In a clear glass vase stood a stalk of tuberose emitting a thick, sweet fragrance and browning at the edges of the pale green-white blooms. Twelve women stood in a circle surrounding the tub with arms intertwined, their eyes half-closed and humming an indeterminate tune, but with great intention and synchronicity. With each escalating moan the women began anew, starting at a muted high pitch and slowly bringing their voices lower and louder as the contraction took full grip. The effect was similar to that of a weight lifter grunting, or a martial artist yelling out at the kick.

Callie alternated her position in the tub between sitting upright with her arms outstretched, moving her hips in ever increasing circles, and falling forward on all fours screaming. The scene was exactly as she had planned it. All of her good friends were present, all of her favorite flowers were scattered throughout the room, and it was nearing dawn. The only light came from the candles and the rising sun filtering through the lace-covered windows. She could feel her baby working with her to emerge from her body, pressing his feet against her womb and pressing his head toward her opening. Each contraction brought with it the spiraling sensation of energy up and down her spine and she worked with it, not against it, as her midwife had coached her. She had been laboring for eleven hours and was nearing the time to push.

There was just one thing amiss, and that was the expression on Gus's face. She had had to convince him to go along with the home birth and midwife, the birthing tub, having all of her friends present, and saving the placenta. But this expression was something she hadn't seen before. It wasn't the incredulous expression that he reserved for her birth plan, or the blank expression that he exhibited when discussing paint colors for the baby's room. It wasn't fear, exactly, and she didn't flatter herself that he was scared for her or impressed by her process of giving birth. Instead, he seemed preoccupied. Callie had grown to anticipate Gus's resistance to her ideas, especially when her hippie ideas clashed with his traditional Greek ethos. The clash arose in every discussion, every decision, from circumcision to baby-naming.

Just a few short days ago, a very pregnant Callie had sat in bed reading from a stack of baby-naming books while Gus sat by her side reading *The Millionaire Real Estate Agent: It's Not About the Money . . . It's About Being the Best You Can Be!* Callie caressed her belly, amazed that the baby she could feel moving inside her womb would soon be born, and she could finally look at him and hold him.

She turned to Gus. "Hey, honey . . . have you thought any more about baby names?" she asked hopefully while flipping through the pages of her book.

"There is only one name. Manoli," he said with a flourish. "That was my father's name and that will be the name of my son. That is how we do it."

"But there are so many interesting and beautiful names in the world. Why limit yourself?"

6

"I'm not limiting myself. I'm fulfilling something. It's a cultural thing. You know. You know? I'm Greek."

"Yeah, I know. I know you feel an obligation to name the baby for your father. That's the way you do it. But I thought you guys weren't that close . . ." Callie paused, not sure whether to continue her question. "Gus, didn't he leave when you were a kid?"

"Callie, don't talk about things you don't understand," Gus said gruffly.

"Ouch."

"Listen. Of course I wanted my Dad to stay. It was complicated. But I didn't get a choice."

"But don't you want to have a choice now for your son? There are thousands—maybe even millions—of names to pick from. Why not pick a name with a positive association?"

"Well how about we narrow it down to Manoli—or Manoli?" He closed his book. "Sometimes too many choices is a bad thing. Whatever my father did, right or wrong . . . it doesn't matter now that he is dead."

"What about Marley? That starts with the letter *M* just like Manoli. We could honor your father that way."

"You want to honor a stoned Rastafarian instead of my father?"

"Hey! Bob Marley was a great musician who wasn't afraid to speak his truth about politics and religion. He spread a message of love throughout the world. He was also very spiritual."

"He was still a stoner. And by the way, my father wasn't afraid to speak his truth about politics and religion either." He laughed, mimicking his father pounding his fist on the table while arguing politics with his friends.

"Did you know that cannabis is a sacred sacrament in the Rastafarian tradition?" she asked.

"Well then, why don't we name him Cannabis?" He turned toward her and fixed a tangled red curl. "What's wrong with a good Greek name?"

"Okay. Okay. We can narrow it down to a Greek name." She closed the *Pick a Pretty Indian Name for Your Baby* book and picked up *The Greatest Baby Name Book Ever*. "There are so many Greek names with interesting meanings. How about Kosmo? It means 'perfect order, harmony.'"

"You like harmony? Then pick Manoli. Why do you have to make this so hard?" he grunted.

"It *is* hard. There are so many choices. And he'll have to live with this name the rest of his life. I want him to like it. I want it to be special."

"Picking a name isn't about making choices. It's about honoring the people that raised you," he harrumphed, giving her *New Age Baby Name Book* a little kick with his foot, both annoying and bewildering Callie.

She kicked it back, and taking a deep breath said, "*Manoli* rhymes with *cannoli*. There. I said it."

"What's Cannoli?" he asked incredulously.

"Cannoli! Cannoli. You know. It's a long tube filled with cream, and it has a big cherry on the end. I don't want him getting teased because he sounds like an Italian dessert that looks like a penis!" Her face was red and she was rubbing her forehead. "I mean, no offense to Italian people. Cannoli are delicious. I just don't want our son to sound like one."

"Is that what you're worried about?" He laughed and pulled her in close to him. "We wouldn't use Manoli at school. We'd use the American version. You know, how my Greek name is Constantino, but I go by the American version, Gus?"

"Oh." She paused. "How do you get Gus from Constantino?"

"Good question!" Gus laughed. "But I don't think they sell the *Greek Immigrant Name Translation Logic Book* at Barnes and Noble."

Callie smiled. "Well, what's the American version of Manoli?"

"Emmanuel. Manny for short."

"Emmanuel . . . I like that. But what does it mean?"

"Don't ask me. Look it up in one of your books here." He picked up the *Millionaire Real Estate Agent* book and resumed reading.

Callie riffled through *The Greatest Baby Name Book Ever* until she found Emmanuel. "Emmanuel. Emmanuel means . . . God is with us. God is with us." She thought about their sweet baby and the miracle of him growing in her womb, and the feeling of peace she'd experienced as he nestled within her. With his conception she'd experienced a love that came from the inside out, perfect and complete. No doubts, no conditions. Just pure love.

"Yes. Emmanuel. Yes. It's perfect."

He grabbed her hand and squeezed it. He looked into her eyes and said, "I told you so."

They had settled that debate without too much pain, but now Callie was seeing that familiar distance in Gus's eyes, and she wanted to feel completely connected to him as she labored to birth their child.

"Hey, Daddy. What's on your mind?" she managed to pant, emerging from her labor trance long enough to whisper across the surface of the splashing water. He looked at her intently and just shook his head.

A laboring woman is not in her right mind. She enters a different dimension of existence and perception. And because of the extreme nature of her task patience is in short supply. Callie didn't have the time to tease it out of him. "NOW! Tell me now!" With that she lunged forward and gripped the sides of the tub and let out a scream inches from his face.

"Uh. Okay. Well, it's just that . . ."

"Not NOW! Not NOW! Not NOW!" she spat as she began pushing out their child.

Between contractions Callie could see that Gus was clearly rattled. She saw him desperately reaching for the cigarette he had hidden in his swim trunks. She could tell Gus wanted to turn his back on her as she labored and press the cigarette to his lips, smell the tobacco, and deeply inhale its smoke.

Callie felt the next big wave hit and she went into a full squat, unleashing all of her energy into a push, and screaming "Gus!" She was birthing his baby, and the least he could do was watch.

She could hear the midwife saying, "You're doing great, you're doing great, keep pushing, keep pushing."

Callie let out a huge breath and relaxed back from her squatting stance, putting her weight onto the side of the birthing tub. The doula wiped the sweat from her forehead and wrung cool water from a fresh washcloth over her chest. The midwife was quietly giving her instructions on the next big push. Her friends hovered around the perimeter of the tub with varying expressions of joy, wonder, and fear. Some were crying from the intensity of the experience while others looked around the room for something to keep their minds occupied between pushes.

"Okay. Tell me now. Tell me now before the next contraction." She had a glazed, yet piercing look in her eyes. "I want my giving birth to be just right. It can't be just right with you sitting there looking . . . looking . . ." The doula helped her back up into a squatting position and she pushed, hard. The women hummed a low vibrating tone, and it filled the air with a buzzing sensation. Gus rose from his crouching position and started to pace the room. Callie watched him start for the door, then turn back toward her, rubbing his forehead. He looked as if he wanted to bolt from the room. Gus started to fan himself.

"Gus, you look like you're about to faint." Callie gestured for him to come closer. "Are you okay?" Callie felt a lump rising in her throat. Maybe Gus didn't want any of this, or maybe he just didn't want her. Her face started to crumple with pain as the next contraction gripped her. The midwife reminded her to relax and breathe through the pain. Callie grimaced and asked Gus again, "Is everything okay?"

"Yes, yes. It's okay. Okay?" Gus managed to spit the words out, and while Callie wasn't convinced, she had more important things to deal with.

"Welcome!" she screamed to the baby. It was the word she had decided to focus on during labor, as she felt the baby kicking and fishing its way through the birth canal. "Welcome!" With that she collapsed again against the side of the tub.

As if seeking to reassure himself, Gus repeated, "It's going to be okay." The midwife turned to the women surrounding the tub and asked them to please sing a supportive phrase for the father. She led them through it, and they were soon singing,

"It's okaaaaaaaaaaaaaaaaay!
It's okaaaaaaaaaaaaaaaaay!
It's okaaaaaaaaaaaaaaaaay!
It's okaaaaaaaaaaaaaaaaay!"

Callie was breathing hard from the exertion of pushing. Her eyes were puffy, and her red hair was hanging in sweaty strings. The tub water was tinged with her blood. Callie prepared for the next big push and started to sing with the women, "It's OKAAAAAAAAAAAY!" The midwife took a medium-sized green fish net and started dragging it through the water, fishing out a couplet of small turds before the next big contraction. Callie turned her head in time to see Gus drop to the floor in a dead faint. And before she could say a word the midwife reminded her it was time to push. Callie moved into a full squat and, while Gus lay unconscious, pushed their son out into the world, a glorious little boy with a full head of red hair and his father's eyes. Callie leaned back in the tub of water, holding her son to her breast, her red hair a halo of electricity framing her face, looking like a modern-day Madonna with her child.

Into the Pot

Gus groped in the dark as if he were fighting his way out of a wet burlap sack. The shrill screams had startled him awake.

"Callie . . . Callie . . . the baby is crying." He reached his arm over to nudge her awake but found the bed empty. He groaned and rubbed his eyes, wishing the baby would magically stop crying. "Callie!" he yelled, and the baby screamed louder. *Where is she?*

"Argh!" Gus reluctantly swung his bare legs over the side of the bed and stumbled over to the co-sleeper. Picking the baby up always scared him a little. What if he accidentally snapped his neck or dropped him? He gently wedged his hand under Manoli's back until he was cradling his neck in his hand, and carefully lifted the baby's bottom with the other hand. The baby continued his crying, shaking the house with his desire.

"Okay, little guy. Calm down . . . calm down. Manoli, are you hungry?" He looked around for something to calm him with, but Callie refused to use pacifiers or bottles, preferring to deftly lift Manoli to her breast for comfort whenever necessary. Manoli was always content to suckle her breast, his mouth moving rhythmically, his gulps just audible. Gus had watched them so many times, relaxing into each other and at peace. Gus felt a sudden panic rise up his chest.

"Where's your mama, huh?" He walked toward the door to search for Callie, but Manoli was crying so hard his little body was shaking, and his cries had become hoarse with fury. His need was immediate. "Oh crap." Gus tried to bounce the baby and pat his back. He tried walking back and forth across the room, all the while wondering where Callie was. Finally, he wiped his hand on his pajama bottoms and placed his pinkie in the baby's mouth. The baby voraciously sucked Gus's finger, and Gus marveled that a being so tiny and fragile could have such strength in its mouth. "Shhh . . ."

Gus was so relieved that Manoli was no longer crying he nearly wanted to cry himself. He wiped his forehead with the back of his hand and pushed his breath through his lips. The house was silent except for the suck and whimper of the baby. When he looked back at Manoli, he realized that the baby was gazing up at him, and the look in Manoli's eyes could not be mistaken for anything but love.

Gus inhaled, almost gasping, as if he couldn't take breath in fast enough. He realized that his whole life was now about that moment. His son loved him, trusted him, and relied on him. It was no longer about reaching over to Callie's side of the bed when he was feeling amorous, grasping her breasts greedily. It was no longer about staying out late drinking a good scotch and smoking cigars with his buddies at the Middle Eastern bar. It was no longer just about him. It was all about his son now, and the thought was strangely terrifying and comforting at the same time.

And with that Gus knew there was no turning back. Even though he wasn't sure if things would ever feel quite right with Callie. He felt guilty keeping secrets from her, but he couldn't bring himself to tell Callie about his mother and their phone conversation months earlier.

"*Mana, thelo na sou po kati.* I'm not sure how to tell you." Gus had clenched an unlit cigarette between his callused fingers. His mother didn't want him smoking, but times like these begged for a good smoke. He put down the cigarette and pulled a humidor out of a mahogany cabinet in his home office.

"*Ti einai, pedi mou?*" He could hear his mother's voice crackling through the telephone line. He imagined her sitting on the veranda with a demitasse cup in front of her, turned upside down, drying the coffee grounds so she could read the future. "What is it, my child?" she asked in a familiar tone. It was one of motherly alarm, concern tinged with anger.

It didn't matter that Gus was forty-two. To his mother he would always be a child. He cleared his throat.

"Well, you remember that girl I was dating? The redhead?"

"*E Amerikanitha? Asfalos. E Putana.*"

"Mana, she is not a whore. She's just a girl I dated." Gus didn't tell his mother that the redhead was down the hall in his bedroom at that moment, asleep in a crumpled heap of sheets that smelled vaguely of vomit.

"Listen, I just spoke with Effie Papadopoulou's father. He is a very wealthy man you know. He can help you. He would be a good *petheros.*"

Gus picked up the unlit cigarette again and squeezed until a small break formed in the wrapping paper. "*Mana,* I told you I don't want to marry Effie Papadopoulou so I can have a rich father-in-law. I have my own business."

"Hah, real estate. One year up, one year down. There is no security. Effie is a good girl. She will take care of you the way a woman is supposed to." Gus could hear her moving about in her apartment in Athens overlooking the *Syndagma* shopping district. After living in Oakland for nearly forty years, she'd repatriated to Greece four years earlier, leaving Gus to miss his mother.

"*Mana.* I have to tell you something. I hope you'll be happy." Even as he said the words, he knew that she would not be happy. She would be furious. The cigarette lay in two pieces on his desk. He caressed the lid of the humidor before putting it back in the cabinet. He reached for the bottle of Johnnie Walker instead.

"The only thing that will make me happy is to see you married to a good Greek girl and with children of your own. All of my sisters have grandchildren. I am the only one left. What are you waiting for?"

Gus could hear her banging pots around in her kitchen. "Mana, I can barely hear you. What are you doing?"

15

"I'm making lunch for the priest and his wife today. *Avgole-mono*. Once he tastes it he will put you in his prayers so that you can start a family of your own."

Gus could picture his mother moving around her small kitchen, the phone pressed between her ear and shoulder while she prepared to drop a chicken into a pot of boiling water.

"That's the thing, *Mana*. I have news." He was thinking now about the tiny being curled up tight inside of the redhead's belly. He imagined it sucking its thumb, even though he knew it might not even have thumbs yet. And dark hair and dark eyes like his. Surely his mother would overcome her dislike for the mother of his child, would forgive the fact that Callie held long-forgotten roots from various Scandinavian countries. She was carrying his child and would soon give his mother the grandchild she so wanted. And he would have a child, maybe a son, God willing. He involuntarily smiled, even as his pulse found its way to his throat, constricting his speech.

"*Mana*, I know you want me to marry Effie Papadopoulou, but I can't do that right now. You see, there's a problem. Well not a problem exactly. It's a good thing. A wonderful thing! A very happy tiny thing . . ." He gulped down a shot of the Johnnie Walker. ". . . person."

"What are you talking about, *pedi mou*?" Her voice was growing harsh with irritation. She always became angry when she was afraid.

Her tone of voice made Gus feel like the chicken she was wrestling out of its paper wrapper, pale, pink, and goose-bumped, with its legs up in the air. He took a deep breath and blurted it out. "I am going to be a father."

"Yes, I hope so. Once you are married to a good woman like Effie. But not now. You are not going to be a father now."

He imagined her plucking the last feathers off of his wings.

"You will not shame me, bringing home a redheaded pregnant *putana*. She is just tricking you into marrying her so that she can get your money. Are you so naïve?"

Gus paused, holding the phone receiver in one hand and the bottle of whiskey in the other. He felt heat rising to his face.

16

"I know you," she continued. "You believe what the pretty faces tell you. Remember what happened when that *Sultana* told you she was desperate for help? Her family home was in trouble and she had to save it?"

His mother was right. He had lost a lot of money that time. It was a source of embarrassment that he'd been fooled into giving her so much cash. It was supposed to be a temporary loan, but she'd left town the next day and he'd never heard from her again.

"You listen to me," his mother said. "I want a Greek daughter-in-law and then I want a Greek grandchild—in that order. I don't want you to bring home your mistakes and bring shame on the family. You understand?"

Gus could hear the water surging as his mother grabbed the chicken by the thigh and plunged it into the boiling pot of water.

"Yes, *Mana*."

"*Endaxi*. I have to go now. I have a lot to do before the priest gets here."

"Yes, *Mana*." He had hung up the phone and examined his hands, the hands of a man defeated. Just then, Callie had entered his office, wrapped in the creamy sheet, and sat on his desk. She took one look at his face and the Johnnie Walker bottle. "Talking to your mother?" she asked.

Remembering Callie that way, slender and freshly disheveled from an afternoon in bed together with her beautiful blue eyes looking at him with understanding and desire, brought Gus out of his memories and back into the bedroom he shared with Callie, Manoli asleep in his arms. It all seemed so long ago. But the problem remained the same. He had decided to wait, to wait until whenever—to wait as long as he could. There was no good that could come from telling Callie about his conversation with his mother. No good in telling her that she and this child might never be accepted by his culture. How would this woman, this wonderful and carefree *we are the world* woman, ever understand the pressures he was under? How would he ever explain? He had broken the rules, for a woman who didn't share his world. She

17

wanted to, but she never truly could, *could she*? Could someone *become* Greek?

The question haunted Gus the rest of the night and all the next day while he was out scouting properties for clients. Now that he had Manny there was no turning back. He had to find a way to bring his two worlds together. Arriving home, he grabbed the mail from their box next to the steep staircase leading to the front door of his house. He slowly ascended the stairs as he shuffled through the bills and junk mail, looking for the letter from his mother he was hoping for but that never came. When Manny was born, Gus had sent his mother pictures of her new grandson, hoping that seeing the baby would melt her stony refusal to accept his relationship with Callie. He'd invited her to come and stay with them, both because he missed her and because he desperately wanted her punishing silence to end. He knew that he and Callie weren't a perfect match, but they'd had a lot of fun in the beginning, and then they had Manny. And he was determined to be a good father to his son, a father that stayed.

He'd never forgotten that day when his father had left. He drove off in their old station wagon and never came back. Once in a while he sent a comic book or a new shirt for Gus. When Gus was fourteen, they got the call from the hospital that his father had died from a heart attack. He never knew what his father had been thinking. Why had he really left? Whether he'd left to get away from them or to get to something or someone better. Whether it had been worth it.

He rubbed his eyes and fit the key into the lock. On the landing outside the front door, he noticed a small box wrapped in brown paper and embossed with several colorful stamps. Picking it up, he realized that the writing on the box was very familiar, the strange looping twos, the extra round *C,* the ink pen firmly and carefully pressed into the package. It was the careful immigrant English handwriting of his mother. The waiting was over—she had finally written! Dropping his briefcase, he tried to rip the package open right there outside the front door, but the clear packing tape escaped his short fingernails over and over again.

He pushed the front door open and ran up the stairs into the kitchen where he searched for scissors. Unable to find any, he grabbed a ten-inch chef's knife off the block and carved the brown wrapping paper open. Inside was more tape holding the box closed, and Gus shook his head and chuckled as he recalled Christmases growing up. His mother would use extraordinary amounts of tape to make it hard for him to open his gifts, finding his excited desperation amusing. "Always the same, *Mana*. You like to make it hard for me," he laughed as he finally got the box open and the smell of Greece filled his nostrils.

One by one he removed the objects from the box: a bag of oregano, some of his favorite cookies, *moustokouloura* made from grape molasses, and down underneath a layer of crumpled paper a pair of hand-knit baby booties with a letter rolled up into one of the feet. "My dearest Manolaki, please tell your father that I am coming to visit you on June 15th. I would like a ride from the airport. Love, *Yiayia.*"

"She's coming. She's coming!" Gus yelled out into the house. "Hey, Callie? My mom is coming!"

Callie came bounding down the stairs from the bedroom, Manny in her arms. "What's going on? You scared me."

"My mom is coming! Manolaki, your *yiayia* is coming to see you!" Gus hopped around the kitchen.

"Wow. I've never seen you so excited." Callie giggled. "When is she coming?"

"June 15th!" Gus said loudly and grabbed Manny from her. He kissed the baby's cheeks. "*Yiayia* is coming!"

"June 15th?"

"June 15th! In seven weeks!"

"Don't you have a real estate seminar in the wine country on June 15th?" Callie asked.

"Screw it. I can go next year. We have to get ready!" Gus laughed.

"Well, at least one of his grandmothers is coming to visit him," Callie mumbled as she tugged on her tube top. "You know, I'm not even sure which commune my mom is at right now?"

Gus stopped smiling. "Maybe we shouldn't mention the communes while my mom is here, okay?" The last thing he needed was for his mother to decide Callie was some weird cult hippie.

"Well, what if it comes up in conversation?" Callie asked.

Gus started making a mental checklist of topics to avoid while his mother was visiting. He was going to have to get Callie to go along with it. There were so many things she'd need to learn if she was ever going to win his mother's approval.

"Cal? Seriously, we have to get ready." Gus grabbed Callie's arm. "We have to get ready. You have to get Greek right away."

"What?" Callie stopped smiling.

"You know, learn to cook all the Greek dishes, learn some Greek phrases like, 'welcome, how are you,' etc." Gus was getting nervous. "And maybe get some new clothes, you know, respectable lady kind of clothes."

"What do you mean, Gus, 'lady clothes'?" Callie's tone was becoming terse.

Gus looked her up and down. She was wearing a tube top, short denim cutoffs, thongs, and her hair plaited into two braids pulled back behind her ears. "Oh you know, a little more respectable?"

"I thought you liked the way I dress?" Callie said wrinkling her brow.

"I do, babe. You're totally hot." Gus realized suddenly that this visit might be harder than he expected, carefully balancing the egos and desires of Callie and his mother. "I was just thinking that, you know, to make a good first impression, that maybe you could wear something a little more traditionally . . . mother-like?"

"Would you like me to get some high-waisted jeans, a pink polo shirt, and a short, carefree haircut? And some granny panties? I bet you'd like that," Callie huffed.

"Hey babe. Please don't take it that way. You know how long I've wanted my mom to come visit," he said in a pleading voice. "I really want it to go well." Gus knew that he was asking a lot of Callie, but in that moment he felt like an earnest little boy missing his mother, and he needed Callie to help him. Callie softened her stance, reaching out to run her fingers through Gus's curly hair. "I want it to go well too. I'll try my best, Gus. And I'll buy a new dress or two. Respectable ones." She smiled.

"Thanks, Cal." Gus drew Callie into his arms and held her close to his chest. Manny chortled at the group hug, and Callie smiled as she tickled his chubby cheeks. "Maybe she and I will hit it off. We could really click, you know."

Gus thought about his stubborn traditional mother and her insistence on things done "the right way," and thought, *This is going to be a disaster.*

The Vision

In the dark predawn hours, in the liminal space between dreams and reality, I kneel in an eastward-facing corner of my bedroom, before a low table where I have carefully arranged my sacred objects. I lift the lid of the golden incense burner and light the black charcoal. As I drop a rock of *livani* onto the heat, an ancient scent perfumes the air. I carefully arrange the flowers cut fresh from the garden into a small crystal vase. The roses droop under the weight of their velvety red heads, and the jasmine emits an insistent and seductive fragrance. I light the wick that floats within the chalice of life-giving olive oil, mesmerized by the undulating flame that adds one small source of light to the darkness. My bare knees press into the rough carpet, and the sensation of pain keeps me centered. Everything is in place. I make the sign of the cross and, staring up at the icon of the Madonna and child on my bedroom wall, I pray.

For the past two years I have desperately whispered the same unanswered request into the dark silence. My prayer is simple, yet forged from a state of longing, an unsatisfied wish that pushes on my heart. The scents, the smoke, the pain, the years, my fervent prayers—all of it adds up to this moment of pure desire. I can only hope that this time God will see me, that He will see my devotion and answer my prayers.

I close my eyes and imagine holding my baby in my arms, as I always do. I hold my arms in a perfect cradle position and visualize my baby, with its soft, deliciously fragrant head nestled safely in the crook of my arm. I stay in this position until I notice my arm muscles starting to burn. But this time something is different. My arms are tingling and heavy. This time I can *feel* the warm weight of its body pressing against mine. This time I can *feel* it breathing! I hold my breath so that I can feel the rise and fall of my baby's breath against my chest. With equal parts of terrible hope and fear I slowly open my eyes to look down into my arms. At that same moment the icon of the Virgin Mary is inexplicably illuminated in the darkness of the room. Her crimson and blue robes trimmed in gold reflect the light as she tenderly turns and tilts her head toward her baby, and then turns to smile at me. Trembling, I am overcome with unadulterated joy and certainty. I begin to swoon, and I fall to the ground, nearly losing consciousness. When I open my eyes I see her kneeling over me holding her hand over my belly. I see her lips move and I hear the words, "the right hand can perform miracles," and millions of sparkling particles float slowly from her outstretched hand within a bright shaft of light toward my womb. I notice a slight pressure on my vagina, but rather than startle I relax and let myself open. I'm certain that the divine has entered my body and that at last my dream has come true. I, Xeni, am a pregnant virgin.

When I regain consciousness, I grab the box of pregnancy tests from inside of my hall cabinet. As I rip the plastic wrapper off of the test stick I can hardly breathe. I take the stick into the bathroom and carefully sit on the cold toilet seat. When I think I get it wet enough, I take it to my altar. I place it under the icon of the Virgin, between the lit wick floating in the chalice and the fresh flowers I picked this morning. It lies there, white and plastic and lifeless, next to my sacred objects. I will the pink line to appear. I kneel on the floor and genuflect three times before I kiss the icon of the Virgin. Did I really see her turn her head to smile at me? Did she really kneel over me? I felt something miraculous enter my body. I know I did.

But everything feels cold. The air is cold. The carpet under my knees is cold. The test stick looks like a sharp icicle. The flame flares and dies out, despite the generous amount of olive oil that it floats on. Even before I pick up the stick I know.

I run my trembling hands down my body, my breasts, my belly, my thighs. I search for the changes that will show me that God loves me, that dreams can come true. I am suspended in this moment, my breath gathered in my chest, eyes squeezed shut. But my breasts are not sore, my belly is just plain fat, and my thighs remain clamped shut. My nipples are dry and my throat is choking. There is no movement in my womb, neither slight nor impatient. I am dry and barren, a vine without flowers or fruit. A woman without purpose.

I am reminded each month when I bleed instead of growing bigger with child. My baby dream sinks and clots into a bloody pad that I reluctantly throw in the trash and cover with a soft tissue. My arms are interminably empty except for my Doll. She may be the only baby I will ever have. Maybe it's best that way. She'll never get sick or leave me. She'll never hurt me. But she'll also never learn to cook with me. I'll never watch her grow up. And she'll never be able to say, "I love you."

I don't know anyone who wants a baby more than me. But sometimes I doubt that God will ever listen to me. I don't know, and so the rest of the time I try to think of ways that I can get myself a baby.

I wish I could just wake up and find a baby on my doorstep or an abandoned baby at the mall. There are always women with their babies at the mall. The mothers usually seem tired or absentminded. A lot of times they leave their babies in a shopping cart all by themselves while they go wandering down an aisle looking for something like a birthday card or a blouse. Sometimes, when the mothers have wandered a few yards away and no one else is around, I think about snatching the baby. I wonder if the child would cry. But, if it was meant to be my baby, I don't think it would.

One day at the grocery store I see a baby sitting in a shopping cart. He has a nice round head, red hair, and big brown eyes. I slowly walk by him in the cart filled with diapers, tofu, and kombucha. I look up and down the aisle, but his mother is nowhere to be seen. I even check the next aisle over. Then I see her—a tall, slender woman with long red hair bent over a pile of spinach, a wilted bunch in each hand. She's talking to herself about something and not even watching her baby.

I reach out to touch his fat cheek. I need to feel the soft, plump skin of a real living baby. I just lightly graze his skin with my fingertips. It is as soft as black velvet. Like the black velvety horizon on an ultrasound screen dotted with white stars and the shape of a baby curled up in a deep sleep. I am so overcome with emotion that I turn my back and start to softly cry. I hear footsteps and I know his mother has returned. Her shadow blocks out the sun, the moon, and the stars.

An Odd Job

Callie strode through the supermarket pushing the shopping cart before her, talking to Manny, who was reclining in his infant car seat firmly wedged into the cart. "Daddy is so excited about your Greek Granny coming. I wonder what your Granny likes to eat. What do you think, little honey? Would Daddy like something Greek for dinner tonight? Maybe we can surprise him with something good!"

Manny pushed his fist into his mouth and gurgled, smiling with his eyes.

"I thought you'd agree." Callie ran through a list of Greek dishes, not letting the fact that she didn't know how to prepare them deter her enthusiasm. She'd eaten them all in restaurants that Gus had taken her to, and then sat and listened to him complain that they didn't come anywhere close to his mother's cooking.

"What do they say? It's a good sign when a man loves his mother . . ." She paused under the fluorescent lights of the supermarket, trying to remember the exact phrase. Shrugging her shoulders she started walking again, making silly faces at Manny as he giggled. "I can't believe you're already five months old!"

"So let's see . . . there's moussaka, there's kabobs, there's spanakopita—mmm, spanakopita. Let's make that. Daddy needs more vegetables." She chuckled as she turned her cart toward the green mounds of produce. "What do you think goes into spanakopita besides spinach? Cheese, filo . . . maybe there'll be a recipe on the filo package. Or maybe we'll wing it. We could improvise and add some interesting and new stuff. How about tofu—or cranberries?" Callie smiled and kissed Manny's plump toes.

Callie stopped by the freezer section and found the filo. The recipe on the box was for a mushroom strudel. "Huh. Well, I was kind of counting on that spanakopita recipe, wasn't I, as a guide . . ." Callie wrinkled her brow and checked a few more packages just in case they displayed different recipes. "Mushroom strudel, mushroom strudel, mushroom strudel. Crap. I thought for sure they'd have the recipe. Too bad Mommy forgot her phone at home. I could have googled it." She put the filo back in the freezer and took a few steps away. Then she went back and grabbed the filo box. Then she put it back in the freezer. Then she grabbed the filo box again and put it in her cart. Then she pulled it back out and put it in the freezer again. Looking about, she was relieved to see that she was alone in the aisle with her confusion.

"What do you think, Manny? You think I can pull off spanako-pita without a recipe? Maybe I'll go look at the spinach first."

Callie turned the cart again and headed toward the produce section. This time her walk wasn't quite as sunny, her banter a little more subdued.

"Maybe we should have macaroni and cheese instead. That always makes me feel better when I'm grumpy." But she knew that macaroni and cheese wouldn't warm Gus's stomach or heart. It had to be Greek. And it had to be good. Good enough for Gus and for his mother.

It was these thoughts that kept Callie up at night, unable to sleep in the unnatural stillness of the house, lying awake listening to the sound of baby Manny's soft breathing. The night before she had turned to look at Gus, who lay sleeping on his back. "Hey baby daddy, are you awake?" She rested her hand on his chest and felt his heart beating beneath the surface. He stirred and turned away from her, his eyes still closed. His olive-skinned ribs caged his heart, and she wasn't sure she'd ever quite reach him. Since Manny was born, she had found herself feeling alternately overwhelmed by the consuming task of being a mother and increasingly disconnected from Gus. She wanted to feel whole and settled in her new life and family, but in the quiet night hours she couldn't deny that there was some soul connection missing. And she wasn't even entirely sure what she wanted anymore.

She would rise from bed most nights and sneak into the moonlit living room where she would sit in mediation trying to remember who she was. She'd wind her arms above her head and remember herself the sexy belly dancer that Gus had first been attracted to. She had been carefree and sexually adventurous when they first met. But she'd been feeling herself shrink, feeling her sexual power leave her, feeling less than she wanted. At night, alone, she would stand and extend a slender arm out, rotate her hips in a generous figure eight, then undulate her soft belly and shimmy her glowing shoulders. She felt her power return, even if only for those brief moments when she was alone and fully herself.

During the day she tried to be a good mother, to meet Gus's expectations of a good Greek wife, and fought against her own instincts to run free. During the day she tried to be everything that she didn't know how to be. But at night she danced.

Manny shoved his fist into his mouth and squealed, startling Callie. She ran her fingers through his red curls and said, "I don't think we can make mac and cheese today, Manny. Today it has to be Greek."

Callie swung the cart to a stop and wandered over to a pile of spinach where she picked up a bunch in each hand. It suddenly made her think of Popeye the Sailor Man, standing with his feet planted firmly on the ground and making a mighty muscle after eating his can of spinach. "This will be fine. I think it will be fine. Will it?" she said.

Callie wandered down the aisle looking for a plastic bag, and when she returned she noticed a woman a few feet away talking to Manny. The woman turned her dark intense eyes away from Manny to look in Callie's direction. Callie couldn't quite tell what her expression was. The woman wiped her eyes, pursed her pillowy lips, and seemed as if she was going to say something. Instead she pulled her long, wavy brown hair back and quickly plaited it into a braid. Even though she was wearing shapeless drab clothes, Callie could see that the woman's body was soft and curvy. *She's beautiful in a way that people might not notice*, thought Callie, surprising herself with a sudden desire to speak to the woman. But before Callie could decide on something friendly to say, the woman spoke.

"You can't buy that spinach."

"What?" Callie asked, still clutching a bunch in each hand.

"The spinach. It's all wrong."

"Why?"

"Well. Look at it. It's limp. It has no life." The woman took the spinach from Callie and shook it, causing the flaccid leaves to droop even further.

"But that's all they have," Callie protested. She was both mildly offended and curious about this stranger who was telling her what she could buy.

"What are you making?" the woman asked.

"Spanakopita?" Callie replied as if she was no longer sure.

"Spanakopita?" the woman laughed. "Why?"

Callie shifted her weight, trying to stand a bit taller. "I wanted to surprise my partner. He's Greek. And he's always talking about his mother's cooking. Always. Especially after he's eaten something I've made. No matter what I've made." Callie found herself speeding up like a car with no brakes. "I just think that if I could make something Greek for him he could see me. He could see me as someone. He could see me and not be thinking about his mother. You know? And now his mother is coming to visit in, like, six weeks, and I have to cook for both of them!" She realized that she'd said too much, letting her internal thoughts spill out all over the supermarket floor. She heard a little chuckle.

"Are you telling me that you are trying to please a Greek man? No, wait. You want to rival his mother's cooking?" The woman laughed.

Callie started to flush. It was one thing to feel inadequate in the privacy of her own thoughts and quite another for a beautiful yet bossy stranger to laugh at her.

"It's not funny. Don't laugh at me," Callie said quietly and realized her eyes were becoming wet.

The woman became quiet. "Okay. I'm sorry. It's just—"

"What?" Callie asked.

"What did you say you want to make? Spanakopita?"

"Yes," Callie sniffed.

"Okay, let me show you a few things, all right?" The woman put the spinach bunches back onto the pile.

"What can you show me? You don't know me," Callie said, straightening up.

"I don't know you. But I know spanakopita." The woman turned her attention to Manny and playfully pinched his chubby thigh. "You look good enough to eat!" Callie's eyes brightened as she watched the woman play little games with Manny.

The woman led Callie through the supermarket and showed her how to pick the best ingredients to make a spectacular spanakopita. In the organic produce section they found fresh, vigorous spinach and bunches of savory herbs. From the dairy section she selected salty feta cheese, fresh farm eggs, and plenty of creamy butter, explaining along the way what to do with each ingredient, how to mix the filling, and layer the filo. Manny sat and listened attentively from his position in the cart, mesmerized by the woman and her stories.

Callie noticed how the woman's hands lingered over the fresh produce until she found just the right bunch of spinach, how she closed her eyes as she brought the feathery dill to her nose and inhaled deeply. She gently squeezed the cheese to test its firmness, and checked each peachy brown egg for cracks. She never selected the item from the top of the display, instead searching the pile until she found the choicest ingredients.

"How do you know all this?" Callie asked. "Are you a chef?"

"No. Not a chef," the woman smiled.

"Well, what do you do?" Callie asked.

"Oh, I have odd jobs. My main one is to house-sit. I have one main family I work for in exchange for an in-law unit and a little cash each month to take care of their house and garden."

Callie looked into the woman's dark eyes and felt as if she were drowning in a pool of melted dark chocolate.

"Sometimes I cook, and sometimes I teach private cooking lessons. Sometimes I take care of babies. I'd be happy to take care of this little guy." The woman smiled at Manny.

There was something familiar about the woman, the color of her hair, the texture of her skin, the way she cocked her head when she said yes.

"Did you say you teach people how to cook?" Callie asked, forming an idea as the words left her lips.

"Well, yes. But only Greek food," she replied.

"Do you know how to cook a lot of Greek dishes?" Callie asked.

"I know how to cook *all* of the Greek dishes," she replied. "I'm a Greek woman!" and she laughed.

Suddenly Callie realized why the woman seemed familiar. She could be a long lost cousin of Gus's, with her dark hair and eyes and olive skin. "Of course. You're Greek . . ." There was something more about the woman that Callie couldn't put her finger on, but wanted to. She felt tempted to reach out and touch the woman's arm, to feel the muscles below her skin as she grasped the handle of the grocery cart.

"I know this might seem kind of strange since we just met and everything. But I have a feeling about you. Maybe you can show me some things." Callie looked at the baby still sucking his fist in the shopping cart. "What do you think, Manny? Should we ask our new friend to help us?"

The woman wrinkled her nose at the words "new friend."

"Would you consider taking on one more odd job? Would you teach me how to be a good Greek woman?" Callie backtracked, flustered. "I mean, how to cook good Greek food?"

The woman looked at Callie for a moment and then shifted her gaze to the baby in the shopping cart. He was sitting pedaling his chubby legs and happily tugging at his mother's sleeve, which lifted higher, barely showing the edges of a tattoo.

"Oh, I'm not sure. I've been doing more babysitting lately."

"I can pay you for cooking lessons! Of course I'll pay you. How about if I pay you fifty dollars if you teach me how to make spanakopita today?"

Callie felt that perhaps it was fate that had put her in the path of this Greek culinary goddess. She held out her hand and said, "I'm Callie and this is Manny. What's your name?" Callie's outstretched arm seemed to glow.

"Xeni. I'm Xeni." She smiled.

"Xeni. I'm so glad to meet you," said Callie as she reached out and put her right hand on Xeni's arm, revealing a luminous tattoo of an olive-skinned Virgin Mary holding baby Jesus.

Xeni froze at Callie's touch, her eyes trained on Callie's tattoo.

"Won't you please teach me to cook?" Callie put her hands together in prayer, begging Xeni to say *yes* with her oceanic blue eyes. "I think it was a sign that we would meet here today, don't you?"

Xeni rubbed her arm as if Callie's fingers had burned a mark on the muscles below, her eyes still wide at the sight of the tattoo. "Well, yes I suppose it was." Then she turned to Manny, grabbed his chubby leg and said, "*Tha se faw!*"

Tha Se Faw!

I follow her home in my truck. There is plenty of room in the truck for a whole lamb, crates of strawberries, or whatever good thing I find while I'm out. They live up in the Oakland hills, surrounded by trees, and I'm wondering if there is good mushroom hunting on the forest floor. I roll down the windows and inhale deeply. Maybe I can smell them. Maybe not.

Their house is perched on stilts, two flights of stairs up. She hitches the baby onto her back and picks up a bag of groceries. I grab the rest and trudge up behind her. The baby's legs are crammed through the carrier holes, and I can see the soles of his feet. Pink and creased. Padded fat, fat, fat. He must like to eat to have such plump, delicious thighs, perfect for roasting. One per person would be plenty. Boiled new potatoes with fresh herbs, garlic, and butter. And maybe a little bitter green, like dandelion, to balance the sweetness of his flesh.

I almost trip because I'm so distracted. Not a good idea to go tumbling. I like my legs very much. They take me through orchards and markets, carry me closer to hot ovens and frigid lakes full of fish.

We stand side by side in her kitchen arranging the ingredients on her counter, and I feel a strange prickling sensation making its way up my spine when our hands accidentally touch. She laughs a little, puts her arm around my shoulders, and presses me closer to her body, just for a moment.

"Xeni, thank you for agreeing to teach me to make spanako-pita. This is the most comfortable I have ever felt standing in my own kitchen." She smiles at me, and I look away.

I begin by showing her how to wash the spinach in a big bowl to get all the grit out, the way the women in Greek villages do. I tell her stories about women rolling out filo by hand into sheets thin enough to see through. I tell her how my aunt slaughters roosters, slitting their throats and throwing them into the brambles to drain their blood. A wood-fired oven makes the best roast chicken, freshly killed. I look at the baby and wink. *Tha se faw! Tha se faw!*

"Wait! What does that mean? *Tha se faw?* Is that how you say it?"

"It's a common Greek endearment expressed to babies." I pause to tickle under Manny's chubby chin. "It means, I'm going to eat you!" She smiles, and it feels as if the sun has flooded the room.

"You know, I love him so much, sometimes I do want to eat him up." Manny laughs as she grabs his foot and puts his fat little toes into her mouth. "My sweet tasty baby!"

I can see that she really loves her baby, so I decide she's okay even though she was dumb enough to marry a Greek guy. Now she has to learn everything I learned growing up. How to cook Greek food, clean house, serve your husband, the proper hierarchy of serving guests hors d'oeuvres and cocktails—male guests first by order of age and importance, Greek husband next, women guests next, etc., etc. Children last. How Greek babies get so fat is a wonder. I sigh.

The butter is sizzling in the pot, ready to be spread on the filo. The filling is ready, emerald green and fresh smelling, studded with good chunks of feta. The hard part has arrived: handling the filo. I show her how to work quickly, gently releasing one thin sheet from the fragile pile of filo and covering the rest with a damp towel. I show her how to brush just enough butter on the filo so that it bakes up crispy and rich, instead of brittle and taste-less or soggy and dense. She looks a bit panicked and with good reason. But the secret to filo is that if the inside layers are some-what messy, you can always cover them up with one perfect sheet on the outside, and it disguises so many flaws. "Right, baby!?" I click my teeth at him, like I'm chewing. This makes her laugh.

The baking spanakopita fills the kitchen with the smell of a hundred Greek grandmothers. As it cooks, it rises, spreading out the filo layers into a golden crisp puff. She is so excited she's squealing, and in that moment her eyes remind me of an abundant cerulean ocean fertile with fish.

"I can't wait to show Gus!" she exclaims.

She can't wait to serve her husband. Oh brother. I give the baby a squeeze on the calf before I head out the door.

SPANAKOPITA

"The secret to filo is that if the inside layers are somewhat messy, you can always cover them up with one perfect sheet."

2 tablespoons extra-virgin olive oil
1 bunch green onions, chopped
2 pounds fresh baby spinach, washed to remove all grit and chopped
1 tablespoon chopped dill
1 tablespoon minced mint
10 ounces sheep's milk feta cheese, crumbled
2 eggs, beaten
1 pound filo dough
3 tablespoons melted butter
3 tablespoons extra-virgin olive oil
Salt and pepper to taste

FOR THE FILLING:

Heat 2 tablespoons of olive oil in a large pot. Add the chopped green onions and sauté until they become soft. Add the chopped spinach, and cover with a lid, stirring occasionally until the spinach is wilted. Transfer the greens into a colander and let cool. Use your hands to squeeze out any excess moisture from the spinach and transfer it into a large bowl. Add the dill, mint and the crumbled feta cheese. Add salt and pepper to taste. Add the beaten eggs and stir to distribute evenly.

PREPARE THE FILO:

Create a filo pattern for your 9-by-13-inch pan. Put a piece of wax paper in your pan. Press it into the bottom and corners and fold it over the edges of the pan, creating creases on the outside perimeter. Remove the wax paper and cut around the creased edge to create a pattern.

Lay a large piece of wax paper down on a flat work surface. Unroll the filo onto the wax paper. Cover it with another piece of wax paper and top it with a damp cotton dish towel. Do not let the damp towel directly touch the filo, and always keep your filo covered. Using the pattern you created, cut ten sheets of filo to size. When you are done, place the filo back under the wax paper and damp towel.

ASSEMBLE YOUR SPANAKOPITA:

Melt the butter and olive oil in a small pot. Remove one sheet of filo and place it flat on your work surface. Make sure to cover the remaining filo. Using your pastry brush, lightly coat the entire sheet of filo on your work surface with the butter and oil. Take another sheet of filo and place it on top. Brush it with the butter and oil, and repeat this pattern until you have used all of the precut filo. Place it in the pan so it nicely covers the bottom and sides. Pour the spinach mixture into the pan of filo and spread evenly.

Cut the remaining sheets of filo in half width-wise. Using the same method, create a layered stack of buttered filo, and when the last filo has been buttered lay it over the top of the spinach. Roll the edges of the lower crust over twice onto the top crust creating a seal. Brush butter and oil on the rolled edge. Using a sharp knife, score the top layers of filo into 12 pieces. Take care not to puncture the filo all the way down to the filling.

Bake at 375 degrees for approximately 45 minutes or until golden.

Inhale deeply and enjoy the delicious scent of your Spanakopita.

Beep!

Beep!

"Constantino, I'm coming in thirty days. Last time I was there the bed was too hard. If I wanted to sleep on the floor, I'd go back to my village home and sleep *stromatsatha* on a pile of hay on the floor with all of my brothers and sisters. We didn't have a choice back then. But you live in America. Macy's has a good mattress department."

Beep!

"Constantino, you still have plenty of time. Don't forget that I love those cookies they sell in the shopping mall. The kind with walnuts. Don't forget."

Beep!

"Constantino! *Christos na me filai*! Christ protect me! The airline put me in a middle seat. I don't want to be trapped in my seat like a sardine between all those people. Call them and get me an aisle seat, close to the bathroom, but not too close."

Beep!

"Constantino, I want to go to church and see my grandson baptized while I am in America. Just because you are living in sin doesn't mean that he can't go to heaven. He is just an innocent child. He didn't do anything."

Beep!

"Constantino, remember that even though you are a big man and I don't like many things you do, you are still my little baby and I love you."

Beep!

Link of Loukoumathes

Callie is all excited because he took her to the Greek Festival over the weekend. "Oh it was so much fun, oh you should have seen the dancing, oh the food was so good. I want to learn to do all of it. Listen, listen—I learned a new word. *Loukoumathes!* Loukoumathes! What a long name for doughnuts! They are so yummy! Can we learn to make loukoumathes today?"

I give her a hard look. "Callie, let me remind you that we are making a red meat sauce scented with cinnamon to serve over fancy buttered rice molds," I pause, "and loukoumathes are *not* doughnuts."

I've been coming back at least twice a week, teaching her new dishes: moussaka, youvetsi, youvarelakia, plaki. She wants to learn everything before the mother-in-law comes. I feel sorry for her because she'll never really be a good Greek wife. I'm not about to teach her how to be subservient.

Each week the baby gets fatter, grows a little hair, and gets to know me. He's gotten so that he smiles when I come over. I always bring a little treat for him and tell him, *"Tha se faw!"* Every time he starts giggling and bouncing in his high chair, his legs swinging to and fro. I talk to him in Greek, and now she is learning to pick up what I'm saying, too. *"Tha se valo stin catsarola!"* Ha ha. "You're going to put him in the cooking pot! Why do Greek people joke about eating babies so much?" she asks.

"Oh, we're not joking," I tell her. "We eat our babies alive."

It is still early in the afternoon, and we have time to make both the cinnamon-scented meat sauce with rice as well as the loukoumathes, but I'm not feeling cooperative. I'm in charge of the lesson, not her. She gets up close to me and squeezes her eyes shut and clasps her hands together. "Oh please, oh please, let's make dinner *and* loukoumathes!" I wasn't going to relent, but then she says, "Manny loves them too!"

Manny. He is sitting on the floor in the kitchen clutching a red and blue plastic toy hammer and shoving it into his mouth. His cheek is pushed out on one side, and with his reddish-brown hair he looks like a squirrel storing nuts for the winter. I want to bite his cheek it is so round. Round and delicious and soft like loukoumathes. I imagine my teeth sinking into the warm puffs. I crouch down near the baby and playfully bite his cheek. "Well, if Manny loves loukoumathes, then loukoumathes it is!" He gurgles.

"What do you think goes into loukoumathes?" I ask her.

"Well, I would guess flour and water, maybe an egg? And honey, nuts, and cinnamon on top." She bends down and plays with Manny's curly hair, the color of rusty cinnamon. "Except for Manny—we'll coat his in cinnamon and sugar."

"What makes them rise?" I ask.

"Baking powder?" she guesses and kisses Manny's fat cheek.

"It's the magic of yeast," I correct her. "Without that ingredient, they would never come to life. It's just like Manny. You picked the ingredients. You combined yourself and his father, but God sprinkled in the magic that made him come to life."

She becomes quiet. "What if you don't have yeast? Could you use something else?"

"If the ingredients aren't right, no matter how hard you try, it'll fall flat," I tell her. "Loukoumathes are simple to make, and the ingredients that go into them are common. We just go to the supermarket and pick up whatever we want and never think about where the ingredients came from. We forget the farmer that threshes his wheat, and the bees that collect pollen from thousands of flowers to bring back to the hive. Most of us don't even know that cinnamon is a bark that has to be collected with care before it is ground and put into labeled bottles with holes in the plastic top for sprinkling. We take ingredients for granted, but we should not. Ingredients can change lives."

Callie is nodding, her blue eyes intent. She wants so badly to learn to be a good Greek wife. She is on the right track, learning how to cook Greek food, but she will never master subservience, and it is too late for her virginity.

She is standing close and puts her hand on my arm. "What if you think you have the right ingredients, but then in the middle of the recipe you realize that you are missing something? Should you give up or keep trying?" I move my arm away, but I can still feel the imprint of her fingers on my skin.

"Each ingredient represents a choice. You choose which jar of honey has the best flavor. The bee selected which blossoms to collect pollen from. The gardener decided whether to put pesticides in her garden. God decided if it should rain to grow the flowers. It is all a chain. We are linked."

She nods, but she looks confused.

"Another way to look at it: when I found you at the supermarket, you were picking limp spinach, feta from Wisconsin, and light olive oil. All of those choices affect the flavor and quality of the finished spanakopita. You see? And when you have choices available to you, make sure to take advantage of that—make the best choices. The freshest ingredients, the purest flavors, will make the happiest stomach."

She looks away toward the window over the sink. It overlooks a canyon of green trees thickly huddled together. She says, "You're right. We have all the choices in the world." Manny bangs his hammer on the floor. "I try to make the right choices, but sometimes it seems hard to know what the right thing to do is."

The truth is that I do feel sorry for her, but I'm not going to tell her that. Here she is a free, adventurous American woman, and she chose to marry a Greek man—and all he wants is for her to be just like his traditional Greek mother.

"It could be worse," I try to console her. "All you did was pick some limp spinach. You could always throw it away and start all over again." Manny bangs the floor again. She nods.

"Just think, what if you were born a poor olive farmer, or worse yet, a poor olive farmer's daughter like my relatives in Greece?"

Callie grabs my hand and asks, "What do you mean? Tell me about them. I hardly know anything about you . . . or your ingredients." She smiles.

So while I show her how to dissolve the yeast into the warm water and then gently add the flour and salt, I tell her. I tell her until the batter has doubled in size and formed bubbles all over the surface.

I tell her about my *Papou* and *Yiayia* and their eight children. My mother was the youngest of the eight. They were poor farmers who lived on the land they farmed in the Peloponnesus region of Greece. Their small clay brick house was surrounded by their olive groves, line after line of gray-green queens, whose fertility and generosity controlled whether there would be enough to feed the family for the whole year. As the olives reached their feathery branches into the sky, their gnarly trunks gripped firmly in the dry ground, as if caught in an eternal choice between staying rooted in the familiar Earth or flying upward and away toward the unknown universe.

Their lives were hard, not just because of the legacy of four hundred years of Turkish occupation, or the German invasion, or even civil war, but because there was never enough to eat. Eight children, sixteen hands and sixteen feet. An army squad of their own to feed. My grandparents raised them with the firm grip of religion and the belt, hard work and sacrifice. The boys worked in the fields, digging, planting, watering, guarding against inclement weather. Running out into the precious rows of corn and grapes at midnight yelling insults at the booming thunder and unraveling crackling sheets of hard cloth to protect the ripening fruit from the impending rain. Each plant they protected, each tomato or cluster of grapes represented the difference between being hungry or starving. Each cob of corn saved would produce dry, shiny kernels that would feed their chickens that would lay eggs for their sustenance and would later float, legs up, in a steamy pot when there was cause for celebration.

The girls cooked and cleaned and tended to the livestock: beautiful brindle chickens with full breasts and wary eyes, and sneaky roosters that pounced with their bright red cockscomb quivering and strong beaks that held the chickens down. The girls knew all the secret places the chickens hid their eggs and stole them with quiet apologies. Sweet goats with trusting eyes ate whatever was given them, trash, old shoes, or a field of wild green weeds, and yielded sweet, warm milk that the women transformed into hard wheels of salty white cheese and hid in briny dark barrels. The eggs and cheese kept them alive.

"That's so amazing . . . they really lived off the land." Callie pulls me to the couch and sits down next to me while we wait for the loukoumathes batter to expand. She grabs my hand and laces her fingers with mine. I sit silently staring at our inter-twined fingers which remind me of the gnarly roots of an olive tree. My face flushes, but I let my hand stay there a few moments too long. Why did I do that? When she asks me to continue the story, the spell is broken, and my hand comes back to me like a winged bird and rests over my pounding heart.

I tell her how the blood in their veins was the olive oil. Each September the family gathered beneath the branches of their olive trees, warily and gratefully eyeing the fruit that would both break their backs in labor and give them the bright green elixir that would bring them profit at the local olive press. It would cook their food, baptize their babies, and keep the wicks lit at their family altars and headstones. The olive trees fed them in life and in death. In the early morning it was easier to approach the task with good spirits and resolve, imagining the price the oil would fetch at market. As they spread the large cloths beneath the trees to catch the falling fruit, they sang folk songs celebrating their perseverance through this hard life. The women took one last look at their callused hands, all shades of brown after a long summer tending to their crops and animals in the burning sun. Soon they would be black with the juice of kalamata, and stinging, bursting cracks of hard skin. As the men shook the branches of the trees with long canes, shaking loose a shower of black fruit, the women murmured their prayers and made the sign of the cross before they knelt down in the dirt and started picking.

Everyone helped when it was time to harvest the olives. Neighbors and relatives all gathered to help harvest a crop, and rotated between their respective groves. Children were taught to pick the good fruit and leave the ones that had shriveled on the trees. The oldest women stayed back and cooked huge pots of food to feed the laborers—hot, creamy *trahana* or fried eggs with hunks of bread and cheese. Decrepit old men supervised from the side, working their wooden worry beads with one hand and pointing angrily with the other, yelling at whoever was within earshot that they were doing it all wrong. At the end of the day weary workers fell to the ground in relief and the harvest was protected as it lay in big burlap sacks under sheets of cloth. After many days, the grove would be stripped clean and the entire crop collected. The men would drive their big trucks with olives piled up high in the back to the nearest olive press, and when they returned the celebration would begin.

"How much did you get? How many barrels did you press? Where is our oil?" The majority of the oil would be sold, but each family kept a large barrel for their own use, blessing the oil and cursing the Communist soldiers who had blasted through their homes and stuck their dirty gun barrels into the life-giving green liquid, looking for hidden weapons or money, or knocked over their stash of golden grain and stomped through it with their heavy black boots. Once the price was discussed and the reality of their cash resources for the next year had sunk in, the women set to work making loukoumathes, the traditional way to celebrate the conclusion of the olive harvest. Remembering the soldiers plundering their oil and grain for the year made them anticipate and savor the fried balls of fluffy dough all the more. The sweetness of food can take away our pain, even if just for the moment.

I rise from the couch to check the loukoumathes batter. It has bubbled and risen like a cratered moon. I call Callie into the kitchen to show her how my mother learned to make loukoumathes from her mother, and now I am going to show her. I bring her into the chain, and we follow the same steps as the women before us.

My grandmother, my *yiayia*, would quickly stir up a batch of the yeasty batter and set it aside to rise while her daughters admired the cloudy chartreuse color of the freshly pressed olive oil. One sister chopped walnuts while another swirled the amber honey loose of crystals for the syrup. The rich, fruity aroma of the oil thickened the air as it heated in a deep pan on the petrol stove. My *yiayia* would wash her hands thoroughly just as the oil reached the perfect temperature, and plunge her fist into the cool batter. She pumped her fist like a beating heart, and with a spoon in the other hand captured a dollop of dough to drop into the hot oil. The puffy balls of dough bobbed on the roiling green surface of the oil, turning from pale white to golden and crisp.

While the loukoumathes cooked, the whole family gathered around the table in anticipation, jostling to be closer to the big ceramic bowl that would hold the delicious morsels. Yiayia would scoop the hot dumplings out of the oil and pour them into the bowl. She would drizzle generous amounts of honey syrup over the golden balls, and then sprinkle them with chopped walnuts and plenty of aromatic cinnamon. When the honey and cinnamon merged with the heat of the loukoumathes, an intoxicating scent filled the air that allowed everyone to forget the labor of the last weeks and that they were poor farmers. For the smell of honey and cinnamon wafting through the air of a warm, glowing kitchen can make even ordinary laborers feel as if they are rich, as if they are privy to the food of the gods.

I tell her, "Each time you pick up a bottle of olive oil in the grocery store, remember the history. Remember the labor. Remember the people whose lives are hard so that yours is easy. Remember their cracked skin and their backs burned by the sun as they bent over to pick their crops. Remember that we are linked to them. Remember and be grateful."

Callie and I sink our hands into the batter just like my *yiayia*, squeezing the batter through our fists and dropping it into the

51

burning oil where it sizzles and sings as it transforms into something delectable to be eaten with eager tongues.

Our hands move together to prepare the loukoumathes, and they are finally ready, bringing a bit of the past into our present. As we bite into the golden puffs, our teeth break through the crispy, sticky, honey-drenched crust, and a puff of yeasty steam releases into our mouths. They are too hot to eat and too good to wait for. We exhale through our mouths like panting dogs as we continue to savor the chewy dough and crunchy walnuts. Callie blows on a little piece sprinkled with cinnamon and sugar and gives it to Manny, who has by now abandoned his hammer for a wooden spoon. He sucks the treat from his mother's fingers, and makes a happy high-pitched sound and bangs his spoon until she gives him more. We eat until we are too full to stand up anymore.

We set aside a small bowl of loukoumathes for Gus, and go sit down on the cream-colored couch in the living room. Callie lays Manny down on his favorite fluffy flokati rug and he plays with the fringes. As soon as we sit down, she gets back up to get the loukoumathes that she had saved for Gus and brings them out to the couch with her. "We can always make more for Gus another time, right?"

I watch her pop another in her mouth. Well, at least she can eat like a Greek.

"Sure, why not," I say. "We can do whatever we want. We live in America."

She looks down and softly says, "I wish we could do whatever we wanted."

I find myself blushing as I remember Callie's fingers intertwined with mine, and I wonder what feelings are hidden in her downcast eyes.

When we are done with the loukoumathes, she picks up Manny and curls up on the couch with her feet tucked under a cushion and Manny nestled in her lap, nursing. The sun is setting over the canyon, and the room has become dusky. I can see the curve of her bare breast and Manny nuzzled against her softness. I long for that closeness and peace. Callie sits staring at me, and

I try to avert my eyes from her nakedness. Manny has fallen asleep and is breathing softly in her arms. You can barely see his outline in the dark room.

"You know, Manny was a surprise. I didn't really 'pick the ingredients' like you said, but once I was pregnant I knew I wanted him to have a father. I mean, otherwise I could have just gone to the sperm bank. I thought about doing that. I could have gotten pregnant without a man. But it worked out this way. People get together under difficult circumstances all the time, and it turns out all right. Right?"

She could have gotten pregnant without a man? Without waiting for me to reply, she continued.

"When I got pregnant, he was so excited about having a son. It seemed like the best choice for us. There were so many things I didn't know. There are still so many things I don't know. So many things to learn."

"And here we are," I say. "Do you wish you had gone to the sperm bank instead?"

"You know, I feel confused a lot of the time. I don't know what's right anymore. All I know is that when I'm with you . . . I can finally feel like myself. It feels good." She smiles at me and then turns her face away from mine.

Sitting there in the dark, I don't want to train her to be a good Greek wife anymore. I imagine Manny lying close to her breast, safe in her arms. I can hear her breathing, can feel the warmth of her exhaled breath. The room smells of cinnamon, honey, and regret.

LOUKOUMATHES

"It's the magic of yeast—without that ingredient, they would never come to life."

    1 package dry yeast
    1 1/4 cup warm water
    2 cups flour
    1 teaspoon sugar
    Dash of salt
    Cooking oil
    Honey
    Chopped walnuts
    Cinnamon

Dissolve yeast in the warm water, and wait for it to foam with life. Combine the flour, sugar, and salt in a bowl. Add the yeast and stir it with a spoon until you see it is well incorporated. Cover the bowl with plastic wrap and then a clean towel and place it in a warm place. Let rise until it doubles in size and forms bubbles, approximately two hours.

Heat a few inches of oil in a deep frying pan until just before the smoking point, about 375 degrees. If you are right-handed, submerge your left hand into the batter and scoop up a handful of batter. Squeeze the batter so that it emerges from the circle formed by your index finger and thumb. Imagine your heart beating. Using a teaspoon, scrape a ball of batter from the left hand and drop it gently into the hot oil.

Dip the spoon into a glass of water between each ball. Do not crowd the loukoumathes in the pan. Turn them as they cook to achieve an even golden color. Remove them from the oil and allow them to rest on a bed of paper towels. Set the paper towels on top of a cookie rack to drain any excess oil.

Place the loukoumathes in a serving bowl and drizzle them with honey. Sprinkle them with chopped walnuts, and cinnamon to taste.

Eat them with your fingers, and feel free to lick the honey clean.

Baking a Baby

I can't let myself think about what Callie said: It feels good to be with me? I have to push those thoughts out of my mind. Callie is married. Callie is a woman. I can't let myself blush and stammer and have a racing heart. I have to focus. I have to show God that I am pure and deserving of a baby.

Seeing Callie hold Manny to her breast, peacefully enraptured with her baby, just makes me want a baby even more. But I'm afraid it will never happen. I'm past my prime and my eggs are losing their vitality. I know how important fresh ingredients are. Just as yeast makes the loukoumathes rise, I need all the right ingredients to make my dream a reality. Why is this recipe so hard? Did I leave out some step or forget to perform a necessary ritual? It's been over two years now that I have been praying for a miracle.

Callie said she could have gotten pregnant without a man. She said she could have gone to the sperm bank. As much as I worry that it will be interpreted as a lack of faith, I have to try something different. I'm always telling Callie that you have to pick the right ingredients if you want your recipe to succeed. Would it be cheating to add a secret ingredient? I'll still pray. It will just be a boost, like sprinkling *mizithra* on your pasta or adding olives to your salad. It would still be a salad without them, but the olives take the salad to the next level, and I need to get to the next level.

Or maybe this doesn't have anything to do with God. Maybe it's all science, like baking. Add the right ingredients in the correct amounts and bake as directed for perfect results every time. I just need to get to know my ingredients better. I'm an excellent baker. I know that I can do this.

I arrive at the sperm bank late, with the last of my savings in my pocket. Sitting in the waiting room, I focus on my hands folded in my lap. I don't want to look up. I don't want people to see me here and think that I am losing faith. I will still be an Ever-Virgin. I am still keeping my vow that no man will ever touch my body. It will still be a virgin birth even if I get a little help . . . won't it? In the end, it's God who makes the final call, who gives me a baby or keeps me barren regardless of what science says.

There are no tellers at the sperm bank, only women wearing Birkenstocks. One of them calls my name, but she says it wrong.

"Zee-ni?"

"No, it's Kseh-nee," I correct her, and look down at my feet.

She tries to repeat after me, "Okay, Seh-nee, follow me and we can get started." She smiles at me when I look up at her and leads me into a small room with a window in the door. There is a metal tank sitting in the corner.

"Now when it's time, you'll come and get the sperm in one of these tanks. It will have liquid nitrogen in it to keep the sperm frozen for up to seven days. Be careful handling it because the nitrogen can hurt your skin if you touch it."

I nod my head as she shows me how to lift the vials from the tank.

"How many of those do I use?" I ask her. "They are so small." I start calculating in my head as if composing a recipe.

"It's up to you, but we recommend two vials to increase your chances."

I make a note to myself . . . *two vials of sperm, and one egg* . . .

"Now you can use a glove or a towel to hold the vial because it will be very cold initially." *I should wash my oven mitts.*

"After the sperm has thawed, you can tuck it between your breasts."

This strikes me as odd, or at least immodest. "Does it have to be between my breasts? How about in my hand?" I ask.

"You can hold it in your hand, but your breasts will keep the sperm at just the right temperature." She smiles so wide her face crinkles, and I wonder why that makes her so happy. I know that having the right temperature is critical in baking, so I decide to follow her instructions.

She seems helpful enough, but she has some weird ideas about how to become pregnant. Charts, thermometers, sticking your fingers into your vagina to check your mucus! That can't be right. I can't believe that the miracle of life begins with probing your private parts. I've never even heard of some of the things she is talking about. If I was meant to know about my cervical os, then I would be able to see it. I'm not sure this is a good idea, but then I see the bulletin board with all the pictures of babies and I turn my attention back to her.

She shows me how to draw the sperm up into a syringe and inject it into my private parts.

"After you inject the sperm, you should lie quietly with your legs up in the air." I imagine myself lying on the bed like a trussed chicken being basted with a magical marinade.

"Okay! Now here is the fun part! Have you had a chance to peruse our donor profiles yet?"

"I have looked a little. But . . . I'm not sure how to pick."

"Well, just look through. Maybe you'll find someone that clicks for you. If it were me, I'd try to pick someone who looks like Jason Momoa." She chuckles as she leaves the room.

Looking through the binder of sperm donors, I grow more confused about how to pick. Eye color, hair color, height, hobbies? The donor information profiles tell me what they study, if their grandmothers have diabetes, and if they play basketball, but it doesn't tell me if they are decent human beings. After looking through a binder full of donor profiles, I pick one that reminds me of Jesus. The description says he is a student of religion and serves food at the homeless shelter in his spare time. I reserve three vials of frozen sperm to represent the Father, the Son, and the Holy Ghost and say a little prayer. I imagine the sperm bank lady lowering my vials into a cave of swirling mist, the cold keeping my future frozen, until that time when I can retrieve them and they will rise, bringing with them my baby.

I follow their recipe, and when the time comes I rush to the sperm bank to get the final ingredient. Early the next morning I put on my mittens and take each of the frozen vials out of the big beige nitrogen tank. They are so small, not even two inches long, about as wide as a pencil, and at the bottom, there's just a little pea-sized bit of pink ice. It's hard to believe that the miracle of life could be contained in such a small space. I warm up the first vial between my breasts like they told me to until the ice turns into a little pink liquid puddle. When I look at it closely with the light going through it, it looks like a tiny swirling universe in there, moving in slow motion, and it makes me choke up a little. According to the papers they gave me there are twenty-two million little sperm bodies in there swimming around, coming back to life after being suspended in death, resurrected for this moment.

BAKING A BABY

"Maybe this doesn't have anything to do with God. Maybe it's all science, like baking."

1 uterus
1 ripe egg
3 vials of frozen, defrosted sperm

Take vaginal temperature using a basal body thermometer every morning immediately upon waking. Note temperature on chart. Insert two fingers in vagina while squatting, and touch the cervix. Note the shape and position of the cervix. Note whether the os is open or closed or in transition. Collect cervical mucous, and with eyes closed rub it between the fingers and thumb. Note the texture, quantity, and temperature. Smell and taste the mucous. Note all data on chart.

Starting on seventh day, using first morning urine, urinate on fertility monitor ovulation test sticks for ten days. When the test sticks indicate high fertility, collect saliva sample on microscope slide. Begin testing evening urine with backup ovulation test sticks, paying particular attention for a positive evening reading, so as not to miss the beginning of ovulation.

When the ovulation monitor has peaked, the backup test stick is positive, the saliva has ferned, the cervix has risen, the os is open, the mucous is copious and resembles raw egg white, but before your morning temperature has risen, and at the moment of mittelschmerz (a pain in the abdomen that accompanies ovulation), administer orgasm, insert defrosted sperm into the vagina using sterile syringe, and stand on head. If standing on head is not possible use the rotisserie technique: Lay with hips elevated above the head for two hours, turning position every fifteen minutes to thoroughly baste the cervix with sperm.

Bake for two weeks and test for doneness on the first day of the missed period.

Papoutsakia

The following week, I arrive early in the morning with several brown paper bags clutched tightly to my chest. The steep staircase to the house on stilts seems especially treacherous and gray. I place each foot firmly as if walking a tightrope until I reach the top of the stairs. Looking behind me, I swoon a little and imagine myself falling backward with produce and bottles and sacks hovering in the air above my head before landing with a thud on my broken body. I shake off the vision and knock on the front door. While I wait for an answer I double-check my ingredients and try to smooth my hair, which the misty fog is causing to rebel and curl out of my tight braid. The longer I stand there the more out of balance I feel. The sperm bank lady told me I'd have to wait two weeks before I'd know if my recipe worked. In the meantime we cook.

It is several long minutes before I hear Callie's muffled footsteps on the carpeted staircase coming to let me in. My heart is beating soundly against my ribs in rhythm with her steps. I have to admit that I've come to enjoy these cooking lessons, almost as much as visiting the fat little baby.

When Callie finally opens the front door, she looks as if she's just emerged from her warm blankets, hair tangled, and wearing a striped men's pajama shirt unbuttoned nearly to the waist and big sheared wool and suede boots. I have the sudden sensation that air is being sucked out of my lungs. Taking a deep breath, I blurt out, "Good morning! I have something for Manny!"

"Is it time for our lesson already?" Callie asks as she rubs sleep out of her eyes.

"Well, I'm a little early. I was at the farmer's market this morning and I found the most perfect, firm, glossy *melitzanes*. They are just the right size and shape, and a beautiful deep purple color. I've planned a special lesson today. Unless . . . you don't want the lesson today? Are you feeling ill? I could go . . ." I look back at the steep staircase, and imagine free-falling back down the bumpy steps.

"No! No, of course not! Please come in!" Callie takes a heavy bag from my arms and leads the way up the last set of dark, twisting stairs. "I must have overslept. Manny woke up really early this morning, and I brought him to bed with me and nursed him back to sleep. I guess I fell asleep too. Nursing always makes me feel sleepy and relaxed, too. I guess that's nature's way of ensuring the survival of the species, huh?" She chuckles as she mounts the steps.

"Yeah, that sounds really relaxing," I say, imagining the warmth and softness of Callie and the baby puzzled together under the covers.

As I follow her up the stairs, I notice her long legs emerging from the furry boots, the way her calves flex with each step, the absence of freckles behind her knees, and her hot pink panties peeking out from under the pinstriped pajama top. I shake my head and focus my eyes on the stairs, willing myself not to trip and fall. I have always been extremely modest, and Callie's ease with her own body both mesmerizes me and makes me uncomfortable. "I'm probably supposed to know this, but what's a *melitzanes*?" Callie asks.

"I'll show you in just a minute," I reply.

We put the bags down on the kitchen table, and one by one I pull the ingredients out. "Today we are making *papoutsakia*, a very special dish, because you have to find *melitzanes* of just the right size and shape." I pull from the bag two small eggplants that nearly glow with freshness and generously fill each hand. "Notice how the skin is so shiny and firm? The color is beautiful and deep. You can see your reflection in these—look!"

Callie looks into the beautiful surface of the eggplant and grins. "You really love food, don't you?"

Unable to contain my happiness, I continue to pull out more of the perfect *melitzanes* until there are eight. "Aren't they beautiful?" Also emerging from the bag are three fleshy red tomatoes, a yellow onion, a snowy white head of garlic, a bunch of frilly parsley, and a package of freshly ground beef from the butcher. "You still have plenty of the extra-virgin olive oil and the dried Greek oregano that I brought, don't you?"

"Of course. If I've learned one thing so far, it's that I can't keep a Greek kitchen without olive oil and oregano!" Callie says.

"What kind of olive oil?" I quiz her.

Callie smiles. "Extra-virgin olive oil from the first cold pressing, preferably from Greece, but Italian will do in a pinch."

"And?" I prompt.

"Don't tell the Italians."

"What about the oregano?" I ask as she caresses the rounded curves of the shiny *melitzanes* with her long fingers.

"Only wild oregano collected from the mountains of Greece. It should be a vibrant green color even though it is dried. If it is dull and gray, it is last year's harvest."

"Excellent! I am glad to see you are taking your lessons seriously!" I remove a large chunk of mizithra cheese, a half-gallon of organic whole milk, a dozen fresh eggs, and a pound of butter from the sack, and ask her to get the flour from the cabinet.

"Okay. So what is the dish that we are making today, papou—?"

"*Pa-pou-tsa-kia*. It means little shoes. Baby shoes. We take these lovely *melitzanes*, and we cut them in half and fill them with a delicious ground meat filling and top them with béchamel sauce and bake them. It sounds easy when I say it that way, doesn't it? It isn't. You are learning two lessons in one today. Papoutsakia and béchamel sauce. Once you learn how to make béchamel, you can make pastitsio, moussaka, and many other delicious dishes."

"And béchamel sauce is . . .?" Callie asks with a serious look while scratching an itch on her exposed thigh.

"Béchamel is the most creamy, delicious sauce. The French and Italians both want to claim that they invented it, and the French call it one of the four 'mother sauces' from which all other sauces originate. But the Greek version of béchamel differs in that we add mizithra cheese, white pepper, nutmeg, and egg to finish it."

"Mmm . . . I think I've had that before when I went to a Greek restaurant."

"You haven't had béchamel until you've eaten it fresh from the oven while it is still steaming hot and the texture is delicate and soft. It is still tasty after you reheat it, but the first bites are always the best. That's why I always skip a meal when I cook a dish with béchamel, because I know that I will eat until I am ready to burst when the dish comes hot from the oven."

"Wow. That does sound like a high recommendation." Callie smiles.

I often find myself getting carried away when sharing the cooking lessons with Callie. Being near her seems to give me some permission to express myself freely, allowing my passion to expand.

I feel her eyes on me for a long moment before she says, "I love that about you. Your passion, your belief. You feel so strongly about food it almost seems like a religion."

It's as if I am being seen for the first time. I look down, trying to hide the emotion in my eyes. "Yes, in a way, it is. We can create miracles in the kitchen." I shake myself and looking around ask, "Where is Manny?"

"Still sleeping. I better go check on him. And put on some clothes!" Callie laughs.

"I'll be here." I have brought a special surprise for Manny—one perfect sunflower, almost as tall as he is.

By the time Callie comes down the steps from her upstairs bedroom, wearing a halter top and shorts, and carrying Manny, the fog has cleared outside and a bright sunshine is filling the kitchen. "Say, 'Good morning, Xeni,'" Callie prompts Manny, and laughs since the baby is nowhere near enunciation yet. But Manny does give me a prompt smile and his face stretches out into a huge grin once he sees the sunflower that I brought him.

"Wow. That is one beautiful sunflower, huh, Manny?" she says as he reaches out his fat fists to grab at the flower.

"It reminded me of you," I tell her. *Why did I do that?* I hold the flower out so Manny can touch the soft yellow petals and the bumpy texture of the purple center that later would have developed into seeds. His little fingers crush the petals and poke at the center, and he tries to grab the thick stalk with his fist. Avoiding Callie's gaze, I smile and give him a quick squeeze on his blubbery, delicious thigh. Callie sets him down in his playpen with the flower, where she can watch and interact with him while we cook.

My eyes linger on Manny, wondering if I could be pregnant, and what my baby would look like. I tie my apron on and hand another to Callie.

"Okay, let's get started. Gus's mother is going to be here before we know it."

"Papoutsakia . . ." I say as I hold a *melitzana* down on the cutting board and make quick cuts, removing the stem end and then dividing the fruit neatly in half, ". . . means little shoes. When we cut the eggplant in half and stuff it with filling, they end up looking like little baby shoes." I hand Callie the knife and supervise her technique, guiding her hands with mine as she cuts the rest of the *melitzanes*. "That's why they have to be the right size, so they look like little shoes when they are done." Next, I show her how to scoop out the flesh of the eggplant, leaving a shell the width of her pinkie finger.

By the time we finish scooping, she is already blowing the hair out of her face and commenting that the dish is a lot of work. I laugh. "We're just getting started." I direct her to start chopping up the meat of the eggplant into little pieces. "Since I don't want you to start crying yet, I'll chop the onion."

I arrange the eggplant shells on large baking sheets and sprinkle them with salt. "When working with *melitzanes*, you always salt them and let them rest for twenty minutes. This draws all of the bitterness out of them."

"Really? That's amazing."

"Yes, sometimes I wish it worked on people too." I sprinkle a little salt on my hand.

"Are you bitter?" Callie asks.

"Oh yes, but that's another story," I reply.

"You know, I have realized that you have never told me anything about yourself."

"What are you talking about? I told you all about my family history the other week."

"Yes, I know. And it was so amazing. But I want to know more about *you*. Where did you grow up? Do you have siblings? Tell me about your childhood. Family pets?" Callie asks hopefully.

"No. I don't like to talk about those things. Try to chop the *melitzana* a little finer." I will tell her all I know about Greek cuisine, but other things are better left unsaid.

"Oh. Okay." Callie chops the eggplant studiously, "I was just wondering if you have family of your own. A lover, maybe?"

"No. No lover. I love God and the kitchen. That's all I need." I look longingly at Manny, my arms suddenly feeling empty and useless.

Callie puts down her knife and picks up Manny for a quick hug and asks, "Do you think that you would ever want to have a baby?"

I pause, trying to find words that I can say in a normal voice, that won't reveal my emotions, my deepest hope. "It would be my greatest blessing." I move farther from Callie and Manny and cut into an onion, my eyes stinging. "Why don't you tell me about your childhood instead?" I try to imagine Callie as a young girl with curly red ponytails and her sunny smile.

"Oh, nothing special. It was just me and my mom. We have family in the Midwest, but Mom and I left when I was little. She dreamed of California where she felt she could really be free. She was sick of all the small-town culture and rules. I still remember certain things, like when we stayed with my Aunt Margie and Uncle Ed. They had a big old house with a backyard and a dog named Homer. Aunt Margie didn't have kids of her own, so she always liked it when I stayed there, and I'd stay there some summers if Mom had other things going on."

"What do you mean, other things?" I hand Callie a washed bunch of parsley to chop as I finish chopping the onion. I can't imagine what kind of mother would leave Callie behind while she went to go do "other things."

"Oh, you know. She liked to move a lot, and she made friends easily. We lived a lot of different places. Sometimes with new boyfriends, or sometimes the boyfriend didn't want me around, so I'd get to go stay with Aunt Margie. One boyfriend she had got her hooked on checking out his commune. She really liked that idea, of communal living, everyone taking care of each other." Callie stops chopping the parsley long enough to rub a spot on her nose, the knife edge rising and falling next to her face. "But she never was one to stay in one place for too long. So for a while we traveled up and down the coast checking out different communes. Different places, like rural Oregon, out of the way parts of northern California, and the Santa Cruz Mountains. The kids ran around naked all the time and it seemed like the adults weren't around much. It was fun some of the time."

I have finished chopping the onion and garlic and I'm washing the tomatoes. "Sounds ... different?" I can't imagine such an environment and how someone as naïve as Callie has emerged from it.

"Yeah, it was different. There were definitely weird parts. Okay, I'm done with the parsley and eggplant."

"*Melitzana*," I prompt.

"*Melitzana*," she repeats.

I quarter the juicy red tomatoes and push half of them into the food processor. "Fresh pureed tomatoes are always best. Most recipes call for tomato paste or sauce, but since we live in California, we don't have to use canned tomatoes. Your dish will always taste more delicious and lighter with the fresh tomatoes."

I push the pulse button on the food processor. Pausing the pulsing tomatoes, I ask, "So, what was weird?"

"Oh, well, you know. Boundaries are really different on the commune. Free love, free everything, really. I remember this one place I was staying with my Mom. She found out about it through this guy she met at a bar. He took us there, and we stayed in these cabins that reminded me of barracks. They had bunk beds inside, and she had me sleep on the top and they squeezed into the one below me. I could hear them, you know, doing it. That was always kind of weird."

"Always?" I press the pulse button again, sending the tomatoes into a red frenzy in the clear bowl of the processor. I press my lips together and try to hold my tongue but can't. "I'm sorry to say something disrespectful toward your mother, but that's totally inappropriate! To expose a young girl to," I sputter, "to, to *that* kind of thing. It's wrong. She should have protected you."

Callie looks down at her hands. "Yeah. It was pretty weird. But there were some good things about being at the commune too."

I couldn't believe that there was anything good in such a place of debauchery. "Like what?"

Callie smiles. "Well, for one thing I got exposed to world cultures, which I still love. And at this one in Santa Cruz, I met this woman named Shameena. She said it meant sweet smelling, which was kind of funny because no one at the commune smelled very good." Callie laughs. Seeing I'm not laughing, she gets serious. "Well, she's the one who taught me how to belly dance. I loved it. I escaped into the music through my body and didn't think about anyone or anything when I was dancing." Callie twirls through the kitchen, giving her hips a quick shimmy as she seems to float toward me.

I turn my attention back to the food processor, fiddling with buttons and avoiding Callie's outstretched hand. "Was she Middle Eastern?"

"Oh no. She was probably from Jersey. But no one used their real names. There was usually some spiritual leader who renamed people at will." Callie wipes her hands on her pants and shrugs.

"What about your name? Is it real?" I frown.

"It's real. But it isn't my name given to me at birth. Callie is short for Calliope. Someone renamed me that after they saw me dance. I was told it means 'the muse of epic poetry.'"

"It suits you," I say, watching her as she gracefully turns toward Manny and tickles his soft folds. "What's your real name?" I ask.

"Hmm? It's something boring." Callie pulls at Manny's toes and tickles his chin.

I long to stand close to her and join her in playing with his plump feet. "Has your mother met Manny?"

"No, I haven't seen her in a while. She ended up in Hollywood, where she hooked up with this group that started a commune in Hawaii. I haven't much seen her since. But I send her a letter once in a while, and when she heard about Manny, she sent him a little tie-dyed onesie. But she's never come to meet him." She pauses, and I wonder how any woman could ignore her grand-child.

"So anyway. I always thought to myself, when I had a kid I would try the more traditional route." She turns to me and smiles. "Well, as much as I can muster anyway, not being the most conventional person in the world. But I'm really trying."

I have the sudden impulse to hug her tightly, but instead I say, "Yes, you are. Well, let's get back to some traditional cooking then."

"Yes. Let's do that," Callie answers. "Thank you, by the way, for everything you are doing, for teaching me."

"It is my pleasure," I reply.

"Our time together is so . . ." she pauses, searching for the right word, "delicious."

"Yes, the food is delicious," I agree.

"No, I mean, I love spending time with *you*. In so many ways I think we are so opposite, and yet when I am with you, I feel so good in my own skin."

"Oh." I smile, unsure what to say. "I am enjoying this time too. With you and Manny." I'm thinking, *It feels like home*, but I'm not about to say that and sound crazy. Instead, I show Callie how to

71

brush olive oil onto the eggplant shells and put them into the oven to soften and bake while we make the meat sauce. Browning the onions and garlic in olive oil fills the kitchen with an irresistible smell, and as we add the freshly ground beef, the aroma of the meat browning makes our mouths water. Callie picks up Manny and dances around the kitchen while I stir the parsley and oregano into the meat. Then she hands Manny to me and I show him the vibrant red tomato puree as Callie pours it into the pot. Stirring different elements together and adding a little heat can transform almost anything into something better.

"I love how the smell of good food cooking can make any house feel more like home," Callie says.

I nod, smiling. We let the meat cook in the sauce, so the flavors of the tomato and onion and herbs can deepen and thicken, and in the meantime begin the most difficult part of the dish, the béchamel sauce. I hold Manny close as I instruct Callie, inhaling the scent of his hair. I tell her how to brown flour in butter until it reaches a golden color, and then add hot milk, quickly whisking out the lumps. I have her repeat this step many times until she masters the timing. Then we get to the hard part. I tell her to carefully add a little bit of the hot béchamel sauce to a bowl of beaten egg while stirring constantly. "This way, the egg gets warmer and warmer slowly until it gets used to the heat. Before you know it, it will be hot enough to add to the sauce—but you have to continue stirring quickly. You can ruin the whole thing if you don't warm it up gradually."

"Well, I have been told that I sometimes come on too strong," Callie jokes.

I want to ask what she means by that, but instead I urged, "Keep focused. This is a critical moment."

Callie nods and stirs with all of her focus on warming the eggs gently. "Is that better?" she murmurs.

"Much," I answer. With the eggs safely added, we reach the last phase of completing the sauce. "Now add the grated mizithra, and using that same whisk, stir it in so it melts." Callie slides the cheese into the thick, hot sauce and stirs until it melts. "Now taste it," I command.

Callie licks a bit of sauce from a spoon I hand her. "Mmm. That is the creamiest, most delicious—"

"We're not done yet. It gets better. Now, we'll add salt and white pepper to taste, and lastly we'll add a little nutmeg. But not too much!" I direct. "Okay, okay, that's good. That's perfect!"

We work up a sweat working in concert until the sauce is complete and delicately, perfectly seasoned. When we are done we stare at it in wonder that something can taste so good.

"Yum, that is so good, it's practically better than sex. I think I need a cigarette," Callie jokes.

I imagine Callie lying in bed with the sheets tucked under her bare shoulders, a tendril of steam rising from her fingertips. I shake my head, pushing the thought away.

"Well, we aren't done quite yet, so don't get too relaxed," I scold.

"Okay, what comes next?"

"We fill the baked melitzana shells with a bit of the stewed meat, and then we top it with a thick layer of the cream sauce, and put it all back in the oven until the top turns a golden-brown color."

"And then?"

"And then we pour a glass of wine, toast our good work, and sit and eat and eat until we cannot eat any more."

Callie reaches for a bottle of wine and two glasses. "Can I help quench your thirst?"

PAPOUTSAKIA (Little Shoes)

"Look for small eggplants that nearly glow with freshness and generously fill each by hand."

6 medium eggplants, approximately 6 inches long
4 tablespoons extra-virgin olive oil
1 onion, finely chopped
3 cloves garlic, minced
1 pound ground beef
3 ripe tomatoes, pureed
1 teaspoon dried oregano
1/4 cup parsley, chopped
Salt and pepper to taste
1 recipe béchamel sauce (see recipe)

To make the little shoes, cut the eggplants in half lengthwise. Scoop out the meat of the eggplant with a spoon, leaving a 1/4–1/2-inch shell. Sprinkle the eggplant innards and shells with salt to draw out any bitterness. Let them sit for 20 minutes. After 20 minutes, rinse the salt off. Blot the eggplant dry. Finely chop the eggplant innards. Brush the eggplant shells with 2 tablespoons olive oil and place them on an oiled baking sheet. Bake at 375 degrees until they become soft, approximately 20 minutes.

Heat 2 tablespoons olive oil in a large pot. Add the chopped onion and minced garlic and cook until soft. Add the ground beef and sauté it until it is browned. Add the chopped eggplant, pureed tomatoes, oregano, parsley, salt and pepper, and 1/2 cup of water. Mix well. Let the mixture simmer until most of the moisture is absorbed, approximately 30 minutes. The meat sauce will fill your kitchen with a savory aroma that will make your mouth water.

Fill the eggplant shells with the meat mixture, and then top them with the béchamel sauce. Add 1/2 cup boiling water to the pan around the eggplant shells. Bake at 375 degrees until the béchamel sauce has turned a golden brown, approximately 30 minutes.

Sit down with a glass of wine and enjoy your little shoes.

BÉCHAMEL SAUCE

"You can ruin the whole thing if you don't warm it up gradually."

6 tablespoons butter
6 tablespoons flour
4 cups warm milk
2 eggs, beaten
1/2 cup grated mizithra cheese
1/2 teaspoon salt
White pepper to taste
1/4 teaspoon nutmeg

Melt the butter in a large pan over medium heat. Stir in the flour and cook it until it gains some color and starts to smell nutty, around five minutes. Gradually add the warmed milk, whisking earnestly to remove any lumps. Beat the eggs in a small bowl, and gradually add a tablespoon of the sauce, stirring constantly. Add a few more spoons of sauce to gradually warm the eggs. This is critical: slowly drizzle the eggs into the pan of sauce, continually whisking, or you will end up with scrambled eggs in your sauce. After you have incorporated the eggs, whisk the mizithra cheese into the sauce. Stir in the salt, white pepper, and nutmeg to taste.

I dare you not to lick the spoon and pan.

Béchamel Sauce

Callie is so excited that she has finally mastered béchamel sauce. Browning heaping spoonfuls of flour in pools of butter until it all turns into a nutty paste is not the hard part. It was pouring in the hot milk in spurts and quickly incorporating it into the paste to create the creamy sauce that had her stumped. I made her practice over and over again until it all came together—dumping out one pan of lumpy goop after another until finally she learned to feel with her body how much liquid to add, how long to stir, and when to take the pan off the fire. We did it until making the creamy delicious goo became second nature to her. I showed her how to sprinkle in the tangy mizithra cheese at the end and stir until it all melted in. I took a clean wooden spoon and dipped into the sauce. My first taste of her sauce made the saliva spurt in my mouth.

When I was done licking the spoon clean, I dipped my finger into the warm pot and gave her a taste. When she closed her lips around my finger, her eyes became drunk with joy. It was delicious. In our excitement, we screamed with delight and hugged each other close, spinning around the kitchen, almost falling onto the hot stove. She had finally mastered béchamel, and I was afraid she was beginning to master my heart.

Roosters and Hens

The next time I go over for our cooking lesson he is sitting there at the kitchen counter. He is tall and looks very typically Greek. Dark curly hair. Swaggering dark eyes. I think about turning around and running down the stairs and never coming back. Then I remember my *thea*, my aunt, and how she slaughters roosters. Their meat is tough and stringy, but when stewed long enough with fresh tomatoes and onions it becomes delicious and savory.

He stands up when he sees me at the top of the steps, his face placid. "So you're the one," he says, and reaches out a big bear claw at me. I think about biting his fingers until the filling oozes out.

"Yes, that's me," I say.

"So what's on the menu today?" he asks with a smile.

"Well, I was thinking about roast billy goat, but I have a hard time finding it this time of year. Then I was thinking about stewed rooster, or oxtail soup." I can hear his testicles retract.

"Really," he says. "Well, why don't you teach her how to make yogurt from fresh milk, or bake some chicken breasts with lemon and oregano?"

"I thought about that," I say, "but instead I decided to show her how to make sausage from scratch, so that a sausage she'd never lack."

He struts over to me, "Oh, that won't be necessary."

"Why," I ask, "don't you like to eat sausage?"

"Why no," he says, "I prefer homemade bread made from yeasty punched-down dough."

Just then Callie emerges from the bathroom with the baby, all freshly bathed and sweet-smelling. "Ah, I see you've met," she says.

"Yes," he says, "you know, she reminds me of my mother?"

I'd rather poke myself in the eye than remind him of his mother. So I do, just to get out of there. "Ouch! Oh. Wow. Silly me. That was an accident." I smile as I cover my eye with my hand. "I need to use your bathroom. Excuse me."

"Sure," she says and gestures the way.

The bathwater is still in the tub, and I imagine bringing it to a slow simmer on the stove. I stay in there as long as I can, hoping he'll be gone when I go back out. But he is not. He is right there in the kitchen, holding the ever-fatter baby. He is laughing and biting Manny's leg, and saying "*Tha se faw! Tha se faw!*" My stomach sinks. I offer to hold the baby so he can go do his thing.

"Oh no," he says. "I'm staying for the lesson today."

"Well," I say. "Why don't we bake the baby then? He looks about big enough for the roasting pan." They both laugh and smile at their son. I reach over and grab Manny's foot and tug on it.

"I love this," she says. "It feels like one big Greek family."

"Yeah," I say. "It's just like this."

STEWED ROOSTER

"Rooster is tough and stringy, but when stewed long enough with fresh tomatoes and onions it becomes delicious and savory."

1/4 cup extra-virgin olive oil
1 onion, cut into thin slices
1 fresh rooster, plucked, gutted, and cut into pieces
3 ripe tomatoes, pureed
Salt and pepper to taste
2 teaspoons dried Greek oregano
2 cups *hilopites*, a small square-shaped noodle, or other small noodle
Mizithra cheese

Heat the olive oil in a large pot. Add the onions and sauté until they become soft. Add the rooster and cook until it is browned. Next, add the pureed tomatoes, 3 cups of water, salt and pepper, and oregano, and bring to a boil. Immediately reduce the heat and simmer the rooster until the meat becomes tender and falls off the bone, approximately two hours. Remove the rooster to a serving bowl and keep warm.

Add 4 cups of water to the pot and bring to a boil. Add the hilopites and cook until they are tender and have absorbed all of the liquid.

Generously sprinkle the hilopites with grated mizithra cheese and serve alongside the stewed rooster. Given enough time to stew, even a rooster can become tender.

The Family Tree

Gus was reading the newspaper and enjoying his coffee at the breakfast table. It was a good morning. He put the newspaper down and listened to his voice mail again. *"Beeeeeep!* Constantino. I don't have any more of the icy hot patches that I like. They don't have them here. Make sure you have some when I arrive. How is the baby? Good-bye." His mother was definitely warming up.

He smiled broadly when Callie came downstairs with Manny. He took the baby from her arms and snuggled him close, inhaling his fragrant scalp.

"Good morning, Daddy!" Callie stroked Gus's hair as she passed him on the way to the coffeepot.

"Good morning, yourself. It's a great day!" Gus kissed Manny's nose. "Hey Manoli! Want to go watch the windsurfers at the Berkeley Marina?"

"I had another really great idea." Callie paused.

"Oh yeah? What is it?" Gus kissed Manny's cheek before handing him back to Callie. "I just need to run to the post office before I do anything else."

"Well . . . you know Manny is getting older now, and I know you think it's gross, but I think it's time to plant his placenta."

He stared at the screen of his phone, scrolling through to find a good picture of Manny to send to his mother. "You're right. I do think that's gross."

"Gus, can you put down the phone for a second and talk to me, please?"

"Oh fine." Gus turned off the phone. He had already gone along with the hippie water-tub home birth witnessed by a whole coven of her friends. Wasn't that enough? Did he really have to go along with this too? "Isn't it going to be smelly and slimy after all this time?"

"Well, it's been frozen."

He had seen the bloody, lumpy placenta after Callie had given birth, and he didn't feel the need to see it again. "I don't know. I need to go buy some icy hot patches."

"Icy hot patches? Gus, we're talking about a precious organ that nurtured our son while he was in my womb!"

As Callie's voice escalated, he could tell he wasn't going to be able to get out of the placenta planting. He sighed and put the phone in his pocket.

"What did you have in mind?"

"I love the idea of planting it under an apple tree in our back-yard."

Gus stiffened at the words *apple tree.*

"Every year it bears fruit it'll remind us of when I was pregnant, and how wonderful it was when Manny was born."

Gus looked at Callie. He knew there was no dissuading her from the idea. "Okay. But no apple tree. Pick some other tree."

"But Gus, apples are like, the quintessential American fruit! We could make apple pie! They're so crunchy and sweet, and think how much fun it would be to pick the apples right off the tree and eat them."

"Please pick another kind of fruit." Gus didn't want to explain to Callie why he hated apples. It had started out a good morning, and he didn't want to think about apple trees or that day all those years ago when the ripe apples had filled the air with the heavy scent of fruit and rot.

Hanging low from the gray branches, the golden orbs tempted bugs, birds, squirrels, and even raccoons to feed on their sweet flesh. Gus was twelve, and he'd been sent out to pick the ripe fruit from the tree before the creatures could damage them beyond use, and to collect from the ground any overripe fruit that he had missed from his previous harvest. He would have rather been playing baseball or chasing friends down the wide streets of their Oakland neighborhood on his bike. His parents came from farming families, and every piece of fruit was important to them, as if each apple had a quarter taped to the stem. He figured they were free, so who cared?

He got sick of apples anyway. His mother would put one in his lunch bag every day, and peeled and quartered them for the family after dinner every night, passing the pieces to them skewered on the pointy blade of her knife. She tried to make her Greek version of apple pie—*milopita*—with filo dough from the dusty old Greek store in the bad part of town. His father would take her there to shop where she would pick out ingredients for the milopita, and jars of preserved quince, baby citrus, blocks of feta, *bastroma*, and *halvah*. While she shopped, his father would sneak off to the porn store next door and look at the pictures of naked blond women with big breasts and parted lips. Once his father had tried to sneak a magazine into the car in a brown paper bag. Gus had found it and gazed at the pictures while riding in the backseat of the car on the way home, his skin prickling with discomfort and excitement.

Picking apples was old country, and he was sick of the old country. He didn't want to hear about how everything tasted better there, and how they were forced to come to *Ameriki* to make a rich life for him. If they were rich, they wouldn't care about wasting some apples, and he wouldn't have to pick them before they rotted. Just that morning his parents had been fighting about sending money home. His mother wanted to send her family one hundred dollers, but his father said it was too much and they should send forty dollars. They always fought. He made a promise to himself that he'd never get married, or if he did that he wouldn't have an arranged marriage like his parents. He'd choose all by himself, an *Amerikana* like the pretty ones in his father's magazines, buxom and agreeable.

After he had finished his math homework that afternoon, he went out the back door into the yard, stopping briefly to grab his baseball bat, planning to go find his cousin Jimmy for a game of ball once he'd finished with the apples. It was sunny outside, even though it was late in the afternoon, and he could hear the buzz of bees collecting pollen in the flowers planted below the apple tree. There were dozens and dozens of apples, all golden ripe and ready for him to pick, high in the branches of the tree. On the ground were another dozen brown apples, rotting into the earth and covered with tiny black bugs, feeding. He would need at least three bags to collect them all: two for the good fruit and one for the decaying apples. He would have to hide the rotten fruit deep in the garbage can outside of the house so his parents wouldn't see how much fruit he'd let go bad because he didn't pick it in time. He put down his baseball bat next to the tree, feeling sorry for himself because he'd never get a chance to play ball that afternoon.

From the open kitchen window he could hear the voices of his parents. They were arguing again. He shrugged his shoulders against the inevitable bickering and made toward the kitchen to get the bags. He assumed they were fighting about the hundred dollars again and rolled his eyes. He imagined the same old refrain, "*Prepe na stelome lefta*! We have to send money!" Every other phrase out of his mother's mouth started with "*prepe*," a word with the combined heft of "we should, we have to," and "if we don't we'll be shamed." His mother always did things the right way, the Greek way, and she insisted that the family do the same, that they not lose sight of their heritage, customs, and social rules. But most importantly, they must never shame the family.

As he mounted the stairs by the open window, he heard his mother crying. This was unusual as she prided herself on being right, and being right narrowed down the possibilities for feeling remorse or sadness. His father was speaking quietly now, and he froze near the back steps to hear what was being said that could make his mother cry.

" . . . sick of your cold ways . . . she's nothing like you . . . ice in your veins . . . you should have kept the church out of our bedroom . . ."

"You're perverted. . . dirty magazines and *putanas* calling here . . . I should have never . . ." his mother hissed.

"*You* should have never!" his father thundered.

Gus shifted his weight as he stood there, trying to make sense of what he was hearing.

"Never! I should have never run off with you!"

"I wish! I wish! There were so many other girls in the *horyo*, but none of them would come to *Ameriki*. Stupid village girls. Only you were greedy enough to come."

"Greedy? I came for love. Like a stupid, stupid girl! I refused the *proxinio* my parents arranged for me—with a good groom too, richer than you. I insisted on you! Ha! I married for love. I ran off with you in the middle of the night, and now look what you are doing to me!"

His mother had told him a story about how his parents had been match-married a thousand times. She said the village matchmaker had come to her father's house on a beautiful spring day to request her for a very important groom, one that had lots of land and money. She said it was a prestigious match for her, and she had elevated her family's standing in the village by marrying him. She said that her father had approved the match and had toasted the marriage with ouzo and rifle shots in the air. She had repeated this story over and over again. She told of the other village girls that were so jealous of her match that they turned their backs when she walked by. She said they were married in the village church built by the hands of her grandfather and his brothers with rocks from the surrounding mountains and stained glass and gold brought from *Athena*. *It was all a lie?* Gus rubbed his ears and shook his head in confusion. *What else had she lied about?*

"You ran off with me because you wanted to leave the village and were greedy for *Ameriki*. You never loved me. *She* loves me!"

"Don't talk about her in my house! Don't talk about her in my house!"

"Your house! Your house! Your garden! Your apple tree! You never say 'My husband'! Only your house, your car, your money!" His father spit on the kitchen floor and burst out of the back door, blindly pushing past Gus. Gus heard his mother scream out, "If you leave now, don't come back!"

His father stormed toward the garage, passing by the apple tree with all of its abundant fruit. His mother was still screaming in the kitchen and now crying, "Wait, come back, come back!" He noticed his father was wearing his Sunday suit and good brown shoes even though it was Wednesday. As he marched determinedly toward the garage and the waiting car, he suddenly slipped on a rotting apple. The slimy flesh of the fruit smeared under the thin leather soles of his shoes, and he rose feet first into the air before landing on his back next to the apple tree.

Gus watched his father lie there for a moment with his chest rising and falling under the plaid suit jacket. Then his father rose, picked up Gus's baseball bat and started swinging at the apple tree. As he pounded the tree, the fruit began to rain down on the ground, crushing the flowers below and setting the bees into a startled flight. The apples landed with force, some rolling away and others bursting their skins on the hard ground.

Gus stood silently and listened to the wails of his mother and the *thunk* of his baseball bat hitting the apple tree and knew that this moment would not come again. It was a singular moment that would not be repeated or retold. It would be replaced with a new story by his mother. The story would start and end with the word *prepe*. He vowed never to pick another apple again.

Gus pulled himself out of his reverie and repeated, "Please just pick another kind of fruit."

Babies R Us

That day in Callie's kitchen making papoutsakia keeps coming back to me—the look of excitement in her eyes when she finally mastered béchamel, the warmth of her sauce against my lips, that feeling of belonging, holding Manny close to me, nuzzling against his soft round cheeks, and the warmth emanating from that kitchen. I want that feeling again. I'm tired of waking up in my little cottage alone. But I know I have to resist her if I want God to make me pregnant, and there are still a few days left before I can take the pregnancy test. I have to distract myself.

Sometimes I get up and go, not knowing where I'm headed. Sometimes it's the farmers' market or the specialty butcher shop. Sometimes it's the baby store. Parking in front of Babies R Us is always exhilarating because I know that when I step on that welcome mat, the front doors will slide open for me as if by magic. The doors say, we know, we just *know*, that you'll be a mother one day. As I lift one foot to cross over that magical threshold, it's as if my whole identity changes. No one there knows me. They don't know about my life, my weaknesses. All they know is that I am there to shop for baby things, and that maybe, probably, I am expecting a baby of my own, and maybe I am. As I cross that invisible line, I transform from a lonely single shopper to expectant mama.

Sometimes I wear a maternity outfit when I go. It makes the trip so much more special. Maybe just some jeans with a maternity panel, and a long top with a modest scoop neckline in a pretty pastel, like pink or baby blue. I have one of each. On the days when I feel that a little boy might be on his way to me I wear baby blue, and on the days I just know a little girl is coming, oh a little girl, I wear sweet, sweet pink. I get misty just thinking about it.

I could be pregnant with twins, fraternal twins, a boy *and* a girl. This thought puts me into a tizzy because I don't have a pink and blue shirt. Only one or the other, so I wear both, one right on top of the other. That seems right because the twins would be cuddled up one right on top of the other inside of my belly until it was time for them to come out. I pull on some good sensible shoes because carrying twins is a lot of weight. As I fasten the Velcro straps, I smile and sigh as I realize that in no time I may not even be able to bend over to put on my shoes, and make a mental note to buy some slide-on shoes. I splash some water on my face, tuck Doll into my diaper bag, and head to Babies R Us. I am going to need two of everything.

I love taking Doll with me. It's so much more fun to shop when you have company. She fits perfectly in the diaper bag. It's big enough for her to sit down and still be able to see out the top. It's sunny and bright out, with the slightest breeze. Doll is snuggled comfortably in the bag, with a pink rattle in one hand and a blue pacifier in the other. With each step we take closer to the store, my maternity blouses catch in the breeze a bit and float around my body, as if they caught some life force. With each step Doll winks her eyes over and over again in excitement, and the sound of the rattle is sweeter than a blue jay singing.

We cross the dividing line between only me, and me and my growing family. Inside the store the lights are very bright and make the linoleum floors shine. It is dazzling. Stuffed animals of every size and shape are stacked against the walls. Thousands of tiny outfits hang on display racks. Frilly little dresses and patent-leather Mary Jane shoes for girls. Rough-and-tumble overalls and baseball caps for boys. As I walk through the aisles toward the newborn/infant section, I notice people sneaking glances at me and smiling. Yes, that is right. I have a secret. A secret is growing inside of me and will blossom into fresh, soft babies. I love the way people look so happy and interested in you when you are being acknowledged as a pregnant woman. I can't blame them. What could be more miraculous than creating life? It is the closest thing that we can do to what God does. And only women can do it.

Even when Arnold Schwarzenegger became pregnant in that old movie *Junior*, he became more and more like a woman, and less like a man. He became soft and emotional, but fiercely protective when someone wanted to take his baby away. I loved it when he turned to the camera and said, "My body, my choice."

But really it isn't our choice in the beginning. In the beginning it is God's choice. Only he decides whether to plant the seed of a soul in your womb. Women do all kinds of things to get pregnant these days: inject the urine of menopausal strangers, spend the equivalent of a down payment on a home to have a doctor mix their eggs with some sperm in a cup, or have surgery to untie tubes that they tied for some other man. Even I tried the sperm bank, but that doesn't count. Because no matter what you do, it still comes down to God. You can do all those things and more, and if He doesn't see fit to bless you, it doesn't matter. You can hop on one foot under a full moon in the sign of Gemini, and sprinkle your feet with unicorn poop and it won't matter. Trying isn't what gets you pregnant; it's believing. I still believe that prayer is the best strategy for getting pregnant. You don't need money or a man for that. You need only to believe.

I really want to find some matching outfits for the twins, but all of the clothes are so different for boys and girls. I don't want to put them in yellow, which is so ambiguous. I want them to look the same, but different. Like Donnie and Marie on the reruns of their old variety show. Their costumes were made of the same fabric and glitter, in the same colors, but cut differently. Marie might have on a white V-neck jumper dress with silver sequins and a blue silk shirt underneath with French cuffs and Donnie would have on a white V-neck vest and long pants with silver sequins and a blue silk shirt with French cuffs. They would both be wearing white ice skates and big toothy smiles. That is the kind of coordination I am looking for. No, two shapeless yellow onesies is not what I am looking for. Doll agrees. Her nose is turned up so high you can see her nostrils.

Phew, I am getting tired from standing on my feet for so long under all of these bright lights. I start to feel dizzy and the room seems cloudy. I grip a circular rack of boy's pajamas to steady myself but, phew, it is hard to hold on. My stomach is turning and churning and my breakfast is on its way up. I don't want anyone to see me out of sorts so I crawl inside of the round rack and sit on the ground. My stomach is spasming and my throat is clenching. I can feel my insides coming out. I pull Doll out just in time and heave my breakfast into the diaper bag. After a few minutes, I have to heave again. The bag has a waterproof lining, but it will never be the same again.

I wipe my mouth with a wet wipe from the special side compartment. My stomach is still in turmoil, and I am confused. I had had toast and freshly squeezed orange juice for breakfast. Could the oranges have been contaminated with E. coli? But I had washed them before cutting into them. I don't understand why I could be so sick. Unless . . . *could I really be pregnant?* Could renewing my faith in God have worked this quickly? I look to Doll to see if she has any ideas. Just then the circle of light above me is shaded, and I see the outline of a man's face floating above me where I am sitting under the round rack of boy's pajamas. I can't make out his features, but I am sure it is a sign. Maybe it is a vision of God!

I hear him say, "Are you all right? Hey, is that you? I told you it was her. I can't believe it. What are you doing down there? Are you nuts?" There is a rustling in the pajamas to my right. That's when I see Callie with Manny, peering in at me. She looks concerned and is saying something to Gus, but I can't hear either of them. I try to hide the bag of vomit by shoving Doll in on top.

"I wasn't feeling well. The lights are so bright that I needed to get to a shadier spot. I'm not sure what's wrong . . ." I try to offer some excuse for being on the floor.

I hear Callie say, "Are you feeling faint, Xeni? If you are feeling faint, just stay there until you feel better, okay? Don't rush. That happened to me once when I felt faint." She gives me a reassuring smile, but Gus is shaking his head and asks, "What are you doing here anyway?'

"I'm sure I'll be fine," I tell her. I cross my arms over my chest to cover the maternity shirt. I tell Gus, "No big deal. I'm here shopping for a friend's baby shower. I'll be fine."

Manny has crawled over and is pointing at me. He looks at me with a big goo-goo smile on his face and starts making happy sounds. He is a real baby. Seeing the three of them there together makes me think that I am dreaming. I'm not pregnant. I am just sick to my stomach. They are a real family, and I am a lonely desperate woman with a belly full of fake babies. *Aren't I?*

A Flashing Light

It's finally the day I will find out if I am pregnant. I'm sitting on the toilet holding the pregnancy test stick in my hand. But after all the waiting and wondering, I'm actually afraid to look at it. What if this didn't work, and I'm right back where I started? I take a deep breath, make the sign of the cross, and slowly open my eyes. The second I see the plus sign on the pregnancy test I fall to my knees in thankful prayer, crumpled up on the bathroom floor and heaving happy tears. I wrap my white nightgown around my knees and squeeze myself tight. White, white, I can wear white. There is not a drop of blood in sight. The only red is a plus sign, a sign of the cross on the pregnancy stick. I feel reborn and pure. God has blessed and entrusted me with a baby to love and protect!

I start nesting right away, organizing all the baby clothes I've accumulated into stacks according to size. I reread all of my pregnancy books. I stock up on newborn diapers and soft cotton blankets. I clean my little home from corner to corner and set up the baby monitor. It doesn't take long to assemble the bassinet once it arrives in the mail. The little sheep hanging from the mobile swing to and fro as I rock it back and forth singing soothing lullabies. I pin an icon of Mary and baby Jesus on the bassinet so the baby will always be safe.

∾ ∾ ∾

I've been walking on a cloud of happiness since the day I missed my period, and now here I am at my second ultrasound. I've been anxious with anticipation to see my baby again, to see how she or he has grown. Lying on your back with your feet in stirrups is very embarrassing. But it's the only way I can see my baby's heartbeat. When I lie this way, an image is projected from my womb up onto a screen. The doctor rubs a cold gel on my stomach, and somehow it soothes me and makes me feel less nervous. At the last appointment, I saw my baby for the very first time. Its heart pulsed on the screen like a little flashing light. It was so fast, I could barely believe my eyes. After all of this time, my prayers have finally been answered. There is a miracle growing in my womb.

I am lying there on the table with my feet in the air when they tell me they don't use the ultrasound screen at this appointment. This time the doctor will use something like a microphone to pick up the sound of the heartbeat. He presses the microphone onto my belly several times and in different locations, and then he mumbles something.

"What did you say, doctor?"

"I'm having a hard time hearing the heartbeat."

My face feels hot, and I think, *this can't be happening*.

"I think it's because I have gas. Or maybe I'm too fat, and you can't hear the baby through my bulgy tummy. Please try harder," I ask him.

The doctor is rubbing the cold gel on my stomach again, but I still have butterflies because I haven't heard the heartbeat or seen the flashing light yet. He has a weird scowl on his face.

"I'm going to have to take some blood tests."

I sit up, clutching the hospital gown to my chest. "But I want to see the heartbeat first. Please!"

He shakes his head. "There is no longer a heartbeat."

That doesn't make any sense to me because it was there. I saw my baby's heart beating with my own eyes at the last visit. There has to be a heartbeat. He must be wrong. But when I look at his face again, I realize his scowl is actually resignation. It feels like my body is on fire, and I fall to the floor, keening. My baby is dead? God must be punishing me. Is it because I used the sperm bank? I promise I'll never do it again. Just please bring back my baby.

Back home, every time I turn around I see another reminder. The empty bassinet sucks the air out of my lungs. The stacks of clothes and diapers threaten to fall over and crush me. I've gotten to where I can't stay at home anymore. But when I go out, all I see is gloriously happy pregnant women waddling down the street getting ready to give birth, preparing to nurture their precious bundles. When I think of that little light going out I can't breathe.

Bread

At communion you drink of His blood and eat of His flesh. Wine and bread. The magical alchemy of life. Round grapes crushed and fermented become His blood. Yeast and water, sweetness and flour, transform into His flesh. From simple beginnings to holy beginnings. And when we eat of His flesh, we understand that all things are possible.

I told Callie that there are all kinds of magic in the world, but not everyone wants you to know about that. Most people keep it to themselves unless they're trying to trick you out of your money, and usually those people don't really know magic; they just know how to make you feel naked. I know because I've been to my fair share of fortune-tellers, gypsies, and psychic readers. I even used to have a Ouija board, but I finally got rid of it because all it ever did was spell out swear words. Stupid things like, A-S-S-W-I-P-E and D-I-C-K. I had one simple question that was never answered: "When will I have a baby?"

As far as I can tell, there are only two kinds of real magic in the world—the magic of God and the magic of food. Who am I to explain the magic of God? He is almighty and we are His children. He speaks to us and guides us, through the Virgin Mary and Baby Jesus. He has saved me on more than one occasion through them, but that is not something I go around sharing with perfect strangers. But I do think that if I ever have a girl, I'll name her Mary. Surely there is no sweeter and braver name for a girl.

Food is easier to explain but also unexplainable. For instance, yeast. I can tell you that when you mix dried-up, smelly, crumbly, inert yeast with a little warm water, a spirit is resurrected. And if you feed it something sweet like sugar or honey, it will bubble up with life. And if you keep feeding it with the golden grain of wheat, its body will begin to take shape. It will stop being a primordial, foamy, bubbling liquid and it will take a form that will rise and grow. And when you add some love to it, helping it to integrate liquid with solid, blood with flesh, massaging it, *needing* it, kneading it, turning it over, and patting it, it becomes of an elastic flesh that takes in breath and grows at a phenomenal rate. Rising like a luminous moon over the valley of the bowl, rising and expanding the possibilities of life. It needs warmth, and careful attention, and rest . . . quiet.

Sometimes you lose things that you really, really love and the wind gets knocked out of you, but you have to keep going. It's like that with the yeast. After it has risen, its glistening crown anointed with holy olive oil, you have to punch it back down. What was once hopeful and full of promise deflates and seems to die. But what is not visible to the naked eye is that its spirit still hovers, waiting. And so you lovingly caress the mass of loose skin and cover it again with cloth and desire. Sometimes when you check back, you see that it really has died and will never, ever come back. And yet you always hope that when you check, peek under the cover, you will see that once again it is rising with a full luminosity that is truly astounding and brings you down to your raw knees.

With the gentlest of motions you cradle it and place it in the oven, hoping that this time all the magic will fall into place, that the form you are baking in the oven will become a baby that you can lovingly eat alive.

BREAD

"You will see that it is rising with a luminosity that is truly astounding."

1 1/4 cups lukewarm water
2 packets of yeast
1 teaspoon sugar
3 cups flour
1 teaspoon salt
2 teaspoons extra-virgin olive oil

Mix the warm water, yeast and sugar in a bowl and set it aside. The yeast will resurrect and bubble. Mix the flour with the salt, and then stir the flour into the yeast until the dough is smooth and no longer sticky. Turn your dough out onto a floured surface and knead it for 10 minutes. While you are kneading the dough, remember that each push of your hands brings it to life. Place your dough in a bowl coated with olive oil, turning it so the dough becomes coated with oil. Place a sheet of plastic wrap over the bowl and then top it with a clean towel. Put it in a warm place to rise. When you see that your dough has doubled, it will fill you with wonder, but you must punch it down. Put the dough into an oiled bread pan, and allow it to rise again, until it doubles once more. Bake it at 375 degrees until it is golden brown and makes a hollow sound when thumped, approximately 30–45 minutes.

Cradle your warm loaf in a clean towel and sniff the crust before you tear off the first delicious piece.

Sweet Sour Pie

Manny is sitting in his high chair with a big round biscuit in his hand, banging it over and over onto the little table in front of him. His eyes are crinkled up from smiling and spit bubbles are on his lips as he gurgles with joy. "GAAAA! Ha ha ha hhhhhhhh! Ah!" I look at him intently, and he stops his banging long enough to stare back at me.

"What do you feel like cooking today, Manny? Do you have any favorites in mind?" I tickle him under his chin and he giggles, showing off a new tooth.

Callie is standing at the kitchen counter with a cardboard box of organic produce that has been delivered that morning. One by one she takes out the contents, naming each fruit or vegetable, "Swiss chard, corn, summer squash, oranges, strawberries, and rhubarb —oh, let's make a strawberry rhubarb pie!"

My stomach turns. I do not want to make pie, but I notice that Callie looks unusually happy, her blue eyes twinkling, her wavy red hair resting on her shoulders, talking about how her aunt used to always make strawberry rhubarb pie and how it was her favorite when she was a little girl. Callie's nose wrinkles a little when she smiles, and all the tiny freckles across her nose dance.

I shake my head. "We aren't making pie. Strawberry rhubarb pie is not Greek, and Gus's mother will be here before you know it. *In a week.* You have to get ready, right?"

105

Callie grabs me by my shoulders and brings her face up close to mine. "Oh come on, please!" I can smell her minty breath and wonder if her red lips taste like strawberries. I feel as if Callie's fingers are sinking into my flesh, and for a moment I feel hot and cold at the same time and a rush of energy zooms up from my stomach and into my throat, choking me. The fine hairs on my neck and scalp stand up. Spots float in the space between my face and Callie's.

"Whaddya say?" Callie asks, but I can't move my tongue or my jaws, I am frozen in her grasp. Callie's face changes. Her smile turns into a little pout, her eyes turn to her feet, and ever so slowly her hands release my shoulders. As they drop, they skim my arms from top to bottom until her hands find mine. When she looks up again, her eyes are sad and watery. She whispers, "I need a break from being Greek right now. No offense." I notice dark circles under Callie's puffy eyes, and wonder if she's been crying.

"I just need to feel like me again," Callie says.

I can't argue with that. "All right. But you're going to have to chop up that fruit yourself!"

Callie squeezes my hands and kisses my cheek, surprising me. I stand a little taller and try to suppress the smile that is trying to take over my face. I haven't smiled since it happened. I haven't told anyone I lost my baby. Callie takes my hand, pulling me toward the kitchen counter and the box of produce.

"Come on, I'm gonna show you how to bake my aunt's pie. It'll make you feel like you have a little bit of heaven in your mouth. It's sweet and tangy at the same time, and when you bite into a plump, juicy strawberry, all your troubles go away!"

"Well, I don't know anything about strawberry rhubarb pie. We never made things like that when I was growing up and I was learning to cook. That was too American. We only made Greek food, but to us it wasn't Greek food; it was *food*." I lift Manny out of his high chair and give him a squeeze. "Let's watch Mommy make a yummy pie, Manny. Do you like pie? But you better behave. You know what happens to children who misbe-have. They get baked into pies, and evil fairies eat them!" Manny grabs a handful of my hair and tugs. "Oh no, Manny! You don't want the evil fairies to eat you, you know why? Because I'm going to eat you!" He giggles while I blow raspberries onto his pudgy belly.

Callie throws the strawberries into a colander and rinses them off. She is humming a little tune under her breath that I can't make out. She chops up the deep red rhubarb stalks and the sweet strawberries and puts them into a big yellow ceramic bowl. "Now make sure you mix them up good with the tapioca balls and the sugar and let it set for at least fifteen minutes," Callie says. I poke my foot against the cabinet door and squeeze Manny a little closer. It feels unfamiliar having Callie teach *me* how to cook. But I find myself feeling curious about the rhubarb and about Callie. And I want a break from being me. I put Manny down on the rug, and he starts pulling on the fringy edges right away.

"You know what I love about strawberries?" Callie asks. "They remind me of my aunt's dog, Homer. I loved him so much. When I'd come home from school, as soon as I got through the door, he'd practically knock me down and lick my face with his rough tongue." She picks up a big strawberry. "His tongue was rough like this strawberry with all the little seeds on the surface." She licks the rough strawberry with her soft tongue. "If I close my eyes, it's like I'm back in my aunt's house with Homer."

With her eyes closed Callie looks like an angel floating on a cloud in heaven, licking that strawberry.

"You want to try?" she asks and holds the strawberry out toward me. The strawberry is vivid red and plump, full of juice and vigor. She holds it between her thumb and middle finger, with the pointy end toward my mouth. It looks like a tongue, a thirsty, rough red tongue. I imagine taking it into my mouth, like a French kiss, with Callie's fingertips at my lips.

"Go ahead, take a bite," Callie prompts.

107

"No. I'm not hungry."

"It's really sweet . . . and juicy delicious." Callie has a little smile on her face. She steps closer to me and holds the strawberry near my lips. I can feel Callie's breath on my cheek. "Try it . . . I think you might like it."

"B—but, I'm not hungry."

Callie softly says, "Are you absolutely sure?" and puts her arm around my shoulders.

"No."

"You're not sure," Callie whispers.

"No. I mean. I'm not sure. What am I supposed to be sure about?"

Callie laughs and rubs the rough strawberry skin against my lips. "Come on. Take a bite. For me?"

The scent of the strawberry is intoxicating. Redolent of spring and lush fertile fruit, and I never wanted to take a bite of anything so badly.

"Look, I'll take a bite, and then you'll take a bite, and before you know it the strawberry will be gone." Callie smiles, opens her lips, and takes the strawberry into her mouth with her tongue. The sound of juice breaking free from flesh is audible as her white teeth sink through the berry. "Now you."

She holds the gaping berry up to my lips. The inside of the strawberry is truly beautiful. Under its bejeweled skin, glistening red flesh with brilliant white streaks surround a speckled pink cavern. Callie squeezes the strawberry, and its juices bubble up and drip from the fruit. I instinctively catch the sweet liquid on my tongue and swallow, licking my lips.

Callie says, "Open wide," and I do, enjoying the delicious fruit.

Callie exhales and wipes her hands on the sides of her hips and quietly says, "Well, what do you say we finish that pie now?"

"Uh, huh. Okay." I turn away from Callie and straighten my shirt. My lungs feel full to bursting as if I've stopped breathing. I slowly exhale. Looking around the kitchen, I remember the baby. "Manny, Manny! Whatcha doin'? Want to watch Mommy make a pie? Huh?" Babies aren't confusing. They want either love, food, or a clean diaper. I hug him close and say, "Do you love me? Because I love you!" He feels warm and safe in my arms. I carry him to the big window above the sink and look out on the horizon. "What do you see, Manny?" A lone hawk sails through the sky. "See the birdie?" I wonder if it is flying for the pure joy of it, or if it is searching for prey.

I notice Callie taking a tube of prepackaged piecrust out of the refrigerator, but don't say anything. This is her pie, after all, her memories. Who am I to judge what makes her happy, and brings her comfort? I squeeze Manny closer.

"Now, I know that prepackaged piecrust isn't as good as what you would make from scratch . . ." Callie looks a little embarrassed. "But that's how my auntie made it, and that's the only way it tastes right to me." She straightens her shoulders and pops open the can.

"Hey, we agreed that we aren't being Greek today. There will be no punishment for taking the easy way out," I say. "I mean, we're doing it your way, and that's just fine." I want her to know that I mean it.

"Okay—because I really want you to like it . . ." Callie looks like a little girl, open and earnest. I squeeze Manny's chubby body closer. "Strawberry rhubarb pie, coming up!" She rolls out the fatty piecrust into the round pan, and fills it with the chunks of thickened glazed fruit. She shows me how her aunt taught her to weave a lattice top for the pie and crimp the edges with her fingers. She washes the top with milk, sprinkles it with sugar, and it is ready for the oven. Callie is so proud of herself that she dances around the kitchen, giggling and singing, "Shoo Fly Pie and Apple Pan Dowdy" while it bakes.

"Shoo Fly pie and Apple Pan Dowdy!"

She grabs Manny and twirls him around the kitchen.

"Makes your eyes light up and your stomach say howdy."

She cheers—"Come on, let's dance!"—and grabs my hand. "Sing with me!" I don't know the words but manage to cry out, "Shoo fly pie!" at the right time. I imagine that this is what a happy family looks like. I see Callie's full radiance now that she is being completely herself, dancing joyfully, her body and spirit free. Manny feels solid and at home in my arms. I hold him and deeply inhale his scalp, warm and intoxicating, like the irresistible smell of a fresh loaf of bread from the oven. I let the magical comfort of bread and babies envelop me. I feel happy, even content, for that one moment. *Yes, this is what a family should feel like.* As I allow myself some joy, a bit of sadness creeps in and surprises me as I try to imagine what my baby might have felt like in my arms had it not been taken away too soon. I push the thoughts away and hold Manny closer to my heart. A real live baby. By the time the pie is done, we are burning our tongues trying to eat it hot out of the oven, on the floor laughing and screaming out, "Shoo fly pie!" Even Manny tries to get into the act, with his high-pitched squeals and cries. The pie is scrumptious. You can taste all the love and happy memories in each bite. The piecrust is fine, flaky and rich against the gooey, tangy-sweet red filling. I like how Callie is so cheerful, so different from me. Callie is like the sweet strawberries, and I am like the sour rhubarb. Together we make a pretty good combination.

CALLIE'S SWEET SOUR PIE

"The scent of the strawberry is intoxicating—redolent of spring, and lush fertile fruit."

4 cups strawberries, hulled and sliced in half or quarters depending on size
2 cups rhubarb, trimmed and cut into 1/2-inch slices, peeling off any strings if necessary
2 tablespoons minute tapioca
1 tablespoon flour
1/2 teaspoon lemon zest
1/2 teaspoon lemon juice
1 cup sugar
2 frozen deep dish piecrusts
3 tablespoons butter, cut into small chunks
1 tablespoon milk
1 tablespoon sugar
Preheat oven to 425 degrees.

In a large bowl, mix the strawberries, rhubarb, tapioca, sugar, flour, lemon zest, and lemon juice together. Let it stand for 15 minutes. Breathe in the perfume of spring.

Let the piecrusts thaw while the fruit thickens. Turn one piecrust out onto a piece of wax paper and roll it flat with a rolling pin. Cut it into 12 strips. Fill the other piecrust with the strawberry rhubarb pie filling. Dot your pie filling with chunks of butter. Lay six strips of crust across the top of the pie. Lay the remaining strips in the opposite direction and weave them into a lattice top. Tuck the ends under the lower pie crust and crimp them together.

Brush milk over the lattice and then sprinkle sugar over the top of the pie. Bake your pie at 425 degrees for 15 minutes, then reduce the heat to 375 degrees and bake until the pie is golden and the filling has thickened and is bubbling, approximately 30 minutes.

Cool before serving, if possible.

An International Visitor

Callie busied herself in the dimly lit kitchen, preparing breakfast for the woman who held her fate. Gus had picked his mother up from the airport late last night, after Callie and Manny had gone to bed. As the rest of the house slept, she hurried to ready the meal before they awoke. It was the first meal she would prepare for Gus's mother, her child's grandmother. Gus's mother had finally agreed to come all the way from Greece to meet Callie and Manny. Callie practiced saying the word for grandmother that Xeni had taught her, *Yiayia*, remembering to put the accent on the second syllable. "*YiaYIA*! Not YAH-yahs. Not getting my yah-yahs. *YiaYIA*!" She pulled a few yellow bananas from the bunch, peeled them, and cut off the bruised parts. "*YiaYIA*!" She noticed her hands were shaking as she poured the oatmeal into the boiling water. "*YiaYIA*!" There were only three eggs left in the box. She was so busy planning a big Greek welcome dinner that she had completely forgotten to plan something good for breakfast. Now she was stuck putting together odds and ends to create something impressively tasty and welcoming. *I hope you like oatmeal, YiaYIA!* She was out of milk. Luckily she kept a box of soy milk as a backup. Expressing her breasts was out of the question for this meal.

There was a jug of Odwalla orange juice in the fridge. She grabbed it and the tub of strawberry goat yogurt. There was also a box of soy chorizo, but she thought better of it. She looked in the cabinets for some forgotten treat to add to the meal but came up empty until she spotted a dusty jar of preserved baby oranges in the way back of the cupboard. "That's Greek!" she announced, "*Na-RAHN-tzi!*"

As she set the table with her favorite serving ware, she kept repeating a phrase over and over again in her head: "Breakfast is the most important meal of the day. *Kali-MEH-ra YiaYIA!*" She laid lavender cloth napkins on the handcrafted green ceramic plates and topped them with the bamboo-handled silverware. She set the blue-rimmed Mexican glasses from Oaxaca to the right of each plate, and filled the matching pitcher with the orange juice. In small white Chinese bowls decorated with blue fish she ladled the goat yogurt, the narahntzi, and the chopped bananas. She poured the steaming hot African rooibos tea into a petite black iron Japanese teapot. The soy milk sat in the cow-shaped pitcher with blue windmills that she'd gotten in Solvang. It reminded her of one her grandmother had, and she loved its little blue hooves. She smiled at her creation, a tabletop of all nations. What better way to welcome an international visitor? In the further recesses of her mind, she knew it had to be perfect. She wavered. Would she be good enough? Did she actually want to be a good Greek wife?

The oatmeal sat in the pot, creamy and hot, and the table was ready, boasting her improvised feast. The house was perfectly still. It was one of those rare moments when no one needed anything from her. She sat in her favorite chair, sipped her rooibos, and tucked her hand into her blouse. Cupping her breast had always felt comforting to her. She tried to relax, eyes closed, inhaling the fruity aroma of the African tea, while she tried to release her nervousness and doubt. She could hear the birds chirping in the trees outside the kitchen windows and imagined them in flight soaring through the fresh morning air, untouched by the day. Just then she heard Manny start to cry in his bedroom and felt the sensation of her milk letting down. She paused before rising, savoring her last moment of peace before the day started in earnest.

When she opened her eyes there was a person standing before her, watching her. Flustered, she rose and dropped her teacup in the process. She'd been caught in a private moment, eyes closed, hand on her breast, which was now leaking milk through her thin nightgown. Searching for the right words, she spit out "YAH-yahs!" Gasping, she tried again, "*Kali-MEH-rah*, YAH-yahs! Oh crap. I mean, *YiaYIA*!"

The old woman looked her up and down without saying a word. She didn't have to. Callie knew that the most important meal of the day already had a bitter taste. "I was just resting for a moment, and then the baby cried, and my milk let down. I wasn't touching myself inappropriately. Look, I made breakfast! But we are out of milk. I mean cow milk. Did you see my cute little pitcher? I mean my milk pitcher. Not my milk, but the … Actually there's soy milk in there. Are you hungry?" Callie wanted to kick herself for sounding so idiotic. It wasn't what she'd planned at all. She'd wanted to appear welcoming, world aware, culturally competent, and instead she looked like a morning masturbator caught in the act.

"*Kalimera*. You may call me Mrs. Horiatis. Has Constantino left for work? And why are you letting my grandson cry?"

Callie stood frozen in place, her tea in a puddle at her feet. "Um. Well, Gus is upstairs sleeping, actually. I was getting some breakfast ready, and Emmanuel just woke up. Would you like to sit down?"

"I would like to see my grandson, Manoli." The old woman continued to scowl as she surveyed the room. "Don't you have a chair with a cushion on it? Those wooden chairs are so hard and uncomfortable." Callie rushed to grab a cushion from the neighboring room to soften the old woman's landing. Mrs. Horiatis took the cushion and placed it on the chair at the head of the table, sniffing her disapproval as she took in the tabletop.

"Why don't I go get Gus? I'm sure he'd be so happy to have breakfast with you." Callie scurried out of the kitchen, leaving the tea and her pride behind. Mrs. Horiatis shook her head from side to side and tsk-tsked as she looked at the mismatched plates and linens on the table. Before Callie started climbing the stairs to the bedroom, she paused to take a breath. She noticed her heart was beating soundly in her chest, and despite her best efforts to believe herself a composed, confident woman, she could not help but feel deflated and small. She gripped the handrail and placed one bare foot on the first step. She found herself staring at her pink, glittery toenail polish for what seemed like a long time. She could hear Manny crying and Gus snoring, but most loudly she could hear Mrs. Horiatis's disapproval. It hovered in the air like a thick, suffocating blanket. She wrapped herself in it until she nearly melted into the floor.

Callie didn't want to be a bad person. She wanted to be a good person. A person who was liked. The sensation of a tear rolling down her cheek broke her reverie and reconstituted her back to action. There was no point in feeling sorry for herself, she thought. Manny needed her, and Gus loved her. He would stick up for her, and his mother would learn to like her. Ever the eternal optimist, Callie rationalized that Mrs. Horiatis must be jet-lagged from her flight, and that would explain her cranky demeanor.

She took the stairs two at a time, burst through the bedroom door, and landed on Gus's chest. "Wake up! Breakfast is ready, your mother is downstairs, and you have to go keep her company! Tell her that I'm learning to cook Greek food! Tell her!" Then she rushed to Manny's room where he sat waiting for her to come. His red ringlets framed his chubby face, wet from crying. He broke out in a huge grin when he saw her, and she apologized for keeping him waiting as she hugged the weight of his body against hers. As they settled into the glider for a nice nursing session, Callie could hear Gus groggily making his way down the stairs to sit with his mother. She rocked back and forth in the peaceful room with her son rhythmically sucking at her breast. She felt sure that by the time she brought Manny downstairs Mrs. Horiatis would be happy to start all over again with a cheerful hello and perhaps an apology for her testy behavior.

❧ ❧ ❧

Gus looked at himself in the hallway mirror before entering the breakfast room. He looked older. His curly brown hair was sprouting some gray, and the wrinkles beside his eyes were getting deeper. His olive skin looked dull, and the stubble on his face cast a dark shadow. He ran his fingers through his hair and tied the belt around his robe to conceal his hairy chest. He was a man—a man who had begged his mother to come and meet Callie, to see their son. He'd called her many nights after Callie had gone to bed. And she'd resisted for months, but now she was here. That showed that she'd softened, didn't it? He cleared his throat, pulled his stomach in, and pushed his chest out.

"*Kalimera, Mana.*" He walked toward his mother, leaned over, and gave her a kiss on the cheek while hugging her around the shoulders. "Did you sleep all right?"

"*Ach, pedie mou.* That bed you have feels like rocks. Where did you find it, the Salvation Army? I slept better on the plane."

"I'm sorry, *Mana.* That bed is brand-new. I thought you'd be comfortable."

"Just because something is new doesn't make it better. You young kids always want the new things when the old ways are better." She sighed loudly and mopped her forehead with one of Callie's lavender silk napkins.

"Sometimes the new ways can be good too, *Mana.* You just have to give it a chance." He forced a smile and instinctively reached to his chest pocket for a cigarette. But he had no chest pocket or cigarette, only a plain robe protecting his heart.

"And my grandson, where is he?"

He hoped this was a safer topic. "Oh, Callie must be nursing him upstairs." He grabbed a piece of chopped banana and popped it into his mouth.

"Still? How old is the child? She doesn't need to nurse him anymore. Three months is plenty."

Gus felt like a mouse in a glue trap. No matter what his movements were they only sunk him deeper down into the inescapable.

"Would you like some *café, Mana*?" Gus sidestepped his mother's judgment.

117

"Are you going to make the *café?* Don't tell me the *Amerikanitha* cannot even fix one *café?*" She snorted. "Well, at least she is good for one thing."

"*Mana*, please don't start with that." Gus decided to change the subject. "I was thinking that today we could go to Fisherman's Wharf and have lunch. Remember how you used to love the fried prawns at the Lighthouse? We could see the sea lions on the pier."

"Oh yes. That would be nice. We could go, the three of us— me, you and Manolaki—and show the baby the sea lions. *Bravo*."

"Yeah. Uh . . ." It was only 8:13 a.m. and Gus was already tired of fighting. "Yeah. Uh. Callie might come with us. Or maybe she'll stay home and cook. I know she has a big welcome dinner planned for you. Isn't that nice?"

Mrs. Horiatis looked at the breakfast that Callie had prepared and said, "I'll make sure to eat a lot at lunch."

Gus rubbed his chest where Callie had straddled him and said, "You know, Callie has been learning to cook Greek food. She's not bad."

"I'll be the judge of that."

Callie swept into the room. Gus noticed how her long, pale blue silk robe contrasted with her fiery red hair and complemented her ocean-blue eyes. Manny clung to her hip and tangled his fingers in her hair. Callie always looked so natural with Manny on her hip, but this morning Gus could feel her nervousness, and he suddenly felt sorry for her. She would try her best, and it would never be good enough. Callie stood a few feet away from Gus and his mother and smiled brilliantly.

"*Kalimera* again, Mrs. Horiatis." Manny squealed at his mother's voice and shyly flung his arms around her neck. "This is our son, Emmanuel . . . your grandson, Manoli." He peeked out at his grandmother, his *yiayia*, for the first time.

Mrs. Horiatis was silent, but Gus could see that her eyes were glistening as she set them upon her grandson for the first time. He held his breath as she took in Manny's curly red hair, dark brown eyes, and chubby cheeks. "Would you like to hold him?" Callie asked.

"Yes. Yes. I would like to hold my grandson." Mrs. Horiatis rose from her chair and stretched her arms out toward Manny. Callie kissed him sweetly on his forehead and nose, and held him out toward the old woman. As Mrs. Horiatis held her grandson for the first time, she lit up like the sun on a long summer day. As if in slow motion she turned her back on Callie and walked away with Manny, and Gus was overcome with relief and pride, seeing Manny cradled in his mother's arms. But there was that other emotion too: guilt.

Gus saw Callie looking to him for reassurance, and he held his breath, looking from one woman to the other. He felt like a liar as he smiled at Callie, and gave her an okay sign with his fingers, and then a wink.

Mrs. Horiatis bounced Manny up and down in the air and sang a tune that Gus remembered from his childhood. "*Pie lagos na pye nero, mes tou* Manoli *to lemo!*" and she tickled his throat, pretending to be the little rabbit drinking water from his neck. Manny giggled, and this encouraged her to sing it again. Mrs. Horiatis sat down with Manny on her lap and sang, bringing back long forgotten memories for Gus and creating new ones with Manny.

Gus watched Callie move to the stove, where she stirred ground coffee and sugar into water boiled in a small *briki* pot until the foamy coffee rose to the top. She poured it expertly from high above as Xeni had taught her, into the small demitasse cups, and brought them to the table on a tray the way any good Greek wife would do. Noticing the beauty of Callie's long creamy neck and the ardent joy beaming from his mother's eyes, Gus allowed himself to exhale. Perhaps it would be all right after all. Perhaps he would find a way to merge his two worlds, reconcile his two women, his lover and his mother. Perhaps.

Callie placed the cup with the large bubble in front of Mrs. Horiatis and said, "Look, you have the *mati*, the eye. It's good luck!"

Mrs. Horiatis squeezed Manny tight to her breasts and said, "Yes, I do."

Time Capsule

Gus's mother arrived late last night, and Callie has been so atwitter waiting for this day. It makes me want to puke. "Oh, I hope she'll like me. Oh, I hope dinner will be okay. Oh, I can't believe that she is finally coming." It's obvious that she must not care about me at all if she's trying this hard to please Gus and his mother. Little does she know that she is about to go through a test that will make the SATs, GREs, and labor all look easy. She is going to attempt to please a Greek mother-in-law, trying to prove that she is a worthy replacement. It would be hilarious except that it's so pathetic. She doesn't know what she's up against. Every detail of her being will be evaluated and found unworthy.

First her appearance: her fiery red hair and cool blue eyes will be compared to the devil. She is tall and thin, so no fat comments at least. And luckily Callie isn't taller than Gus, so her mother-in-law can't compare them to Sonny and Cher. Of course, she'll be wearing something the mother-in-law, her *pethera,* will consider immodest, so oh well. Hopefully she'll wear a bra. And hopefully she won't pull out her round breast and nurse the baby in front of the old woman. He loves to nuzzle up to her and suckle away until he sleeps. He has found the most peaceful place on Earth, but it will raise the old woman's hackles to see the baby nursing past three months.

Then her personality: that's where we really get into trouble. Sure, she's caring, sweet, funny, and gentle. She has a way of making people feel safe . . . and there is some kind of magic that stirs the air when she walks into a room. But it won't matter. Gus's mother won't see that.

Callie will totally blow it, no matter how many times I've tried to explain to her how to be deferential and anticipatory of *pethera*'s needs. Always offer before she asks. Always anticipate and supply what she needs before she even realizes what is missing. This is a concept that she doesn't understand. "But I'm not a psychic! How can I know what she needs before she does?" You study her every move. If she moves toward a chair, you put a table next to it for her coffee. If she fans herself, offer to take her coat or open a window. If she looks around the room with her eyes going from corner to corner, point out the embroidery you worked on for your dowry. "But I don't have a dowry! This is America! It's the twentieth century!"

Sometimes I forget. Greek-Americans live in a time capsule, following the customs in place when their parents left the homeland thirty, forty, or fifty years ago. We live in our own frozen version of Greece. When our parents stepped on a boat or plane to come to America, they took a snapshot of the cultural laws at the time and used it as a map to raise their children in the new land. That's why so many of us first- or second-generation Greeks are so messed up. We've lived in two time zones, two dimensions of space simultaneously. We grew up in a Greek village called America.

"This is confusing!" she cries out. Yeah, tell me about it.

Then there's the woman's assets: who says that dowries are out of style? Doesn't everyone evaluate what other people have? Someone with a house is a better catch than someone living in a trailer, right? I would love to live in a little house in the wine country with rows and rows of grapevines lining the land all around me. In September the air would fill with the smell of ripe grapes begging to be picked, a fragrant aroma that would set me thinking about biting into juicy, plump grapes, their juice squirting into my mouth as their skin pops between my teeth. But Callie doesn't have land or a house. All she has is Manny. Though he's the most precious possession of all—his sweet baby spirit a gift from God and the universe. He is more valuable than land or money. He carries her blood, Callie's blood, but also the *pethera*'s blood. And in the end, that rich intermingled fluid is the only thing that will save her. She may bumble and snort. She may forget to notice the small things and demur. But the Greek blood in the veins of that baby might buy her a few years of tolerance from the old woman.

But perhaps not a lifetime's worth. It makes me sad to think about Callie being barely tolerated for a lifetime. *She should be cherished.* She'll try so hard and will never be good enough. Will she ever get tired of it? Would she ever walk away? I wonder what her dream life would look like and how she would get there if she could. For a moment, I imagine her as part of my wine country dream life, the two of us walking together between rows of grapevines hanging with sweet fruit. Is it wrong that I am helping her try to succeed in a life that will only bring her misery? Too many questions. It's all confusing, confusing. I'm confused. One step at a time. This is what she wants. She wants Gus and to impress *pethera*. And I'm supposed to help her.

The first step is dinner. She has to make every dish she has learned until now for the *trapezi*. The table must be laden with delicious food until it can barely take the strain, to properly honor and welcome her guest. *Tiropitakia:* golden, puffy filo triangles filled with melted feta cheese. *Dolmathakia:* grape leaves filled with rice, ground meat, and herbs. *Horyiatiki salata:* the juices of soft ripe tomatoes, green pepper, cucumber, and red onion all breaking down in a bath of olive oil, oregano and salt. *Psomi:* freshly baked bread to dip into the pulpy salad juices. *Pastitsio:* layers of buttered pasta, ground beef perfumed with cinnamon, more slithery pasta, and topped with a thick blanket of creamy béchamel sauce spiked with shredded mizithra cheese, white pepper, and nutmeg. *Kota me patates:* a whole chicken marinated in lemon juice, olive oil and oregano and roasted until crisp in a pan lined with tender and tangy potatoes. Small plates of salty feta cheese, puckery olives, anchovies bathed in vinegar and oil, and mild green peppers fried until their skins burst and the meat becomes tender. *Bira kai crasi*: Frigid cold bottles of beer and homemade wine.

But the most important course of all is the plump, delicious, tender, juicy baby. He must be bathed in a warm tub of water, his arms and legs slathered with creamy lather. Rinsed clean and rubbed dry. His skin made tender with oil. His ringlets combed through and twisted. His toes kissed. His tummy tickled. His cheeks caressed. He must see himself reflected in teary eyes overflowing with love and hunger. Dressed in soft clothes and innocence. Of all the delights at the table, the one most coveted and adored will be the baby. A very small person that is bursting all of our hearts. But will he be enough to guarantee Mrs. Horiatis's acceptance of Callie?

A Captured Spring

The dinner table is nearly groaning under the weight of the feast that Callie and I have prepared. We worked all day while Gus and his mother went about town enjoying the sights with Manny in tow. We are sweaty and hot from the peeling, the boiling, the frying, the baking, the stirring, the constant motion that we've been in, dancing in sync around the small kitchen. Every surface is covered with a platter of prepared food. The sun is setting and spreading pretty pink and gray hues throughout the horizon. Gus and Mrs. Horiatis have still not returned, and the house is finally quiet and still. No activity, no more tasks. We collapse on the couch together, wearing our aprons and exhausted expressions.

"Oh my God! I'm so tired! If she doesn't like this meal, I'll kill myself," Callie groans.

"If she doesn't like this meal, I'll kill *her!*" I smile. "And then I'll stuff and roast her on a spit."

"Eww . . . gross!" Callie throws a pillow at me.

"What's really gross is that I'm helping you try so hard to please Gus's mother." The words feel heavy with truth. "I mean, you already gave her a grandchild. What else does she want?"

"Speaking of the baby, I am so engorged. I haven't nursed Manny since noon. What time is it now? Five? I think I'm going to explode." Callie grabs handfuls of her breasts and rubs them, trying to alleviate the pressure.

I want to turn away but am fixated on Callie's efforts to get comfortable, and I suddenly wonder what it would have been like to nurse my baby. Just the thought of it triggers that familiar stabbing pain in my heart.

"I'm sorry," Callie says. "That must make you feel uncomfortable. Sometimes I forget how to act in proper company."

"Uh . . . no, I don't mind. Go ahead." I pause. "What else can you do to relieve the pressure?"

"Well. I could go pump, but I'd rather wait and nurse. I much prefer the natural way. Besides, I'm so exhausted. I don't want to do one more thing that involves a food-preparation device." Callie laughs, then looking dreamy, "Mmm . . . maybe a warm bath would help."

"My feet hurt." I stare down at my feet in my sensible brown lace-up shoes. "They're pounding."

Callie grabs my foot and starts to untie the laces. "Here, let me rub them."

"Oh no. That's okay. You don't want to do that." I pull my foot away.

"Of course I do. You worked hard to help me so that I wouldn't fall flat on my face. The least I can do is rub your feet!"

"They probably smell."

"That's okay. I won't inhale." Callie laughs as she pulls my feet up onto her lap and unties my laces and pulls off my socks. My shoes land on the ground with a *thunk, thunk.* I notice my heart rate speeding up. I feel exposed with my bare feet up on Callie's lap.

"Come on, loosen up. I'm pretty good at this," Callie says in a soothing low voice. Callie's shirt has come unbuttoned, and I can see her pink satin bra. She starts rubbing my aching arches with firm strokes.

"I thought that all nursing bras were ugly. Just plain white."

"Do you like this one?" Callie opens her shirt and shows me the satiny bra. It perfectly cups the soft curves of her breasts. "I bought it at a specialty shop. It was so expensive! But I like to feel pretty. So I decided I was worth it."

"Yeah. I think it was worth it." I am in a zone, getting light-headed, my breath becoming shallow. Callie rubs my toes, one by one. Her hands are so strong. I feel myself melting little by little until I finally start to relax and close my eyes.

"You know what would be really great?" Callie asks.

"What?" I mumble, already feeling great.

"A warm bath. We have a double Jacuzzi bathtub upstairs. It came with the house. Doesn't that sound great?"

"Okay. You go take a bath and I'll clean up in the kitchen."

"No, silly. I mean, we could both go up and take a bath. It's a double tub. Big enough for two. Like a hot tub."

"Doesn't that seem kind of unusual? Taking a bath together?" I pull myself upright, removing my feet from Callie's lap. Callie grabs them back.

"Well, it depends on your point of view, I suppose." Callie smiles at me in a way that make her eyes sparkle.

"I'm not sure what my point of view is. I've never done anything like that before." I fiddle with the buttons on my dress.

"I'll tell you what. If you don't want to get in the bath, you can just talk to me while I take a bath. How's that? The water would feel so good. Come on. Let's do it before they get back! We still have about forty-five minutes or so."

Callie grabs a bottle of wine and two glasses and leads me up the stairs where I reluctantly follow her into the master bedroom. She steps out to run the water in the tub in the adjoining bathroom. I have never been in the master bedroom before. I notice the aubergine comforter on the king-size bed, fluffy pillows, and the soft glow from the brushed silver bedside lamps. There is an antique dressing table with lotions and makeup on it, and a frosted white bottle with a gardenia etched into it. "I love gardenias. They smell so heavy. Like a fruit so ready that it will drop off the tree if you don't save it and devour it at the perfect moment."

Callie reenters the room. She has taken off her clothes and is standing there in her blue silk robe. "You surprise me sometimes, Xeni. You're so passionate about food . . . but . . . why don't you have a lover?"

I turn my back to Callie. "I think I should go."

"No. No. Stay. We'll listen to some music and relax. Have a glass of wine. No more questions." Callie pours two glasses.

"Don't you think they'll be back soon? Maybe we should be doing something useful."

"Relax, honey. It's just us." Callie hands me the glass of wine. "Soon they'll be back and I'll be doing a tap dance to get Mrs. Horiatis to like me, and you'll be garnering compliments on your cooking. Let's just take a minute to celebrate our hard work . . . and our friendship."

I am confused. It seems unusual to drink wine with Callie in her bedroom while the bathtub is filling with warm water. But at the same time, deep down I want to be here. If I were brave, I'd take off my clothes and get into the bathtub. But I'm not brave.

"Do you ever feel confused?" I ask Callie.

"All the time. Especially lately." Callie looks into my eyes and reaches out for my hand. She leads me toward the bath. She has lit candles, and the bubbling water is sprinkled with dried flowers that are blooming as they suck in the hydration. The petals unfold like a slow motion film: a captured spring is unfurling in the tub. I gasp at the scene, the motion of life, the thirst of the colorful flowers thrusting themselves into being after a long drought.

"It's amazing."

"Yes." Callie drops her robe and enters the bath. The petals cling to her pale white skin, and with her red hair and blue eyes she looks like an astonishing flower herself.

The sight of Callie in the bath is startling, so exposed and yet so open, her breasts full of life-giving milk. She is mesmerizing. I stand in exactly the same position for an entire minute while Callie smiles shyly at me, holding her hand out toward me. I want to run, but my feet are firmly rooted in place. I feel like a potted plant that has never gotten enough water. Thirsty and brown around the edges. There is Callie, like a beautiful flower that got plenty of sun, and water, and nutrients. And here I am in a pot that is too small.

"Get in," Callie says simply, but her eyes convey a million emotions I've never seen before.

I am choking, thirsty, cramped. I untie my apron and let it drop. I lift my hands and unbutton my dress, opening it to reveal my heart beneath. I am embarrassed by my plain white bra. I feel like a daisy, while Callie is a stargazer. Biting my lip, I shyly unhook the bra and let Callie be the first person to ever see my breasts.

I hear Callie deeply inhale and say, "You're beautiful."

I hear her say the words but I can't believe them. My body is a vessel for God. He is supposed to bring me a baby, and now somehow I am standing naked in front of another woman getting ready to . . . to what? I shake my head.

"What's happening? How did I get here? I don't think I'm supposed to be doing this."

Callie repeats, "You're beautiful."

I grab my clothes from the floor and hold them up against my bare breasts. "Look, let's pretend this didn't happen. I'm confused. I don't know why I did that."

"Xeni . . . nothing happened. It's okay."

"But if I got into that tub with you, what would happen? I took off my clothes. That happened!" I close my eyes and start to silently mouth the words, *Dear God, please forgive me for my behavior. I don't know what I was doing. I was hypnotized by the flowers, and this woman makes me feel things I don't understand.*

"Xeni, it's okay." Callie rises from the water. Flower petals cling to her skin, and water drips down her exposed body. Her hair lies in wet ringlets against her full breasts. "It's okay." Her eyes are welling with tears. "I'm sorry I upset you. I don't want to hurt you. I'm sorry."

Her tears stop my praying. I don't want to hurt Callie, either. I don't like to see her cry. I want her to be happy and appreciated and loved. I want to comfort her, even more than I want to comfort myself. I step toward the tub. I inhale deeply, taking in the scent of the flowers. Callie is standing in the tub, the water bubbling around her legs, her skin illuminated from within, glowing with some ethereal quality I can't quite name. I slowly drop my clothes to the floor and step into the bathtub to get closer to her.

"Please, don't cry," I whisper.

"I don't want to hurt you. I act like such an idiot sometimes. I'm so confused. Please don't hate me," Callie whispers back.

I pick a flower from Callie's skin. "Do you know what this is?"

"A flower?"

"It is a flower that dried up and thought it was dead. It thought it was dead until it found itself near you, and then suddenly it started to bloom and grow in ways it never thought it could."

Callie puts her arms around me and brings me close. "That's how I feel about you."

We hold each other in the effervescent, surging water. Our bodies squeezed together as if pressing flowers for a scrapbook, preserving the moment for later days when we will find ourselves apart and thirsty.

Dinner at Dionysis

Just before six o'clock, Gus walked through the front door and was confronted by the aroma of melting feta cheese, roasting lamb, and fresh flower arrangements strewn throughout the house. He was balancing Manny on his hip, and corralling his mother's many parcels from their tourist excursion with his other hand.

"*Ach, Mana*! It smells so good in here. It reminds me of when you would cook for Easter or Christmas when I was growing up."

Mrs. Horiatis waited outside of the door until Gus turned to look at her.

"What's wrong, Mana?"

"Well, we had such a nice day. You, me, and my grandson. Why spoil it? Let's go have dinner at Denny's."

"*Mana.* You have to be kidding. Callie has been working all day cooking to impress you. I can't believe you'd want to eat at Denny's instead."

"Don't tell me that this Callie can cook Greek food. Do you have a *skili*? Maybe he can sit under the table, and I can feed him what I can't eat. And then you can take me to Denny's after the *Amerikanitha* goes to sleep." Mrs. Horiatis removed her embroidered handkerchief from her pocketbook and blew her nose into it.

"Oh come on, *Mana*. It will be delicious. Xeni has been here all day teaching her how to cook. She's an excellent teacher."

"Xeni? Who is Xeni? *Einai Ellinida?*"

131

"Yes, of course she's Greek. With a name like Xeni? Of course. Come on. Come in. Let's sit down and have something to drink." Gus put down the bags in the foyer and transferred Manny to the other arm. "You're getting heavy, little man!"

"*Ela etho, manari mou.* Let *Yiayia* hold you." Once they climbed the stairs, Mrs. Horiatis took the baby from Gus and entered the living room where she nearly tripped over Xeni's shoes. "*Para ligo na skototho!*"

"Well, I don't know if you would have died from the fall, *Mana*."

"Well, where are they? I don't see any women here." She pinched Manny's cheek.

"I don't know. Maybe they're in the kitchen." Gus called out, "Callie! Where are you, babe? We're back! Callie?"

"I'm coming! Just a minute!" A few moments later Callie came down the stairs with her hair pinned up and a flower tucked behind her ear, wearing a strapless short dress and no shoes.

"You look great, babe. Did you forget your shoes?" Gus was trying to sound pleasant, but could tell from Callie's face that she could sense the tension underlying his question.

Manny started to whine and struggle in Mrs. Horiatis's arms.

"Hey, baby boy! Mommy missed you so much!" Manny held his arms out toward his mother. Callie deftly took him from Mrs. Horiatis and gave him a big hug. Manny wrapped his arms around her neck and squeezed. "Oh I love it when you hug me, baby boy! Mommy loves you so much!" Callie sat down on the couch, pulled down the top of her dress to expose one breast, and Manny happily latched on, hungry and tired from his outing. Mrs. Horiatis gasped and genuflected, turning away from the sight of Callie's exposed breast.

"Did you guys have a fun day?" Callie asked, brightly smiling.

Mrs. Horiatis remained silent for a moment. "Why don't I give him a bottle?"

"Oh, well didn't you already give him a bottle of breast milk while you were out? Besides, he likes it straight from the source. Don't you, sweetie?" Callie stroked Manny's hair as she spoke to him.

Mrs. Horiatis looked at Gus. "That was breast milk? You said it was formula."

"Oh no, we don't give Manny formula. Just breast milk," said Callie proudly.

"Well anyway, formula, milk, whatever. Same difference," Gus said.

"It is *not* the same!" both Callie and Mrs. Horiatis cried out.

"Okay, whatever. He had a bottle and now he's nursing. When's dinner, Cal?"

"Dinner's ready. We've just been waiting for you."

"Where's Xeni? I want my Mom to meet her. She's staying for dinner, right?"

"I think so. She's upstairs getting changed. I lent her a dress to wear. We got so sweaty cooking all afternoon."

Mrs. Horiatis excused herself, calling over her shoulder, "Don't forget, Constantino, I want to go to *Dionysis*'s house after dinner!"

"Who's *Dionysis*?" Callie asked.

"Oh, just an old friend. We used to call him Denny."

"Doesn't your mom want to stay in tonight so we can get to know each other better? I've hardly seen her since she arrived."

"Yeah, babe. Don't worry. The food smells great. We'll have a little wine. She'll warm up." But Gus doubted that she'd warm up and was starting to think that there was no amount of wine in the world that could bring these women together.

In Callie's Panties

Gus and his mother are downstairs with Callie and the baby, and I'm standing here wearing my white bra and Callie's panties. They are leopard print with black lace on the edges of the leg holes. I've never worn anything so exotic in my life. I was going to say slutty, but Callie isn't slutty. She's something I don't understand yet. But she is good to me. She treats me like I'm normal, no matter what I say or what I do. She doesn't turn away when I open my heart to her.

My clothes are a wet mess on the floor near the bathtub. I shove them into my bag and look again at the outfit that Callie has selected for me to wear. I don't know if I can do it. But what choice do I have? My dress is drenched and I can't go downstairs in my bra and her panties. Of course, that isn't my mother-in-law down there. I can do whatever I want. Standing in the tub with my body pressed against Callie's showed me that. The house didn't collapse, no icons fell from the walls, and there was no aftermath. Only that exact moment of . . . she called it "connection," when it felt like our hearts were beating in unison and our bodies were melting together, and I was lost in that embrace, and I never wanted to find my way out of it.

I wonder if God would ever let one woman get another woman pregnant.

Hurricane Horiatis

Mrs. Horiatis slowly climbed the stairs to the guest bedroom, shaking her head from side to side, imagining the barbaric life her grandchild would lead with the devil *Amerikanitha* for a mother. She was aghast at the way the redhead pulled her breasts out all the time. "We saw them already!" she said out loud as she reached the top step. "Put them away, *hristianie!*" Then Mrs. Horiatis realized that she didn't even know if the *Amerikanitha* was a Christian. "*Hristos na filai,*" she gasped as she genuflected. *My grandson must belong to the Greek Orthodox Church. I cannot leave until he is baptized,* she thought. *Po! Po! What a mess my son has made. Well, I needed to lose some weight anyway.* She was affirming her choice to starve rather than eat soy chorizo when she rounded the corner and bumped head-on into Xeni.

"*Me sinhoris.* I'm so sorry!" Xeni placed her hands on Mrs. Horiatis's arms. "Are you *endaxi?*"

"Yes, *koritsi mou.* I'm fine." Mrs. Horiatis was stunned. Not because of their collision, but because there standing in front of her was a classic Greek beauty with thick brown hair and intense dark eyes, a sculpted nose, and full rosy lips. Her hips were curvy like a fertile, ripe pomegranate. *This* was the kind of woman that she'd hoped her son would find.

"I'm Xeni. You must be *Kyria Horiatis.*"

"Yes. *Heroume poli.*" Mrs. Horiatis looked Xeni up and down. She approved of the dress Xeni was wearing. It was not too long

137

and not too short. She wasn't showing too much cleavage. The maroon color brought out her eyes and lips against her olive skin. Very respectable.

"So nice to meet you, too. *Kalosoresate*. Welcome. Did you have a nice trip?"

"Oh. It could have been better. They squash us like sardines in those airplanes."

"It is a hard journey between Greece and America." Xeni hugged herself.

"Tell me, Xeni. What village are your people from?"

"*Pirgos*. In the Peloponnesus."

"*Ach! Pirgos! Eimaste* from *Amaliada*! We're neighbors. What is your father's name?"

"*Christopoulos*."

"*Christopoulos . . . Christopoulos . . .* No, I don't know any *Christopoulos*. But it is a beautiful name."

"Yes." Xeni smiled. "Are you hungry? We prepared the *trapezi* for you. So many wonderful dishes. I hope you will enjoy them."

"Since *you* prepared them, *koritsi mou*, I'm sure I will!"

"Well, we prepared them together. Callie is a very good cook."

"Oh, come on now. It's one thing when an *Amerikanitha* looks up a recipe in a book, and it's another when an *Ellenopoula* like you cooks. It's in your blood!" Mrs. Horiatis smiled and pinched Xeni's cheek. "My son deserves the best."

"It sounds like you have already made up your mind."

"Oh *koritsti mou*, you know when a Greek mother comes to visit it is like a hurricane. Only the strongest unions survive!" Mrs. Horiatis laughed.

"Sounds like trouble!" Xeni smiled and hugged Mrs. Horiatis.

Mrs. Horiatis was surprised by Xeni's sudden hug, but returned the hug warmly. "Xeni *mou*, we are going to get along just fine. I can tell already. Let's go and taste some of the delicious food you prepared."

The Dinner Scene

Dinner was delicious, each dish better than the last. Gus sat with his mother on one side of the table, while Xeni and Callie sat on the other with Manny in between them. Gus noticed his mother staring from Callie to Xeni and back throughout the meal, and could just imagine the tirade going through her head. *How could my idiotic son have picked the* Amerikanitha *when there was a beautiful* Ellenopoula *right under his feet, cooking in his kitchen and caring for his son. How does he expect to pass on our culture, our language?* Gus sighed heavily.

Callie offered Mrs. Horiatis servings of every dish and tried to explain how she had made this or that. Gus could see that Callie was feeling nervous. He wondered if she had noticed that his mother had been staring at Xeni all night and didn't seem to notice when Callie tried to start some conversation with her.

"Mrs. Horiatis, what do you think about the *tzatziki?* Is it too salty?" Callie would ask.

"I don't know. What do you think, Xeni? You look so pretty in that dress."

"Well, I think it's just right. Callie did a great job."

"What about the stuffed squash blossoms, Mrs. Horiatis?" asked Callie.

"Did you make the *kolokithanthi gemisti,* Xeni? They are delicious. What a romantic dish—stuffed flowers! Xeni, I wish I had your beautiful skin."

And on and on they went, Callie seeking approval, Mrs. Horiatis courting Xeni, and Xeni deflecting attention to Callie. Gus watched with irritation as the women turned the same corner over and over again.

"Okay, enough ladies! Everything tastes good, Callie did a good job, and Xeni looks great tonight. Big deal! You're giving me a headache." Gus couldn't wait for the evening to end. He excused himself from the table, but the women hardly took notice.

I can still smell the scent of the flowery bathwater on my skin as I sit at the dinner table watching Mrs. Horiatis and Callie in their awkward dance. As much as I want Callie to succeed, there is another part of me that wants her to fail, for Mrs. Horiatis to drive a wedge between Callie and Gus. I rub my arms where Callie touched them as we embraced. I wish that everyone else would go to bed and that Callie and I could quietly clean the kitchen together.

Manny suddenly adds his two cents by throwing his spoonful of cereal across the table and accidentally hitting his *yiayia* in the face. Her hands fly to her mouth.

"What kind of table manners do you have around here? It is a mother's responsibility to teach her son how to behave!"

"Oh, I'm so sorry, Mrs. Horiatis. He didn't mean to hit you," Callie begs.

Callie's ingratiating attitude toward Mrs. Horiatis snaps me out of my reverie. *Why is she letting the old woman pound her into the ground . . . ?*

"Can I get you an ice pack?" Callie asks.

. . . if she cares that much what the old woman thinks . . .

"Does it hurt?"

. . . then she must really want to be with Gus . . .

"Manny, say you're sorry!"

. . . and she can't really care that much about me . . .

"I'm leaving. I have to leave. I can't take it anymore." I can't believe that I am wearing Callie's leopard-print panties and that I'd—I can't even think it, what I've done. Callie and Mrs. Horiatis try to convince me to stay, but I am determined to leave. I can't take another minute of watching Callie woo Mrs. Horiatis. There *is* an aftermath, the house *is* collapsing, and the virgin is falling.

STUFFED SQUASH BLOSSOMS

"What a romantic dish—stuffed flowers!"

1 cup feta cheese, crumbled
1/2 cup cottage cheese
2 teaspoons finely minced mint leaves
2 eggs, beaten
Salt
Pepper
20 squash blossoms
1 egg, beaten
Flour
Extra-virgin olive oil

Mix together the feta, cottage cheese, mint, two eggs, and salt and pepper in a bowl.

Gently open the blossom and fill it with the creamy filling. Dip the flower into the beaten egg and then drag it across the flour, carefully shaking off any excess. Fry the flower in hot olive oil until it becomes gorgeous and golden on both sides.

Place the flower between your lips, being careful not to get burned.

Belly Dance

Callie smoothed gardenia-scented lotion onto her arms while looking absentmindedly into the mirror above her dressing table. Gus watched her from the bed where he was lying thinking about his mother, who could not be more different from Callie. He wondered if he might have some kind of defect in a heart valve because it felt impossible for the two women to coexist without causing him palpitations. Callie poured more lotion into her palms and warmed it between her hands before rubbing it into her calves and then thighs. He noticed the way she moved her hands up and down her legs, following the definition of her muscles, gliding over her velvety skin. She had amazingly soft skin.

Callie put the lotion down on her dresser and wrapped her robe closer to her body. The silk fabric caught in the air, hovering slightly before settling down upon Callie's body. It sparked a memory for Gus—the first night he'd seen Callie. He'd gone to the Grapeleaf Restaurant for a drink and some *mezethes*. He liked the music there. They played some Greek songs but mostly Middle Eastern. Sometimes when he was feeling lonely, going there for an ouzo and the drumbeats made him feel good. The bartender knew him by name, and when he'd walked in that night, he'd said, "Hey, Gus, you picked a great night to come!" and laughed as he plunked a shot of ouzo and a bowl of peanuts down in front of him on the bar.

145

"Oh, yeah? How come? Are you giving out free ouzo?" Gus winked at the bartender.

"Oh come on, you know it's student belly dance night."

"Wouldn't miss it." Gus smiled. Student belly dance night was always good for some entertainment. The local belly dance teacher brought her students into the restaurant for a dance recital a few times a year—earnest girls dancing around in jerry-rigged sequined costumes trying their best to look exotic. Usually the students were blond or overweight. And they all took on fake Middle Eastern names for the performance. They never knew the words to the songs because they couldn't understand the languages being sung. They all wanted to look sexy, and so they danced toward the single men sitting at the bar, sometimes draping their veils over a bar patron's head and dancing faster than the music called for.

"Better give me an extra shot," Gus chuckled. Just because many of the dancing girls were ridiculous didn't stop Gus from going home with one or two. He felt it was a public service to make their fantasy of a dark-haired, olive-skinned, bouzouki-playing lover come true. He always spoke to them in Greek as they screwed, and he insisted that they keep their costumes on, shaking their breasts so their coined bras jingled.

That night it was the usual performance of clumsy, sexy girls dancing their hearts out to the drums. Gus and the bartender rated the girls on their performances with peanuts, and the first to run out of peanuts downed a shot. It was around Christmas, and one girl had made herself a costume out of red velvet and trimmed the bra with white marabou feathers. The bartender pushed a few peanuts forward to reward her originality. After the usual suspects had all come out and danced, shimmied, and thrust their hips toward the bar, Gus was ready to go. None of the girls had interested him that night. Then the teacher, a plump woman with dark eyeliner and long, dyed black hair, came out to introduce the last student. "Won't you all please welcome my newest student, Calliope!"

The crowd clapped obligatorily as the slow music started to

flow from the speakers. Callie emerged from behind the curtain with her wavy red hair cascading down her back. She was wearing a sea-foam green skirt that floated over her long legs, and she held a sheer veil over her upper body as she slowly stepped towards the stage, lifting and dropping her hips with each step. Her softly curved stomach undulated with the music, and as the tempo picked up she lifted her veil above her head and twirled, revealing her ample breasts contained within a silvery blue net.

Unlike the other students, Callie seemed lost in the music, almost oblivious to the audience. Gus stared at her intently, willing her to look in his direction. Her arms snaked above her head as she slipped into a sensuous backbend, her body arched in an impossible curve, throat exposed, mouth open. Gus's head was throbbing from the ouzo, and his body strained from desiring her. The music swelled and she twirled in circle after circle until her veils caught the air and hovered around her like a surging tide. The bartender slid five peanuts toward Gus. Callie ended the dance on the downbeat of a drum, one slender arm extended up into the air, and the other out toward the bar, pointing at Gus. As the audience applauded with genuine enthusiasm, Gus shoved all of his remaining peanuts at the bartender, knocked back his ouzo, leapt off of the stool, and walked a straight line toward Calliope, mesmerized.

The night felt more like fantasy than reality. Gus brought Calliope home and led her into the living room where he asked her to dance for him. She was still in her costume and willingly undulated before the picture windows with the moonglow behind her, framing her lithe body with a fractured spark that made him gasp. He enticed her with passionate Greek phrases as they shared a bottle of *mavrodaphne,* the sweet wine tipping their senses into a buzzing drone of hypersensitivity. Each touch felt like a searing push into their physical bodies, each kiss a challenge to their borders. They lost the ability to maintain their margins, lost all white space, and merged into a tangled mess of legs, heartbeats, and breath. Was it a sin? It had felt like one, and that made it all the sweeter.

Gus was startled from his reverie by the sound of Callie accidentally dropping her brush onto her dressing table. Her long red hair hung in seductive waves as she started to brush through it, the hair glistening more with each stroke. Even though he cared for her, and she was certainly beautiful, he felt conflicted about this life, this moment.

He sighed and wondered how he'd gotten caught so easily. How one evening, a few shots of ouzo, and a dance had gotten him a live-in lover, a baby, and a mother who was spinning out of control. He rubbed his eyes, his face, as if trying to wake up from a dream. But he'd already left dreamland and was entrenched in domestic disturbance. *Damn those peanuts,* he thought. *Damn those peanuts and the ouzo, too.*

Callie absentmindedly finished brushing her hair, thinking about the night, the dinner, Xeni, and their argument. Callie's confusion seemed to be mounting by the day. She had been so focused on impressing Mrs. Horiatis that she felt like she was losing herself except when she was with Xeni. She found herself reaching for Xeni instinctively, as if seeing herself reflected in Xeni's eyes was the only thing anchoring her to the Earth. And now Xeni was upset. Callie hadn't noticed Xeni becoming angry or anticipated her eruption at the dinner table at all. She had to patch things up with her. It wasn't because she needed her help to impress Mrs. Horiatis. It was because Callie could not risk losing Xeni.

Callie sneaked a peek at Gus. He was lying on the bed clutching an old copy of *Time* magazine with Barack Obama on the cover. His curly brown hair was still damp from his shower and hung on his forehead. She walked over and pushed a curl back. He didn't seem to notice, his face caught in an expression of confusion. She put the lotion down on her bedside table and sat down on the bed next to him.

"Will you hold me?"

Gus's eyes came back into focus. "Huh?"

"Will you hold me? I feel scared."

Callie could sense Gus's distance, but she curled up onto his chest anyway.

"Why are you scared?" he asked reluctantly.

"Well, Xeni is really mad at me. I don't want her to be mad at me." And silently, she said, *I want her to love me.*

"Yeah. You guys are friends, babe. It'll be all right." Gus started to take his arm away from her shoulders and yawned.

"I don't want you to be mad at me either."

"Callie, I'm not mad at you."

"But what if you *get* mad at me?"

"For what?" Gus asked.

"I don't know. Whatever." *I want her to love me.*

"Well. What if you get mad at me?" Gus asked.

Callie turned to look at him. "Why would I be mad at you?"

"I don't know." Gus looked away.

Callie curled up tightly against Gus until they fell asleep, and then she dreamt that they were having the same dream, that they would stay together forever, and that they would both be very, very sad.

Mirage

My stomach feels so hollow. So empty. Is it possible to be filled with emptiness? Can it inflate your insides until they want to burst from the pressure? I don't know what I was thinking. I must have been delirious from working in the kitchen, sweating out my good sense. I must have lost my judgment stirring the roux for the béchamel sauce, or fallen into a hot pan of butter, melted and burned. Manny, Manolaki, you are the one that brought me to this situation. But instead of finding pleasure biting your thigh or sucking your toes, I have fallen into a cooking pot of boiling water, sprinkled with flowers and flavored with one cinnamon-sprinkled *Amerikanitha*. The freckles across her nose travel down to her chest and lighten around her breasts, round and creamy as fresh mounds of mizithra cheese. It was one thing when I was helping Callie learn to cook, but what is this that is happening? I thought I was teaching her to be a good Greek wife. But instead she is teaching me to . . . what? I don't know.

Would it be wrong to pray? Pray to God to help me understand my feelings? I think I feel too much for Callie. What does it mean? It must be wrong. Sometimes when I'm washing a roast, my hands linger too long on the firm flesh. When I pick tomatoes, my fingers curl around them and don't want to let go. Eating a cluster of grapes, my tongue curls around each round fruit, licking the smooth skin, and then pushing through to the wet, sweet insides. I want to stay there in luscious, juicy ecstasy and suck and devour and get lost.

I don't understand. I want a baby. A young Easter lamb is tender and delicious. Older sheep are gamy and tough. I want a baby. I want a baby. I can't want Callie. She is married, an *Amerikanitha*, so different, shameless. Without shame. How did she get to be a grown woman without shame? With an open heart?

My heart is closed. It will stay closed. It will only open when God blesses me with a baby, and He will never bless me if I go astray. If I indulge in . . . baths . . . with another woman. The water roiled and lifted the flower petals up around our thighs as we stood there embracing, like a double Aphrodite rising from the water. Perhaps this is a test that God has placed before me to see if I have the moral strength to receive parthenogenesis. Does holding another woman in a bath of warm water constitute moral weakness? Is it a sin if she places her hands on either side of my face and brings me so close to her that I can feel her breath on my lips? Is wrapping her wet ringlets around my fingers and pulling them back so far that her neck is exposed . . . because I don't want her face too close, too close, close enough to kiss? Is it bad that I leaned in and brushed my lips against the moist skin of her neck, licked the drops of water collected in the well of her neck? I was so thirsty.

If someone is lost in a desert and they've run out of water, they start to hallucinate. A mirage will suddenly appear before them, perhaps at a distance, wavering in the hot sun, offering their deepest desires. Water, food, comfort, safety, pleasure. Is it wrong for them to grasp at the unattainable? If they know that they can never have what they want, is it wrong for them to keep wanting it? Or is it a pitiable attempt at survival? Dear God, tell me. Is this a mirage? Or is it real?

Green with Envy

Gus pulled up to the Green Envy Ranch just as the sun was hitting high noon. He sat behind the wheel of the SUV cursing the internet for faulty driving directions to Sebastopol. He looked sideways at his mother sitting in the passenger seat beside him and wiping her forehead with a handkerchief that smelled of lilacs and sour sweat. She had gotten carsick on the ride. Nausea had leached the color from her face and emptied her belly of the coffee and the sticky roll she'd had for breakfast. She dabbed the creases next to her lips, carefully avoiding the pink lipstick that she'd just reapplied. Gus noticed it smelled like cotton candy, and just the thought of the airy confection was enough to make him want to gag just a little into her hand-embroidered handkerchief.

Gus crumpled the driving directions into a ball and threw them at the windshield, where they bounced off and landed in the back of the car on the floor between Callie and Xeni's feet and under Manny's car seat. In the rearview mirror he could see the two women look at the mangled paper and then at each other and roll their eyes. Manny poked at a stuffed dog attached to the car seat and then arched his back, crying out against the belts restraining him.

"Was that just the longest hour and a half of my life?" Gus muttered as he rolled down the window to get some fresh air. Gus had been tense since his mother's arrival. He'd run to the Greek store four times in the last three days, fetching small items that would make his mother more comfortable: Greek magazines, a religious icon for her guestroom, olive soap, and chunks of halvah. As his mother scolded Callie during the ride, Gus gripped the steering wheel harder and occasionally turned back to ask Xeni to *do something*, as if she had some magical power to mollify his mother. He had insisted that Xeni come on this outing, hoping that her presence would create some kind of buffer between his mother's disapproval and Callie's lack of understanding. Xeni had been working with Callie for weeks, teaching her how to cook Greek food, to speak some of the language and to understand some of the customs, but once born an *Amerikana* always an *Amerikana*. He sighed. And the fact that Callie wouldn't tell him the details of this outing . . . He started thinking about smoking again. Imagined the deep drag he'd take on the Marlboro, holding the smoke in his lungs for a good while before slowly blowing smoke rings into the air.

"*Ayori mou, pou me eferes? Sto gabo?*" His mother interrupted his smoke fantasy with her question. "My boy, where did you bring me? To the fields?"

"No, of course not, *Mana*. Why would I bring you to the fields?" He laughed nervously while reading the sign before them: Green Envy Ranch.

Callie looked pleased with herself as she announced, "We're going apple picking! And then we'll have a picnic! And tonight I'll make us a good old-fashioned American apple pie! From scratch!"

Gus groaned audibly at the words "apple picking" and turned to his mother. "I'm sure there are some nice restaurants here in Sebastopol for lunch. We'll go find one."

"NO!" Callie shouted. "I mean, no. This is going to be fun. I planned it all out. I have a picnic lunch for us. We'll eat it under an apple tree once we finish picking. It'll be pastoral and reminiscent of earlier times." She reached forward and poked Gus in the ribs with an umbrella she found on the floor of the car.

"Earlier times? Whose earlier times?" Gus was not charmed by her plan. He had never wanted to pick apples as a kid, and

154

he didn't want to do it now. Then he realized that she must be referring to his mother's earlier times. "You know, I don't know that *anyone* wants to remember earlier times." He shoved the umbrella back at her.

"Well, we are going to. We're here now."

Callie quickly unbuckled the restraints on Manny's car seat, and Xeni offered to carry him through the verdant orchard on her back like a tasty sack of fruit. Callie helped adjust Manny in the carrier, and she and Xeni walked forward toward the Green Envy Ranch with arms locked. Gus watched them move on ahead of him while he helped his mother out of the SUV. She complained about the car being too high, but Gus couldn't take his eyes off of Callie. She was walking with her arm around Xeni's waist and whispering something in her ear. They laughed together, and Xeni tilted her head toward Callie in a gesture that was at once imperceptible and unmistakable. Their foreheads touched for just a moment and Callie blushed before pushing a curl back behind her ear. She smiled and held Xeni's gaze a moment too long, he thought. They had been getting close, maybe too close. Xeni seemed to understand Callie in a way that he never had. He felt a searing heat rising up from his neck and into his face.

"*Ella pedi mou*—help me get down." His mother interrupted his thoughts.

"Yes, *Mana*. I'm sorry." He helped her touch her feet down on the dusty parking lot. "I came to *Ameriki* so that I could come to a village," she grumbled. "Why are they walking ahead of us? Why don't they slow down so I can see my grandson?" She looked forward into the entryway of the ranch that was flanked by two vibrantly green apple trees and saw only their healthy strong backs and the baby bouncing farther from her reach. "Why don't they slow down?" Gus noticed that his mother seemed heavier than he remembered, and she was walking with a slight limp. "I can't go any faster. I wish I could go faster. I'd dance circles around them and race my grandson to the farthest tree."

"*Mana*. Manny can't walk yet, much less run."

"*Skaseh*! You know what I mean."

Gus could see that with each step his mother fell behind, and the more upset she became. Seeing her struggle made him realize his mother was no longer the powerhouse she once was. She was aging. He put his arm around her shoulders and tenderly kissed her cheek.

As Callie walked arm in arm with Xeni through the apple orchard, she thanked the Goddess for this second chance with Xeni. Callie was determined to hold onto pieces of herself. Even though she had committed to the path of pleasing Mrs. Horiatis—who, after all, was always going to be Manny's grandmother—she didn't want to lose herself or Xeni in the process. Xeni had refused to answer Callie's calls all the next day after the welcome dinner for Mrs. Horiatis. When they finally spoke, Callie tearfully begged Xeni's forgiveness for acting so foolish. She had wanted to please Gus and to win his mother's approval. She had wanted to give Manny the kind of family she had never had, but she was realizing that she wasn't willing to completely lose herself in the process.

As if to prove it to herself and Xeni, she realized she needed to get back to her roots, her version of family and culture. She decided to bring everyone apple picking, something they could all do together. Green Envy Ranch had Arkansas Black, Granny Smith, Pippins, Gravenstein, Red and Golden Delicious, Rome Beauty, and Macintosh. That was more varieties of apples than she had ever tasted, but she knew that she could make a good old-fashioned double-crust apple pie with the Granny Smiths, using twelve apples just like her Aunt Margie had shown her. With all those apples the upper crust would elevate to an impressive four inches tall. Making pies always made her happy, and she was good at it. And she needed to feel good at something on her own terms. Or maybe she'd make her famous apple crisp with a buttery cinnamon oat topping. The luscious apples contrasted perfectly with the cinnamon crunchy top.

Callie hadn't planned to lure Xeni into the bathtub that

evening, but she could never be sorry for that moment of true connection. It wasn't the first time that her spontaneity had taken her to unexpected places, and she knew with certainty that it wouldn't be the last. She often replayed the scene in her mind, her body and heart awakening each time. Xeni had lowered her walls and trusted her, and Callie flashed back on that moment endlessly, even as she was serving Mrs. Horiatis and Gus the dinner they'd prepared. Callie had always been able to love more than one person at a time, but she could feel her feelings shifting toward Xeni in a way that surprised her. Holding Xeni in her arms made Callie feel vulnerable. She wanted to protect Xeni, and her own heart. She wanted to do the right thing for everyone, even though she didn't know what that was.

Walking with Xeni through the apple orchard, inhaling the scent of ripening fruit, felt like a perfect moment. Knowing there was no easy solution to her dilemma, Callie decided to be present. She lost herself in showing Manny the red, golden, and green apples hanging from the low branches of the trees. The sun was shining through the vibrant green leaves, shooting from every open spot on the tree's frame. Manny reached for a bright green apple, but couldn't quite wrap his small fist around it. His fingers all moved together, open and closed, open and closed. He hadn't yet developed a good one-handed grip for something so comparatively large and hard to grasp. He made a loud excited "aaaaaaaahh!" sound.

Callie looked back at Gus and his mother. He was tenderly offering her his arm as they walked the uneven pavement toward the ranch. His mother looked unhappy about something and barely acknowledged his arm. He placed his hand on his mother's back. When he looked at his mother, he looked like a little boy again—eager to please her, afraid to disappoint her. He never looked at Callie that way. She used to care, but she was beginning to let go. At some point in the past she would have been jealous, but not now. She was tired of trying to please everyone.

Apple Wishes

I spend most of the ride either looking out of the car window while caressing Manny's plump hand, or occasionally stealing a glance at Callie and her softly curling red hair or the freckles scattered across her nose that remind me of strawberry seeds.

When Callie announces that we are going apple picking, it almost makes the car ride worth it. Even though I am stuck spending the day with Gus and his bossy mother playing cultural interpreter for Callie, I will enjoy being out in the fields picking the ripened fruit. There is nothing I enjoy more than searching out the freshest ingredients and creating something delicious with them. Apples are luscious when baked with butter, chopped chocolate, and mint tucked into the core. Apples are refreshing in a crisp salad with hearts of romaine, pomegranate seeds, and creamy gorgonzola. Apples sit heavy in the palm of the hand and offer a satisfying mouthful of sweet tanginess as teeth burst through skin and crush firm flesh. I steal another glance at Callie. The love apple, red and juicy.

The fields are fragrant and the trees heavy with fruit. The trees are beautiful mothers dangling their tasty babies from their branches. I carry Manny as Callie and I walk deeper into the orchard surrounded by the soothing, leafy green canopy. Callie's smiling face shows a look of utter contentment as she spins with arms outstretched under the apple trees. I try to pretend everything is normal, even when our faces come close and foreheads touch, even when her hand rests on my back.

I pick a green apple and hold it close to Manny's face. It appears perfect and unblemished, pristine and innocent, just like Manny. I wish that I could go back to being free from damage. I wish that I were a fragrant apple contained within a resilient green skin, with sweet flesh, and seeds of potential slipped inside of my body.

GREEN ENVY APPLE CRISP

"Apples sit heavy in the palm of the hand, and offer a satisfying mouthful of sweet tanginess as teeth burst through skin and crush firm flesh."

Butter
10 green apples, peeled and cut into bite-sized chunks
1/2 cup oatmeal
3/4 cup flour
1 teaspoon cinnamon
1/4 cup sugar
8 tablespoons butter, cut into small pieces

Preheat oven to 375 degrees.

Butter a small baking pan and fill it with the peeled and chopped apples.

Mix together the oatmeal, flour, cinnamon, and sugar. Add the chunks of butter and, using your fingers, massage it into the flour mixture until it resembles crumbles. Top the apples with the crumble mixture.

Bake for 45 minutes, or until the topping is golden brown and crisp and the apples are bubbling in their own juices. Serve warm with vanilla ice cream.

Heart Attack

Mrs. Horiatis bustled about the kitchen preparing breakfast. It was barely dawn and the other members of the family were still sleeping in their beds. She had peeked into Manny's room before she came down to make breakfast. He was lying on his back with arms thrust above his head, his brilliant red curls lying gently against his pale cheek. She feared for her grandson, wondering what little amount of her culture might trickle down to him. *Kids today,* she thought. *They leave their customs and culture behind. To chase after—what?* In his sleep, Manny found his thumb and started to nibble, finding his flesh a comforting snack.

Down in the kitchen Mrs. Horiatis stabbed raw egg yolks with a fork before beating the eggs in the bowl and laying strips of pork belly in the searing hot frying pan. Slices of white bread sat on a plate awaiting their fate. The house vibrated with desire, dissatisfaction, bewilderment, and dreams. As the fat began to sizzle, filling the air with the smell of smoky flesh, she recalled all the Sunday mornings that she had prepared American breakfast for her husband, Manoli, and Gus. Manoli would absently read the paper, and Gus was always fascinated with the flame burning hot on the stove. As she would turn her back to grab a plate, he'd stick his finger as close to the fire as he could without burning it. He would push forward just enough to make her furious and then withdraw when she'd shout with fear. The child was always challenging her in his cowardly way.

This situation is no different, she thought. *He is in bed right now with that* Amerikanitha, *but he will withdraw. He never had the courage to get burned, and he doesn't have it now.* She poured the beaten eggs into a hot pan splattered with bacon fat drippings. She swirled the yellow clotty liquid into the black-flecked amber fat and watched the speckled curds form. *The only good thing in this situation is my grandchild,* she thought. Sometimes you could put two nauseating things together and find something pleasing. She stirred the eggs until they formed fluffy mounds, wholesome and flavored with savory smoke. She removed the crisp bacon from the other pan and laid the strips side by side on a bed of paper towels to drain.

"Constantino!" she yelled up the stairs. "I'm making the bread now. Come eat!" Mrs. Horiatis grabbed the plate of bread, and one by one she fried each slice in the bacon fat until it was golden brown and crisp. Her doctor would not approve of this technique, but it was delicious, and she was sure that Gus hadn't enjoyed this kind of a breakfast since he was still living at home with her. *I'd like to see the* Amerikanitha *make a breakfast like this,* she harrumphed. *Now, the* Ellenopoula . . .

She indulged her fantasy of Xeni walking about the kitchen in a blue-and-white striped apron preparing breakfast for Gus and Manoli. She imagined Xeni caressing Gus's curls as she set a plate before him of bacon-fat fried bread, her wedding band glimmering on her right ring finger. "Sweetheart, why don't we please ask your mother to come and live with us? She would love to spend more time with Manoli, and I'd appreciate her help in the kitchen. She's such a great cook." Mrs. Horiatis smiled at the scene playing out in her head and imagined herself joining her family at the table, Gus pulling out her chair, and Xeni placing a fresh-cut rose in a vase near her plate. "Good morning, *Mana!* Could I make you some eggs? Would you like to hold the baby? I'm so happy that you've decided to stay here with us. I could really use your help," and Xeni would kiss her hand and rub her feet. Mrs. Horiatis's chest filled with oxygen and deflated just as quickly.

"*Mana.* You don't have to yell, you know." Gus lumbered into the kitchen. "Everybody is asleep. Why are you cooking so early?"

"Well, I'm not asleep. There is work to be done. Sit. Eat. We have to talk about something." Mrs. Horiatis shoved a heaping plate of bacon, eggs and fried bread before him.

"Wow, *Mana*. I haven't seen this kind of breakfast in years. Wait a minute, let me just get my heart medication." Gus chuckled at his own joke.

"What? You don't like it now?" Mrs. Horiatis snorted.

"I love it, *Mana*. I haven't had this in forever. Just don't make it again for a while so that I can live past fifty, okay?" Gus hugged his mother to his side and popped a crinkled piece of bacon into his mouth. She giggled freely, knowing that she had pleased him, and for a moment allowed herself to soften.

"*Ayori mou* . . ."

"Yes, *Mana*?"

"Manoli is so precious. He makes me so happy with his little smile and funny faces."

"Yeah, he's a great kid." Gus bit into the fried bread, crunching through the crisp outer layer into the doughy white insides. "Mmmm . . . this shouldn't be so good."

"He is so precious, and no matter what the circumstances of his birth . . ." She paused to clear her throat, ". . . he deserves to be baptized. No. He *must* be baptized."

Gus put his slice of bread down on the plate. "I don't know, *Mana*. I don't know if . . . I don't know."

"Don't know what? What is there to know?" Mrs. Horiatis stiffened again.

"I don't know," he took a breath before completing the sentence, "if Callie would want that."

"Would the *Amerikanitha* want your child to wander aimlessly in purgatory for eternity because he wasn't baptized? What's wrong with you? Who's in charge of this house?"

"*Mana*. Hold on—"

"You expect me to sit and watch while you let that red devil ruin your child's chance to enter heaven?"

"*Mana*."

"*Mana*, what? There is no this or that. There is one way. He is

Greek. He must be baptized in the Greek Orthodox Church. See what happens when you get involved outside of your culture? Trouble, nothing but trouble. It could be a lifetime of trouble unless you do something about it. Why don't you give her some money to go traveling? Or buy her a house in hippietown? Give her what she wants so that she gives you Manoli and goes away. I can help you raise him. Or, Xeni . . ."

"Mana! Stop! Please! Callie would never give up Manny. Never. She lives for that kid. And, she's a good mother. I don't want to take her away from him. I couldn't do that to him. *Mana*. Can't you help me try to make this situation work instead of making it worse?"

"*I* make it worse? I come here to try to accept your child that you had outside the proper bounds—*I* make it worse?" Mrs. Horiatis was so mad that she wanted to take his finger and put it in the flame so that he could finally understand what it meant to play with fire.

"*Mana*. Calm down."

"I make it worse! I better calm down before *I* make it worse!"

"*Mana*."

"Do you know what baptism does? It releases the child of all sin and fills him with the Holy Spirit. Considering the way he came into the world, I'd say he needs all the help he can get."

"Manny didn't do anything wrong, *Mana*."

"No, but you did. And he carries your sin until you help cleanse him of it."

Gus was silent, and she knew she had him in her grip.

"I give up. What the hell. If dunking the kid in water a few times and rubbing him with oil will make it all okay, we'll do it. Okay, *Mana*?"

"Well, don't do it for me. Do it for Manolaki's eternal soul," she said reproachfully. She turned her back to Gus and smiled. He was always such a simple boy, she thought. It was a source of his charm—and his stupidity. Mrs. Horiatis flipped another piece of fried bread onto his plate, hugged his shoulders, and pinched his cheek. "*Tha se faw!*"

Pig Heaven

"Hey Cal, I had a great idea this morning." Gus walked into the bedroom rubbing his bursting stomach. Callie was lying on her side in the bed nursing Manny. He grasped at his toes as he sucked at her breast, filling his stomach with sweet mother's milk.

"Yeah?"

"Yeah. I was thinking it would be really great to baptize the baby while my Mom is here. It would make her so happy, and uh"—Gus grasped for another good reason—"it would cleanse him of sin and fill him with the Holy Spirit." By the look on Callie's face, he knew he'd picked the wrong one.

"Sin?"

"Uh. Yeah, you know." Gus tried to remember his Sunday school lessons. "We're all born with sin, etc., etc."

"Please, Gus. Take a look at your son. Does he look like he's a sinner?"

Manny was lying on his side against his mother, suckling and fiddling with his big toe. Seeming to feel that eyes were upon him, he turned toward his father and smiled, a fat droplet of white milk rolling off of his pink lips and down his chubby chin.

"He looks like he's in pig heaven." Gus rubbed his stomach one more time and sighed. "Look, it's important to me and my mother that we baptize the kid. Whaddaya say?"

"Fine. I was thinking about it myself. I think it would be very uplifting to introduce him to the community through a baby blessing at Glide Memorial Church in San Francisco."

"Glide Memorial?"

"Yeah. You know, they do really great work in the community and they welcome all people there."

"Don't they welcome drug addicts and homosexuals and homeless people there? Can you see my mother sitting in church next to a homeless person on one side and a big queen on the other?"

Callie sat up and pulled Manny close to her chest. "I don't want to have this conversation with you in front of the baby. I don't want him to see how prejudiced you are. I don't want him growing up that way." Manny pulled at Callie's robe, exposing her breast.

"Ah, come on, Callie. All I was saying is that—"

"I know what you were saying." Callie pulled her robe firmly shut. "Since when are you so homophobic anyway?"

"I'm not homophobic. Lighten up."

"Well, what was that 'big queen' comment for then?"

"Ah, come on."

"Did you know that I used to be with a woman? Her name was Nylah and we were together for three years."

"Hey, that's kind of hot." Gus grinned.

"Typical."

"Okay, I'm sorry. I'm sorry. I don't mind if you were with a woman."

"Have you ever been with a man?"

"Hell no! Are you kidding?" Gus balked.

"Well, why not?" Callie got up and bounced Manny around on her hip.

"For one thing, that's gross. For another, it's against my religion."

"How is it against your religion? I didn't even know you had a religion."

"Of course I have a religion. I'm Greek Orthodox. Even if I never set foot in that church, I still belong there."

"Unless you sleep with a man?"

"Well, yeah. But it doesn't matter because I don't plan to. What is up with you today?"

Callie hugged Manny close, kissing his forehead. "You know, I thought that . . ."

"What?"

"I thought that you loved me and our son."

Gus hedged. "Where's that coming from?"

"I don't think you respect my point of view."

"What does that have to do with love?" Gus snorted.

"Can you give me one really good reason why we should baptize Manny at the Greek Orthodox Church instead of blessing him at Glide Memorial?"

"Because he is Greek, and he has a right to his heritage. It is my job to make sure that he retains it, and that he doesn't get lost in some blank, white American lack of ethnic identity."

"So, it really is important to you?" Callie asked.

"Yes, it is important to me," Gus stated, and realized he was speaking the truth.

"Well, okay. But on one condition."

"Okay, whatever."

"I want Xeni to be the godmother." Callie smiled.

"Really? What about my friends, like Thanasi or Alexandros?"

"Xeni spends a lot of time with Manny. She loves him." She added, "In a way, she's his second mother."

Gus noticed that Callie was suddenly blushing and flashed back on the intimacy he had noticed between her and Xeni at the Green Envy Ranch. He wondered if it was the cooking that had brought them together, or something else.

"Anyway, that's my one condition. Take it or leave it."

Gus knew when to stop arguing with a woman. "I'll take it."

Macy's, a Holy Place

The bustle in Macy's San Francisco created a steady roar. Each element of the shopping experience added a ring to the cacophony: the hunger and hope of the shoppers, the flirtatious dance of the sales associates offering goods and suggestions, even the sound of perfume spraying from the mouth of signature bottles and onto the customers. It seemed that no matter what day or time it was, there were always people looking for something to fill them up, to take away their boredom, sorrow, and fear and to replace it with a kind of euphoria.

Mrs. Horiatis always came to Macy's San Francisco whenever she was back in the United States. She loved the cosmetics counter with all the makeup ladies standing at the ready to help bring out her beauty, and she always had a list from relatives with their special requests from Estée Lauder, Clinique, and Lancôme. Callie and Gus accompanied her, and she'd insisted that Xeni accompany them as well. Xeni had finally agreed to come when Mrs. Horiatis reminded her of the culinary cornucopia and cooking equipment that covered the lower floor of the store called, "The Cellar." As she shopped, Mrs. Horiatis handed Gus her purchases as she made her way through the store. Mrs. Horiatis barely paid attention as Callie tried to make small talk while holding Manny in the baby carrier.

As the group passed the fine jewelry section Mrs. Horiatis paused to admire the gleaming gold jewelry and sparkling gemstones. She stared wistfully at the diamonds and looked at her ring finger, which still hosted her plain gold wedding band. There had been no money back then for an engagement ring, and Manoli had left before he ever made it up to her. Letting go of old dreams came hard for Mrs. Horiatis, and she lingered for several moments, silently staring at the promises in the case. The old feelings always came back at unexpected moments, and she wondered if she would ever be able to feel at peace again.

Mrs. Horiatis walked along the jewelry cases admiring the rings, the bracelets, and the necklaces, and imagined the happy women who would receive the trinkets as gifts and gestures of appreciation. She'd even heard of some men giving their wives "push presents" after giving birth to children. *What a ridiculous American stupidity. The gift is the baby.* She caught her reflection in one of the many mirrors propped up on the counter—an old woman, tired and dull. She needed something shiny and new, something to show her that her life had been worth it.

There was a selection of crosses in the display case, some plain, others with diamonds, in gold, platinum, and silver.

"Constantino," she said, "who will be Manolaki's godparents? I want them to see this cross. It is so handsome." Mrs. Horiatis pointed to a large slender cross with a single blue aquamarine in the center.

"We thought we'd ask Xeni," Gus murmured, checking his watch.

"What!" Mrs. Horiatis exclaimed.

"What?" he mumbled, tapping his watch face, and then holding it up to his ear. "Is this thing working? Have we really only been here one hour?"

Mrs. Horiatis reacted before thinking. She yelled, "Constantino Horiatis! *Tha se skotoso*!" The jewelry associates stopped to stare.

Xeni giggled. "What did he do now? It must be pretty bad if you want to kill him." She smiled.

"Hey. I didn't do anything. I was just telling her that we want you to be Manny's godmother," Gus grumbled.

"Gus! That's so unceremonious! I can't believe this is how you want to ask her!" Callie said in a whisper hiss while smiling at

Mrs. Horiatis. Callie took a deep breath and turned toward Xeni, who had remained silent during this exchange.

"We want you, Xeni, to be Manny's godmother."

Mrs. Horiatis interrupted. "Nothing personal, sweetheart," she said to Xeni, "but," she turned to Gus with a fierce look in her eyes, "I don't think that would be appropriate. Don't you have some other friend, Constantino?" Gus put the shopping bags down with deliberate slowness, as if he was approaching danger, and Mrs. Horiatis resisted the temptation to pinch her son. She shook her head and sighed as she realized he could not look her in the eyes.

I'm not sure whether to be offended, relieved, or flattered. I wonder whether this is God moving in some mysterious way, making me a mother of sorts. Could God be saying that he wants Callie and me to *share* Manny? I ponder the question while the others continue their arguments.

"No, *Mana*. Xeni is the one. Callie wants her and *only* her," Gus adds with great emphasis. He pats his empty shirt pocket and mumbles to himself, "*Why* did I quit smoking?"

"Well, what if, let's say that you and Callie break up one day," Mrs. Horiatis starts.

"*Mana*! Stop!" Gus implores, beginning to bite his thumbnail nervously.

"I must speak. I am thinking of my grandchild." Mrs. Horiatis commands his attention. "What if you and Callie break up . . . and what if you and . . ." Mrs. Horiatis turns to look at me, "Xeni . . . want to get together."

Gus and me get together? She is going too far. I wouldn't let my parents marry me off, so I'm certainly not going to let Mrs. Horiatis arrange my marriage with Gus, even if only in her fantasies.

"No really. You can stop now, *Mana*. I would never want Xeni." Gus laughs, and spits out a cuticle. "I've never thought of Xeni that way. Well, except maybe for that night she came down wearing Callie's clothes and makeup and smelling good. No offense." He nods to me.

"Gus!" Callie shouts. "Have some boundaries!"

Why am I suddenly the topic of this conversation? We are supposed to be shopping. I was going to look for a new whisk, but now I feel like perusing the knife section. I pull my sweater closed over my chest.

Mrs. Horiatis presses forward. "Xeni is a lovely girl. She's Greek. She can cook and keep house. But if she baptizes Manolaki, she will be considered your spiritual relative. The church would prohibit you from marrying her. It's just not done!"

"Well, that's okay by me!" Gus laughs incredulously, and starts looking around for the store exits.

I am beside myself trying to keep my laughter and outrage contained within my body. It's classic Greek behavior, marrying off women without their consent or consideration. But this time it's different. This time there is Callie in the mix. And she looks like someone has drained the blood out of her body and left her on a cold sidewalk to frost over.

Callie interrupts. "First of all, Gus, you would be lucky to be with Xeni. *Really* lucky. Second, Mrs. Horiatis . . ." Callie pauses and looks at me intently. I wonder what she is thinking in that moment. Is she imagining his hands on my skin, his mouth on my shoulders? Callie shakes her head vigorously. "NO! This discussion is over. Xeni is mine! I mean, my choice for godmother and that's that. She and Gus will not get together, not if I have anything to say about it."

I feel as if I've fallen into a deep bowl of *petimezi*, the thick, dark molasses that results from hours of boiling down fresh-pressed grape must. I'm not sure where to reach out for a hand. Why is God doing this to me? I wonder. Why, God, did you bring me to this house, with these people? Why did I meet Callie, with her eyes that look like blue planets and hair that flows like lava? When it hits the water you can hear a sizzle. Callie just said, "Xeni is mine!" How can I belong to her, when she belongs to Gus, and I belong to you? If I become Manny's godmother, I will be responsible for his religious education. I must be an impeccable example of morals and Christianity. But if Callie and I—

"Xeni. What do you think? Would you be willing to be Manny's godmother? You already are a second mother to him," Callie pleads. She looks at me so intently that I feel as if a silvery veil has encircled us, giving our eyes privacy despite the fact that we are still standing in the midst of a bustling department store, with Gus and Mrs. Horiatis staring at us. "Would you do it, for me?"

My chest is bursting. A good Greek woman follows the edicts of the church. I found ways to avoid marriage, and I thought my prayers for a virgin birth would come true—that I could have a family without the oppressive thumb of a husband. I thought that if I believed enough and loved God enough that it would eventually happen. I thought it would be simple. But it hasn't been simple, and things are suddenly becoming more and more complicated. There are certain things that I know are not okay in the eyes of God. I try to avoid them with all of my might. I cannot risk my chances for parthenogenesis. Mary must have been so pure to be chosen. I must be pure too. But the purest emotion I've been having lately is love. For Callie. And I feel clean. Cleaner than I've ever felt. I feel like I am unfurling with new life. But I know it is wrong in the eyes of the Church. I feel as if I am being asked to choose between God and Callie. But God is love, and I love Callie. Does that make Callie God? I am getting lost in circles and don't want anyone to see that I am coming undone.

"Xeni?" Callie repeats. "For me?"

Looking into Callie's blue eyes, I am reminded of the *mati*, a Greek charm in the shape of a round blue eye that is worn as protection from evil. God's eye. I feel as if I am floating away above the crowding shoppers, above the noise, above it all. "Yes, I will be Manny's godmother if it is God's wish," I reply. Callie reaches out and touches my arms, then hugs me, Manny between us in the baby carrier. "Thank you, sweetheart," Callie whispers. My soul returns to my body and while in her embrace I notice that the three of us look like a modern-day Mother and Child, but with another Mother.

Pork Rump

Mrs. Horiatis sat on the queen-size bed in the guest room of Gus and Callie's home and rubbed her feet. Bending over that far put great pressure on her stomach and lungs and made it hard to breathe. She took a break, lying back on the plump new pillows that Callie had provided earlier that evening, and imagined how nice it would be to have a daughter-in-law who took care of her. Her feet throbbed from shopping at Macy's and Union Square all day. Her stocking feet were happy to finally breathe after a day confined in too-tight shoes and released an aroma not unlike the smell of a baking pork rump. Wiggling her toes, Mrs. Horiatis closed her eyes and indulged in a daydream of a different life . . .

Xeni would poke her head through the door and ask, "*Pethera*, could I bring you a coffee and a sweet treat? You must be so tired from shopping today. You bought such generous and thoughtful gifts for everyone but yourself. Let me do something for you."

"Please, *koritisi mou*. Call me *Mana*. We aren't strangers anymore."

With a blushing nod, Xeni would advance into the room. "*Mana*." She would pause and smile shyly, her hands playing with the neckline of her blouse. "Would you allow me to rub your feet? They must be so tired from all the walking. Or maybe . . . I could wash them? My feet always feel so much better after I wash them. I could bring in a crystal bowl from the buffet table and wash them right here. Wouldn't that feel nice?"

"Yes it would, my sweet. But you have worked hard enough

177

today carrying all of my parcels and fanning me when I got too hot. Besides, you have a more important task to accomplish."

"What is that, *Mana*?"

"Well, I have always wanted a granddaughter. Do you think you could give me one?"

"Oh *Mana*! I am so glad that you brought that up. I just found out, and I haven't even told Constantino yet."

"What is it? You can trust me. I won't tell Constantino."

Xeni would blush again and step closer to the bed.

Mrs. Horiatis would gesture toward the floral bedspread beside her feet. "Xeni, sit down here beside me. I am like your own mother. You can tell me."

Xeni would gingerly sit down next to Mrs. Horiatis and with a little smile begin to rub the older woman's feet. "Well. I guess it is only right that you are the first to know. I just came back from the doctor and . . ."

"Tell me, my sweet."

"He said I was pregnant with twin girls. Oh *Mana*. I want to name them both after you. Would that be okay?"

Mrs. Horiatis would raise her palm to her mouth and then genuflect three times before laying her hand over her heart. "At last my dream has come true. Xeni, you are the best daughter-in-law a woman could ask for. Why don't we keep this a secret between you and me for now? Constantino doesn't need to know just yet. Let's enjoy it ourselves for a while."

"Yes, *Mana*. That sounds perfect. It will be our secret."

Mrs. Horiatis let a sigh escape from her lips and came back to reality, rubbing her own aching feet. With Constantino and the *Amerikanitha* asking Xeni to be Manoli's *nouna*, there was little chance of her fantasy ever becoming a reality. She asked herself for the thousandth time how Constantino could have picked the *Amerikanitha* when such a fine-hipped *Ellenopoula* was right beneath his nose. With the baptism Xeni would become a relative, and it would be impossible for her and Constantino to wed. If only there was some way to make Constantino see Xeni through different eyes, she thought, before it's too late.

Maya

The moon illuminated the stairwell as Mrs. Horiatis snuck down to the kitchen and quietly opened the door of the refrigerator. Holding her breath, she looked on the top shelf toward the right side. There, as she remembered, were two bottles of fresh milk. Not just any milk, but the milk of a woman nursing a firstborn son. Taking one of the bottles, she clutched it close to her chest as she gathered her other items: wheat flour and yeast. Measuring out the powdered ingredients, she said a small prayer, and mixed them into the milk before pouring the mixture into an opaque coffee cup with the word "*Opa!*" printed on the side. She took out a piece of paper and wrote out the following words in her neatest handwriting: "As the infant now cries and throbs with desire for the milk which fails him, so may you throb with desire for me." Mrs. Horiatis hoped that her friend, Mrs. Papadakos, who dabbled in Greek magic, otherwise known as *maya*, knew what she was doing.

The next morning Mrs. Horiatis crossed her fingers that all would go according to plan. She rose from her bed and put on a fresh housedress, brushed her hair, and pinched her cheeks in the mirror above the dresser. She practiced smiling and looking sincere. Then she practiced looking nonchalant. And finally she practiced looking innocent. Feeling like a silly old woman in a bad American movie, she sent her fears to the devil, left the quiet of her guest room, and descended the stairs to the kitchen.

"*Kalimera!*" Mrs. Horiatis announced. She was pleased to see that Constantino was already seated at the table reading his paper. Xeni had already arrived at Mrs. Horiatis's invitation. She was making Greek coffee, and Callie was nowhere to be seen. It was perfect.

Both Xeni and Gus jumped a bit at Mrs. Horiatis's sudden greeting. "*Kalimera, Mana.*"

"*Kalimera, Kyria Horiatis,*" Xeni replied.

"Xeni, my dear. Would you please make me a cup of coffee?" Mrs. Horiatis requested as she sat down next to Gus.

"Of course. You can have this cup here."

"Oh. I don't mean to trouble you. You don't have to give me your coffee. Here let me help you." Mrs. Horiatis reached out her hands.

"No trouble, Mrs. Horiatis. I was making coffee for all of us." Xeni smiled.

"What a sweet girl, huh, Gus?" Mrs. Horiatis smiled at Gus and, receiving no response, became firmer in her resolve.

"Constantino."

"Yes, *Mana.*" Gus sighed and put down his newspaper.

"Constantino, I want you to be more healthy. I worry about you."

"Then why did you make me eggs and bread fried in bacon fat the other morning? That breakfast alone shaved five years off of my life."

"Oh. *Ayori mou,* I know. I just thought you would enjoy a breakfast from your childhood. But starting today, we will all be more healthy, right?"

"Yes, *Mana.*" Gus heaved a sigh through his lips.

"Good. Because I have made a health drink for you. I hope you like it." Mrs. Horiatis smiled and squeezed his shoulder. She opened the refrigerator door and found the "*Opa!*" cup behind a head of broccoli where she had hidden it. As she removed the piece of plastic wrap from the top, a noxious yeasty smell rose and dissipated as she stirred the fatty liquid in the cup.

"Now, Constantino, I don't want you to complain. This is a very healthy drink. I made it especially for you, and I insist that you drink it." Mrs. Horiatis used her most pleasantly commanding tone.

"That doesn't sound good. What do you think, Xeni? Should I drink it?"

Xeni sniffed the pungent, yeasty drink and chortled. "Mother knows best, Gus."

"Here, Xeni, do you mind giving this to Constantino? I want to enjoy my coffee here by the window. Oh, and here is a napkin for him."

"It would be my pleasure, Mrs. Horiatis." Xeni took the cup and napkin that Mrs. Horiatis offered and placed it in front of Gus, suppressing a smile.

"All right, anything to make you happy, *Mana*. Here goes," Gus toasted and took a big swig of the drink.

"*Ach Mana*! Are you trying to kill me?" Gus sputtered and protested.

Xeni stood before him, her mouth open in laughter, tears streaming down her face. "That's disgusting! What is this?" Gus grabbed the napkin to wipe his mouth, but it was stuck to a piece of paper with strange writing on it. Squinting to read it, he recited, "'As the infant now cries and throbs with desire for the milk which fails him, so may you throb with desire for me.' What is this?" Xeni was doubled over laughing as Gus's milk moustache highlighted his gagging mouth.

"Oh. I'm sorry, Constantino. That piece of paper wasn't for you. I don't know what that was. Here, here, my son. Have a napkin. You didn't like the drink?" Mrs. Horiatis tried her best to hide her smile of triumph. She'd gotten Gus to drink the potion and recite the incantation. She took the piece of paper from him and crumpled it up. She prayed that the love spell would work instantaneously and that Gus would turn to Xeni with a look of love on his face.

"Ugh, that was disgusting. *Mana*, what kind of health drink was that?" Gus tried to wipe his tongue off with a paper towel. "What are you laughing at, Xeni? You know, if you think it's so funny, why don't you try it?" Gus shoved the cup at Xeni, accidentally spilling a bit on her shirt.

"Because I'm already healthy enough. I don't need a special drink." Xeni laughed, wiping the milky blotch from her shirt. "But maybe you should drink more—for long life!" and she shoved the cup back toward Gus, spilling a long streak on his green polo shirt. "I heard that you're a crying infant with a throbbing desire for milk!" she cackled.

"Oh yeah? Well, how about this? Who's crying now? Who wants milk now?" Gus grabbed the cup and spilled the rest of the liquid between Xeni's breasts, and started laughing heartily.

Mrs. Horiatis' sface was a contortion of mixed reactions. Was it good that they were laughing? Was it bad that they were spilling the potion? Was it good that Xeni was shoving Gus across the kitchen? Was it bad that Gus was turning on the faucet? Was it good that Xeni grabbed the spray faucet and pulled it out by the built-in hose and was drenching Constantino? Was it bad that Constantino was shaking his head like a dog and lunging at Xeni? Would it end in a passionate embrace?

At that moment, Callie walked into the kitchen with Manny on her hip, and both Gus and Xeni stood frozen by the sink, drenched in water and the health drink, which unknown to them was really Callie's doctored breast milk. "Good morning?" Callie ventured, surrendering Manny to Mrs. Horiatis's outstretched arms.

"Good morning!" Xeni called out cheerily, patting her clothes and attempting to straighten her ponytail.

"I've had better," Gus growled, and then, catching Xeni by surprise, squirted her with the spray faucet one last time while howling his victory and doing a little dance.

"Uh." Callie looked from Xeni to Gus and then back to Xeni again. "Okay! Who wants breakfast? Mrs. Horiatis? Could I make you something to eat?" Callie offered.

Xeni shoved Gus. "Yeah, Gus, why don't you tell Callie what you want to eat? Gus wants milk! Gus wants milk!" cried Xeni sputtering with laughter.

Mrs. Horiatis touched Callie's hand. "Callie, why don't you make me a piece of toast? We can have breakfast while these two play." Mrs. Horiatis was reminded of puppies and junior high when boys shoved girls because they were pretty, and girls were too shy to say hello. She remembered a time when playground brawls resembled some kind of mating dance, and she smiled broadly as Gus purposely bumped into Xeni on his way to go get cleaned up, and Xeni tried to trip Gus as he collided into her.

Friends

Gus loaded the bags of food into the back of the car and rubbed his forehead. It seemed as if his mother's visit was now going well enough. She was spending a little more time with Callie. They'd had breakfast together that morning while he and Xeni got cleaned up. "Of course, she still has her demands," he mumbled to himself. Mrs. Horiatis insisted that the whole crew accompany her on a visit to an old friend who lived in a grand old apartment building in the Tenderloin district of San Francisco. Once a high-class neighborhood, it now was home to drug addicts, prostitutes, a large population of Asian immigrant families, and a number of senior citizens who lived alone in isolated government-subsidized apartments. The balance of the families and seniors versus the prostitutes and drug addicts was constantly shifting as one more Vietnamese restaurant took hold while the XXX live theaters changed headlining acts, one more playground got cleaned up of syringes, and another homeless person found shelter for the night in a storefront alcove.

Mrs. Horiatis used all this to make Gus, Callie, and Xeni feel sorry for her elderly friend who watched the drug deals and curbside pickups from her bedroom window all day and night. She'd convinced them all to bring her friend a portable Greek feast and visit with her for an afternoon. Gus dreaded being trapped in the old Greek woman's apartment and imagined the stale smell and dusty doilies that would blanket the place.

Xeni had prepared the meal according to Mrs. Horiatis's request, a roast pork loin with garlicky potatoes and lemon, *kolokithokeftedes*—deep-fried patties made from grated zucchini and feta cheese—a lettuce and dill salad, freshly baked bread. And for dessert, homemade yogurt served with a drizzling of honey and sprinkled with chopped walnuts and brilliant pomegranate seeds. The food smelled delicious, and Gus was tempted to break into the foil-wrapped packages for a sampling of the old woman's meal. Just then Xeni emerged from the house with one more package for the trunk containing a bottle of wine and a bottle of water. Gus snickered. "What, my mother doesn't think they have water in the Tenderloin?"

"Well, you'll notice that this is not just any water, Gus, but a fine artisan water from the mountain springs of Lake Arrowhead," Xeni quipped, "and a fine bottle of screw-top wine hand-selected by your mother."

"Hey, have you ever gone to Greece and seen those mountain springs the old-timers are always going on about?" Gus asked.

"You mean, the 'water of God'?" Xeni volleyed back. "You should have heard my father go on with his idealistic recollections of his mountain village."

"Man, the old-timers are always going on about their mountain springs, and then you go there to see and the whole mountain is covered in goat crap. So gross. Give me municipally treated tap water any day. At least I know that there have been no goats anywhere near it."

"Yeah, just freeways and urban pollution," Xeni retorted.

"Hey, there's fluoride in our urban-pollution water. I might get cancer, but I'll keep all of my teeth until I die." Gus shuddered to think about the lack of dental awareness he'd witnessed in his mother's village, young men and women toothless and too poor to buy dentures.

Xeni raised the wine bottle and toasted, "Here's to teeth!"

"Here's to teeth!" and Gus smiled widely.

Gus and Xeni were still smiling when Callie emerged from the house with Manny and Mrs. Horiatis. "I'm not so sure I'm used to you two getting along so well. Was there something in the coffee this morning?" Callie joked.

Mrs. Horiatis cleared her throat and shoved another bag into Gus's hands. "Put this in the car, Constantino. It's See's Candies. Mrs. Papadakos loves them."

"I love chocolate so much, sometimes I think that I could just sit in a room surrounded by chocolates and eat for days," Callie said. Gus saw his mother's head turn sharply to give Callie a disapproving look. "I mean, I wouldn't really. It's a fantasy."

"Well, that's good because we want you to fit into a nice conservative dress for the baptism, right, Gus?" said Mrs. Horiatis.

"Huh, sure. Why not?" Gus was still focused on the aroma rising from the warm food and his gratitude for proper American dental care.

"Okay. Let's go! What are we waiting for?" Mrs. Horiatis excitedly prodded everyone into the car. "I want to sit in the back with Manolaki and Callie," she announced, which caused Gus to raise an eyebrow. Callie climbed into the backseat and settled Manny in the center, while Gus helped his mother with her seat belt. As they drove, Gus could hear Callie and his mother muse over Manny's perfection until the baby fell asleep, and then they fell into a quiet and unfamiliar companionship until the rocking of the car soothed Callie into a light slumber as well.

The ride over the Bay Bridge to San Francisco was uneventful. The traffic was light, and Gus glided through the carpool lane.

"Why don't you take the Ninth Street exit?" Xeni asked Gus.

"Because I want to take the Fell Street exit," Gus replied.

"But it's out of the way," Xeni asserted.

"I just prefer the Fell Street exit, okay?"

"Well, okay, but the food will get cold," Xeni grumbled.

"Do we get to eat some?" Gus hoped.

"No! It's for your mother's old friend. Maybe she'll have a stale *loukoumi* to serve us." Xeni chuckled.

"Ugh! I hate *loukoumi*. They're so sticky and usually stale." Gus grimaced. "Only old ladies serve *loukoumi*."

"Well, maybe she'll have something better. Maybe she'll have a jar of *narantzi*," Xeni said sarcastically and smiled.

"Only one thing worse than *loukoumi*, and that's *narantzi*. Who ever thought to invent jarred bitter baby oranges in a sickeningly sweet syrup?" Gus shuddered.

When Gus arrived at Hyde and Ellis, he noticed plenty of hookers and drug dealers, but not a parking space in sight. Mrs. Papadakos's building stood resolutely in the midst of the human rubble, a grand old lady holding onto her dignity under difficult circumstances.

"*Mana*, why don't I drop you off with Callie and the baby, and Xeni and I can find a space and bring the stuff up. Do you mind, Xeni?" Gus asked.

Xeni nodded her head. "Sure, that's okay. I can help carry the food."

Gus double-parked in front of the building and roused Callie and Manny, then helped his mother to the curb. He protectively walked the women and baby to the building and stayed there while they waited for Mrs. Papadakos to buzz them into the building. Xeni waited in the idling car as Gus guarded the women and his son. When Gus looked back at the car and saw Xeni sitting alone with a faraway look on her face, he couldn't help but wonder if she had anyone to protect or care for her. As he waited for Callie and his mother to be buzzed into the building, Gus turned back toward the car and held his hand out, pressing the automatic lock button on his keychain, locking Xeni in.

A Prayer for Gus

Mrs. Horiatis shuffled into the lobby of the building with Callie and Manny in tow. They made their way to the old elevator with the painted outer door, and the steel accordion inner door. An "Out of Order" sign hung from the small window in the door. Mrs. Horiatis read the sign.

"'Elevator gets stuck on the basement level.' *Ach*. That's terrible. How will we get to the third floor?" Mrs. Horiatis asked, dismayed.

"I'll help you. You can hold my arm, and we'll go slow," Callie offered encouragingly.

"But you have the baby," Mrs. Horiatis protested.

"I'll be fine," Callie assured her. "Manny, hold on tight, okay? Manny grinned at his mother and hugged her around the neck.

"Well, okay. Let's try. But what about Constantino and Xeni? They'll be all by themselves with all that food," Mrs. Horiatis worried.

"They'll manage just fine. They'll probably get there right after us. And if they don't, at least we know that they won't go hungry!"

Mrs. Horiatis laughed at Callie's joke and started to turn toward the stairs. "You go ahead, Callie. I'll be right there. I need to catch my breath." As she inhaled deeply, Mrs. Horiatis recalled the car ride over. She'd sat contentedly in the backseat observing Gus and Xeni chattering back and forth like an old married couple. She'd closed her eyes and shrugged her shoulders in delight.

The feast for Mrs. Papadakos was a small price to pay for her magical consultation. Mrs. Horiatis made a note to herself to go to church with a generous offering and to ask forgiveness for getting mixed up with *maya*. But it was an emergency, she thought.

Mrs. Horiatis weighed her options and thought about fate. Taking a deep breath, she removed the "Out of Order" sign from the elevator door and made the sign of the cross. "Please God, forgive me for my desperate acts. I just want what is best for my son, and I know if he spends some time alone with Xeni he'll see I am right about her. Please keep him safe." And then she added, "You think you could dim the lighting in there?"

The Elevator

Gus and I circle the block and then the surrounding blocks in search of a parking space. Along the way we see several mothers walking down the street with children in strollers, and the old Greek import shop that was there before the surrounding porn shops, as well as the usual downtrodden element. After a white sedan leaves the corner with a new occupant, we finally find a spot across the street from Mrs. Papadakos's building and with a sense of resignation and irritation start loading ourselves down with the parcels of food. Struggling under the bulk of the shopping bags packed with multiple foil trays, we make our way across the street on the green light. A homeless person offers to help me carry my load of bags for ten cents while a tired-looking woman with bleached blond hair asks Gus if he wants a date. Relieved to set the parcels down temporarily, I ring the buzzer and wait for the response, warily watching the people meandering on the sidewalk behind us. I quickly push open the fortified door as soon as the buzzer sounds and push inside the building, relieved to get off of the street. The lobby has a seating area and fireplace on one end and a reception desk and elevator on the other.

"Let's take a quick breather, okay?" Gus asks.

"They're waiting for us, don't you think?" I reply, ruefully eyeing the couch. I notice a large stain on the upholstery and, wrinkling my nose, say, "Come on. Let's just get it over with. Maybe she'll share the See's Candy with us."

"All right." Gus walks over, and seeing that the elevator car is on the lobby floor, opens the door wide so that I can pass through, and then follows me inside. We both startle when the heavy accordion door slams shut behind us.

"Do you remember the floor?" asks Gus.

"Three," I reply.

"Okay, elevator up!" announces Gus as the elevator starts to go up the shaft of the building.

"Does it make sense to put the bags down for a minute so that my arms can get a break, or should I tough it out because we'll be there in a few seconds?" I ask.

"Ah, just tough it out. We'll be there before you can put them down," Gus replies. And with that, the elevator lurches and makes a screeching sound. The car suddenly is traveling faster than would be expected for such an old elevator—and in the wrong direction. We brace ourselves against the walls of the elevator car, dropping the bags to the ground in the process. The lights blink on and off until finally settling dimly in between as the car crashes to a halt somewhere in the bowels of the building.

We both stay perfectly still for what feels like several minutes until Gus says, "Oh. Hell. No."

I immediately fall to my knees and start praying for forgiveness. I am sure that this is another test or punishment from God for my feelings for Callie. I'd been working so hard on suppressing them, and while I realize that my sin is a major one I am also feeling a bit irritated that God continues to punish me even when I am being good. I also pray that the food has not spilled out onto the elevator floor.

"Oh, Christ. Will you get up?" Gus implores. "There must be an emergency call button here." He presses the button and finds that there is no obvious result. "We'll be fine, just fine. They'll come and get us before you know it. Someone will have noticed the *boom*. Callie will worry that we've been gone so long. They'll send the cops. Or the firemen. It's fine." Gus pats his shirt pocket for a stray cigarette, and finding none starts biting his nails.

I grope around in the dimly lit elevator on my hands and knees. Luckily the food has remained mostly intact. I wrapped it well with double tinfoil and packed it tightly in the bags. Just the loaf of bread and the stack of napkins have fallen out. I quickly pick them up, dust them off, and place them back inside the bags.

"What if no one comes?" I ask.

"Someone will come."

"What if we're being punished?"

"For what? I didn't do anything," Gus snaps.

"Well . . . you did have a child out of wedlock."

"Oh please. What about you? What did you do?"

"Nothing. I didn't do anything," I insist, feeling my face flush at the memory of Callie in the bathtub. "Maybe I should have gone to church more."

"Oh, whatever. We're trapped in an elevator, not in hell."

"Well, when you think about it, this is a kind of purgatory," I suggest.

"Not really. If it were purgatory, we'd be in the lobby. Or in the basement or something. That would be hell," Gus asserts. "But on the other hand, Mrs. Papadakos is on the third floor, so you'd think that would be heaven, and I'm pretty sure it's not," says Gus.

"Do you believe in God, Gus?"

"What does God have to do with anything?"

"Maybe he put us here for a reason."

"Maybe we should figure out how to get out of here. I'm gonna try my cell." Gus reaches for his phone. "Crap. No reception. This *is* hell."

"Press some of the other buttons. Let's see what happens." I reach out to press "L" for lobby.

"No, don't touch the buttons. What if it goes berserk again? Besides, I'm pretty sure this thing is staying right here. Let's try to pry open the door." Gus tries to open the accordion door, but it is locked shut. "Does that mean we're in between floors?"

"Purgatory? We still have a chance."

"Oh, please. Why don't you try your cell to see if it has reception?" Gus asks.

"I don't have a cell phone."

"Huh?" Gus looks at me as if I've grown an extra head.

"I don't need one."

"Uh, you need one right now!" says Gus sarcastically.

"Uh, you have one and it doesn't work," I reply.

"Okay. You know what? In the movies there's always a trapdoor and the guy escapes up the top. Do you see one?"

"It's kind of dark in here, but I don't see anything." We feel the walls, and on tiptoes search the ceiling for a way out, but find none.

"What time is it?" I ask.

"What, you don't carry a watch either? Just cooking utensils wherever you go?"

"A butcher knife would be handy right now . . ."

"Okay, back up there, gal!"

"No, I mean, maybe we could use it to hack at the door lock." I begin searching through the bags. I empty the foil-wrapped containers out of the bags and start to spread them on the floor.

"What are you doing?"

"I'm looking for a knife."

"Do you *really* carry knives with you? I was just kidding, you know."

"Ha. Ha. So funny." I continue unpacking the bags looking for the knife I was sure I'd tucked in one of them for slicing the freshly baked bread.

"Hey, wait. Let's put those on my jacket. That floor has to be crawling with germs." Gus removes his jacket and places it on the floor with the silky burgundy lining facing up.

"Good idea." I continue searching. In the end I don't find a knife, but I find candles, the wine, dinner, and dessert. "Who put these candles in here?"

"Hell if I know. If no one comes in half an hour, let's eat," Gus announces.

"Forty-five. And stop mentioning hell."

"Forty."

"Okay, forty." I sit on the questionable carpeted floor of the elevator and tap my fingers against my knees. "Or, maybe thirty-five," I say and smile weakly.

Gus sits down beside me to wait. "Should we be doing something?"

"I don't know. I already prayed. We could pray together?"

"That's okay. Maybe after we eat dinner. If no one is here yet after we eat, then we'll start praying." Gus elbows me like he is just joking, and we settle in to wait.

"What time is it now?" I ask. The aroma of the roast pork and garlic is teasing my nostrils.

"Ten minutes since the last time we checked."

"Think anyone has noticed that we're missing yet?"

"Yeah, probably. Or no, maybe not. Maybe we should eat."

"How long has it been?"

"Eleven minutes." Gus sighs.

"How many minutes did we decide to wait?" I ask.

"Thirty. But I think that's too long. What do you think?"

"We could pass out from hunger. I could always make the old woman a new dinner," I offer.

"That's a good idea. These are extraordinary circumstances," Gus replies stealing a sideways glance at me. "You know, you look pretty in this light."

I blush in the darkness. "You can't even see me."

"No, I can. Maybe for the first time."

I start to feel nervous, my pulse finding its way to the surface of my skin. "I think we should eat. It'll be good. Maybe we're getting light-headed."

"Yeah, maybe so."

"Can I serve you?" I ask out of habit.

"Do you have plates?" Gus jokes.

"Oh. No, I don't. I guess we'll be eating with our fingers, Moroccan-style."

I pull back the foil wrappings to reveal the feast I prepared earlier. As each package is uncovered, the aroma of the food fills the air and makes our stomachs seize with desire. We dig into the containers with gusto, licking the garlicky lemon pork juices from our fingers, savoring the tangy feta and zucchini fritters with our tongues, and dangling long strands of dill-speckled lettuce over our hungry mouths. We tear into the freshly baked bread and dip it into the juices from the roast and the salad. And against my better judgment I unscrew the bottle of wine. I worry that it might spoil the meal, not believing that wine can taste good without a cork. But we are thirsty and pass it back and forth throughout the meal until the bottle is empty.

"This is heavenly," Gus moans while sucking his fingers clean.

"I wouldn't go that far. I thought we were still in purgatory."

"Well, this meal erases our confinement, our possible imminent deaths, and the real possibility that we find ourselves in purgatory. How'd you learn to cook like this?"

"I spent a lot of time in the kitchen growing up. I felt comfortable there. And I'm good at it. I can feel the food with my body. I can smell when something is done and feel it in my skin when a dish needs something more."

"Sometimes I wonder if I'm good at anything." Gus unscrews another wine bottle and takes a swig.

"You must be good at something. Isn't everyone?"

"Apparently, my biggest talent is seducing belly dancers."

"Oh." I pause. "Can I have some of that?" Gus passes me the bottle. "Is that how you met Callie?"

"Yeah. One night changed my life forever."

"I know how that is."

"Yeah?"

"Yeah."

"Who changed your life, Xeni?" Gus asks.

"Oh, I don't want to talk about that. Let's talk about other stuff."

"Have you ever been in love?"

"Gus, why are you asking me these questions?"

Gus shifts his body so that he is looking into my eyes. "I just wonder if I really know what love feels like. I want to know what it feels like when you are totally overcome with love for another person."

"What about Callie?" I ask with trepidation. "Don't you love Callie that way?"

Gus looks away. "Callie is great. I love her, but we're so different. I wonder sometimes what it would be like to be with someone . . . Greek." He takes my hand and places it on his chest. "Can you feel the blood pumping through my heart? Can you feel it in your skin if I need something more?"

I leave my hand on Gus's chest and close my eyes. I try to sense with my body if Gus is "done." But he isn't a pan of moussaka, and I can't tell if he needs more spice, less oil, or time in the oven to brown. "I'm sorry, I can't tell." I take my hand and place it on my own heart. "I know that I need something more, though." Gus nods and puts his arm around me, and we relax against the back of the elevator.

"Aren't we supposed to be scared right now?" Gus asks.

"I am scared. I'm always scared," I reply.

"Where's that butcher knife when you need it, huh?"

"Yeah."

"Hey, what's for dessert? I want something sweet."

"Yogurt with honey, walnuts, and pomegranate. And Mrs. Papadakos's box of See's chocolates."

"Hey. Maybe we'll eat the pomegranate seeds and we'll be delivered from this underworld," Gus jokes.

"See, Gus, that's the problem. We don't live in mythology or the ancient world. We're only modern-day Greek Americans trying to survive without all of our legendary tricks. We can eat the pomegranate seeds, but they won't deliver us from Hades. We're stuck here."

"Well, if the old myths don't work in the new world, then let's try chocolate. It always makes me feel better."

"Gus, you sound like a girl," I slur, not even caring that I sound drunk.

"Does that make you like me better?"

"Yeah, it does," I say, yawning.

I half-open my eyes when the firemen finally pry the elevator door open, finding Gus and me asleep in a pile, the remains of our feast spread over the burgundy silk lining of Gus's jacket and the box of chocolates still unopened.

ROAST PORK WITH POTATOES

"We dig in with gusto, licking the garlicky lemon pork juices from our fingers."

3–4 pound pork loin
3 cloves garlic, sliced
2 teaspoons extra-virgin olive oil
Juice of two lemons
Salt
Pepper
Oregano
4 large russet potatoes, peeled and cut into eighths

Preheat oven to 375 degrees.

Put the pork loin into a large baking pan. Cut slits into the pork loin and insert the garlic slices into the cuts. Drizzle olive oil and lemon juice over the pork and then sprinkle with salt, pepper, and oregano, covering all surfaces of the roast. Toss the potatoes in a bowl with olive oil, lemon juice, salt, pepper, and oregano until they are well coated. Arrange around the pork loin in the baking pan. Bake for 45 minutes and then turn the potatoes. Bake until the potatoes are tender when pierced with a fork, and have developed a nice crispy exterior. The meat thermometer should read 170 degrees after approximately 90 minutes.

Let the succulent meat rest for 10 minutes before devouring it, so it will be juicy and moist.

The Next Step

Everyone seems to feel a bit rearranged after the adventure at Mrs. Papadakos's apartment building. I'm in the living room behind the sofa playing a game of peek-a-boo with Manny. I wonder how I find myself spending so much time with this family since Mrs. Horiatis's arrival. I'd expected to see Callie less, was bracing myself against missing Manny, and anticipated feeling left out and dejected. Instead, I'm being wound tighter and tighter into the family, something I would have normally avoided.

Mrs. Horiatis is sitting on the couch in front of the TV set watching *The Greek Hour* on public access television. She seems to be largely ignoring the presence of Callie, who is seated on the far cushion of the couch, gamely attempting to watch the program that exemplifies perhaps better than any other means of expression the downfall of our glorious ancient Hellenic past. Callie is sitting casually, but every few minutes or so she readjusts herself or a cushion, or offers Mrs. Horiatis another glass of 7-Up or a cup of coffee until the old woman finally shushes her, pointing to the TV screen.

After ten minutes of fuzzy, outdated music videos from Greece, the host of the program introduces Paul Smith, a man who would provide Greek cooking lessons from his houseboat. He resembles Santa Claus with his rotund stature and full white, bushy beard and ruddy complexion. He speaks with a British accent. Callie interrupts my game of peek-a-boo with Manny to alert me to the upcoming lesson. I poke my head up from behind the couch long enough to assess the skills of the jovial old man. As he fingers a plump eggplant and discusses the gender differences of the fruit, my eyes begin to narrow.

"Did they say whether he's Greek?" I ask.

"I'm not sure . . ." Callie trails off, concentrating hard on his gesturing hands as he begins to slice the eggplant.

I rise from behind the couch, place Manny in his mother's lap, and leave the room stomping loudly as the old man points to the seeds inside the firm flesh. Entering the kitchen, I'm surprised to find Gus sitting at the counter drinking his coffee and reading a newspaper.

"Don't you have to work today?" I ask gruffly.

"I work every day, but right now I'm taking my doctor's advice and am trying to relax," Gus replies sarcastically.

I grumble under my breath while reaching for the refrigerator door handle and then slam it closed.

"And no offense, but you're kind of spoiling the mood here," Gus adds.

"Do you know what they are showing on *The Greek Hour* right now?" I demand.

"One of three things: footage of archeological discoveries in Greece, old-ass music videos, or ads for all the Greek businesses in town. Why? Did you see the ad for my real estate firm? It's a pretty good picture of me, huh?"

"They have some old white hippie with an affected British accent who lives on a houseboat showing how to cook Greek food."

"Yeah? So?"

"So? Who is watching this program?"

"Oh, come on. You know who watches the program."

"Right. The only people who watch that show are old Greek ladies looking for some connection to home. What are you drinking?"

"Coffee and Jack. Don't tell Ma."

"Don't you think it's kind of ironic or insulting that they would put up an old hippie to show our mothers and grandmothers how to make Greek food? What does he know about making Greek food that we don't know?"

"Yeah. But she's still sitting there watching, isn't she? Any taste of the homeland, no matter how moldy or ridiculous, anything with Corinthian columns or the Greek flag."

"Well not just any taste of the homeland. Callie's dishes have been perfect, but your mother won't even try—"

Gus interjects. "Want a sip of my coffee and Jack? It might help you relax."

"Nothing bothers you, does it?" I accuse, as I eye his steaming cup. "Why don't you put some whipped cream on that?"

"Cause then it would look like a foofy coffee drink versus a medicinal tonic that is getting me through the days around here surrounded by demanding women." As if on cue, Mrs. Horiatis calls out, "Constantino! Constantino!"

"Yes, *Mana*?" he replies and takes another gulp of his coffee and Jack.

"Hurry up! Come here!"

We walk into the living room just in time to catch the last few seconds of an ad for a Greek restaurant in the city. Mrs. Horiatis turns back to look at us where we are standing behind the couch and smiles enthusiastically.

"I have an idea!" Mrs. Horiatis had been trying to decide the next steps in her scheme to help Gus and Xeni fall in love. She couldn't let the love potion go to waste or count completely on magic. She had to capitalize on the good start it'd given her. "Gus, I want you to take us all out for dancing tonight!" she stated, pleased with herself.

"Dancing? What do you mean, *Mana*?" he asked reluctantly.

"Take us to Mythos tonight. We'll have dinner and dancing. They have a live band on Saturday nights. All of us." She squeezed Xeni's elbow over the back of the couch and winked.

Xeni paused. "Oh, thank you so much, Mrs. Horiatis, but I don't dance. But that's a great idea. You'll have fun."

"I insist that you come with us, Xeni!" Mrs. Horiatis demanded with a smile.

"I'll stay here and watch Manny," Xeni offered. "He's too young for nightclubs."

"Don't be silly. In Greece, children come to nightclubs with parents all the time. We'll all go." Mrs. Horiatis countered.

"Well, I guess we could bring Manny with us . . ." Callie offered.

Xeni shifted her weight and tried another tack. "Oh, you are so generous. But I really have nothing to wear. You go have fun without me."

"I'll lend you something to wear, Xeni," Callie offered. "Why don't we get ready together? I'll do your hair and makeup. It'll be fun!"

"Yes, that's a good idea. But nothing too slutty. Xeni has natural beauty," Mrs. Horiatis added, with a lift of her eyebrow.

"I don't know if I'm up for going to Mythos tonight, Mana . . ." Gus attempted to interrupt the women. "I have an open house tomorrow, and I'm still worn out from that elevator thing yesterday."

Mrs. Horiatis turned toward Gus, staring at him intensely and expanding her chest with breath, her tongue on the roof of her mouth, but before she could expel her response, Gus backed down.

"All right, all right. Whatever you want, *Mana*. But let's get a sitter for Manny. I'll bet the music doesn't even start until after nine."

"Okay! You'll thank me later, Constantino. We're going to have a beautiful, unforgettable evening, you and Xeni and the rest of us." Mrs. Horiatis glowed.

Beauty Before Comfort

That Mrs. Horiatis has a way of getting her way all the time. It doesn't seem to matter that neither Gus nor I want to go to Mythos. Or be together for that matter! Why do Greek mothers always get their way? And at the same time get nothing? They get nothing they want, so they make their children give them everything. They eat us alive.

I am trying to be upright and proper, a good example for Manny, and here I sit in Callie's bedroom before her dressing table and mirror, staring at the gardenia perfume sitting on the glass top. Trying not to remember the sight of her body sparkling with droplets of water and flower petals. Trying to act as if nothing unusual happened between us. The sheets of her bed are rumpled and stale from her nights sleeping by Gus's side.

Callie is in the closet picking out clothes for me to wear. She is humming a song low under her breath and has a tiny smile turning her lips upward. She asks me if I want to take a shower before I get dressed. I grab the bottle of gardenia perfume and spray it on the inside of my wrist, my elbow. I smell fine. I smell redolent of thick-petaled flowers, creamy and bursting.

She selects something for me to wear. A lavender blouse with a low draped neckline and no sleeves, and a matching narrow skirt that flares at the knees. I refuse. A black halter dress with no back. Never. Reluctantly, she offers me a dress that she's worn and hasn't had time to take to the cleaners. It smells like her, like strawberries and musk and cinnamon. I slip it on over my plain bra and panties behind the closet door. I emerge a different woman. In clinging crimson jersey, I feel like someone else. I sit in the chair before the mirror, one shoulder exposed as she stands behind me and brushes my hair. I can feel each strand of hair tugging against my scalp with every stroke of her brush. The tension between my hair and her hand tightens and slackens, and I find myself breathing in rhythm with the motion of her hand. She abandons the brush and pushes her fingers through my hair, her fingers pressing against my neck, my crown, and resting on my temples. She drags her fingers back through my hair and pulls it up. My neck is weak, and my head follows her direction, lolling from side to side. Finally, she pulls my head back until I'm looking straight up and all I can see is her face, her lips. Her hands hold me steady as she comes closer. Her breath scatters over my skin. Her lashes on my cheek. Her lips grazing my mouth. She sinks to the floor behind me and I stay there head hanging back, lips parted.

Mythos

Gus played with his car keys as they all stood outside of Mythos in the brisk San Francisco night air. Even though he had reluctantly agreed to bring the ladies to the nightclub, there was a part of him that was looking forward to the music, the food, and the ouzo. Gus flashed on his nights at the Grapeleaf and El Monsour and other belly dance spots in the city, and the undulating bodies and delicious food he enjoyed there with his bare hands.

"Ah, we all look very nice!" Mrs. Horiatis exclaimed. She looked each of them up and down, nodding and smiling. "Gus, you look so handsome in that black jacket with your hair combed back. You make your mother proud!"

"Thanks, Ma." Gus replied, a little embarrassed, but pleased by his mother's praise. They did all look very nice. Callie looked beautiful in a silver halter top with a long teal skirt. Gus noticed that she was fingering her silver purse and that she almost seemed nervous as she smiled, looking back and forth between Xeni and Gus. Xeni hung back a few feet, in a crimson dress that framed her blushing face and loose hair. Gus realized that Xeni was actually very pretty. As if she could read his thoughts, she abruptly grabbed a rubber band from around her wrist and pulled her hair back into a tight bun, spoiling the effect. Gus turned back to his mother who wore a royal blue dress with a sequined flower brooch at the neckline and sturdy black sandals.

"Are you ready to dance?" she said as she twisted her plump body into a feisty little turn.

"Okay, Ma. Let's go in." Gus chuckled as he followed his mother inside. She entered the restaurant as if she were royalty, pausing at the door and waiting for the maître d' to come and do her bidding. He held his breath as she took in the surroundings, the blue and white paint, the mural depicting bouzouki-playing musicians, the hanging plastic grape vines, the Corinthian columns, and the small stage and dance floor.

"Home away from home. Isn't this nice? Eh, Constantino?" and she sighed a deep breath of satisfaction.

"Yeah, Ma. It's nice," he muttered, relieved that she hadn't found anything to complain about.

Mrs. Horiatis turned to the maître d' and proclaimed, "A table by the dance floor, please, and a bottle of champagne!" Gus exchanged a look with Xeni behind his mother's back, half-bemused by her display of grandiosity and half begrudging her excitement at all the Greek kitsch.

"Does this remind you of your childhood?" Gus asked Xeni in a low mumble.

"Yes, except that we had many more pictures of the Parthenon and maps of Greece displayed at our house," she replied as they shared a snicker. But at the same time Gus understood his mother's excitement. Though cliché, the symbols of their culture did warm him. Gus sat next to Xeni at the table and enthusiastically mocked and appreciated the decor as they peeked from behind their menus.

Callie sat across from Gus and Xeni, next to Mrs. Horiatis. Gus stopped his joking when he noticed Callie, her silver halter top shimmering in the blue atmosphere like a fish, looking lithe and lost. She had seemed a bit out of sorts lately, though Gus chalked it up to the pressure of constantly trying to please his mother, who seemed to have eyes only for Xeni.

"I wonder what Manny is doing right now," Callie said as she fingered the blue cloth napkin in her lap. "Probably curled up in his bed with his favorite stuffed giraffe?" Gus thought that he might have seen a glimmer of tears in Callie's eyes, but lost his train of thought as his mother suddenly exclaimed, "Skordalia!"

"*Mana*, skordalia is pure garlic," Gus protested.

"I know, I know! It's so delicious. I can't wait to eat it." Mrs. Horiatis scanned the menu for other favorites. "What do you want to try, Xeni, honey?"

Xeni looked out from behind her menu. "I think I'd like to start with the ochtapodi xidato, saganaki, and a plate of the fried smelt. And for dinner the grilled baby lamb chops. And a salad of course."

Gus whistled. "You don't mess around."

"What are the first three dishes you mentioned?" Callie asked.

"The first is a cold appetizer of vinaigrette-marinated octopus. Saganaki is a special cheese that is grilled then flambéed with brandy. The smelt is a small silver fish that you can eat whole; even the bones are tender," Xeni replied from behind her menu.

"I'm going to order the stuffed peppers and a few appetizers that we can share," Mrs. Horiatis announced.

"I'm gonna order the New York steak. And some ouzo," Gus sighed and rubbed his stomach. "How about you, Callie?"

Callie looked at each at them and then back down at the menu. "I think I'll order the pastitsio. I worked so hard to learn to make the béchamel sauce. Do you remember that afternoon, Xeni? I love all the alternating layers of pasta and meat spiced with cinnamon and nutmeg."

Xeni looked up at Callie. "That sounds good, Callie. Nice choice."

"I'm sure it's not as good as yours . . ." Callie murmured.

"Oh, I don't know, tried one pastitsio, tried them all. Try something different," Gus interjected as he tore into the basket of bread sitting on the le. Seeing the women turn their heads sharply towards him, he backpedaled. "Oh calm down. I'm just kidding."

"It is good to sample other dishes. You learn what you like and what you don't like, eh?" Mrs. Horiatis added, nudging Gus, "or who the best cook is!" His mother shimmied her shoulders as a classic Greek tune was played over the sound system. "I wonder what time the band will arrive. I want to dance!"

"You're in a good mood, *Mana*. What are you celebrating?" Gus asked.

"Everything! My grandson, my son, new friends," she said and she raised her glass to Xeni. Gus noticed Callie shift uncomfortably in her seat.

Xeni raised her glass in return and said, "Well, I toast to Callie, who brought your grandson into the world and learned to cook like a real Greek."

Callie smiled her appreciation for Xeni's gesture and cleared her throat. "I toast to all of you, who have opened your hearts, your culture, and your arms to me. Cheers!"

"*Salut!*" Gus toasted.

"*Yia mas!*" Xeni raised her glass.

His mother readjusted her sequined brooch and took a demure sip of champagne, looking away from the table and Callie's waiting eyes.

As dinner proceeded and the champagne bottle was drained, a trio of middle-aged Greek men emerged and started setting up equipment. Xeni was showing Callie how to split open the tiny smelt and peel out the spine before popping the whole fish into her mouth. Gus was spearing chunks of fried cheese with his fork and swigging ouzo. As the band began to play the first song of the night, Mrs. Horiatis blurted out, "Constantino, why don't you and Xeni dance?"

"Huh, are you kidding? They finally brought my steak. I'm starving," and he pushed a bloody hunk of meat into his mouth.

"I already told you I don't dance, Mrs. Horiatis. I'm here for dinner and company," Xeni interjected.

Just then a female singer with a long black wig and liquid eyeliner came onstage and started singing a spirited *tsifteteli*. Callie wiped the corners of her mouth with the blue napkin and started to bounce in her seat to the music. The singer caught sight of her and called into the microphone, "*Ella na horepsoume!*" and gestured toward her, beckoning her to the dance floor. "Come on, let's dance!" Callie blushed and paused, looking at Gus.

"Go for it, babe. Take Xeni with you." When Xeni threw him a dirty look, he winked and whispered, "It's payback time for telling me to drink that nasty health concoction."

Xeni grimaced. "I guess I owe you one."

Callie reached out her slender white arm toward Xeni, silently willing her to rise. Her fingernails shimmered with the reflected light of the candles, and a stack of bangles slid down her soft skin and landed with a jingle at her wrist below her tattoo of the Virgin Mary. She waited there for a moment with her arm extended over the table, her heart pounding in her chest, until Xeni finally pushed back her chair and stood up.

"Okay. But I really don't dance."

"Don't worry. I've got you," Callie murmured as she took Xeni's hand and led her to the dance floor. Standing under the muted lights of the parquet dance floor, Callie lifted one arm over her head and twirled her wrist. She kept her eyes on Xeni's as she slipped her other hand onto Xeni's back.

"Just swing your hips side to side, like this, see?" and as Callie demonstrated, her skirt swung freely like the slapping tail of a silvery fish. "And raise your arms until your heart is lifted inside of your ribs." Callie spoke into Xeni's ear. "Close your eyes and forget that anyone else exists. Just feel the music in your body, and let it take over your heart, let it pump the blood through your veins." And as Callie spoke she felt Xeni relax into the music, and her hips were loosened from their petrified state and swung.

Callie's bangles jingled in time with the music, her exhale finding Xeni's skin as they danced dangerously close to each other. Callie's mouth curled into a sly smile as Xeni opened her eyes. "You look gorgeous. I knew you could dance." And then Callie reached back and gently pulled the rubber band out of Xeni's hair, watching as it cascaded down around her shoulders, moving in time to the music. Callie released the stress of the last month of trying to please Gus and his mother, allowed herself to stop thinking about Manny for the length of a song, and let her body and mind find Xeni. She let the champagne and the warmth of Xeni's dancing body envelop her in a lovely hazy, sensual glow.

"You look like a beautiful mermaid tonight in the middle of the Aegean Sea, surrounded by ridiculous Greeks," Xeni whispered. Callie danced with Xeni as if no one else existed, and complications had evaporated into the beat of the dumbek. The singer, inspired by their dancing, continued her medley of *tsiftetelia*, encouraging the women to dance with her shouted praises, "*Yiassou koritsia!*"

A Shiny New Penny

Another party, a family of Greeks, had joined Callie and Xeni on the dance floor. Gus watched from the table, his vision slightly blurry from the ouzo and the fatigue of trying to accomplish his mother's many requests. He watched Callie and Xeni dance, remembering that night he first met Callie, and sighed. He watched with amusement as he witnessed Xeni loosen up for the first time, shaking her shoulders and swinging her hips. And then his attention shifted to the others on the dance floor. A few young men danced in a group and egged each other on to jump higher, dip lower. There was an older man, perhaps a father, dancing with his grown daughter. Gus remembered his own father, his retreating back, his weary countenance, but shook those thoughts away quickly. The woman was beautiful with dark almond eyes and lustrous black hair. She embodied the music with subtlety and a slow sensuality. The older man clapped as she twirled and swayed, and the singer called out "*Yiassou* Panayiota!" from the stage. The woman blushed, hiding her eyes behind her glossy black lashes. The older man looked proud and clapped with renewed gusto. "I can't believe they are out dancing and making such a big show," Mrs. Horiatis harrumphed.

"What do you mean, *Mana*?"

Mrs. Horiatis leaned in close to Gus. "That girl, Panayiota, see her? They call her Penny." she whispered from behind her napkin.

"Yes, she's beautiful."

"Beautiful. Too beautiful for her own good. Her father let her run the streets at night with an *Amerikanos* who got her pregnant. Two times. And where is he now? They never got married, she lost her virginity, and now she's raising two babies alone. *Drope tis*. She should be ashamed to be out dancing at a nightclub."

"How do you know all this, *Mana*?"

"Everyone knows, Constantino. People talk."

"Her life isn't over, *Mana*. Some things happened. I'm sure she's trying to make the best of it," Gus replied. Inwardly, Gus looked at the woman with new eyes, judgmental eyes, and felt ashamed of himself.

"She should go home and take care of her babies. Shame on her," Mrs. Horiatis said.

"You know, *Mana*. If we didn't look at her and judge her or gossip about her, she wouldn't have to feel ashamed. She'd be just fine."

"Why should she feel fine? She ruined herself, and for nothing."

"But now she has two great kids. Something good came of it," Gus defended Panayiota.

"Two kids with no father."

"Well, what's the difference between me and her?" Gus asked.

"What do you mean? Everything is different."

"Well, I have a baby with an *Amerikanitha*. And I get the feeling that you wouldn't mind if we broke up. Wouldn't I be a disgrace then?"

"Of course not. You're a man," she replied. "For men it's different. You can leave and no one faults you. They all wonder what the woman did wrong to lose her husband." Mrs. Horiatis took a deep swig of champagne. "That Xeni can really dance, *eh* Constantino?" and she nudged him with her elbow.

Gus fell silent. He slugged back another drink of his ouzo. His gaze shifted back and forth from Callie and Xeni dancing together to the old man dancing with his daughter and suddenly felt weary.

"*Mana*? Why did you bring us here tonight?"

"Oh, for a good time, Constantino." Mrs. Horiatis smiled. "Why don't you go dance?"

214

"What would it be like if Dad was here? Would he dance?" Gus asked.

"I don't know about your father. Maybe he would dance if his blond bombshell was here with him. But he wouldn't dance with me." She sniffed and looked away from Gus's inquiring look.

"I just wonder how things would've turned out if we stayed a family," Gus admitted.

"Constantino. We don't have what didn't happen. We have what did happen. Just make the best of it."

Gus looked at Callie again, her silver halter top shimmering under the lights, her arms weaving into the air. Then he looked again at the dark-haired woman dancing with her father, and a sudden chill shook him.

"What if. What if something happened, but we aren't sure if we should stick it out, or if we should try something new?" Gus wondered if his father had pondered that same question.

"Constantino. If you are unhappy, try something new. Try something new tonight! Come on, let's dance." Mrs. Horiatis dragged Gus behind her, jostled onto the dance floor next to Xeni and Callie, and muttered to herself, "He didn't tell me the *Amerikanitha* could dance!"

Shaken out of their cocoon, Callie and Xeni made room for Mrs. Horiatis and Gus beside them. Gus watched with amusement as his mother shook her large behind in time with the music, suddenly losing the limp and heavy gait of an old woman, and gaining the momentum of a young mountain goat. Gus rubbed his eyes and danced with his mother, who both embarrassed and delighted him with her spirited steps. She danced her way toward Callie, separating her from Xeni.

"Gus, why don't you dance with Xeni?" she prodded.

"*Mana*, we're all dancing together. Stop pushing me on Xeni. Let's just have fun, okay?" Gus looked over his mother's head toward the woman with the dark almond eyes and red lips, and the smell of cloves filled his nostrils. His eyes followed her every move, and for a moment his life vanished, and he imagined a new beginning. As if he'd found a shiny new penny.

215

She looked at Gus, her only child, her only son. She thought to herself, if they'd stayed in Greece, he'd be married to a good Greek girl by now. And like every other elderly Greek mother she would have a place in her son's home where she'd be taken care of for the rest of her days. But they weren't in Greece, merely a Greek nightclub in *Ameriki* festooned in blue and white.

Mrs. Horiatis could see that Gus's attention was nowhere near Xeni. She realized that she had to face the awful truth: the love potion had worn off or had never worked in the first place. Or perhaps it was the magic of Callie's hips bumping in time to the music, hypnotizing him. Mrs. Horiatis felt her chest deflate. She had been defeated before and had risen back up again to fight. But this time, she wondered if there was any point in continuing. Maybe, she decided, this girl was not the right one. Maybe there was someone better for her baby, her Constantino. There were so many beautiful young Greek girls back home. Surely she could find the right one. Or maybe she shouldn't give up on Xeni too soon. In any case, Mrs. Horiatis accepted her defeat for the evening and comforted herself with dancing as she hadn't in years. She danced until the nightclub owner bought their table a bottle of champagne, and the singer laced their names into the lyrics of her songs. She sang their praises and lifted them higher into the glad horizon of *kefi*, the state in which a Greek person loses their worries and surrenders to joy.

Now or Never

"Xeni, honey, why don't you come and sit by me?" Mrs. Horiatis calls out to me as I pass by the kitchen table with an armful of Manny's dirty laundry. "Sit down, sit down, honey," she says smiling.

I hesitate for a moment, searching for an excuse to escape Mrs. Horiatis's concentrated attention. "Well, I uh, have to put Manny's laundry in the washing machine."

"Xeni, honey. Are they paying you to do Manolaki's laundry?"

"Well, no. But I like to help," I reply uneasily, sniffing Manny's soiled play clothes.

"Sit down. I need to talk to you," Mrs. Horiatis gently commands. She looks right and left as if to see if either Callie or Gus are within earshot.

I drop the pile of laundry on one end of the table with a sigh, and sit down opposite Mrs. Horiatis and wait. The sun is blazing through the windows and onto the top of the table, casting a windowpane pattern on the wood. The cross hovers there as Mrs. Horiatis prepares to speak, and I concentrate on it with all my might. I have no idea what Mrs. Horiatis wants to talk about. Perhaps she disapproves of the way I had danced with Callie at Mythos that night or, even worse, can sense my ongoing struggle to resist the pull toward Callie, toward oblivion. Or maybe she wants to discuss the baptism. That would be a safe topic. Unless Mrs. Horiatis senses that I am impure, and therefore unfit to be a godmother. All of my guesses always come back to Callie and the attraction, which at times seems as strong as the ocean's undercurrent pulling me under.

"Xeni, what are your plans?" Mrs. Horiatis asks.

I am shaken from my reverie and look up at the old woman, "What do you mean?"

"You are a beautiful young woman. You can cook and clean and keep a house." As she continues, my heart begins to sink. It's the classic conversation delivered to any Greek woman of a certain age. "I see you keeping this house as if it were your own. Can I ask you a question?"

I want to say no, but know it doesn't matter what I want.

"Haven't you ever thought about getting married?" Mrs. Horiatis reaches out and puts her hand on top of mine, her hand blasting through the cross of dark and light above the le.

"You know, Mrs. Horiatis, I don't think that marriage is for me." I offer a weak smile. *Marriage has never been for me. And still, the question never stops.*

"But why not, dear? Sometimes we think that until we meet the right person, and then everything changes."

I eye Mrs. Horiatis's hand on top of mine and wish that I could move out from under her. Perhaps I can fake a sneeze.

"You know, you can trust me, dear," says the old woman as she squeezes my hand again. "I've been getting the idea that maybe you have a secret crush on someone?"

I jump, taking my hand from Mrs. Horiatis and looking for a way to escape the conversation. "No. No. I don't have a crush on anyone. No. That's silly."

"Oh, don't be ashamed, my dear. I lived in America a long time, and I've seen a lot of things. You can't deny love when it comes, even if the situation might seem complicated."

"But, *Kyria Horiatis*, I'm sorry. You must be mistaken." I start to rise from the table.

"Sit down, Xeni. It is time to be honest."

Something in the old woman's voice makes me respond. I sit down heavily in my chair and am surprised to find myself welling up with tears of relief. Perhaps now I will not be alone in my secrets. But how can the old woman possibly understand my deepest desires, my unspoken and foolish desires.

"I can see that you have a deep longing inside your heart, young woman."

I shake my downcast head, hiding my glistening eyes.

"I can help you."

I wonder how Mrs. Horiatis can make my dreams come true. Only God can give me a virgin birth, and God certainly would disapprove of my pull toward Callie. How can Mrs. Horiatis understand, or help me with my longings?

Mrs. Horiatis clears her throat and smiles and takes my hand again, holding it and stroking it with both of her hands. "Now I know it seems complicated, but I think I can help you be with the one you want." I look up expectantly. "If we work together."

I can't imagine how Mrs. Horiatis could make it all right with the Lord that Callie and I . . .

"I'm sure that Constantino feels the same way."

I'm confused, "Constantino?"

"Yes, Constantino." Mrs. Horiatis gives me a wide smile and pinches my cheek.

"Gus would want to go along with it?"

"I think so. I think that he can see his future with the *Amerikanitha* is short. And Xeni, dear. Don't you want a family of your own? A baby that cries out for you and calls you *Mama* and brings you endless joy for the rest of your days? There is nothing more sweet in life than having a baby."

"Yes, Mrs. Horiatis. I want a baby more than anything," and for once, I feel as if I can speak the truth. But I can hardly believe that I'm having this conversation with Mrs. Horiatis. It is as if Mrs. Horiatis can imagine a future for me when all I can see is dead ends.

"That settles it. Nothing would make me happier than to help you be happy."

"But how can you help me?" I ask.

"Those two are hanging on by a thread. All they need is a little snip, snip and it is over. Then Constantino will be free and the *Amerikanitha* can do whatever she wants . . . and you can finally be with the one you love."

"Mrs. Horiatis, how can you be so understanding? Aren't you angry?"

"Why would I be angry, *koritsi mou*? My girl, nothing would make me happier than to have you as my daughter-in-law!"

"Your daughter-in-law?" I realize my mistake. Mrs. Horiatis doesn't understand at all. No one understands. No one can understand my desires, my wishes. Not even God, it seems.

"Yes, sweetheart!"

I'm not sure how to tell Mrs. Horiatis that I don't love Gus without admitting my feelings for Callie. I know I have to squash Mrs. Horiatis's dreams on the spot, and for good. "Oh no, Mrs. Horiatis. I can never marry Gus. My parents wouldn't allow it. I'm sorry, but they would never approve of me marrying someone who already has a family. They would never allow me to break up a family."

"But it isn't a real family!" Mrs. Horiatis exclaims, "It isn't a real Greek family!"

I recoil. "What do you mean by that, Mrs. Horiatis?"

"Oh, you know I love Manolaki. He is my sunshine. But his mother isn't good enough for Constantino."

"Callie is a good woman! She is kind and gentle. She is a wonderful mother."

"That may be true, but she isn't Greek. And no matter how many cooking lessons you give her, she never will be Greek. You can't transfuse Greek blood, Greek history, Greek passion into her."

"Well, what does that make Manoli?" I demand.

"What do you mean?"

"Manolaki is half-Greek, and half-Callie. He will never be all Greek. His mother's blood runs through his veins. He will love her and favor her with the same devotion and loyalty that Gus shows toward you. You cannot erase his mother."

Mrs. Horiatis sits silently contemplating my words.

"And what about you, Xeni? Who do you love?"

I hold perfectly still, holding my breath.

"Who will give you a baby?" Mrs. Horiatis demands. "If no one is good enough for you, who will give you a baby?"

I pull my shoulders back and answer calmly, "God will give me a baby. He will give me a baby when the time is right. Soon, I think. When he sees that I deserve it."

"Such a religious girl. You know, Xeni, God doesn't always answer our prayers. He sometimes ignores them. Or worse, he crashes them down in front of our faces and drinks an ouzo while we cry."

"No. God makes dreams come true when we deserve them, when we have proven ourselves good enough."

"Xeni, don't you know? We are never good enough."

"But I want to try. I want to try to be good enough. And I know that I can never interfere with this family and still be a good person in God's eyes. So I can't do what you want, Mrs. Horiatis. I can't. I'm sorry."

Mrs. Horiatis, shakes her head at me and tsk-tsks as she picks up her Greek magazine and leaves the room. She can't be right. God would never crash my dreams on the ground and sit back drinking ouzo. What does Mrs. Horiatis know?

God.

God. Are you listening? Normally, I wouldn't be doing this. I know that you are all-knowing and benevolent and kind. You are capable of miracles beyond my understanding. And I know that sometimes things happen for reasons that I can't understand. But didn't it make you kind of mad when Mrs. Horiatis said that you don't care about our dreams? And, by the way, do you drink ouzo? That can't be right.

I am trying my best. I am trying my best to resist Callie and not interfere with this family. But I am only human. When I make mistakes, I try to get right back on track. Even when I make the same mistake over and over again. I know you are testing me to see if I am worthy of virgin birth, worthy of a baby. There are so many people out there who don't seem worthy, but they have babies. How does that work? I know I can't have Callie, but please give me a baby. Haven't I proven myself to you yet? I can't begin to understand your master plan, but please God, let's just do this now. Let's do this now or never. Make me pregnant. Show me that my efforts to remain pure of heart are worth something.

I'm not really giving you an ultimatum. I need to know if I am being crazy. If I should move on. If feasting on baby flesh is an idea that I should let go of. Holding and rocking a sweet baby, tickling their toes and squeezing their fat thighs. Kissing them from head to foot, whispering "*Tha se faw, tha se faw.*"

It's now or never, God. Do it. Do it now. Do it now so I don't lose my mind.

Pregnant at the Park

All the stress of Callie and Mrs. Horiatis, and waiting to see if God will punish me for my ultimatum, is getting to me. I take Manny to the playground so I can get back in touch with myself and my real goal of having a baby. I never intended to get caught up in all of this family drama. That's what I always wanted to escape! I need to focus on a virgin birth instead of Callie's oceanic eyes and warm embrace and everything will be fine. I need to show God that I am serious and of pure intentions.

I'm gently pushing Manny in a baby swing near the tall red-wood trees when one of the mothers at the park asks me when I'm due. "Do what?" I say. She asks me when my baby is due and points at my stomach. It is a bit rounder and my shirts are fitting tight, but I thought that was because I'd been having a lot of strange cravings lately and eating like a cow quite honestly. I tell her I'm not sure, and she starts talking about how her second child was a surprise, too. I start to feel dizzy and the sky starts to get dark, like my vision is shutting down. I rub my eyes and focus on a little girl on the next swing. She is wearing a pink gingham dress and has pink satin ribbons tied around her ponytails. She swings higher and higher as the lady talks about her pregnancy.

"And I'm telling you, it was a complete surprise. We hadn't planned on having another. It was a total accident. I mean, don't get me wrong. We're happy to have little Jeffrey of course." She smiles and starts rubbing her temples. "He is a handful, just like his father." She laughs to herself.

I'm still focused on the little girl swinging backward toward the trees behind her, sucking in her breath, feet tucked under her, and then pushing her legs forward with all her might, feet flexed, letting out an excited whoop. "So this accidental pregnancy . . . was it an accident because you hadn't had sex, or you were drunk, or what? How did you do it?" I asked. The little girl flies higher with each push.

"Well, I didn't *do* it. It just happened." She lowered her voice. "And between you and me, the doctors had said I couldn't have any more children. It's a miracle!" Her eyes were wide as she confided in Xeni.

A miracle? Is this a sign?

"Wait. I was just wondering. How did you know? What was the first symptom you had?" The girl glides forward, and I give Manny another push on the swing.

The woman pauses and smiles. "Well, I remember I woke up one morning, and my breasts felt sore and my back was hurting. At first I thought it was PMS, but then I started to feel nauseas. When I thought about it, I realized that I was late, but I hadn't noticed. I put two and two together and got Jeffrey!" The woman laughs and looks out toward the slide where Jeffrey is pushing another little boy out of the way so that he can slide down first.

Sore breasts, missed period, nausea. Maybe *I* have all of those things and just haven't noticed. "How far along were you with Jeffrey when you began to show? Do you really think that I'm showing?"

The woman is still looking at the slide and Jeffrey and at the little boy that Jeffrey has pushed. He is lying face down in the sand at the bottom of the slide ladder. His arms and legs are spread out like a snow angel. "Jeffrey!! What have you done now!!?" She starts to run toward the little boy, but I grab her arm.

"Wait! You have to tell me. Do you think that I'm showing?"

She screams "Yes!" with such passion that I know she really

means it. I look over at the girl on the swing again. She is flying really high now. So high she can touch the tops of the trees with her toes.

Could it be that God has finally blessed me with the parthenogenesis that I've prayed for so long and hard? I had truly fallen into despair thinking that it would never happen. Not with all the feelings I was resisting. But maybe this shows me that my efforts are being rewarded. I have hope again. This woman, the mother of Jeffrey, must have been sent to me from above. She must be a messenger from God. He must want me to know that I am not forsaken, that he has not forgotten me, and that my prayers will be answered. Are answered. *Are* answered? I smooth my shirt down over my stomach and feel for the baby. Just as the woman had said, I do have a bump. Until she had pointed it out to me, I thought it was a fatty tummy bulge, evidence of my midnight snacks and ice cream pops on the toilet. But maybe she's right. It could be the miracle I've been praying for, couldn't it? Otherwise, why else would God send a messenger to me in a children's playground? I can't remember my last period. *Am I pregnant?*

"Manny, it's time to go. Say bye-bye, park!" I take him out of the swing and take him back home where Mrs. Horiatis is only too happy to play with him.

After I drop him off I go straight to the maternity shop to look in the mirror and try on a maternity dress. Even though I have my own little bump to fill out the dress, I use their maternity pillow. I attach the thick Velcro straps around my waist and adjust the little white pillow over my belly, just so. I caress it gently and sing a little song to it, "*Amazing Grace, how sweet the sound, to save a wretch like me!*" They say that babies can hear you and get to know your voice and they can even learn to recognize music. After they're born, you can sing them the same music and it calms them right down. "*I once was lost, but now I'm found, was blind, but now I see!*" It's never too soon to start communicating with your baby. I give the pillow a little squeeze.

I pull the maternity dress over my head and down over my

swollen belly. I refuse to look in the mirror until I have it on perfectly. I adjust the ruching along the sides, smooth the fabric over my stomach, and tie the belt above my baby belly until I think it is just right.

I don't know why, but standing there in that dress I start to feel too afraid to turn around and look in the mirror. I've been waiting so long for this moment. My throat starts to close up tight and my eyes get all bleary. I can't cry. I won't cry. If I cry, I'll ruin the dress and I won't be able to see myself in the mirror and it will all go away. There is no way that I am going to let that happen.

I take a deep breath and wipe my eyes on the sorry barren shirt that I'd dropped to the ground in my hurry to undress. Sniffling, I slowly turn around toward the mirror. My eyes are squeezed shut and my fists are tight little balls. I am breathing hard, and I am still holding back my tears. I take a deep breath and say a little prayer. "Dear God, I know that I should be able to look in this mirror with the full confidence and faith that you have answered my prayers. You sent me a messenger and have caused my belly to swell, yet still I hold doubts. Please give me the strength and courage to receive your blessings and to live in gratitude and not fear. Please bless me with a child to call my own and to raise in your image. Give me the strength to look in this mirror and know that all my dreams have finally come true. I now fully realize that you, Lord, are the only one that can make this miracle happen. I cannot push my will upon yours. But please, Lord, let me look in this mirror and know that you have blessed me, finally, with parthenogenesis. Amen."

At that moment a feeling of relief flows through me. My tears dry up, and I feel that I can view my image in the mirror through God's eyes, through love. I slowly open my eyes and I see a blessed miracle in the mirror. My belly is round and luminous under the stretchy maternity dress. My cheeks are flushed and my eyes are bright with realization. I truly look like a pregnant virgin. I sink to my knees and thank God because I know then that all of my dreams have come true.

When I pay for the dress at the register the salesgirl asks me if I am okay. "Oh, I'm great. I'm fantastic. I'm pregnant!" I cry out, shoving my money toward her. "That's great," she says, "but I'm afraid I'm going to have to ask you to return the maternity pillow. It's not for sale." That's fine with me because soon my own belly will be bigger than their silly little pillow. "Sorry," I say as I rip open the Velcro straps. But then I start crying because I am so very happy.

"Oh, now, now, no need to cry. I understand—all those hormones could make anyone a little emotional or forgetful," she says as she hands me a tissue scented with springtime. "When are you due?"

Revealing Life and Death

As a reminder to myself to stay strong and pure of thought, I wear the dress the next time I go to Callie's house. I have to remember that God is watching, and he can take this baby away from me as quickly as he gave it. I have to resist the temptation of Callie. When I arrive she is surprised to see me looking pregnant. I tell her, "It's a miracle!" She is so surprised that she has to put baby Manny down in his playpen. She takes both of my hands into hers and sits me down on the couch.

"Xeni, what's going on? You're wearing a maternity dress."

I tell her about the lady in the park who asked me when I was due and how she hadn't even realized that she was pregnant because it was a miracle! "She said I was showing. I don't know how I missed it. I pray for a baby every day. But here I am. Maybe I've just been so distracted with everything here." The words tumble out, and she is the first person I'm telling. The first person I've trusted.

"But Xeni, how did this happen? I know that you want a baby, but how did—what did you do?" Callie was silent for a moment, her body stiff. "Have you been dating someone?"

"No! Callie, of course not. Look at me! That's what's so wondrous about it. I didn't do anything. God did it. He finally answered my prayers."

I see Callie's shoulders relax. "Have you seen a doctor or taken a pregnancy test yet? It's really important to see a doctor as soon as you can if you are actually pregnant." Callie is stroking my arm and her hand feels so warm. *I can't let her touch me.*

"I don't want to see a doctor."

"But you have to. You have to make sure everything is okay." She gives my arm a little squeeze. *Her eyes are like a deep blue ocean.*

"No, I can't do this. I mean, I won't go see a doctor. There is no way." I pull away from her. Manny pulls up to standing in his playpen, looking at us. "I won't make that mistake again." I am supposed to be happy, but now I'm feeling all confused. "I can't let anyone touch me, and I won't let the doctor take my baby away from me again!" Callie moves closer to me on the couch and puts her arm around me. I can feel her breath on my cheek.

"What mistake, sweetie? What happened? Who took your baby away?" She scooches even closer to me, and her body fits like a puzzle piece up against mine. She is so soft. She feels like a downy pillow that I can rest on. *If only I could rest.* She traces the shape of a heart with her finger into my hand. "Trust me."

I tell her about the baby that I carried in my belly. I tell her about the first and only time that I saw its heartbeat, pulsing like a beacon of light over a dark sea. How that one moment had given me faith that life was worth living. How that pulse was a true miracle. After I saw that light in my belly, I felt like I had the happiest secret growing inside of me. I was no longer alone in the world. I had a child that loved me, depended on me, clung to me for sustenance and life. A child. I had prayed and prayed for a healthy child. I refused to think that anything bad could happen—but something bad did happen. God snuffed out the light. And when the doctor looked inside of my womb, there was only darkness, and the tiny body of my dead child. It had been dead for a month. All that time when I thought that I'd carried a secret light of life, I'd really carried death inside of me. Death and despair.

Callie's blue eyes glisten as I tell her about my secret, but she never looks away from me. Her arm feels strong around my shoulders as if she is holding me up. It is confusing to be so close to her body, to smell her scent.

Manny has been patient long enough and starts to cry behind the barrier of his playpen. His chubby face is all red with frustration. Apple cheeks. Round and firm. Good for pie. Callie gets up and walks toward him. The couch suddenly feels big and cold. I touch the cushion where she has been sitting. It is warm and delicious like melted chocolate lava cake.

"Shhh, Manny. It's okay. Momma's right here. It's okay. See Xeni? Xeni loves you. She loves you so much she wants to eat you up. Come on, don't cry." Callie hands Manny to me, and I'm not sure that I want to hold him. His soft, sweet flesh is too much for me. "Come on, take him." But I can't, and so Callie sits down very close to me and puts Manny on my lap. She puts her arms around me and Manny and the three of us cuddle together like a pile of sad-eyed puppies.

Telling Callie my secret makes me wonder if I am really pregnant after all. Thinking about my dead baby makes it hard for me to believe that something good can ever happen again. That night when I go home, I take off my maternity dress and stand in front of the mirror on my closet door. I look at my body from side to side, trying to see if my belly bump is a baby or just plain fat. I can't tell. So I put on my flannel nightgown, turn out the lights, and try to go to sleep. But no matter how long I wait, my eyes stay wide open in the dark room. My hands find my belly and gently stroke it, telling the baby, if it is in there, to hold on. Hold on.

The next morning I oversleep. I am exhausted. I try rubbing some of the sleep out of my eyes, but it doesn't work. The longer I lie there the worse I feel. My stomach starts to turn, so I decide to get up and have some dry toast with chamomile tea. Doll sits there in the rocking chair, with the sunlight streaming in over her face. She looks so peaceful, absorbing the rays of light, that I decide to join her. I hold her close to my breast and I rock and quietly sing her a lullaby with my eyes closed, imagining that I can feel warmth and movement emanating from her small body. Doll's pink body is hard compared to Manny's, but that doesn't make any difference to me because I love her so.

When you love someone, you accept their differences. You don't reject them. I rock Doll in the chair and sip my tea. I tell Doll that I am finally pregnant. I tell Doll about Callie and how they both have blue eyes. I can tell that Doll likes to be held. It feels good to be held, like when Callie held me on the couch. I love Doll so much, and she isn't even a "real" person. "Loving a real person could be okay, couldn't it?" I ask Doll. As I rock back and forth, her eyes open and shut, her fringy black eyelashes brushing her soiled cheek. It almost looks as if she is nodding her approval.

The Prenatal Visit

I don't know why I let Callie convince me to come to this doctor. She left Manny with his yiayia and brought me to this place. I don't need to fill out forms and let some stranger poke at me to know that I'm pregnant. God has blessed me with a miracle. My period has stopped, I have morning sickness, and my belly is growing. Sometimes when I'm lying real still, like in the middle of the night when the moonlight glows through my window, I can feel the baby moving. I can feel it sleeping in my womb, can feel it turning, and I can almost hear its dreams. Soft, fluffy clouds, kitten meows, and lapping water. The seed of life. All curled up and sucking its thumb, it is safe inside of me and I will never let anything happen to it.

The waiting room is painted pink and blue stripes, and pictures of babies are on every wall. I pick up the copy of *Mother's Milk* magazine on the table beside me and flip through it. There is an article on pumping breast milk at work, complete with pictures of bare-breasted women demonstrating the machines in an office setting. One woman sits at her cubicle desk, smiling and pumping, with a sandwich in her hand. It reminds me of a TV show I've seen about a dairy farm where the cows had long black tubes clamped to their udders that sucked the milk out while they stood chewing hay in their metal stalls. I can never understand how they could seem so nonchalant about that. Looking at that picture makes me decide I will never attach a pump to my breast.

233

The nurse calls my name while standing in the doorway looking down at her clipboard. If I sit very still and ignore her, then I won't have to go in. Callie touches my arm. "She's calling your name, sweetie."

I pull my arm away and place my hand on my belly. "No, I think she called someone else."

"Didn't we talk about how important prenatal care is for a healthy pregnancy?" Callie asks as I fidget in my seat, and the nurse calls my name again and scribbles something on the clipboard.

"Yes, but what if he hurts the baby?"

"He won't hurt the baby, I promise." Callie takes my hand and stands up, pulling me toward the big gray door and the nurse who is standing there drumming her pen against her clipboard. She's wearing a round button that says, "You're special to us!" I want to give the nurse a dirty look, but Callie is pulling me along after her.

The nurse leads us down a long hallway, turns to the right, proceeds forward and then turns left, and left again. I want to memorize our route so that I can escape while pretending to take a trip to the restroom. But it is too complicated. I will never be able to find my way out again without help. Callie is looking at me and smiling, and I can't help but be mad at her. This was her idea. What does she look so happy for? I turn away from her without returning her smile.

The nurse has me stop in a restroom and pee into a cup before we finally stop in front of a door with a picture of a duck with a yellow ribbon around its neck. The room is cold and bright, and the wall next to the exam table has a big handmade quilt on it. There is a procession of little girls with big bonnets marching around the perimeter of the quilt. They are each wearing a dress of a different floral print, and their big bonnets completely obscure their faces. I know it is supposed to be cheerful, but I find it disturbing that I can't see their faces and that they are all marching in a regimented long line, like cheerful Stepford babies without any free will. I whisper to Callie, "I want to go home." She gives me an encouraging smile and whispers back, "You can do it."

The nurse makes me get up on a scale and writes down my weight. I tell her, "I don't usually weigh so much, but I've put on some pounds since I got pregnant."

"Oh really, how many pounds, and how far along are we?"

"Nine. And I'm not sure."

"Nine weeks or nine pounds? What do you mean, you aren't sure?"

"Nine pounds. And I'm not sure how far along I am . . . maybe thirteen weeks?"

"Okay, let's have a seat on the exam table. When was the date of our last menstrual period?"

"Mine or yours?"

"Well yours, of course." The nurse gives me a baffled look.

"I don't know."

"All right. Well the doctor should be able to approximate the due date by measuring the baby from the ultrasound."

Next to the exam table is a big machine with a black computer screen with some fuzzy white circles on it. There is a woman's name on the top of the screen and some measurement, 17 mm LEFT. Rising from the machine is a thick white probe at least ten inches long. The nurse squirts some gooey blue gel from a bottle onto the tip of the probe and then unrolls a condom onto it. I can see the cold blob of gel sitting there on the tip of the probe under the see-through condom.

"Is that for me?" I start to edge off of the exam table.

"Well, of course, dear. How else can the doctor tell how old your baby is?"

"Can't he just measure my stomach or something?" I look at Callie. Why isn't she helping me? She's just sitting there with a reassuring smile on her face. I am really hating her now.

"Well, he might decide to do an abdominal ultrasound, but I want to have the probe ready, just in case!" The nurse is cheerful for the first time, and I want to rip her "You're Special to Us!" button off of her teddy bear-covered smock.

She wraps the blood pressure cuff around my arm, tucks the silver disk under the tight cuff, and starts pumping the black bulb. "Is this your first pregnancy?" The pressure from the cuff gets tighter and tighter, but she keeps pumping. I can feel sweat forming on my upper lip. I start to feel hot and dizzy. She pumps the ball some more. There are dark spots dancing in front of my eyes, and my arm is pounding with pain from the tight cuff.

". . . And who is the father?"

"I don't know."

The nurse pauses her pumping, and the tight band cuts off all circulation in my arm. "You don't know? Can you narrow it down?"

"Well, I can narrow it down to God. He puts all life on this Earth." I give the nurse a hard look, daring her to challenge me.

The nurse gives me a tight smile and releases the pressure from the cuff, *psshhhhhhh*.

"Okay. How about we disrobe completely from the waist down. Here is a privacy panel for you—and the doctor will come shortly."

After she leaves the room, I get up to go, but Callie grabs my arms and makes me stay sitting on that cold, hard exam table and says, "Relax." Easy for her to say. I look at the end of the table at the stirrups. They've covered the hard metal triangles with pink pot holders so it looks like there are two giant hands waiting to catch my feet and keep my legs spread for the doctor. It gives me the shivers. Callie says, "Just take a deep breath." All I want to do is get up with my baby safe inside of me and leave that doctor's office. What can he tell me that I don't already know? God has blessed me with a baby. And if it isn't true, I don't want to know.

Callie insists that I stay, so I make her turn her back to me while I take my skirt and panties off, and climb up onto the cold exam table. The paper blanket makes crinkly sounds as I try to adjust it to cover my naked lower regions, but it doesn't offer much warmth or discretion. Sighing, I put my heels into the pink pot holders and wait. I try to comfort myself with the thought that I am willing to do anything for my baby, and this too shall pass. Twenty-three long minutes pass. Callie tries to hold my hand, but I push her away. *I can't risk anything now.* Finally, the doctor comes in to see us. He is an older man with bushy gray eyebrows and salt-and-pepper hair.

"Well, okay. Your chart says that you're approximately thirteen weeks pregnant, father unknown, excessive weight gain, and hmm . . . high blood pressure. Is your blood pressure usually high?"

"No doctor, but your nurse was making me very nervous with that probe over there. I'm hoping that you don't need to use that."

The doctor laughs. "Oh, there's nothing to it!"

I want to see how he'd feel with that big probe up his private parts. "Well, let's see what we have here. Since you are averse to the ultrasound, why don't we use the Doppler to hear the baby's heartbeat? Why don't you lie down, and I'll use this microphone here to pick up the rhythm." I turn to Callie and we smile at each other. We are going to hear the baby!

I lie down and the doctor lowers the privacy panel to below my stomach. He switches on his machine and presses it to my belly, and I can't help but remember the last time someone tried to hear my baby's heartbeat. Immediately, we hear the gurgling noises of my baby. "Ah, okay. Well, that's the sound of *your* heartbeat . . ." He moves the microphone again, and there is a distinct sound of movement. ". . . and that's the sound of your intestines."

"Okay, now let's hear the baby!" I am feeling excited and impatient. I want to hear my baby. He continues moving the instrument over my belly for a few more minutes.

"Well, okay. No need to worry, but I think we'll go ahead and do an abdominal ultrasound to take a look inside there."

"Then we can see the baby?"

"Yes. Just relax. This is going to feel a little cold. No need to worry." The doctor squeezes some of the thick gel over my stomach, and Callie clasps my hand. He types something into the keyboard of the ultrasound machine and turns the screen toward him. As he moves the ultrasound paddle over my stomach, I crane my neck to try to see the screen and my baby turning somersaults in my womb. I'm sure she is excited to see me, too. It is really quiet in the room, I think because of the anticipation of seeing new life.

"What do you see, doctor?"

"Did you empty your bladder before the exam?"

"Yes. Do you want me to empty it again?"

"No. But I will have to do the transvaginal probe after all."

"Oh no, but why?"

"I'm having a bit of trouble hearing your little bean, and the transvaginal probe will give me a better view."

I start to feel anxious. Why is he having trouble seeing my baby? I look at the giant probe again, and even though I have never had anything inside of me, I am willing to endure the probe to make sure my baby is okay. I look at Callie for reassurance, but she isn't smiling anymore.

"Okay. Please put your feet in the stirrups and move your bum down toward the end of the table. Lower, lower. Okay."

He has me move so that my naked private parts are hovering over the edge of the table, my feet held in place by those pink pot holders. Callie tells me to keep breathing.

"Okay. Here we go." The doctor touches my private parts, and I feel a sharp pain down there as he pokes me with that probe. My eyes tear up from the pain, but I am trying to stay strong for my baby. I put all other thoughts out of my head as he pushes the probe past my resistance and up into my naked interior. I wonder if I am bleeding. I am breathing hard and trying not to cry—but hanging on because I know that I am about to see my baby. Callie is gripping my hand tight.

The doctor says, "Okay, well, we do have an enlarged uterus. Uhm . . . But I'm sorry, I'm not seeing a baby. I'm going to have to do some blood work to confirm these results, but absent some miracle I'd have to say that you aren't actually pregnant at this time." As he removes the probe, it feels as if all of my dreams are being pulled out from inside of me.

"But doctor, I had a positive pregnancy test at home, and my belly is growing. I can feel the baby moving! I know I'm pregnant. God willed it! You're wrong!"

Callie stands next to me, stroking my forehead and holding my hand. The Stepford babies continue their march around the quilt. Everything in the room is the same but horribly different. The doctor is taking copious notes as I continue to protest. Maybe he believes me. I sit up and grab him by the shoulders. "You have to believe me!"

He stops writing and asks me to remove my hands from his shoulders.

"You have to believe me!"

I stare into his blank, flat eyes. There is nothing there. Nothing. I take my hands off of his body, and lean into Callie who wraps her arm around my shoulders.

"Okay. Now this is a highly unusual situation and diagnosis, and we'll have to do some blood tests to confirm it and maybe additional evaluations, but what I suspect may be happening here is pseudocyesis or, in layman's terms, hysterical pregnancy."

Callie gasps, "But Doctor, she has symptoms. What does this mean?"

"Okay, while it is unusual, pseudocyesis does occur. The most common sign of pseudocyesis is abdominal distension, usually attributed to excess fat, gaseous distension, or fecal and urinary retention. This can usually be resolved under general anesthesia. We'll do some tests, but laboratory findings in patients with pseudocyesis show variable results. Estrogen and progesterone values can be high, low, or normal. Prolactin tends to be elevated, and follicle-stimulating hormone (FSH) tends to be low."

I don't understand anything he is saying.

"But what causes this, Doctor?" asks Callie.

"Okay, well there are a few theories behind it. There's 'conflict theory.'" As he names the theory, he makes little quote marks in the air with his fingers. "This happens when the patient's desire or fear for pregnancy creates an internal conflict that actually causes endocrine changes that in turn cause false symptoms. There's 'wish-fulfillment theory,' where the patient interprets minor body changes as proof of the false pregnancy. And then there's the 'depression theory,' where the pseudocyesis is initiated by neuroendocrine changes associated with major depressive disorder."

I pull the paper blanket around my affronted body. "I don't believe this! I'm not crazy! Or depressed! I'm pregnant! I know it . . ."

Callie puts her arms around me and pulls me close. "It's going to be okay."

"No! It will never be okay. He keeps saying okay and you're saying okay, but it's not okay. Why is this happening to me? Why?"

"I'm sorry," the doctor says. "As I said, we can run some blood tests to confirm the diagnosis, but bottom line is—there is no baby." The doctor hands Callie a prescription for something "for my nerves," an order for the lab, and a referral to a psychiatrist.

In the car, the radio is playing that old song, "Don't It Make My Brown Eyes Blue." I stare ahead out of the spotty windshield at the sunny day—women pushing baby strollers, cars driving along in straight lines. It is all a blur to me. Nothing matters anymore. There was nothing. I am nothing.

From the Sea

Callie drove for a long time, unsure which course to take. Instead of turning onto the freeway she took the streets; instead of heading home, she headed west toward the bay. She often got lost when she was flustered, and her confusion was overriding her ability to navigate. The radio became annoying as the car filled with advertisements for things that seemed insignificant in the face of what they'd just heard, and Callie turned it off. They rode silently. Callie clutched the steering wheel until her knuckles turned white. She glanced over at Xeni, who seemed to be staring out the side window to avoid her frequent concerned looks. There was nothing to say and nowhere to go, and so Callie drove them to the edge of the earth.

Crossing the Bay Bridge and driving through congested San Francisco streets, she reached the relative ease of Fulton Street, catching the lights as she traveled across the city and toward the blue horizon, where the houses suddenly stopped and the deep Pacific Ocean took over. Callie pressed the controls and the windows all rolled down, filling the car with salty air and a cold breeze. When they reached Ocean Beach, she got out and pulled two thick fleece jackets out of the back of the car. Emergency jackets. She opened Xeni's door and helped her step down onto the sandy road. "Here, let's put this on you," she said as she guided Xeni's arms into the warm jacket sleeves and zipped her up, pulling the hood over her head. Callie linked her arm through

Xeni's, and they walked toward the short flight of stairs leading down to the beach. They walked on the wheat-colored sand, their ankles occasionally turning, their shoes filling with the grains, until they found an empty place where they could sit and watch the ocean waves run up onto shore and then retreat again.

"Sometimes, when I was growing up, and things felt hard, I'd take off. I'd hitchhike or take a bus. Whatever would get me to a beach." Callie paused to listen to the roar of the ocean. "I'd get so fed up. Moving all the time. Never staying still. Never having a real home. The ocean was one place I could go that stayed the same. It didn't matter if we were in Oregon or California or Washington. The Pacific Ocean was always there for me."

Seagulls cawed overhead and a few landed near them, jutting their heads to the side, waiting to see if a hand would emerge from a pocket with some crumbs or a treat. "But what I really wanted," Callie admitted, "was someone." Xeni stared straight ahead at the ocean, massive and blue. "I wanted my mother," Callie concluded.

"I wanted my mother, too," Xeni replied. "I always wanted my mother, but she always felt miles away." Callie held Xeni as her tears escaped, and Callie imagined them emerging from deep within Xeni's ribcage, from a place where she'd been holding them for decades. The seagulls took flight, leaving them alone again. They sat huddled together, side by side, bracing against the cold wind and breathing in the clean ocean mist for what felt like hours.

"You know," Xeni started, "there is wild yeast in the air. There's a baker in the city that makes bread using it. They have a wild yeast starter, called the mother dough. They've been using the same mother dough to bake bread for over a hundred years. Longer than a lifetime." Xeni licked her fingers and raised her right hand into the air. "Right now there is wild yeast clinging to my fingers, infinitesimally tiny beings seeking nourishment and home. If only I were a bowl of flour and water . . ."

Callie put her arm around Xeni's shoulders. "Xeni, what do you really want? More than anything in the world?" She leaned her head in close to Xeni's so that she could hear the words clearly.

"I want what I cannot have," Xeni replied.

"Tell me. I want to hear the words."

Xeni paused, and Callie imagined Xeni teetering on the edge of honesty with each wave that crested and then retreating into shame.

"Tell me," Callie whispered, huddling closer.

"I'll sound crazy. I can't tell you."

"You know, sometimes when we keep things inside, that's what makes us feel crazy. Sometimes when you share your secret thoughts, you realize they aren't that crazy after all." Callie waited, listening to the wind rushing past her ears.

"We never really know what other people are thinking," Xeni replied. "If we could hear what everyone was thinking, it would be like drowning in sound. So we keep ourselves separate. And safe."

"I would like to know what you are thinking about, what you desire. I won't drown," Callie said. "Really."

"I want a baby. More than anything. But more than that," Xeni paused, "I want a virgin birth."

Callie absorbed the words, taking them into her heart. "A virgin birth? So you want a baby, but without the man."

Xeni nodded, sniffling her nose and wiping a tear away from her eye. "But I know now that it will never happen. I know now that I'm crazy, or not good enough. If I was good enough, God would have given me a miracle by now, so that means I'm crazy."

Callie wrinkled her brow, not sure what to say. "Honey, you aren't crazy. And you are good enough. You just don't know it."

"Then why can't I have what I want?" Xeni turned to face Callie, looking intently into her eyes. "Why do I always want," Xeni paused, "what I can't have?" She locked her gaze on Callie's, and her eyes welled up with tears again. Callie put her finger on Xeni's lips and said, "shhhhhh." Callie felt herself swelling with emotions that she'd been trying to set aside since that night they'd held each other in the bath.

Xeni suddenly yelled as she pulled away from Callie, stood up, and ran toward the ocean. "I don't want to be quiet anymore! I don't want to be confused anymore!"

243

"Xeni! Stop! Don't run away!" Callie yelled and ran after her.

"Why shouldn't I run? What good can come of this? You are going to hurt me!" Xeni screamed.

"No! No! I don't want to hurt you, Xeni! I want to love you. But I don't know how. I'm caught in a situation. I have to see it through. For Manny's sake." Callie's chest hurt as she looked at Xeni, standing like a statue against the horizon, tears freezing on her face.

"Of course, you're right, for Manny." She nodded. "I shouldn't be selfish."

"I want to be selfish, Xeni. I want to be selfish so much. But I can't. I have to find a way to be selfless. I want to be a good mother."

"I want to be a good mother, too," Xeni cried.

"You will be. I just know it," Callie responded.

"How? How will I ever be a mother? Look at me!"

Callie looked at Xeni, standing just feet from the frothy sea, the wind whipping her long brown hair, her face crumpled in anguish.

"I see a beautiful, strong woman with big dreams. Extraordinary dreams. Someone who has given me so much and accepted me for who I am. Someone that I would be lucky to spend a lifetime knowing. Someone who would be an amazing and fiercely loving mother. Someone who has so much love to give." Callie swallowed hard. "And you should be a mother. You will be a mother. If I have to do it myself, you will be a mother one day."

Xeni laughed wryly. "If only you could."

If only I could, Callie thought, her mind churning.

Xeni raised her right hand into the wild yeasty wind once more. "In the Bible, the right hand performs miracles. That's why Greeks wear wedding bands on their right."

Callie raised her right hand and placed her open palm against Xeni's. "The right hand can perform miracles," she said. Then she pulled Xeni into her embrace and softly kissed her divine tear-soaked lips.

Purity

The day of the baptism passes quickly, like a film on fast-forward. I rise in the morning from my bed with a heavy feeling in my chest. I turn toward Doll, who is sitting on the rocking chair, neglected and forgotten. Her eyes stare straight into mine, unwavering, and I take that as a sign that I must have courage to get through the day. I've already delivered the baptismal items to the priest the previous day, the white towels and sheet, the olive oil, the soap, the large decorated *lambatha* candle, the white clothes and the gold cross with the aquamarine in the center. It reminds me of the ocean and Callie's eyes, the *mati*, the protective eye of God.

Mrs. Horiatis is happy for this day to come, even though I'm sure she wishes she were attending a wedding joining me to their family. The thought of it makes me want to laugh. The combination of me and Gus is ridiculous and combustible, like pouring a cup of cold coffee into a pot of boiling oil. Although I imagine we would make beautiful babies, dark-haired and olive-skinned, with crafty eyes and ready lips. But that is only one of many nonsensical thoughts I have this day.

My mind is in a steady state of confusion and contradictory thoughts. If baptism is to cleanse the soul, how could it lead to ruin? If a godparent is responsible for religious education, they must be of pure thought, and if they are not of pure thought, how can they be a godparent? And if the godparent is impure, why must the child suffer? And if the child suffers, why must their purity be taken from them? And on and on until my mind trips upon itself, and old memories, and fear for the future.

But they selected me. And I vow to try my best to be pure and shameless, a good example for Manny. Someone who follows the edicts of the church, of God, and who stays an appropriate distance from women with blue eyes and red hair. Someone who doesn't kiss another woman on the beach. I will prove that a godparent can overcome her own failings to protect and guide her godchild in the teachings of the Lord.

The ceremony is small. Callie and Gus invited their friends, and Mrs. Horiatis is glowing with satisfaction that her grandson is being baptized. Afterward, she will show him off to her old friends, dressed in polyester dresses with sequins and bows, who will smile, showing their gold teeth and creased faces. The widows will genuflect and embrace him against their black bosoms as if sucking his life force into their hearts.

The Reunion

Mrs. Horiatis sniffed away tears of happiness as she held her grandson in the narthex of the church. It was almost time. In moments the baptism would begin, and he would be welcomed into the arms of the Greek Orthodox religion. She looked into his eyes. He had his grandfather's eyes, deep and brown and soulful. She was suddenly overcome with a familiar scent, one she hadn't smelled in years. The commingled smell of his cologne and sweat was unmistakable and triggered a cascade of memories. Seeing her husband, Manoli, for the first time, stomping grapes at a neighbor's farm. Their first kiss. The nausea she felt on the airplane ride to New York. The swell of her belly under her clothes as they got married by a justice of the peace before boarding a train for California. Feeling the baby kick her mercilessly throughout the night. Poking her belly during the day to make him move to know that he was all right. Giving birth in the big hospital where no one spoke Greek. The look on Manoli's face when he saw his son for the first time. Constantino's baptism in the Greek Orthodox church surrounded by strangers. His first cold. Walking him to school and back past the loud cars and fast-talking loiterers. Puberty. Worrying. Late nights. Girls. Cars. Manoli leaving. Struggling. And always fiercely loving.

And now this smell, she hadn't smelled it in so long. She deeply inhaled. *Manoli, you finally came back. This is your grandson.*

He is more precious than you know. And look at your son. He is a man today. But he still needs you. Watch over him when I go home. I tried my best to match him with the right woman, but now it's too late. Xeni becomes family today. It's time for him to fail or succeed without me. She made the sign of the cross and rested her hand over her old heart. She inhaled the scent of her husband's cologne once more, and for the first time in a long time she didn't feel lonely.

Cleansed of Sin

I enter the narthex of the Greek Orthodox Cathedral of the Ascension and light a candle before entering the dark nave of the church. Following the richly robed priest's direction, we begin the baptismal proceedings by rejecting Satan and blowing three times into the air and symbolically spitting three times onto the floor. As I reject Satan, I feel my trembling hands become steady as I hold Manny close to my heart. I know I must also put aside my feelings for Callie, once and for all. When I become Manoli's godmother, we will be family, and my first duty will be to Manoli. I must do everything in my power to be a good and righteous godparent, a protector of his eternal soul, his heart, and his body.

The priest seems surprised when I can recite the *Pestevo* by heart, as many Greek Americans, and Greeks for that matter, need to read aloud the Nicene Creed professing their belief in God. My eyes close against salty tears as I recite the words with great passion. The priest glances at the glimmering ceiling and asks God to make Manoli worthy of baptism, to cleanse away old sins, and to fill the child with the Holy Spirit. I wonder if I could be rebaptized, if I could be cleansed of old sins, old memories. The priest confides in me afterward that he was so moved by my display of emotion that he felt himself renewed and filled with a spirit that had sometimes eluded him in his many years leading the parish.

We stand beside the silver baptismal font, a representation of the divine womb, where Manny will be symbolically resurrected as a child of God. As I hold him in my arms I vow to do everything in my power to raise Manny to be a good Christian and to keep him safe. The church, which is usually so cool, the stained glass dazzlingly blue like the Aegean Sea, feels so hot. I am sweating. The air is rippling with heat, and I feel like I am losing my breath, submerged in a bath of shame.

The day that I was baptized, my godfather, my *nouno*, took his holy vow to protect me. It was the day I was supposed to become safe, the day I escaped hell. It was the day that I was assured I'd go to heaven. He was supposed to protect me, and each time he failed me I was reminded of his vow. I look up at the pounded copper ceiling, the hand-painted portraits of the saints, and the face of Jesus. He looks angry, and I swoon as the heat overtakes me.

Mrs. Horiatis and Callie, in their first cooperative act, undress Manny, symbolically removing each piece of clothing as if he carries layers of their sins. I was too young to remember my own baptism. Being stripped naked and held above the baptismal font, the priest chanting, tracing the sign of the cross on my forehead with his finger and olive oil. Snipping a lock of hair. Salvation through the act of being submerged in water, losing your breath. I imagine dipping my fingers into the cool baptismal water, but know that the water would sizzle and boil over. My entire body is on fire and I can feel the heat rising, my cheeks burning red.

The priest makes the sign of the cross on Manny's luminous naked body, and I lovingly rub extra-virgin olive oil into his skin and pray silently that there will always be peace between Manny and God. I hold my breath as the priest plunges Manny into the blessed water of the baptismal font three times, and exhale only as he intones, "The servant of God, Manoli, is baptized in the name of the Father, and of the Son, and of the Holy Spirit. Amen." And with that, Manny, like Christ, is resurrected and reborn, and placed into my open arms, draped with a pristine white sheet of purity, and I can see the steam rising from my arms.

Gus was overcome with emotions as the priest raised Manoli above the baptismal font and plunged him into the water impregnated with blessings and a small stream of olive oil. He wanted to cry and then laugh with joy as he watched his son consecrated to the church, for Manolaki to enter the embracing arms of the Greek community fully, and to know that whatever happened Manny would now be truly Greek and a member of the church.

The priest continued with the chrismation, and Gus reached over and found Callie's hand. He held it as the priest anointed Manny with the blessed miron oil, dabbing his feet so that he might be blessed wherever he walked. He cut three locks of his glistening red hair in the form of the cross, as a humble gift to God. The priest blessed a piece of Manny's new white clothing and put it on him as he said, "The servant of God, Manoli, is clothed with the garment of incorruptibility."

The priest fastened the gold cross around little Manoli's neck, with the aquamarine stone sparkling with the Holy Spirit against the boy's chest. As the priest lit the *lambatha* candle and walked Xeni and Manoli in a circle around the baptismal font for the symbolic dance of joy, Gus fingered the cross that lay against his heart under his shirt and tie, and said a short prayer for his son, that he might find happiness and love in his life, and that Gus would have the strength to be a good father—and he wanted to say good husband. He wanted to. He pressed the cross deeper into his skin and stole a glance toward Callie. She was following Xeni and Manoli with her eyes as they walked around the font, with a smile and contemplative look upon her face. Gus vowed to try harder. Callie looked over at him, and as if reading his thoughts she smiled brightly. Gus returned the smile and felt suddenly hopeful.

The priest finished reading the scriptures, at which point he signaled to Gus and Callie to come forward. They stood side by side as the priest declared, "I present to you your son, baptized and confirmed, dedicated to God." Gus beamed at Manoli as the priest nodded at Xeni, prodding her forward. Gus wondered why Xeni seemed reluctant to look at them. Following custom, Gus and Callie took turns kissing her hands. First Gus bowed forward slightly and took Xeni's hand in his and kissed her knuckles, and then took Manoli from her arms. Gus watched Callie step forward and take both of Xeni's hands in hers, and tenderly kiss each one before drawing her into a full embrace. Gus's smile faded, and he felt an unease spread through his stomach as he watched Xeni stiffen, and then collapse into Callie's arms quietly crying, and Callie stroking Xeni's hair as she murmured something he could not hear.

God and the Kitchen

Sometimes I wonder about secrets. Keeping them or releasing them. Coveting them or spitting them out. It seems to me that there are so many secrets in the world that it is impossible for them all to be kept before they burst their containment, leaving a sticky, funky mess all over their keepers. There were a lot of secrets in my family. Whispers and warnings and bribery. There were codes—let the phone ring once, hang up, and then call again. There were visitors and long naps. There were angry tirades after the red wine was drained. The wine held secrets loose, and wanted more undone. Then there were hissy denials and cries of martyrdom. I knew never to tell what I saw, because it would only lead to more of the same. The secrets, the lies, the dangerous games. I did what I was told and kept my mouth shut. I was taught very early never to say no.

Some afternoons my *nouno* would come to our house when Daddy was at work at the butcher shop. I loved my *nouno*. He would bring me presents, and he was always smiling. He loved to grab and kiss me and make me sit on his lap. Ha ha, it was always smiles when he was there. My mother was happy too when he was there and stopped frowning so much like when Daddy was home. She would give him anything he wanted. Anything.

I loved him so much that when he came over I would hide his shoes or his keys so that he couldn't leave. He and Mommy would go and lie down in the bedroom, and when he came back out he would look for his keys. "Where are my keys?" he'd ask, knowing that I'd hidden them. I'd giggle and say, "It's a secret!" Then he'd grab me hard and bite my cheek, and his grisly gray beard would scratch my face. I'd squirm away and run to see if he'd chase me and he always did. It was a game we played. My mother would come out of the bedroom straightening her sleeveless white sweater and brown pencil skirt. She'd growl at me, "Give him his keys—your father will be home soon." Mommy's eyes were hard like lava and I could feel the burn of her anger. She taught us never to say no.

When I was ten, we moved to a new house. It was around the corner from my *nouno* and *nouna's* house. Daddy didn't like to be so close to other people, and he didn't like it when people would call the house and hang up when he answered. Moving to the new house made the secrets get bigger. The phone would ring once, silence, ring again and Mommy would whisper-hiss things like, *You broke my heart,* and *I told you not to call at night.* Daddy drank more red wine and cried through his screaming accusations. I didn't like the new house. Doll and I would sit in the dark bedroom and watch the fog drift by the window. The fog surrounded our house like thick insulation. It kept in all the secrets.

One day after school my mother told me that my *Nouno* was sick and that I should go around the corner to keep him company. I thought that she should come with me but she said "No" and to "go get dressed." I had a new outfit for Easter, and I decided to wear it so that I would look nice, even though it was cold outside and the fog was swirling thick. I loved the pink and red stripes on the white short-sleeved sweater and how it matched perfectly with the short red skirt. I combed my long hair which hung past my bottom and used two white flower barrettes in my hair. I looked pretty. It was my first grown-up visit alone and I wanted to look nice. Mommy yelled at me to take a sweater and said it was stupid that I was wearing sandals when it was cold outside. I was a bit nervous to go by myself, so I brought Doll with me. I combed her hair too and changed her clothes so she looked nice. Her shiny blond hair was curly, and I put a barrette in her hair that matched mine. Her dark fringy eyelashes blinked at me as I walked, her blue eyes winking.

When I rang the doorbell, *Nouno* opened the door in his pajamas. They were all wrinkled and his face looked sleepy. But when he saw me he smiled and told me that I looked pretty. "Come in, come on." I followed him into the house, past the living room and the dining room and the kitchen. I followed him down the dark, long hallway past the door to the garage and little pink bathroom. I followed him all the way to the bedroom where the air smelled funny and all the curtains were closed. The covers on the bed were messy, and he crawled under them. I stood there by the side of the bed for a moment before I sat in a chair near the wall. The room looked so big to me, like a dark cave, and I couldn't quite see my way. I crossed my legs at the ankle and folded my hands.

"Where's *Nouna*?" I asked as I looked around the dark room.

"She went to the dentist. Why are you sitting so far away?" he asked me and gestured to me to come closer. I stayed in the chair with Doll and asked him why he was sick. Sick people have bad breath. He just laughed and told me again to sit closer and patted the bed. Above the bed my *nouna* had placed an icon of the Virgin Mary on a little shelf, with a lit *candili* floating in olive oil next to it. It was the old-fashioned kind of icon made out of pressed gold metal that showed the shape of the Virgin's robes and her arms holding the little baby Jesus. There were holes in the metal where their faces peeked through in full color. Seeing the Virgin and Jesus made me feel better. It meant that the room was blessed and that they were watching over me. I got up and dragged the chair a little closer to the bed.

"You don't need the chair. Come sit on the bed." His face was smiling but his voice wasn't, and I knew I was never supposed to say no to an adult or else I would get in trouble. I clutched Doll close to my chest as I walked to the bed. He said, "Leave your doll on the chair." My *nouno* was the same but different. He was acting weird. If he'd been at our house, I wouldn't have hid his keys. I put Doll down on the chair. I made her sit up, facing the bed. Her eyes seemed blank, but it made me feel better to have her watching. I stood a foot away from the bed. He was still smiling. I noticed his eyes looked different: his eyelids were half shut, and I couldn't tell what they were saying. He grabbed my arm and pulled me onto the bed with him. I tried to sit up straight and fold my hands. The bed was high, and my feet dangled off of the side. Doll was looking straight at me. She looked scared.

He was saying, "I like your outfit" and rubbing my back. He slipped his hand under my shirt. My skin got all goose-pimply, and I tried to move so that his hand would fall out of my shirt. He laughed in this quiet way and kept rubbing my back. I tried to ask him again why he was sick, but he told me not to worry about that. I was so relieved when he took his hand out from the back of my shirt, but then he started to rub my chest and slipped his hand through the neck of my shirt. I was antsy, trying to move to get his hands off of me. My heart was feeling fluttery, and I looked at Doll to see what I should do. I wasn't supposed to say no to adults, but my stomach was starting to feel sick and Doll was so far away.

He laughed. "Heh, heh, heh, why are you moving around so much. Relax, relax, I won't hurt you." I tried to take deep breaths and stop moving around so much. He was my *nouno* who loved me and brought me presents. He was my *nouno* with his hand in my shirt, rubbing my chest, my little bumps that were new.

I said, "I think I smell something. I think something is burning in the kitchen. I better go check," and started to jump off of the bed.

He grabbed me back and said, "Nothing is burning in the kitchen," and shook his head no.

I looked up at the Virgin and baby Jesus above the bed, and they looked so calm. *It must be okay. It's okay.* I kept telling myself it was okay as he slipped his hand under my skirt. I thought I heard a noise in the house. I looked toward the doorway, my whole body alert. I think he heard the noise, too, because when I jumped off of the bed he didn't try to stop me. I grabbed Doll off of the chair and ran to the front door, pulled it open, and rushed out into the billowing fog.

The next day when I came home from school my mother told me that he had called. He said he had fun and wanted me to visit again. I told her I didn't feel well, I had homework, I didn't want to go, his breath smelled bad, I needed to clean my room, it was too cold, I wanted to stay home and help her make dinner. She whipped her head toward me and gave me a hard look, and I knew I couldn't say no. She would give him anything he wanted as long as he kept coming back to see her. That day I chose an old red turtleneck that went all the way up to my chin. I tucked it tightly into my long green pants. I put on my lace-up boots. I was covered from head to toe, and it would be impossible for any hands to slip into or under. I left my hair messy, and I told my mother one last time that I didn't feel well, so did I have to go? She told me to go comb my hair and hurry up, that he was waiting.

This time I didn't bring Doll or a coat or anything that I'd have to stop and grab before I left. I would go and sit on the chair and stay for five minutes, and then I would leave and everything would be different. Everything would be all right. Nothing would happen, and he wouldn't tell me to keep our little secret. He wouldn't tell me that he loved me the most and that was why he liked to spend time with me, so I should relax, relax. He wouldn't tell me not to tell, so that other people wouldn't get jealous that I was so special, relax, relax.

As I stood on the doorstep of their house I stopped and looked at the fog surrounding the house. It was hard to see through it, and the mist dotted my face, covering me with secrets—and I knew there was no escaping. Before I could ring the bell, the door opened and he was standing there wearing the same pajamas, his beard a little longer and his body smelling stronger. "Come on," he said and put his hand on my back to lead me down the dark hallway. "Come on. Hurry up." The house smelled like *avgolemono soupa,* hot and chickeny and lemony, and there was a light on in the kitchen.

"Is *Nouna* here?"

"She went to the store. Hurry up," he said and pushed me harder. He closed the door behind us and said, "I liked the little *fousta* you were wearing yesterday. Girls should always wear skirts."

He grabbed my arms and put me on the bed. This time he tried to make me lie down, but I didn't want to. He shoved his hand into my turtleneck, and the stretchy sweater gave in. He shoved his hand into my pants and the button snapped. He was in a hurry. He didn't tell me to relax, relax. This time he told me to be quiet and lie still. I didn't want to. I wanted to be in the kitchen with my *nouna*, making *avgolemono*, squeezing the juice out of lemons, beating the egg whites until they got foamy, slowly mixing in the hot broth so the eggs wouldn't curdle, stirring it all together in the big pot and watching the steam rise.

I thought I heard something, a key turning in a lock, her voice, the pot of soup boiling over and flooding the kitchen. I was praying, *please God help me*. He was hovering over me, and above him I could see the Virgin Mary, servant of God. She was holding Jesus tight. This time she didn't look calm. She looked angry. I could hear the kitchen roiling with surging waves of hot soup crashing against the walls, breaking down doors, burning tongues. I saw her lips move and she told me to say, "No!" and to kick him as hard as I could. When I did, he lost his balance and his hands slammed into the wall burning, and the Virgin came down and smashed him on the head.

I jumped off of the bed and burst open the closed door, running toward the glowing yellow light of the awakened kitchen. The pot of soup was festering, boiling over and sizzling as the tangy drops hit the flames. He tried to catch me, but the soup rose in a cyclone of hot fury blocking his path. Something was burning in the kitchen and I was breaking free. The secrets were too big for me to keep, and I never knew who to trust until I was saved by God and the kitchen.

AVGOLEMONO SOUPA

"I wanted to be in the kitchen, squeezing the juice out of lemons, beating the egg whites until they got foamy, slowly mixing in the hot broth so the eggs wouldn't curdle, stirring it all together in the big pot and watching the steam rise."

  1 chicken, approximately 3–4 pounds
  12 cups of water
  1 1/2 cups rice
  Salt and pepper to taste
  3 eggs
  Juice of two lemons

Place the chicken, legs up, into a pot with water and bring to a boil. Reduce the heat, and partially cover so that the chicken gently simmers. Skim any foam off the top of the broth. Simmer until the chicken is falling off the bone, approximately 1 1/2 hours. Remove the chicken from the pot. Pour the broth through a strainer into a large bowl.

Return the broth to the pot and bring to a boil. Stir in the rice and simmer until it is tender, approximately 15-20 minutes. Add salt and pepper to taste.

Separate the egg whites into a large mixing bowl. Beat them until they are frothy. Add the egg yolks and continue beating. Mix in the lemon juice. Remove the pot of broth from the flame. Ladle out a cup of broth and very slowly add it to the eggs, while continuously beating them until the eggs are tempered. Very slowly add the egg mixture into the cooking pot, while stirring continuously. Shred some chicken meat into the soup and serve.

The soup will have a beautiful foamy layer that floats over a tangy and aromatic broth.

Resurrection

After Manoli's baptism, I pass out the *martirika*, the small lapel pins made of blue ribbon with a cross at the center, to all the witnesses of the ceremony. Mrs. Horiatis proudly passes out the *bonbonieres*, as they were her selection, a porcelain white-and-gold baby bootie tied with blue satin laces and attached to a tulle pouch filled with sweet Jordan almonds. I stay at the reception long enough to appear normal. Gus and Callie present me with a pair of aquamarine earrings. They dangle from my earlobes heavily, constantly reminding me of their presence. I need to leave, to get away from this confounding situation. I thought that Manolaki's baptism might make me feel clean again, but instead it just inflamed my memories, and resurrected my shame. I offer my good-byes and pretend that my stomach hurts when they insist I stay. Mrs. Horiatis tells me to drink a 7-Up and stay. "Stay, stay," they say. I can't stay. I have to find a way to become clean again, to end this burning shame.

I get into my car and drive to Mills College. As I enter the college I let the beauty of the campus sink in. Someone is getting married in the chapel. The bride in her white dress stands by the grassy curb, a smile frozen on her face. Photographers kneel in a circle around her, flashing photos and asking her to pose just so. I drive past the scene and park the car on the wide road framed by gorgeous trees and climb the wood chip-covered slope to the swimming pool. Daring that no one will stop me, I start running toward the pool, dropping my clothing along the way until I am stripped down to my white panties and bra. I enter the gated swimming pool area and sneak past the entrance booth. The pool is shimmering. Each ripple of water reflects the brilliant sunlight and white clouds. As I enter the vast pool I hear a sizzling sound as I slowly step down the wide steps into the cool water, and I pray. I pray for removal of my sins, I pray for purity, I pray to be reborn and resurrected without shame. As the water rises over my hips and waist, above my breasts, I imagine that it is cleansing me. I beseech God to cleanse me of my past. I beg him to make me pure again. I don't dare ask for a virgin birth, because I know I don't deserve it. When the water covers my neck and head and my hair floats freely in the water, I hold my breath until I can hold it no longer. Closing my eyes, I pray for the strength to carry through and exhale through my mouth, pushing all of the oxygen out of my lungs and allowing the water to rush into my mouth.

I shake my head from side to side, struggling to die or live in peace. As I move my head from right to left I feel a tapping on my cheek and then again on the other side. The harder I shake, the stronger the taps. I am distracted long enough to pause in my struggle and lose my concentration, which forces me to rise to the surface. Gasping for air, my body suddenly goes cold, and I realize that I am still wearing the dangling aquamarine earrings from Callie and Gus. The pair of them saved me. The earrings tapped my face as if to bring me back to life, to bring me back to their family.

I float onto my back with my arms spread out wide forming a cross. I float. The gurgling sound of the water hypnotizes me as I lie on the water bobbing up and down. The sun warms my cold skin. I close my eyes against it. I decide to surrender to the will of the water. It carries my body, and for the first time I feel weightless. I feel clean. I have been resurrected.

Gus Grows Up

"Constantino!" Mrs. Horiatis yelled out into the house. Hearing no response, she tried again, "Constantino!" Then she heard the muffled response.

"Yes, *Mana*!"

She smiled. She loved her son. She loved him more than anything or anyone. "I need you, Constantino!" She heard his footsteps coming down the stairs, and felt the floor vibrate as he drew nearer.

"What is it, *Mana*?" Gus asked, out of breath.

"You're a good boy, Constantino." She smiled.

"Uh. Thanks?" Gus was rubbing some ink off of his fingers with a diaper wipe.

"And I love you."

Gus looked at his mother where she stood by the couch in front of the bay windows.

"I love you too, Ma." He put the diaper wipe down on the coffee table and gave his mother a big hug. "Thank you for coming to visit. I'm so glad you're here and that Manolaki is spending time with his *yiayia*."

"Constantino. I've decided it's time for me to go back home."

"But *Mama*, it's too soon. I think you should stay longer. There's no rush to leave."

Mrs. Horiatis drew Gus tightly into her embrace and was

surprised to feel his body quaking against hers, and the warm dampness of his tears against her cheek.

"I know, honey. But there is nothing else I can do here. Maybe I should let you find your own way, instead of interfering. You're a man now."

"I love it when you interfere. You're my mother. You're supposed to interfere."

"I know, *ayori mou*. My sweet boy." Gus's mother wiped his tears with the palm of her hand and hugged him tighter, holding his tears in her fist, treasuring them.

"Maybe if you stay longer, you'll get to know Callie better and it will all be okay."

"Constantino. It doesn't matter if I like Callie. You made your choice." Mrs. Horiatis found herself crying also. "I just want you to be happy. That's why I thought, maybe you and Xeni, you might have more in common than you thought. But now she is family, and that is that."

"Maybe we do have more in common than I thought, Mama, but I don't love Xeni. Not like that."

"I know that, *ayori mou*. I know." Mrs. Horiatis paused. "I was so proud to see you, my son, in church baptizing your baby boy. I can't believe that you've grown up so much. You're a man. I have to respect that you are a man and you make your own decisions. I just want the best for you."

"I know, Mama. But Mama, I don't want you to go. I want you to stay. You can stay in the guestroom for as long as you want. Please stay."

"No, Constantino. I realized when we were in the church that this is something that you have to do yourself. You have to decide if this is the life for you. I can't stay here to make it better or worse for you."

"But Mama—"

"No. If I stay, you'll be distracted by me. Maybe even comforted by me?" Gus's mother smiled, feeling vulnerable, and happy to know that her son did need her after all. "No. It will feel like home. You'll never find out if this is really your home, or if it is just a house. If I go, you will soon see."

Gus nodded, still wiping tears from his cheeks.

"Come on, come here. Sit with me on the couch and I'll sing you a little song." Gus's mother pulled him down next to her on the couch and put her arms around him, rocking him and humming a little song about fishing boats leaving the harbor, "*Vyaine varkoula, e varkoula tou psara, apo to pariyiali, varkoula, varkoula.*" Gus settled into his mother's arms.

"Mama?"

"Yes, sweetheart?"

"I love you, you know."

"I know, honey. I know."

Gus drove his mother to the airport on August 15. He couldn't believe that two months had already passed since her arrival. It seemed so long ago that he'd eagerly awaited his mother's arrival. It was almost four months since he had started pushing Callie to learn, to adapt, to change, to become Greek, all to please his mother. Callie had tried so hard, and yet his mother was leaving, still withholding her blessing. Manny was now nine months old and baptized. In a few months he would be a year old. Where had the year gone?

Gus couldn't understand why his mother had booked her flight for August 15. It was an important feast day for Greeks. It was the day that the Virgin Mary ascended to heaven, and a day they say all Greeks return home to celebrate. Her eminent departure left him feeling unmoored, but he was too embarrassed to ask her to stay again. He knew it was time to be a man. He escorted his mother to the security checkpoint, and as he embraced her one last time he felt as if he were choking with loneliness and the grief of not knowing when he would see her again. He fought the tears and the tight feeling in his throat and forced a smile onto his face, but was somehow comforted to see that she too was overcome by their parting. For once his mother was speechless, and yet Gus felt her immense love envelop him and comfort him even as he struggled to say good-bye. He waited by the windows until he was sure her plane had safely lifted into the sky. He ordered himself an ouzo at the airport lounge, and then another. He stayed there and drank, his mother's body lifted up closer to God, and he prayed for some clarity before he became sober enough to return home, where he knew that Callie and Manolaki waited.

The Virgin's Feast

Perhaps because it is August 15, or maybe because Gus took his mother to the airport and she wants to cheer him up, Callie decides to prepare a Greek meal that will comfort him, and perhaps rival anything that Mrs. Horiatis can make. It seems that Callie has still not learned that there is no woman on Earth that comes before a Greek man's mother. The spoiling, worshipping, and coddling that a Greek baby boy experiences ends only when his mother dies, and no sooner. No wife, and certainly not an American wife, can ever rival the unbridled selflessness of a Greek mother for her son, and that son's loyalty toward his mother.

Still, Callie insists on cooking, and she wants me to be their guest for the night. She plans the menu herself. Roast leg of lamb with potatoes, horiatiki salata, and tzatziki, accompanied by feta, olives, anchovies, and homemade bread. A simple meal for the accomplished Greek cook, it will be a good challenge for Callie. She plans to serve plenty of ouzo and retsina with the meal to blur Gus's thoughts of his mother soaring away from him toward God and homeland. Sometimes all it takes is a few bottles of alcohol to achieve miracles. Callie insists that she do all the cooking herself. She says she wants to cook dinner for me too, that I should just relax with the baby, and to just stop her before she makes any big mistakes.

Manny's plump body is lying on a flokati rug in the middle of the living-room floor when I get there. The shaggy rug looks like a marshmallow cloud fluffed around his sleeping body. I kneel down on the floor with a dull feeling in my chest and curl up next to him, studying his face while he sleeps. His cheeks, once so delectable and tempting, no longer move me. His thighs, with layers upon layers of juicy fat, leave me cold. His sweet red curls and chocolate-kiss eyes only make me sigh. I am losing my appetite for baby flesh, losing hope that I will ever bake a baby, losing faith that God will bless me, and becoming more sure every day that this curse of dead and disappearing babies will continue to follow me. I lie there listlessly staring at Manny until I slip into a fitful sleep punctuated by baby burps and clashing pot lids.

"Well, isn't that cute!" His booming voice makes the floor tremble with sarcasm. I startle awake to find Gus standing over me laughing, with a highball glass of cloudy ouzo on the rocks in his beefy fist, and an exaggerated wink that makes him look like a Cyclops. "I mean, it's the Virgin's holiday, and you look just like the Virgin Mary and baby Jesus. Maybe I should call you Virgin from now on." He laughs, winks again, and takes a swig of his drink. Manny has crawled into my arms while I slept and is snuggled against my chest. The whole tableau is humiliating. The Cyclops's baby crawled into my infertile arms as I slept and now the monster has returned to his lair to laugh at me.

"Hey, Virgin, is this what we're paying you to do? Take naps on our floor? Shouldn't you be helping the little woman with the cooking?" He grimaces and takes another swig of ouzo. "Lord knows she needs help," he slurs.

"You're drunk, Gus." I pull my arm out from under Manny's curly head and get up on my knees. Gus is talking but I'm not listening. All I can see is his big mouth making shapes. From his curly brown hair to his sturdy muscular frame to his big wide feet, he is a classic specimen. He is a grown Greek man, crying for his mother. His hairy chest heaves with each new wail, and the muscles in his legs and arms tense as he squats in his dirty diaper waiting for the next willing woman to clean the poop off of his olive-loving ass. I realize that I feel a little sorry for him. His mother is gone, and he can never have that mother and child kind of love again unless one of them travels halfway around the world to get it.

Callie calls out from the kitchen. "Hey you two, Manny is crying. Can one of you please pick him up?" I jerk out of my reverie long enough to see the Cyclops pick up his offspring and carry him off to the couch where the two of them settle in for a winter's nap. With the natural stone fireplace jutting behind them, they truly look as if they are settling into their cave, father and son. It makes me want Manny back in my arms, and suddenly my indifference for him disintegrates and the familiar barren ache returns.

Unable to watch them, I wander into the kitchen where Callie is frantically stabbing a leg of lamb, swearing under her breath, "Mother fucker, mother fucker, mother fucker."

"NO!" I yell. "Why are you mishandling the lamb?" The kitchen is a mess. There are dirty pans and bowls everywhere. Several of the white cabinet doors hang open. She is sweating, and her red hair is coming loose from its ponytail and falling into her eyes.

"STOP! I'm begging you. The lamb didn't do anything to you. You'll ruin it!"

Callie stops stabbing and throws the knife into the sink. "I'll never do it. I'll never be good enough! No matter how hard I try I always mess everything up. I just want one time to do something amazing and for it to work." Her blue eyes are so miserably sad. I take a towel and wipe the tears and lamb blood from her cheeks.

"No, you will never be good enough," I tell her. "You will never be good enough if you don't love your own ingredients more than your guest's appetite." I put down the cloth and take her hands in mine. "But you will always be good enough—for me." She pulls me tight into her arms. So tight that our knees knock together and I can smell the garlic on her fingers as they clutch me close, and it fills me with hunger.

"He's such an asshole. I kill myself trying to cook his favorite foods, and please his mother, and learn his culture, and make us a real family, and all he can do is smirk and come stomping in here drunk and insulting the way I'm making the lamb—which is actually one of the easiest Greek things to make! I just realized, all this time, I had it all wrong. He never cared about me. He only cared about his mother. And maybe I never really loved him. I just wanted a family for Manny. We'll never be a real family! I give up. He's only good for one thing."

I really don't want to know what the one thing is so I say, "Let's take a look at this poor lamb and see what we can do to save it." But before we turn to the lamb I impulsively kiss her cheek, and Callie smiles and I can feel her tension start to melt. We fill the deep cuts with whole cloves of garlic and then massage the lamb with a mixture of olive oil, salt, pepper, and Greek mountain-grown oregano. We peel and quarter brown russet potatoes, toss them in the same marinade and arrange them in the pan around the lamb where they will soak up the lamb juices while they bake. In the end they'll have a crispy golden exterior that yields a steamy, melting soft inner flesh. They are so good that burning your tongue and the roof of your mouth is a reasonable risk to take, eating them as soon as they come out of the oven, tossing them between greedy, burning fingers.

As the lamb bakes we prepare the other dishes and drink ouzo. Gus has fallen asleep on the couch with Manny slumbering on his broad chest. We are all a bit drunk. The sun is setting, and the sky is brilliant with jewel-toned clouds. Callie wanders through the house lost in thought, lighting candles and sipping from her frosty glass. I clean up the kitchen and keep an eye on the lamb. The house is silent except for the rising aroma of browning flesh and garlic, the clink of ice cubes.

I stand in the kitchen staring out of the arched window above the sink, my hands resting on the rim of the sink. I am caught in the brilliance of the sunset's shimmering edges and the looseness of the ouzo in my body. I don't resist when I feel the warmth of her arms wrapping around me, pressing me back against her body. The moment is unfamiliar and complete, a recipe without a name. I melt into her.

"Please forgive me," she whispers. "I wish I could make everything right. Simple. It's all been so complicated. It's like I've been trying to make the recipe for a family, and even though I have tried really, really hard, and I thought I had the ingredients I needed, it won't come together no matter what. But the truth is that you are the secret ingredient I've been longing for."

She pauses and turns me toward her so we are facing each other. She twines her fingers between mine and holds them close between our hearts. "But you. You make me feel like I can do anything. You make me feel like I can create miracles. More than anything, I want to make all your dreams come true. I think I know the right ingredients for a family now. Do you think you could ever trust me, mind, body, and soul?"

I don't know what to say. There is a certainty in her eyes that I've never seen before. I nod my head, looking down at our entwined hands, noticing how her slender, freckly fingers fit perfectly into my sturdy olive hands, like a warm béchamel sauce draped over grilled eggplant. I nod again. I understand. I understand wanting to try to make something happen against all odds, and I understand wanting something you aren't supposed to have. What I don't know about is this: her. But I do have to confess to myself and to God that she has entered my dreams of what could be. I slowly put my arms around her waist, pull her in closer, and whisper, "I wish you could make my dreams come true." I rest my head on her shoulder, and my body softens as the tears release.

Dinner is delicious. The lamb is tender. The velvety tzatziki burns our tongues with garlic and cool cucumber. We dip our bread into the tomato and olive oil juices in the bottom of the salad bowl and drink wine. The mavrodaphne is the perfect accompaniment to our dessert of vanilla ice cream with a syrup of sour cherries. The melting, sweet creaminess of the ice cream mingles lusciously with the tang of the fleshy cherries on our tongues. Gus is happy to be eating such a good meal and toasts me with his wine glass. "*Yias ta heria sou!*"

"You should be blessing your wife's hands, not mine. She prepared the meal." I am quite drunk and don't feel like holding back anymore.

"She's not my wife, don't you know? We're just living together." He laughs. "Hey, maybe *you* should be my wife! You cook just like my mother." He gestures toward me and accidentally knocks his wine glass over.

Callie shoves her chair back from the table and sits there staring at him. I turn to look at her and then back at him. *Callie and Gus aren't married? But they're Husband and Wife. I don't understand.*

"What! What! I'm just kidding! Can't you take a joke!?" *What is he joking about? Are they married or not? And how can he be so rude to her after everything she has done for him?* My knife is lying on the table inches away from my fingers. I want to grab it and cut his tongue out and feed it to the dogs. Instead I say, "Gus, you're drunk. Maybe it's time to be quiet."

"You're a real asshole. You know that? Thank God we aren't married!" Callie gets up from the table and starts to sop up the spilled wine. Callie is so mad she looks like she's going to cry, but all I can think is, *She's not married!*

"Oh, come on. Calm down. I'm just kidding. Come here. Let me give you a kiss." *His tongue isn't good enough for dogs. I'll feed it to rats.*

"You know, the only good thing you ever gave me was that baby. That's all you're good for!"

"Well let me give you another one then," he says as he reaches out and grabs her ass. *I will feed his tongue to a snake. It will open its jaws and swallow his fat tongue whole. Swallow him whole.*

Callie stands there staring hard at Gus for what seems like a long time, while rubbing her heart with her right hand and says, "*Let you give me another baby?*"

She turns to me and says, "Xeni, can you please put Manny to bed? I think Gus and I need a few moments in private. This won't take long."

Then she takes my hand and leads me out to the hallway and whispers, "I have an idea. Do you trust me?"

I stare into her eyes and realize that I do. "Yes, I trust you."

"After you put Manny to bed, I want to try something. Will you let me?"

I pause, unsure of what she has in mind. She reaches out to stroke my cheek, and her eyes are so round and intent, her blue eyes swimming with excitement and desire.

I whisper, "Yes, I trust you with my heart, my soul, and . . . even my body."

Callie kisses me on my lips and tells me she wants to make my dreams come true. I wander back into the dining room, still glowing from her kiss. I pull Manny out of his high chair and give him a long hug. I cling to his sweetness, and as I climb the stairs I can hear Callie and Gus start to spar, and my heart tightens.

"So you want to give me another baby?"

"Well, if that's all I'm good for!"

Their voices fade as I turn on the bathtub faucet. I give Manny a nice warm bath. Then I take him to his room and change him into a fresh diaper and his jammies and hold him while I sing. I put him in his crib and turn on the nightlight. I pull the trunk on his lullaby elephant, and sweet, tinny music fills the dusky room. Manny gurgles, all happy and sweet like a simmering pot of honey syrup, and I stand crisp and hard like a baked pan of baklava hot from the oven. If you try to cut the filo at that point, it will fragment into shards. But once you pour the honey syrup over the hot buttery filo and spicy walnuts it softens and becomes so sweet that you need a tall glass of water to bear it, and it makes all of the sharp edges go away. Manny melts me. I gently pinch his fat cheek and say, "*Tha se faw.*"

I shut Manny's door behind me and go to find Callie. As I

come down the stairs I hear a strange sound. It's coming from the living room, and like a highway motorist I can't stop myself from rubbernecking at the burning wreck. Gus is stretched out with his Cyclops head leaning over the back of the couch, gripping the beige chenille pillows with his lobster claws and groaning. Callie is on her hands and knees with her head pumping up and down over his lap like an old oil drill. I can't believe this is happening. Is it happening? We are all drunk. Very drunk. Maybe it is a joke. Maybe, maybe, maybe, maybe.

What do I expect? They're together, and who am I? A barren, forsaken, delusional reject of God. It didn't mean anything when she kissed me and said she wanted to make my dreams come true. I am a pathetic, confused person who at this moment wants nothing more than to vomit up every bite that I've ever eaten, every ounce of breast milk, and disappear back into the Earth's womb. *Stop*! I want to scream. *Stop touching him! Turn around and see me standing here!* God forgive me, I want her to grab me by the arms and kiss me with those rosy, cheating lips. I want her to touch me. To love me. To give me a baby. To prove her love for me. But instead she has her mouth on him.

Gagging, I stumble toward the front door, and almost make it there before the room starts to spin and I pass out on the spot.

The Promise

Callie sucked Gus's dick until she hit oil. As she predicted, it didn't take long. By the time she got to the bathroom, Gus's rumbling snore could already be heard from the couch. Callie knew she could either stop at that moment, or never turn back. She grabbed a floral Dixie cup and spit the sticky juice out. The first ingredient. Then she grabbed one of the needleless syringes that she used to give Manny his medicine and drew every last possible bit of the sperm up into it, and tucked it into her bra between her breasts. She grabbed her toothbrush and scrubbed her mouth and tongue clean. Staring into the bathroom mirror she saw a woman in possession of a miracle.

"Xeni! Where are you?" Callie ran upstairs to look for Xeni, but found only Manny slumbering in his crib. She wasn't upstairs. She wasn't in the kitchen or dining room. She wasn't in the bathroom. She certainly wasn't in the living room with Gus. Callie's heart was pounding at the sudden thought that Xeni had left. She hadn't taken into account that Xeni might leave before she could tell her what she'd done. She started to question her sudden inspiration. Maybe it wasn't such a good idea, but the ouzo and the commune baby in her piped up. *We are all one! If one of us really needs something, and someone else has it, we should share, right?"*

Just then she saw Xeni's body sprawled out on the carpet by the front door. Xeni looked like a virgin angel, her face peaceful, her dark eyelashes resting against her glowing cheeks.

"Xeni, wake up! Wake up!"

She was out cold. There could be no discussion. Callie hesitated. *Would she want this? What if she didn't know how it happened . . . what if her dream of a virgin birth could come true? What if she never forgives me?*

Callie could almost smell Ocean Beach as she remembered Xeni standing in front of the crashing waves and their conversation that day.

"I want a baby. More than anything. But more than that . . . I want a virgin birth. But I know now that will never happen. I know now that I'm crazy or not good enough. If I was good enough, God would have given me a miracle by now."

"You should be a mother. You will be a mother. If I have to do it myself, you will be a mother one day."

"If only you could."

Callie knelt down beside Xeni's body and gently touched her cheek. "I do. I do want to make all of your dreams come true— even your dream of a virgin birth. You *are* good enough. You do deserve a miracle, more than anyone I know."

Callie exhaled deeply, suddenly unsure. She knew she had to decide quickly. *Dear Universal Spirit and all that is good, please guide my hand. Please give me a sign. Should I proceed?* She felt a vibration in her heart. Callie brought the syringe out from between her breasts. It was still warm and glowed with an unearthly hue. Callie felt a surge of energy shoot through her arm, illuminating her tattoo of the Virgin Mary, and down into her right hand. The air seemed to sparkle with a million particles of light. *Please help me give Xeni the baby and the love she deserves. I will always give her the best of me. So mote it be.* She brought the syringe closer to Xeni, hovering over her womb. She paused to stroke Xeni's face and tucked her dark hair behind her ear. Callie placed her right hand on Xeni's heart and whispered, "I love you. The right hand can perform miracles. Please trust me. Please forgive me." And with the very best intentions Callie tried to create the miracle that she'd promised Xeni at the beach.

A Soul

As the plunger of the syringe presses forward, millions of sperm enter the pink confines of the vagina and cluster themselves around the cervix. As if on cue, the cervix folds in upon itself and sucks the sperm up into its mouth. From there the sperm start the great race into infinity. Some swirl through the dark liquid atmosphere in a slow, undulating dance following some intuitive pattern toward the open path. Others dart forward in a headlong rush toward dead-end crevices of magenta flesh or swim in frantic cyclones trying to find a way through thick impenetrable walls. Several thousand ride the flush of the syringe all the way up into the long dark pathways leading to the round and illuminated prize.

Only hours before, the egg had rested within a follicular bubble bathing in the magical hormonal liquor that nurtured its growth. The incubus had finally grown so big that it burst, propelling the tiny pearl of DNA into a boundless, bloody universe where it floats in suspension, only to be caught by the long fluttering sleeve of a fallopian tube. Like slow magma, it rolls down in infinitesimally small increments undetectable to the naked eye toward a predetermined meeting place. And waits.

Some sperm die along the way, their fast push wearing them out too quickly. Others are weak and disabled by some disorder of their genetics and never have a chance to make the long trek. And some, like the old tortoise, advance slowly and surely toward the finish line.

Perhaps there is a weak signal transmitted, or it is all random chance which swimmers reach the prize, or some common mystery that determines the outcome. But at some fateful moment, sperm meets egg and the first penetration begins. But it is their heads that lead the way and not their tails, their heads that hold the key to melt the hard exterior of the egg. Or perhaps it is the egg that decides when to melt and let one in. In any case, it is the first taste of power that the egg experiences as the sperm cluster around her, surrounding her, and her first taste of fear. She picks just one to merge with and then the others are shut out forever, her hard shell reinforced. It is those other immigrants that eventually die alone in a foreign land, that forever carry sadness and lost hope.

Tumbling, merging, multiplying, the two opposites that become one expanding whole begin a long journey together through unknown terrain to find a place to nest. Along the way they must make few mistakes and surrender to the instinctual processes of biology, trusting that they will end at a beginning and thus begin an ending. Seven days and seven nights transpire until they find fertile ground, a vast network of bloody nutrients, spongy vessels within which to burrow and grow. As they nose their way into the perfect spot, their efforts release the transforming enzymes that help them to break ground and spring deep roots into their resting spot, their nest. The symbiotic nature of their host allows them to thrive and relax, and somewhere along the way they become one, someone. A soul.

Xeni Leaves the Building

I wake up the next morning with a terrible pulsating headache. I am lying on the couch in the living room with a pillow under my head and a blanket covering my fully clothed body. I have no idea how I got there and only vaguely remember passing out somewhere in the hallway in my frantic rush to get out of the front door and back home and away from my horny hosts. I suppose I should be grateful that they didn't leave me there on the floor, but feel uneasy imagining how I got to the couch. Did Gus pick me up in his hairy arms and carry me? I shudder. I doubt that Callie is strong enough to get me to the couch by herself. I comfort myself with the thought that maybe I got to the couch on my own, but can't exactly remember everything that happened the night before. But why would I choose to sleep on the couch where *it* happened?

I rub my neck and head and say a little prayer under my breath, "Please Lord, forgive me for drinking too much wine. I wanted to leave as soon as the debauchery began. Why'd you make me pass out anyway?" But the more I think about what happened the night before in the living room the madder I get. "And why did you let them do *that* while I was here?" I know I'm not supposed to be mad at God, but I'd be much happier if I could've made it home last night. I could have gotten between my clean white sheets, snuggled Doll next to me, said a little prayer of forgiveness, and woken up at home this morning instead of in Cyclops's lair, having to face his lascivious wife who says she loves me and then does dirty things to him right in front of me.

I yank off the blanket and sit up. Moving too fast makes my head hurt. It is still early. I can't hear anyone moving around so I grab my coat and head for the door. I vow never to come back.

An Empty House

The house held still that morning, as if holding its breath. One Greek mother had left in defeat. A Greek virgin had left in a storm. The combined energy of their emotions was enough to blow any house off of its foundation. Tightening its grip on the bolts that held it firmly onto the earth, the house shuddered, willing its foundation to hold. The stilts it balanced on trembled—imperceptively to humans, but the constant rumbles were unnerving to the structure.

On the outside, the house looked fine. It stood upright at correct angles. The windows gleamed with reflected sunlight. The paint, though a few years old, still presented a neat and attractive façade. The cracks were beneath the house in the dirt on which it stood. And despite the sunny outward appearance, on the inside the house felt chilled, as if the heart and soul of it had departed for some other place, and what was left were the muted wanderings of ghosts.

Gus walked from room to room looking for his mother, knowing that she was gone. He imagined her body in an airplane 30,000 feet above the Earth, transporting her to another life, another time zone. With a feeble smile, he imagined her giving the flight attendants a hard time because the food was cold or her pillow lumpy. But the truth of the matter was that when his mother was away, Gus felt cold and lonely, as if her fiery temper and blazing eyes, the things that most infuriated him, also kept him warm.

When she left to go back home, she took the blazing heart of Greece with her. He was left all alone in *xenitia*, the land of strangers.

Gus pressed "play" on the stereo and a mournful tune began, the drumbeat slow and steady, the bouzouki somber. "*Mi me stelnis Mana, stin Ameriki.*" Words he'd heard over and over growing up, when his mother would sadly sing, "Don't send me, Mother, to *Ameriki.*" He imagined the multiplicity of immigrants who'd sat alone in a small room nursing an ouzo and their heartache, singing those words. Gus stretched out his arms and began to dance the *zeibekiko*, the soulful dance of Greek men, the physical expression of pain and survival, loss, and enduring spirit.

Upstairs, Callie lay curled up in the massive bed, unable to get warm. She pulled the comforter up closer to her chin, and then the throw blanket, and then piled all the pillows up over her shivering body. Her nipples felt like hard stones and she hugged herself, rocking, trying to find a way to soften. She knew without looking that Xeni had left the house, was gone, maybe forever. And she knew that she'd betrayed Gus.

Clutching at whatever warmth she could, Callie knew that she'd sacrificed everything in one night.

Melting

Everything is wrong. My face is wrong. My body is wrong. My desires are wrong. I've spent the last four months in a house with a family that is not my own. They will never be mine. They are a family. They are loyal to each other even when they are fighting or unhappy. Maybe that is what a family is. But I don't want to fight. I want peace, and I pray to God that one day I will find it.

The kitchen is empty. I've been stocking their refrigerator and neglecting my own. There is nothing, nothing to cook, and I need to cook. Ripping the kitchen apart, I find almost nothing to work with. A cube of butter, some oil, a bag of chocolate chips, some nuts. Dumping the chocolate chips into a glass bowl, I stick it into the microwave. No. That's too easy. I pull a pot out of the cupboard, and a metal bowl. I fill the pot with an inch of water and put it on the stove to simmer. While the water heats, I arrange the chocolate chips in a concentric pattern within the circumference of the silver bowl in ever-expanding circles. Round and round. Placing the pointed tips at just the right angle requires enormous concentration. If I place one incorrectly, it will tumble into the center, and I have to put my fingers into the sharp bed of chocolate tacks to extract it. And if I think about Callie, I have to press my fingers into the points. I work on this until the water starts to bubble, and then I stand over the fire gently stirring the brown nibs until they lose all shape and melt into a warm, amorphous mass.

At the Table

Gus sat at one end of the table and ate the stack of *souvlakia* that he'd picked up at Simply Greek that afternoon. He'd bought enough of the skewers of meat to last him a few days. As he tore a chunk of meat off of the skewer with his teeth, he stole a glance at Callie, who sat huddled at the other end of the table eating a huge bowl of macaroni and cheese. Since Xeni had left, Callie had refused to make any more Greek food and had fallen into eating only Americana comfort food, meatloaf with mashed potatoes and gravy, chicken with dumplings, and pie—every kind of pie Gus had ever heard of and more. "Who makes buttermilk pie?" he asked her one afternoon as she stood over her mixing bowl adding ingredients. She had given him an exasperated look and had kept mixing.

Gus couldn't understand why Xeni had left and never come back. She was his *koumbara* now, Manny's godmother, and she wouldn't return his phone calls. Callie refused to talk about it. He rubbed his forehead. He had gone from having three willful, vocal women at the table to this new reality of sitting in silence literally overnight. He wished he could remember what had happened after he dropped his mother off at the airport, but it was a blank hole in his memory. All the ouzo and retsina had burned the events of the evening out of his mind. Whatever happened had changed everything, and Gus missed all the willfulness, the home cooking, and the ruckus at the table.

The Inside

Chocolate when melting loses its form, but you can mold it into whatever shape you want, as long as you keep the temperature at the right level, and keep water out of it. If you add even one drop of water, the tempered chocolate seizes and is ruined. So steam, condensation, and sweat are all enemies of chocolate. I spend my time with chocolate in the kitchen and learn everything I can about it. I seldom leave the house except to buy more chocolate and some groceries to keep me going. And I stay away from people whenever possible.

Once I master tempering chocolate, then I learn to mold it, control it. Truffles are easy to make, as are solid chocolates. The filled chocolates are harder. I never knew that enrobing something in chocolate required such skill. My stomach is growing from all of the chocolate I have eaten, and sometimes growls and kicks in a way that makes me wonder if there is such a thing as too much chocolate.

I don't think about anyone anymore. I am safe here in my kitchen, filling chocolate molds with fondant centers flavored with strawberries, walnuts, and bergamot. After I tap the filled chocolates out of the molds and line them up on a platter, I guess at what they each contain. It's not unlike the childhood habit I had of pushing my fingernail through the bottom of each chocolate in the box reserved for company. Only then, if I didn't like the filling, I'd leave it in the box. The bottom of the chocolate would be crushed, allowing the filling to ooze out, but the top looked perfect. I need to know what is inside. I dissect each piece using my fingernails and teeth, my tongue and lips, devouring the outside layer to get to the filling inside, the mystery and surprise of life.

There are those moments when I involuntarily remember a moment or my body shakes from allowing some words to slip back into my heart. I see blue eyes floating above the flames on the stove at times. But dipping your fingers into melting chocolate quickly erases all other thoughts.

Surrender

"Callie!" She heard Gus speak her name for the first time in weeks.

"What?" Callie yelled from the opposite side of the house.

"What are we doing?"

"I don't know."

"Do you want to go see a movie?"

"No. Do you want to go to the park?"

"No."

Callie looked out the bedroom window and then back to the bed. Each time she did laundry she laid all of her clothes out on the bed as if she were packing for a trip. Then she'd sit and stare at the piles and wonder.

Gus suddenly opened the door to the bedroom. Callie startled at the unexpected intrusion and guiltily began to gather her clothes.

"Hey, Cal. I think I need to go on a fishing trip or something with the guys. You okay with that?"

"Yeah. Yeah. Go ahead. I'll be fine." Callie pulled drawers open and stacked the clothes inside.

"Okay, I think I'll go. See what it feels like to be back out there."

"Yeah. Okay. Just let me know when you're going."

"I will," Gus promised.

"What are you fishing for?" Callie asked.

"I don't know. I just want to eat some great fish by the water and drink a cold beer, like I used to."

"Sounds good." Callie closed her drawer. "I think I might want to do something different too."

The Outside

The chocolate has made me enormous. I cannot hide the fact that I have become a huge woman in the last eight months. I clothe myself with long, flowing dresses and oversized shirts. But when I take off my clothes at night I can't help but stare in the mirror at my body. My legs and arms have remained the same, but my stomach has bulged out farther than I would think possible. Maybe I'm imagining it. My eyes are playing tricks on me. I close my eyes and use my hands to touch the outline of my belly. I refuse to admit that I look—I look almost pregnant. And what kind of joke is that, God? But it can't be. I cannot be pregnant. That doctor told me so. And no matter how hard I try to forget the words *hysterical pregnancy,* they are burned into my skin with the ink of humiliation.

I wish that I could see myself from the outside, instead of always through my insides. I see myself through a haze of self-pity and disgust. All I can see clearly is chocolate. And so it makes perfect sense, doesn't it, to go into the kitchen, melt several pounds of chocolate, and slather it onto my belly, and then stand in front of the open freezer door until the chocolate cools and hardens. It makes perfect sense that I would be able to lift the cast of my stomach away from my skin and take a good look at it. What doesn't make any sense at all is what I see: a baby belly.

Greek Festival

As Gus drove down Lincoln Avenue toward The Greek Orthodox Cathedral of the Ascension, he was once again dazzled by the church's copper dome as it stood solidly in the center of spring. All around it evidence of faith sprouted. A new parking structure for 220 vehicles, with a roof turned *platea*—an 18,000-square-foot plaza of additional space to celebrate Hellenic culture—and a glass elevator from which worshippers and revelers could view the splendor of the San Francisco Bay spanned by the Bay Bridge and fiery Golden Gate. And its crowning achievement, the new glass-domed Koimisis chapel celebrating the bodily ascension of the Virgin Mary to heaven. Unfinished, it stood resolutely awaiting interior adornment, with cement walls and stained-glass windows washed with sunlight from the elevated glass dome. The vault of the dome seemed to create a meeting place that lifted one up into the heavens and seemed to bring God closer to Earth to view the happenings.

Gus imagined that if God was watching that day, he'd see thousands of people streaming onto the grounds to indulge in Greek culture; to dance to live music on two stages; to eat lamb freshly roasted on the spit; to drink beer, ouzo, and Greek coffee; and to stuff themselves with loukoumathes until they burst from the yeasty fried dough drizzled with honey, cinnamon, and walnuts. The Oakland Greek Festival was a weekend of indulgence, a celebration of earthly delights, in the center of which stood the

293

cool-aired church, silent and embracing, and now the Koimisis chapel, a symbol of transformation, a place where one motherly human voyaged from one state of being to another.

Challenging the peacefulness of the chapel, speakers blared the sound of the bouzouki and drums, and the accented lyrics of Greek American singers. Each year costumed church youth danced traditional steps from the homeland, but devoid of the suffering that gave the old-timer-immigrant gyrations depth and soul. It was good to move on, and also sad. The letting go of sadness can be a trial in itself, the forgetting of the beauty and nobility of struggle and the devolution of culture into fragmented memories and piecemeal re-creation. The ache of those that remember how it was and the blissful forgetting of the future. Until it all comes full circle again and one generation remembers that something is lost, and begins to study its history as a foreign language, dance steps full of longing for what is lost. What is re-created is something new again, bearing little resemblance to the past. And once again we seek a way to voyage between homelands.

Gus parked his car in the new parking structure, gladly paying fifteen dollars to avoid pushing Manny's stroller up the steep hill of Lincoln Avenue to the festival. He glanced at Callie, who sat quietly in the passenger seat with a familiar preoccupied expression on her face. Gus's heart beat in rhythm with the music filtering through the cement and rebar of the parking structure. They were three floors below the live band, and Gus felt as if his feet were already on the rooftop *platea* weaving through the crowd hand in hand with other Greeks in a rite of bodily remembrance. He could smell the souvlakia crisping over hot coals and the burbling oil of the loukoumathes pots. His stomach tightened and he realized that he wasn't breathing.

He missed his mother. He missed Greece. He missed everything that was aggravating about growing up a child of immigrants. He had cleaned his life of the vigilance of diaspora and had left very little of the past intact. The festival was a joyous and painful reminder of all that he'd lost in the transplantation. The music called to his body, bypassing his mind and all the tangles there. With his heart beating faster, he opened the car door and leapt out, suddenly needing to be up in the sunlight holding the hand of another Greek in dance.

He looked over at Callie in the passenger seat as she checked her eyeliner in the visor mirror and fluffed her hair. "Hey, Callie. Can you hurry it up? They're gonna sell out of the lamb if we don't get up there quick." Gus couldn't tell Callie what he was really feeling, a separation from her and the life they'd fallen into. Callie, with her blazing red hair and fair skin. Callie who had tried so hard but would never be Greek. It wasn't fair to ever think she could be, Gus thought. He watched her apply more makeup and could hear his mother's voice in his head. "*Vameni san putana.*" Gus pushed the cruel comparison to a painted whore from his mind and tried again. "Hey, Cal. What's the hold-up?"

"Just a minute. Give me a minute. Okay?" Gus got out of the car, released Manny from his car seat, and gave him a hug while he waited. "Ready, little guy?" Gus and Callie rode the ascending glass elevator in silence, their backs turned to the expansive view. Callie held Manny in her arms, while Gus rested his hands on the handles of the empty stroller. Two perfumed older ladies stood near them making faces at the baby, trying to get a smile. Manny studied them seriously and without comment.

"Oh look at that red hair!" one of them said.

"Oh, he must be Irish," the other responded.

"How darling." They nodded and smiled at Callie. "How old is your little . . . boy?" said the lady with the silk flower tucked into her lapel.

"He's about eighteen months." Callie smiled at the ladies.

"Oh, how precious," said the one with the unconvincing wig.

Gus interrupted, "He's Greek. He's not Irish. He's Greek." He shifted his weight and squeezed the handles of the stroller, gritting his teeth.

"Oh really! I never would have known! What a lucky little boy. I wish I was Greek! Do you like to eat spinach pie?" the wig lady chortled. Gus rolled his eyes, wishing Callie would stop trying to get Manny to smile at the old ladies.

The elevator doors opened onto the *platea* swarming with bodies, the gyro booth to the left and the main stage far to the right as they passed through the ticket booth. Panoramic views of the Bay Area surrounded the festivalgoers, and Gus was glad to get away from the old women and enter the throng. He gravitated toward the stage where the musicians were playing spirited dance classics. As he approached, he spotted the usual awkward folk dance enthusiasts taking up center stage, while on the margins the Greeks danced in their own circles, politely escaping the bumbling steps and eager smiles of the folk dancers. The folk dancers had their own culture, with men sporting Greek fisherman's hats and the women wearing embroidered peasant blouses with ruffled cotton gauze skirts from the Greek tourist vendors. They drank in the local color and with comfortable unawareness danced in too-wide circles, leading their pack into all corners of the dance floor, crowding into the Greeks. Then there were the average festivalgoers of every ethnic heritage imaginable, mostly walking about with fists full of food and drink, their bodies soaking in the music and bustle of the festival. For the most part, Gus felt good to see so many different people interested in his heritage, and he walked proudly among the festivalgoers as if he personally were hosting them.

The music was infectious. Gus could feel the drums in his belly and the bouzouki in his feet. He turned to Callie. "Give me the baby."

Callie held Manny a little tighter. "How come?"

"Give me the baby. I want to dance with him. I want him to feel this music in his body. I want him to really feel it."

"Okay. Let's dance." Callie started toward the dance floor, holding Manny close to her.

"No. Someone has to stay with the stroller." Gus wanted to dance with Manny. He wanted to hold him in his arms and repeat the steps he'd been dancing since he was a child. He wanted the baby to absorb the rhythms into his soul so that for the rest of his life he would involuntarily respond with joy when he heard the sounds of Greek music. Gus wanted to dance. Just him and Manoli.

Callie reluctantly handed Manny to Gus and turned away to find a parking spot for the stroller. Gus held Manny in his muscular arms and danced to the music. Manny's mouth was wide open in a smile, and Gus looked into the baby's eyes while he sang to the music. Gus hadn't felt so happy in a very long time.

Gus closed his eyes and sang, holding Manoli close to him. The old songs took him back to childhood, going to the Greek Taverna in North Beach with his parents: dancing the *hasapiko*, watching belly dancers, and sitting on a table while a Greek man lifted and spun the table in the air with his teeth. Gus would hold on tight and watch the room spin 'round, the blue and white of the Aegean, and the darkness of the American nightclub. His parents wouldn't fight on those nights, and they'd applaud as he danced in his little black patent leather shoes, impressing the crowd. He loved the music and the smell of lamb roasting, and the boisterous shouts of the men who'd drunk too much ouzo and yelled "*Spasta ola!*" They threw plates to the ground, smashing them in a gesture of pleasure, abundance, and wholeness—a moment when all of the humiliations of immigrant life faded away and the glory of *Ellatha* returned. *Kefi.* The state of being when all your troubles vanish and you are filled with an expansive freedom that lifts you spread-eagled into the heavens.

Gus was reaching that place when Callie stepped up to him and said, "I don't want to watch the stroller while you dance. I want to dance, too."

"Fine. Go ahead," Gus said, continuing to dance with Manny.

"I want to dance with you, Gus. And Manny." Callie grabbed Gus's hand and attempted to follow him around the dance floor. She studied his feet as he moved ahead of her in their tiny circle. "Hey, Gus. Are you doing the right steps? I can't follow you."

Gus rolled his eyes. "Yes, I'm doing the right steps." *I can't help it if you can't follow*, Gus thought, and tried to lose himself and Manoli in the music once more.

"I don't think you're doing the right steps, Gus."

Gus looked at Callie. She was beautiful, with her red hair curling around her soft neck, but at that moment he hated her. "I am doing the right steps. I'm just taking small steps so that I don't put Manoli's ears right into the speakers." *That is exactly why the Greeks avoid the folk dance enthusiasts.* Gus grimaced. *They want you to lead them, and then they get mad when they can't follow. They have no awareness of space, or judgment when they dance. They see only themselves and their own desires. Then they want to lead the Greeks.* "Callie, if you don't think I'm doing the right steps, maybe you should dance with someone whose steps you like better."

"I don't want to dance with someone else. I want to dance with you. I just want you to show me the steps."

"But if I'm showing you the steps, then I'm no longer dancing with Manoli, see?" Gus stopped dancing, standing still at the edge of the dance floor. As Callie and Gus argued back and forth, the music came to a stop, and the crowd applauded the band. Gus stonily walked toward the stroller and their baggage, while Manny twined his fingers through Gus's wavy brown hair and squealed, "Dada!"

As they wound their way through the crowds, looking at tables of goods and possible foods to consume, and for people they might know, Callie was delighted to see that the church had installed a new playground. "Hey look, Gus. There's a playground. Let's take Manny in there."

"Yeah. That's nice. But let's take him into the church first."

"I think he'd have more fun in the playground. Look at that slide!"

"You know what? Fine. You take him to the playground while I go get something to eat."

Callie winced at Gus's terse tone of voice. "Don't you want to be together?"

"I'm hungry. Do you want something?"

"Well, I wanted to have fun today. . ." Callie pouted.

"But do you want any food?"

"No. I don't want anything." Callie wasn't even sure if she was hungry, but she didn't want to accept anything from Gus in that moment. Gus tried to open the gate for Callie to enter the fenced-in playground, but she pushed inside with the stroller herself while avoiding his eyes.

"Okay then," Gus snorted as he walked toward the lamb sandwich booth.

Callie turned toward the playground, Manny in her arms. There were at least a dozen children sliding, hanging, and jumping off of the play structure, and the sun was blazing on the dark rubber tile floor. There was little shade except for one spot beneath two olive trees growing side by side. The playground was situated between the two performance stages, and the sound from the live bands and the jumpy house across the way was deafening. Manny squirmed as he watched Gus walk away through the chain-link fence, calling out to him, "Dada!" but Gus didn't hear.

Callie shivered despite the warm sunlight and decided to go park the stroller in the corner while Manny played in the dirt between the two olive trees. She fiddled with the baby bag in the basket of the stroller, grabbed her compact mirror, and took a quick look before scanning the crowd for a familiar face. She wondered if Xeni would be there, and reapplied her lip gloss. It had been months since they'd seen each other. Months since the night that Callie had attempted to bring about a miracle for Xeni, interminably long months of wondering and waiting. She found herself nervous, but hopeful that the day would bring a reunion.

As much as Callie wanted to see Xeni, she was afraid of what her reaction would be. The possible rejection. Or the possibility that she wouldn't even be there at all, and she'd be left playing all of her mistakes over again in her head, bathed in regret, while cheery partygoers danced all around her.

Manny lifted his arms for Callie to pick him up and pointed toward the fence enclosing the play area. As she brought him closer, he leaned forward and she realized he was trying to climb onto the fence. He stepped on her chest and arms to reach the fence. His soft leather shoes left imprints on her white blouse, and in his zeal he stepped onto her face and hair. "Manny! Ouch!" He was gripping the fence with all his might, and Callie felt embarrassed that she couldn't pull him away without him issuing screams of protest. She felt the disapproving looks of the old Greek women in black as they walked by. She was tired of being stepped on, but she didn't know how to stop him. She tried to pull Manny down, but he dug his feet into her chest and howled. "All right. All right," said Callie, giving up, her eyes filling with tears. It was hot, and loud, and humiliating, and Callie wanted nothing more than a comforting hug. But no one there wanted to hug her, which made her even sadder.

Callie was still standing at the fence with Manny tenaciously clinging to the wire when she finally saw Gus returning with a half-eaten lamb sandwich.

"Sorry it took so long—the lines . . ." Gus trailed off, noticing Callie's tears.

"I'm so sick of being trapped in this little cage!" Callie cried.

"Okay. Okay. Let me finish this sandwich and we'll go. Want some?" Gus offered a bite.

"No. I want to get out of this cage and walk around. I want to be free."

Gus took a last bite of his sandwich and shrugged, "Okay, let's walk."

With Gus carrying Manoli, they walked past the countless vendor booths offering hand-painted bowls, worry beads, T-shirts, and signs stating, "PARKING FOR GREEKS ONLY." They paused at booths offering tiropita, frappe, loukanika, and cala-mari. There was a booth for the Greek School, and Gus said, "Let's send Manny there once he's old enough." Callie shrugged. There were sunny oil paintings of Greek islands with white-washed churches with blue domes that matched the color of the azure sea. Callie paused at the vendor booth that showcased cotton gauze skirts and billowy blouses and turned away as if she'd caught a whiff of a cornucopia of fruit gone rotten.

"They always have the same things here," Callie said.

"It's only your second time at the Greek Festival. How would you know? There's always something new here," replied Gus.

"Show me something that's new," challenged Callie. "It's the same, the same as last year; nothing changes."

"They're selling those hip wrap things with the coins on them now. Seems like you'd be excited about that." Callie didn't appreciate Gus's sarcastic tone. He used to like watching her dance, the coined hip wrap chiming with each pop of her hips. Now he seemed to be mocking her. Two preteen girls ran past wearing the jingling wraps, followed by a middle-aged woman yelling after them, "Come back here, youth!"

"They had those last year." Callie eyed Gus, holding Manny in his arms, and wondered how life could feel so stagnant in the middle of spring. Despite the festive music, beautiful weather, and opportunities for feasting, Callie felt bereft. "Let me hold the baby."

"I'm holding him."

"I see that. I want to hold him. I need to hold him." Callie's face was flushing a hot burn. Manny held out his arms to his mother and pointed to her eyes, now glistening.

"What's up with you today?" Gus handed the baby to Callie with exasperation.

"Show me something new. I need to see something new." *I need to see Xeni.*

"How about we go to the *Kafenion* and have a cup of coffee and *galaktoboureko*?" suggested Gus.

"That's not new!" Callie shouted.

The crowd of festivalgoers bumped into Callie and Gus as they stood blocking the stream of foot traffic.

"Christ, Callie! Would you get a grip? You're freaking out the baby."

"Am I freaking you out, Manny honey? Mommy didn't mean to scare you. Mommy's just having a hard day."

"Seems like you've been having a lot of those lately."

A woman in her fifties wearing a depressed frown and coined

hip wrap bumped into Callie, nearly throwing her off of her feet. The clash of the gold coins hit Callie like a slap into the future. "I *want* to be happy. It's just that . . ." Callie paused, unsure whether today was a good day for telling the truth.

"Come on, Cal. Let's go get a cup of coffee," Gus interrupted. Callie gave up and followed Gus into the *Kafenion*. The cool room was a relief after the hot sun. She noted that, like last year, there was a cooking demonstration booth set up in the front of the room, near the entrance in front of the floor-to-ceiling windows. Tables with white cloths were set up throughout the room where festivalgoers were dining on desserts and coffee. Along one side of the room was a glass case filled with classic Greek sweets, and behind it was a team of church matrons standing at the ready to serve the confections. Adjacent to the dessert case was a long table where they could order Greek coffee and pay for their confections. Callie and Gus joined the line of people waiting to order their desserts.

"What do you want?" Gus asked. "To eat?" he added.

"It's all the same."

"What's your favorite? Everyone has a favorite."

"It's all the same, same as last year," Callie sulked.

"That's the point, Callie. It's the same every year. One time a year, everyone comes here and gets to look forward to the same things that they can't get for the rest of the year. I'm having *galaktoboureko*. Manoli, what do you want?" Gus squeezed Manny's cheek and chuckled.

"I never learned to make that."

"Well, if Xeni hadn't run off without a word, then maybe you would have learned."

"It's not her fault."

"Okay, let's not get into this again."

"Fine."

"Look, it's going to be our turn. There's only one person ahead of us. What do you want?" said Gus, impatiently.

"Baby Belly."

"Huh?"

"Baby Belly. What does that sign say? Baby Belly?" Callie stretched up onto her tiptoes to see the sign perched atop the glass case, with a neat stack of brown boxes tied with gold ribbons next to it. Gus looked ahead and saw the large, sage green sign with brown lettering. There was a mighty plant trailing up the left side of the sign bearing something unexpected: chocolate babies.

"Well, that's new," Gus snorted.

"What is it? I can't see!" Callie gripped Manny tighter and tried to see past Gus.

"There's a sign. And there's a plant on it, with fruit hanging off. They look like some kind of chocolate babies?"

"Chocolate babies? What kind of chocolate babies?"

"Is there more than one kind? Well, actually, according to this sign, there is more than one kind." Gus chuckled. "It says:
'Baby Belly
Sumptuous Chocolate Baby Bellies of All Colors,
Filled with Unanticipated Flavors.
Eat a Baby Today!'"

Just then one of the Greek matrons asked, "May I help you?" and Callie waited as Gus ordered an assortment of Greek desserts, one piece of *galaktoboureko* to eat on the spot and four pieces to go, in addition to two melomokarona, two kourabiethes, two diples, and four baklava.

"What about the Baby Bellies?" Callie cried.

"What about them?"

"We have to get the Baby Belly chocolates."

"That's not Greek!" Gus protested.

"If they aren't Greek, then why would they be selling them here?" Callie volleyed.

"*Kyria*, can you please tell me . . . what are the Baby Bellies?" Gus asked the church volunteer politely.

"Oh, *pedie mou*. They are *sokolates*. I don't eat *sokolates*."

"But are they Greek?" Callie asked.

"A Greek lady makes them. And the fillings, they have Greek

303

flavors and ingredients, like walnuts, pomegranate, Metaxa cognac, bergamot, and mastica. Except one, that is her specialty. One is not so Greek, with *fraoules*."

"What are *fraoules*?" Callie asked.

"Strawberries. She makes one with strawberries and rhubarb."

Callie's scalp prickled. "Who is this woman who makes the chocolates?"

"I don't know her name. I think she maybe makes cooking demonstration later. Look in the festival program."

"Do we have a festival program, Gus?"

"Anything else for you?" asked the church volunteer.

"I'll have a box of the Baby Belly chocolates!" Callie exclaimed and tickled Manny's stomach. "Did you hear that, honey? Baby Bellies!" Manny gurgled at his mother's tickling and said, "Da!" The church matron handed Callie a box of chocolates from atop the counter, a sturdy brown box with a clear lid, filled with chocolates in the shape of babies—babies lying on their backs, their plump bellies announcing themselves. There was dark chocolate, milk chocolate, white chocolate, pink chocolate, and tan chocolate. The grinning babies lay in a row, side by side as if in a nursery, resting on pink, blue, and lavender tissue paper. "Look, honey. Look at all the sweet babies! This one looks like you." And, indeed, all the babies looked like Manny with his cherubic smile and curly hair, as if he represented all the baby citizens of the world.

Gus carted his boxes of sweets to the register in the stroller, and Callie lingered behind, gazing into the box at all the happy babies. She noticed that each baby had a name engraved in gold lettering on the box: Dark Night. Milk Honey. Strawberry Ruby. Pomegranate Dream. Sweet Regret.

"Gus, do you have the festival program?" Callie asked. But Gus couldn't hear her because someone was introducing a guest speaker who would be demonstrating cooking techniques. She called louder, "Hey Gus! The program?"

"Hang on, Cal, I'm paying here."

Callie tapped her foot, waiting for Gus to finish so he could give her the program. She scanned nearby tables to see if anyone else had a program. All around her people were drinking thick Greek coffee and eating desserts. Their faces looked tired from the excitement of the festival and either anticipatory as they lifted their sweets to their mouths, or groaning as they emptied their plates. At several tables she could see people lifting little chocolate babies up to their mouths and taking greedy bites. Callie didn't see any programs, which seemed to her ridiculous. How could there be so many people and no programs? She clutched the chocolates closer to her chest and gave Manny a little bounce to keep him happy. He'd begun to make his trademark yell, the one that showed great interest or excitement. Callie tried to show him the chocolates and bounce him more vigorously, but nothing would calm him down. He strained against her, pointing his arm forward relentlessly. "Aaaaaaaaaaa!"

"What is it, honey? What's so exciting?" Callie looked in the direction of his arm, followed the fingertip pointing through the crowded room, past the people, the signs, the sweets, and toward one thing. Callie stood stunned as she looked to the left of the cooking demonstration booth near the entrance of the room. There was Xeni. She had her back to Callie as she watched the demonstration, but Callie was positive it was her.

"Aaaaaaaaaaaa!" Manny yelled. *"Aaaaaaaaaaaa!"*

Nearby festivalgoers started to turn their heads toward them. "Aaaaaaaaaaaa!" Callie watched in stunned silence as a ripple effect moved through the large room, until more and more people turned to stare at her and Manny. "Aaaaaaaaaaaaaaaa!" It seemed to Callie that the entire room had stopped to turn their heads toward her, had stopped talking, until all that could be heard was Manny screaming, "Aaaaaaaaaaaaa!" and the voice of the flustered cooking demonstrator, who had stopped stirring her pot to see what the commotion was about. Everyone had turned their heads to stare at them except for the one person who mattered, the one person who seemed to be still as a statue. Callie herself was frozen, as if she'd been caught doing something naughty.

"Hey, hey. Shhhhhh. *Shhhhhhh.* Manoli! Keep it down, buddy."

305

Gus gave Callie a dirty look as he maneuvered the dessert-heavy stroller and a cup of Greek coffee through the crowded tables. "What's going on, kid?" Gus's voice seemed loud in the now quiet room, and he tried to be inconspicuous as he unsuccessfully attempted to shush Manny. "Aaaaaaaaaaaaaaaa!" "Okay, let's get outside! Come on, Callie. Look alive!"

Callie replied in a whispered monotone, "I can't, Gus. I have to stay here."

"Well, give me the baby, and you can stay."

"I can't leave the baby. That's the thing, Gus."

"Well, I'm leaving then."

"Really?" Callie whispered, and a tear escaped her eye and trickled down her cheek.

Meanwhile the cooking demonstrator's pot had boiled over, and Callie caught her breath as the last person in the room finally turned to look. Her dark, downcast eyes took one quick glimpse. Then she slowly got up from her seat near the door and walked out, her long dress flapping behind her. And in the space of a moment Callie felt a surge of happiness spill over her and then a hot flush of dismay as she watched Xeni disappear once again. "Hey, is that who I think it is?" Gus pointed at Xeni's retreating back. Manny's cries reached a crescendo before slowing down to a muffled sound, and the diners returned to consuming their delectable treats. Callie stood rooted, her feet sinking into the marble floor of the *Kafenion*. "Yes, I think so."

"Well, did she see us?"

Wiping the tear from her cheek, Callie replied, "Yes, I'm pretty sure she saw us."

"Well, what's her problem anyway? She's the one that took off without any notice. We didn't do anything to her."

"Gus. Do you remember that last night that we saw Xeni?"

"Not really. We had dinner and a lot to drink."

"I remember it. Every detail. I have to go find her."

I Am the Mother of My Imagination

She can't see me. She can't see me like this. She'll know that I'm crazy, hysterical. She'll know that the doctor was right. I am a crazy woman. My body has betrayed me, mimicking pregnancy, bloating into a huge mass, a bowl of dough risen to monstrous proportions, and overflowing. I should punch it down, punch it down. But I can't. I feel something moving inside. The yeast resurrecting, the curling spine of a crust of bread. Even if this is some hysterical fake pregnancy, I can't hurt my belly, finally big and round, stretched into the shape of a full moon rising and luminous with shiny trails. My belly is a horizon, the night sky shattered by silver lightning and billowing clouds. Thunder and rain hover over me in my darkness and I descend down deep into the loneliest of hells. Except that . . .

There is something there. My imagination or the imagination of another's. I can't crush that, and I can't find out what it is if it means I will lose it. I will stay in this impregnated state forever, keeping my hands full of smooth skin and bumpy shifts of my imagined baby's bottom, just below my breasts. I am happy in this hell, my insanity. As my hands reach to caress every part of my expanded belly, I am filled with a wondrous, delirious joy. Could it be that my dream has finally come true? Has God given me my virgin birth? I am filled with child. From my groin to my heart, I can feel her, stretching her body, becoming more fully realized and conscious in her every pulsating moment.

I believe her to be real. I cannot doubt her fictive existence anymore. I treasure her imposition on my sanity, her invasion of my body. All other thoughts have fallen away. I care for no others. You hear me, God? I care for no others! There is no need to punish me any further. I am pure. Make this dream real, my hallucinations lucid, my mirage embodied. I will not go astray. I have shown you that. I have stayed away, and I will stay away if you just make this virgin birth of earthly substance and not just the hysterical productions of a woman bent on escaping love.

What is love, anyway? Love is a sacrifice. It is not all pleasure and release. Love is Sisyphean. You have to love your boulder to push it every day. Otherwise it will crush you. The way I've been crushed. I was flattened into a dry, black track, always underfoot, and never rising. Maybe I'm not making sense, but I know, God, that there are all kinds of love. Love that hurts like a branding iron searing your flesh. Love that makes you into a crazy monster. Love that makes you go dull and numb, living every day in a haze. There is love that makes you feel trapped, your feet cemented to the ocean floor. Your body swaying side to side as bubbles escape your blue lips, floating up toward the sun along with long swaths of lanky hair releasing from your scalp, eyes upturned and flooding the ocean with salty tears.

Love. I never had too much of it. But I do now. I love this imaginary child of mine. I am happy to stay insane with her in our own little underworld, watery and crimson. My heart beats blood through my veins, rushing love into her heart, my lungs fill with air oxygenating her soul. I will care and feed her with my flesh, my placenta growing old. I will be a woman of one hundred and five, with belly outstretched. I will never give her up, and I will happily push this boulder. No one will notice me. I will become invisible to them, as all crazy people do. I don't mean the crazy people on the street that scare you. I mean the crazy people that carry on their everyday lives, looking normal enough on the surface while inside they seethe with lack. Except that I am not seething with lack anymore as I once was. I now roil with a voracious strength. I will protect my child with my teeth, nails, and growl, protect this state of duality until I die.

I have found comfort in this physical confusion. I have vomited up all of the bile that I held within me. I have rocked myself nauseous and come up empty. My rib cage has expanded, and the bars have lifted. My feet are bigger, more firmly planted on the Earth. As my belly has incrementally grown, my physical body has learned to claim space in the world I never knew I deserved. I am superhuman and unworldly. I carry the spirit of Christ in my womb, no longer shattered and broken. I carry a miracle in my womb. Like red wine that transforms into blood and bread that is of Christ's flesh. My imagination and desire have transformed into a delirious incubation of all that is pure and without shame. I am the mother of my imagination.

Gus Needs His Mother

Gus stood behind the stroller full of sugary treats, throwing his hands up into the air, watching Callie and Manny disappear through the crowd and out of the dining hall following Xeni's trail. Giving up on Callie for the moment, he sat down with his demitasse cup of coffee and *galaktoboureko* and opened up a copy of the *Hellenic Journal*.

Setting it back down again, he surveyed the room teaming with Greeks and non-Greeks. At the next table was a family sitting down for a break. The parents both wore festival volunteer nametags, and the children wore Greek dance costumes. The father was obviously Greek, with his dark hair and eyes and swarthy forearms, ordering his children to sit still and behave, while the wife was blond and demure. She looked weak-limbed to Gus. She must be an *Amerikanitha*, thought Gus. Here she is working the festival. She probably converted to Orthodoxy. She did everything to fit in with her husband's culture. At another table Gus spied on a family with both Greek parents, speaking to each other in a familiar Greek shorthand. Farther on he noticed a non-Greek family laughing as their two young sons pushed each other off their chairs. Everywhere Gus looked he saw harmony, except at his own table. He saw himself alone, his child and the mother of his child running off after Xeni and leaving him to eat his *galaktoboureko* in silence amidst the crowd. Gus felt Callie's absence

311

acutely, and he realized that it hadn't started that day. It had started many months ago. Maybe she'd never really been there, Gus thought. Maybe we made a mistake. Or maybe we were trying to fix our parents' mistakes.

Gus sucked down his coffee, swirled the grounds around the insides of the cup and turned it upside down. While the coffee grounds dried, he pulled out his cell phone and dialed the phone number of the one person who had never really left him. He nervously drummed his fingers on the table as the phone rang, or beeped really, as it does in Greece.

"*Neh*?"

"*Mana*? Can you help me read the *flitzani*?"

"*Pou esai, pedi mou*?" Mrs. Horiatis replied accusingly. "You know what time it is?"

"I'm sorry, Mana. I forgot about the time difference. I'm at the Greek Festival, *Mana*. And I need to know my future."

"How would I know your future? You're a grown man, remember?"

"I'm sorry, *Mana*. I'm confused. I want to do the right thing. I don't know. I love Manolaki. And I love you. Please help me read the cup."

"Okay. Is it dry?"

"Maybe it needs a few more minutes. *Mana*, are you sorry *Patera* left?" Gus heard his mother exhale a deep sigh on the other end of the phone line.

"Sorry? He left me. It was hard. And then it got easier. And there was no more fighting. No more jealousy. He was gone, *me tin allie*. She can keep him."

"I was sad when he left."

"Of course you were. He was your father. Every child wants a father."

"So *Mana*. If that is true, how can I leave Callie? What about Manolaki?"

Gus's mother paused. "You don't have to leave Manolaki. But if you are unhappy with the *Amerikanitha*, then you should leave her and take Manoli with you."

"I can't do that, *Mana*."

"Then share custody and start a new family. With a Greek girl this time."

Gus exhaled. "I think the coffee is dry now, *Mana*."

"Okay. Turn it over."

Gus turned the cup right side up and prepared to receive his fate. Inside the small cup was a dark ridge of coffee grounds. It traveled along the upper edge of the cup and then suddenly dropped. The white gorge on the porcelain cup was wide and then the dark ridge started again. To the right of that stood a small figure with four legs. And on the opposite side was a large cross formed of wavering lines surrounded by a light haze of coffee.

"How does it look?"

"Forget it. This is a stupid idea. I don't believe in all this anyway."

"Constantino. What does it look like?"

As Gus described the cup to his mother, she made little sounds, a gasp, as if what he was describing to her was an affirmation of her suspicions. Each time she made a sound, Gus paused and asked her, "What does that mean?" and each time she'd shush him and tell him to keep describing the cup, that she'd tell him at the end.

"And that's it."

"What is at the bottom on the cup?" his mother asked.

"The bottom?"

"Yes, *ayori mou*. The bottom."

"It is clear. All white."

"Thank goodness," Mrs. Horiatis exclaimed.

"What does it mean, *Mana*?"

"You have been traveling on a dark journey. You have been afraid to fall from the cliff. You don't know it, but the worst is over. Whatever was supposed to happen already happened. But now it will be easier. There is a faithful donkey that will help you for the rest of your journey."

"What journey, *Mana*?"

"This journey with the *Amerikanitha*. Something already happened that will decide the fate of the situation."

"It already happened?"

"Stop talking, Constantino, and listen to me. There is a donkey to help you on your journey, and this will lead you to lighter times. He is leading you to the cross. That is always good. Unless . . . is it an upright cross, or to the side?"

"It's kind of to the side."

"Is it more like a *t* or an *x*?" asked Mrs. Horiatis.

"It's kind of in between a *t* and *x*."

"Hmm . . ."

"Hmm, what?" said Gus growing impatient.

"Well, if it is like a *t*, then you are traveling toward God and protection. But if it is like an *x*, then is has something to do with Xeni. Either way it is good because it is all light, and before it was dark."

"*Mana*. What good can come from Xeni?"

"You tell me."

"*Mana*. Don't start. I'm not going to marry Xeni."

"Xeni is the godmother of your son. You can't marry her. But maybe she can help you in some way with this situation. The donkey brings you to her."

"I don't understand."

"It is not for us to understand. All we can do is try to follow God's will."

"She is here."

"Where?"

"She is here at the Greek Festival. Callie went running off to look for her. We saw her across the room."

"Go find her."

"Why *Mana*?"

"She holds your fate," his mother said. And even though Gus had no idea what that meant, he knew it was true.

"*Efharisto, Mana*. I'll call you later, *endaxi*?"

"Okay. *Sto kalo, pedi mou*. And Constantino?"

"Yes, *Mana*?"

"I love you no matter what happens." It was just what he needed to hear.

"I love you too, *Mana*," and with that he hung up the phone, packed his provisions, and loaded the stroller. Having a sudden thought, Gus looked at the stroller laden with Greek food and Manny's things and asked, "Are you my donkey?"

GREEK COFFEE
(multiply recipe for each cup of coffee)

"Turn the cup right side up and prepare to receive your fate."

1 demitasse cup of water
1 teaspoon finely ground Greek coffee
Sugar to taste:
1/2 teaspoon sugar for bitter coffee (*pikroh*)
1 teaspoon sugar for medium sweetness (*metrio*)
2 teaspoons sugar for sweet coffee (*yliko*)

FOR COFFEE:

Pour the water into a small *briki* pot. Add the coffee and sugar and stir until they are incorporated. Let the coffee simmer until it starts to form bubbles around the edges and begins to rise up the sides of the *briki*. Quickly lift the *briki* from the flames before it boils over and pour into a demitasse cup from a height. A large bubble (*to mati*) brings good luck.

FOR YOUR FATE:

Stop drinking the coffee before reaching the bottom of the cup where the grounds have settled. Swirl the grounds around the sides of the cup and place the cup upside down on a napkin in your saucer and allow to dry.

Find a Greek woman trained in reading the cup to learn your fortune.

Dome within a Dome

The church has always been a sanctuary for me when it is empty like this. Even on festival days, you can find the church solitary and waiting. Entering the narthex with the mosaic icons flanking each wall, I go to the left, lighting a candle under the icon of the Virgin and placing it in the top tray of sand under the icon. I always place it in the upper right-hand corner and light it for the same thing: a healthy baby. And that my mother rests in peace. She isn't dead yet. But one day she will be, and I hope that she finds more happiness in eternity than she did in this life. It seems like the men around us were always disappointing us, except for God and Jesus.

I watched the way Gus was with Callie, and how he didn't see her. He just saw what she wasn't and what he wanted her to be. That can poison a person. It can cripple them and make them crawl on their knees, always trying to please, always knowing that what they are is not good enough. And there was Callie with Gus in that *Kafenion*. I saw her standing by his side. She is still with him, still trying to play good Greek wife, carrying his child around the festival with pride, when he doesn't even love her enough to marry her. I can't be in the same room with them after what I saw that night last summer. She obviously loved him enough to please him, right there in front of me. She didn't really care about me at all. After I left I yanked my phone out of the wall so I wouldn't be tempted to call her. I was merely some kind of Greek puzzle for her, like the lamb knucklebone game we'd play at Easter. Throw it one way and I'm the cook, throw it another and he's the king, throw it one more time and she's the thief. She stole my heart. But I can't let her keep it. I have to get it back. She's holding it in a cage of spun caramel, amber and hard, and carelessly dangles it in the air without care that it may drop and shatter.

Genuflecting three times and kissing the feet of the Virgin, I pass into the inner narthex of the church and then into the nave. I need all of my love back for this baby, real or imagined. I can't let Callie see me. I'll hide in this corner of the church, in a pew beside the baptismal font, and let the blue glass of the church walls envelop me in their serene magnetism. Christ will look down on me from the pounded copper ceiling with his stern expression and tired eyes and watch over me. She will not find me because I can tell that Jesus has tired of all of this foolishness. One woman cannot love another woman, especially when she is devoted to a man, when she is willing to give up her dignity and self-worth to please him. No, she will not find me.

Suddenly there is a shifting in my belly that feels like a foot jamming into my gut, a rolling sensation within my body that I can plainly see. The top of my belly, hard and round as a water-melon, is moving from right to left. Sometimes this sensation scares me. It feels so real that I wonder if I am truly insane. I worry that I may end up spending my days curled into a bloated ball, watching my belly rise and fall, feeling this inside-out sen-sation of movement and propulsion. In those moments my joy turns into a moment of dizzy breathlessness and convulsing sobs. I do not know my body. What is happening to my body?

I try to curl into a smaller ball in the pew, but it is impossible to get very small when your belly expands forward and to the sides and moves independently of your thought and intention. I try to curl forward, but the wooden pew ahead is too close. I am huge, as huge as the domed ceiling of the church, as huge as the sky that holds all the stars within it. I am dumbstruck by my enormity.

On the other side of the church, festivalgoers start to gather next to the display of priestly robes and bibles. They are preparing to watch the demonstration on icon painting. It is a specialized technique that uses natural minerals and egg yolk to bind them. The embryonic yolk of the egg feeds the pigment, helping it bloom into the image of a saint. The dark reds, the golds, the rich earthy colors all come together to form a face, an expression. The egg tempera paint dries into a finish that is amazingly resilient. I wonder if the artist could look at my belly and foresee a face. If they could mix egg and pigment and paint a form onto the dome of my swollen belly, revealing a curved body, an inquisitive face, hands that clutch at the world.

I lie down on the pew barely wide enough to support my girth, and point my belly up toward the ceiling. A dome within a dome. The face of Jesus reflecting on my womb. Or perhaps I could take the juices of strawberries or pomegranates and paint a portrait of my child onto my belly, giving it definition and visibility. I would like to see my baby. At least once. I would like to hold it in my arms, just as I always dreamed, a living portrait of Mary and Jesus. For all mothers accomplish some miracle in the conception and birth of their children and, given the chance, in the nurturing of them.

Lying on my back is as uncomfortable as lying on rocks now, and a thought suddenly occurs to me. What if my belly never stops growing? What if it becomes so huge that I am unable to leave the house, like the eight-hundred-pound man? They'll have to cut a hole in the wall to squeeze me through if I ever do give birth.

I can't fool myself. I will never give birth. This is all a figment of my imagination, a hoax. Just a physical expression of my innermost desires.

The Koimisis Miracle

Callie pushed through the people crowded around the token booth and past the young men loitering in front of the church. A cluster of Greek Americans was just outside the doors of the church blocking the way. One older grandfather was exclaiming, "Give *Papou* a kiss! Where is my kiss?" A young girl with long brown ponytails shyly clung to her mother's legs. The old man, her grandfather, pointed his finger toward his grizzled cheek. "Come on, it won't hurt you!" he chortled. Callie tried to make her way around the family, and her quiet, "*Signomi*" was ignored until she finally and firmly stated, "Excuse me!"—really more of a command than a request. The group gave Callie a stern look as they parted to allow her and Manny to pass. She entered the church foyer and took a moment to push a dollar bill into the donation box beside the hand-dipped yellow beeswax candles. She took a candle and walked toward the icon of the Virgin Mary. Taking a deep breath, she held her wick up to the flame of the solitary candle with the brightest spark and made a wish as she lit it. She placed her candle next to it in the upper right-hand corner, remembering that the right hand performs miracles in the Bible.

As urgently as Callie wanted to see Xeni, she found herself lingering in front of the icon, eyeing the dark interior of the church with hesitation. Clearly Xeni didn't want to see Callie; otherwise, she wouldn't have run away at the sight of her in the *Kafenion. But she doesn't understand what happened that night,*

Callie thought. *If she only knew what I was trying to do . . . Maybe it was a stupid plan. But what if it worked, and Xeni has the virgin conception that she has always dreamed of?* Callie's fear was overturned by her sudden excitement and curiosity. Could it have worked?

As Callie turned to enter the inner sanctum of the church, she noticed that several people had had the same idea, including the old *Papou* and his young granddaughter in the arms of her mother. As they slowly filed in, Callie's impatience was getting the better of her, but she knew that she couldn't push past this family again without looking like a terrible, brutish non-Greek. Before Callie could stop him, Manny reached out and grabbed the ponytail of the young girl, causing her to shriek in surprise. "Manny, no!" Callie tried to apologize, but before the words left her lips she imagined she heard someone mumble the word "*Amerikanitha*." Shamed by her inability to blend in, even standing there in line to enter the church, Callie had a loss of confidence. This was her pendulum, she thought, best intentions and failure.

"How old is your baby?" asked the mother of the girl, kindly.

"Oh. He's eighteen months," Callie smiled weakly. "I'm so sorry he pulled your daughter's hair."

"You should see what she does to her younger brother at home!" The dark-haired woman smiled. "We can't control our children all of the time. They have a will of their own, don't they?"

"Yes, indeed," Callie replied.

"Is he Greek?" asked the woman.

"Yes, he is. His father is Greek."

"Well, it's nice that you bring him here to learn about his culture."

Callie smiled again, touched by the woman's warmness and impatient to get inside. As they entered the main hall, the darkness lifted and Callie found herself surrounded by the blue glass walls and magnificent copper-domed ceiling. She always was struck by the paintings of Christ and his disciples on the ceiling, and wondered why they had to look so stern. Wasn't Jesus a kind and loving man? Pushing those thoughts aside, Callie scanned the church looking for Xeni. People were assembling near the demonstration area, but Callie knew that Xeni wasn't there for the demonstration. She looked toward the baptismal font where Manny had been baptized earlier that year and where Xeni had taken a vow to be his godmother. It wasn't long after that that she'd disappeared. Callie couldn't see Xeni anywhere. Could she have been mistaken? She was sure that she'd seen her enter the church. Callie walked up and down the aisles scanning each pew, but Xeni was nowhere to be found. Then Callie remembered the new Koimisis chapel that was under construction. *Maybe she ducked in there*, thought Callie. *She loves the Virgin Mary.*

Before leaving the church, Callie decided to take Manny up to the baptismal font to show him where he'd been baptized. As she approached the font, she became aware of a rustling sound to her left. Turning to see, she just caught a glimpse of a woman retreating up the aisle and out into the sunshine of the festival. Callie wasn't sure if it was Xeni—this woman was much larger— but she had on a similar dress to what she'd noticed Xeni wearing in the *Kafenion*. "She's larger!" she cried out loud, causing several church visitors to turn their heads.

Following her instincts, Callie made her way to the Koimisis Chapel. She passed the icon of the reclining Virgin and decided that she could look either asleep or dead, in the picture. Callie decided that she'd rather think of the Virgin as peacefully slumbering in the lovely new chapel, with the ability to wake up when she felt like it. There were few people in the chapel as Callie entered, and she didn't see Xeni immediately. Callie pointed up toward the glass dome to show Manny the splendor of the sky, and when she looked back down she saw Xeni there, standing in front of what would become a finished altar. She looked beautiful; her wavy hair cascaded down her shoulders and back. Her eyes were wide and filled with an emotion that Callie couldn't identify. But most noticeably Xeni's body had changed. Her breasts and belly were swollen and her skin radiated a warmth and glow that was unmistakably the result of the divine inhabiting the mundane, the mark of a woman with child.

"Xeni," Callie said, "you look . . ."

"I'm just fat. It's just fat. That's all," Xeni replied defensively, putting an arm around her middle.

"I don't think so, honey."

"Yes. It's just fat."

Manny started to pull his mother toward Xeni, leaning his body forward and pointing to her, gurgling with an excited smile.

"*Yassou* Manolaki. *Ti kaneis?*" Xeni greeted the boy.

Manny stretched his arms out to Xeni and reached for her neck. Xeni smiled, placed his chubby arm in her hands, and took a little bite. "*Tha se faw!* You got so big!"

"Do you want to hold him?" Callie asked.

"Yes, of course." Xeni took Manny into her arms and held him close.

"When are you due, Xeni?"

"I'm not due. This is how I am now. That's all." Xeni hugged Manny tighter and hid her face in his shoulder.

"But, Xeni. Clearly."

"Clearly, it's nothing. Remember what the doctor said?" Xeni looked flushed.

"I know what the doctor said, but you aren't crazy. I did some reading. Do you know what I learned? *Newsweek* did a poll and seventy-nine percent of Americans believe in the Virgin Birth. Parthenogenesis has been documented in seventy species of vertebrates and a ton of insects. Lizards, birds, sharks, bees— they've all done it!"

Xeni shook her head. "Really? That can't be right. I mean, maybe that's all true, but that doesn't explain what's happening to me."

"But maybe . . . your wish came true?" Callie shyly smiled, and her eyes glittered.

"I don't know. I don't know if my wish came true. I'm just fat. I've eaten a lot of chocolate lately developing my new line of sweets. Did you see them in the *Kafenion?*"

"The Baby Bellies? I knew that must have been you."

"Did you see the strawberry ruby?"

"Yes." Callie smiled and started to reach out to touch Xeni's arm. *If only I could touch her, touch her heart, make her trust me again.*

"I have to go now."

"Xeni, please. Don't go. Let me apologize for that last night. I'm so sorry."

"No need to apologize. You were expressing your love for your . . . baby's father."

"No, I wasn't. I was expressing my love for you," Callie said. "I know that sounds crazy. But it's true. I'm in love with you."

"Stop."

"But . . ."

"Stop. We are standing in a Greek Orthodox chapel. I am holding your baby. There are strangers all around who can hear you."

"I don't care."

"But I care, Callie."

Callie was silenced, but only for a moment. "Xeni, I want you to know how I really feel. That night I was really saying good-bye to Gus although I didn't know it at the time."

"Good-bye? You were just in the *Kafenion* with him, buying sweets to eat together, dripping with, with"—Xeni's voice became louder—"honey. That's not what I call good-bye!"

"Please! I don't want to be apart from you anymore. I know things have been complicated. I don't blame you for wanting to run away, but please look at me. I love you. Please don't leave me!"

"Do you know how ridiculous you sound, Callie?" Gus's voice came up behind her. "Obviously, she did leave you. And look, apparently she found herself a lover and got knocked up. He must have balls of gold," chuckled Gus. "How far along are you, Xeni?"

"I'm fat," Xeni insisted and clutched Manny closer to her.

"Even I can tell that you're pregnant. No need to be ashamed. What, did you get pregnant out of wedlock or something?" Gus snickered.

"Gus. Leave her alone," Callie threatened.

"Why? She likes a good ribbing, don't you, Xeni?"

"Leave me alone. Why are you both bothering me?"

"I didn't want to bother you, Xeni. I wanted to see you again and apologize. To see if we could be . . . friends . . . again?" Callie said.

"I'm bothering you because of this!" Gus held out his coffee cup with the dried grounds forming the letter *X*. "What do you think this means?"

Xeni gasped. "I wouldn't know! I don't read the *flitzani*."

"I bet you do!"

"No, I don't. And if you'll excuse me, I need to go." Xeni handed a reluctant Manny over to Gus.

"Xeni. Wait. My mother says that you somehow hold my fate. What does that mean?" Gus implored.

"I don't know. I don't know!" Xeni cried, becoming more upset. "Just leave me alone. Both of you!" Xeni tried to push past Callie and Gus and toward the opening of the chapel. As she stepped forward, she heard Callie cry out.

"Xeni. I'm in love with you. I want to be with you!"

Callie held her breath, waiting for Xeni's response. Xeni didn't say a word but started to sway, her eyes turned upward toward the glass-domed ceiling. Suddenly, she gasped and all eyes dropped to the cement floor of the new chapel, at the spreading puddle of fluid at Xeni's feet.

For a moment there was complete, divine silence. Gus stood clutching his fateful *flitzani* in one fist, and balanced his tired son on the other arm. Callie marveled at the spreading liquid, suddenly feeling extreme joy as she felt the arm of her pendulum stop on the side of good intentions, and ratchet a bit further into an unknown territory: success.

Gus broke the silence, "Are we supposed to clean that up? 'Cause my hands are full right here, see?" He shrugged as he gestured with his chin toward the *flitzani*, the loaded stroller, and his son in his arms. "And by the way, Callie, thanks for the love update. Real classy."

"I'm not sure I understand what's happening . . ." Xeni trailed off.

Callie felt herself well up with an intensity that she was unable to hold back. She clamped her mouth shut, balled her hands into knotty fists, and gripped the hard floor with her toes. She closed every orifice and pore in her body, willed her tongue to be still. She wanted Xeni to have this moment of realization to herself. She didn't want to explain anything at all, and she wanted to explain everything. The push of her emotions found the only outlet that Callie couldn't shut down and pressed itself through her tear ducts and escaped down her cheeks, dropped onto her breasts, and rolled down to drop and commingle with the spreading lake of wishes at Xeni's feet. As their fluids met, a small sizzling sound, barely audible, rose and fell, detectable only to the ears of widowed *yiayias*.

"I must need to use the restroom?" Xeni mumbled. "Maybe I'm getting my period? I feel a little crampy . . ."

"Cal, aren't you going to tell her?" Gus prompted.

"No. I'm not going to tell her," Callie murmured. "I'm never going to tell her."

"Seriously? You two women need *me* to tell you what's happening?"

"Gus. Settle down. Let her experience it," Callie shushed.

"Experience what? Do you know what is happening to my body?" Xeni pressed.

"If none of you are going to tell her, I will." It was the woman that Callie had met in the church earlier. Suddenly Callie became aware of all the people in the chapel, standing in a circle around them witnessing Xeni's drenched and confused state. The woman took Xeni's hand in hers and said, "Hi there, my name is Penny. I'm a registered nurse. How far along are you? It looks as if your water broke."

"I'm not far along. I'm fat. I'm fat, aren't I?" Xeni asked, her voice tremulous and quiet.

"You are pregnant, and you're going into labor," Penny replied. "Why don't we sit down for a moment and get you some water?"

She turned to the gathering crowd and announced, "Okay folks, let's give her a little space, *se para kalo*. Please step back, give her some privacy."

The festivalgoers, disappointed that the curtain was being drawn on the event, reluctantly shuffled away, with a few Greek *yiayias* lingering at the periphery, visualizing their ear canals opening to full aperture to capture any enticing words that might drop from Xeni's lips, which they could pass on as gifts to their friends.

"No. No. I'm not pregnant," Xeni replied her eyes full of shame as she whispered to the nurse. "I have a disease. I'm hysterical. The doctor said so. Hysterical pregnancy. It's not real. It just looks and feels real."

Callie stepped toward Xeni and put her arm around her shoulders. "Honey, you are pregnant. It's real. Your wish came true."

Xeni pushed Callie's arm away. "You know better than anyone that's a lie! You were there!"

"I was there. I was there when the doctor told you that. But that was last year. This is now. This is real." Callie could hold back no longer. "But I was also there the night you got pregnant."

"I gotta hear this," Gus snorted, but then thought better of it. Was the mother of his child trying to say that she got another woman pregnant? "Hey, this is too weird. Shouldn't we go to a hospital or something?" He looked at Penny, hoping that she would be the voice of reason in this situation.

Penny met Gus's eyes. "I think we have a little time here. It doesn't seem as if her contractions are very strong yet." Gus suddenly noticed Penny's dark almond eyes and perfectly arched eyebrows, her fair skin, her nearly black hair, and her cherry red lips. She seemed familiar to him, but he couldn't place her.

"You're Greek, aren't you?" Gus asked, and thought, *a Greek Goddess*.

"Yes, I'm Greek. Those are my two children over there, and my parents."

"Where is your husband?" Gus asked.

330

"Right now, what we have to focus on is this young lady." Penny turned her gaze away from Gus, flushing slightly. "What's your name, sweetheart?"

Xeni paused.

"Her name is Xeni." Gus filled in the empty space that hung in the air.

"Really? I always liked that name. So, Xeni, I think what we should do is have you sit in this chair right here, get you a drink of water, and take some deep breaths. Can you tell me if you are feeling any contractions?"

Xeni shook her head from side to side, in a kind of confused stupor.

Gus dropped the *flitzani* into the loaded stroller seat and clutched Manny more tightly as he stooped to take a bottle of water out of the stroller basket. "Here, Penny, she can drink this." As he handed the water bottle to Penny, Gus noticed Callie rolling her eyes at his sudden attentiveness. He shrugged it off, as she had little room to judge since he'd just heard Callie profess her love for Xeni.

"Thanks . . ." Penny paused.

"Gus. Constantino. But I go by Gus most of the time."

"*Efharisto,* Constantino." Penny smiled at Gus and took the bottle.

Gus felt himself experience a surge of excitement at hearing his name come from this woman's full lips. "*Para kalo,* Panayiota." Gus grinned, pleased with himself for guessing Penny's Greek name. "It's Panayiota, right?"

"Of course. Panayiota translates as seamlessly into Penny as Constantino translates into Gus, right?" Gus and Penny shared an insider's laugh over the imprecision of Greek immigrant name translation.

"Okay, enough. Shouldn't we be focused on Xeni here?" Callie asked impatiently as she brought a chair closer so Xeni could sit down.

"Of course, of course," Penny agreed and turned her attention back to Xeni.

"No, I don't want you to focus on me. I want to go home. I feel, I feel . . . funny. I need to go lie down."

"Please sit down and have a sip of water, and then you can go home to labor for a while if you aren't too progressed or to the hospital if your contractions start to become stronger and more frequent." Penny helped Xeni back down into the small chair. Gus thought it looked as if it could collapse under her expanded size. Penny kept her arms close in case she needed to help steady Xeni. "Is there someone you want to call? The father . . ." Penny asked.

A laugh escaped from Xeni's lips at the word, *father.*

"Well, thanks for your help, Penny. I think we can take it from here. I don't want to keep you from your family," Callie offered and put her hands on Xeni's shoulders.

Penny persisted. "Who is your doctor, Xeni? Maybe we should give them a call."

"I don't have a doctor."

"So, Xeni, honey. Are you saying that you haven't had any pre-natal care at all?" Penny sighed. "You know, I think I'll just ask my parents to take the kids over to the bounce house for a bit while we get straightened out here. Okay?"

Gus watched Penny's hips sway as she walked toward her parents and children and again wondered where her husband was. He suddenly realized why she seemed so familiar. Seeing her with her family, it all came back to him. He had first seen Penny dancing with her family at Mythos. She was the beautiful woman that had captured his attention that night, and here she was again. Was it fate?

He tried to come up with an excuse to follow her. "I'm gonna go for a walk with Manolaki . . ." But Gus realized that Callie and Xeni weren't listening to him at all and felt a surprising amount of relief in being left out. As if by some primal instinct, he found himself following a warm trail that smelled of honey. He imagined his nose burrowing into black hair, and the taste of cloves and cherries on his lips.

The Pulse of Life

Callie huddled close to Xeni, relieved to finally be alone with her again. The festival, the people, the music all disappeared. "Xeni, honey. Everything is going to be all right. I know you are surprised by all this, but isn't it great? It's what you've always wanted, right?" Callie was surprised to find herself ending the statement with a question.

"I don't know. I don't understand what's happening." Xeni looked back up through the glass dome at the clouds. "I saw her. I saw her. She came to me."

"Who, honey?" Callie asked.

"I thought I saw her in the clouds after you said what you said—about your feelings for me—and then the liquid fell. Did it come from the clouds?"

"It came from you, honey. There is an ocean inside of you that contains every beautiful pulse of life. Your baby has been waiting for you. She's inside of you. She's always been there. You've carried her your whole life. Now she's coming to join you out in this amazing world." Callie took Xeni's hand, and this time Xeni let her. Callie's eyes glittered with salty tears. "I've missed you so much."

Xeni whispered, "I have been waiting for so long. But I never thought my dream could come true. That I could find love." Xeni paused. "When that doctor told me that I was . . . I knew I was being punished. I knew what I was feeling for you was wrong. I had to go away. Especially after I saw you, with him, like that."

"I'm so sorry that you had to see that, sweetie. It's not what you think."

Xeni shook her head. "I don't know. I don't know what to think anymore."

"I have been waiting so long to see you. I knew you'd be angry with me and that I didn't have a right to come after you. But I wanted to. I've thought of you every single day since you've been gone. I can't cook without thinking about your hands. I can't breathe without smelling your skin. I love you, and I don't want to live without you."

"I don't know what to say. I'm overwhelmed," Xeni said, and then she gasped and bent over, clutching her belly.

Callie reached out to rub her back. "Breathe. Just breathe. You can do this. Look into my eyes. You can do this."

Xeni looked into Callie's eyes, and Callie held her there in her gaze. Xeni nodded her head and repeated, "I can do this."

The Virgin

I don't think anyone else sees her. It happens right after I hear those words leave Callie's lips. "Xeni, I'm in love with you. I want to be with you!" I hear those words that I never dared hope to hear, and as I do I feel my body get lighter. It seems as if my eyes are swimming toward the glass dome of the chapel, rising toward the sky. I swoon, my swollen and engorged body wavering in the sunlight. I feel as if I might disappear, or, like the Virgin Mary, that I will float upward toward the sky, body and all. My body hovers between the balance of earth and sky, fire and water.

I look upward through the glass of the dome, upward toward the sky. I can just make out the image of the Virgin Mary floating by in a fluffy white cloud, pure and untainted. Her beautiful red, blue and gold robes are draped around her shoulders and framing her peaceful face. Mary reaches out her fingers toward my belly and makes a circular motion. Round and round until I become dizzy. All around me I feel a sudden humidity in the air. And when I look up, Mary has vanished in the clouds and I feel a sudden splash.

I slowly look down at my feet, now drenched, and then lift my eyes back up to the sky. Searching the clouds, and finding no one, I return my attention to the wetness running down my legs and onto the fresh cement, hoping that the parish will not be angry with me for unexpectedly christening their chapel. I look up again through the glass dome ceiling and then out toward the wide open doors of the chapel. "I think I . . ." and then fall silent again. My eyes fill with tears as I am overcome with an intense feeling of joy.

A circular sensation rings itself around my belly, and I feel a deep squeezing down lower. I gasp as a strong clenching force moves through my body. Then Callie reaches out to rub my back and tells me to breathe. I look into Callie's eyes, blue and sure as a summer sky, her red hair and golden skin glowing like the sunlight filtering through the dome. "You can do this," she tells me. I feel the painful clench unwind, and my body floods with a sense of release. I nod my head and repeat, "I can do this."

The Baby Divine

Cramped and curled with feet pressed against the roof of its abode, tightly wound with arms akimbo on knees so close to the chin. The watery elastic womb has gotten smaller and smaller, causing a pause in the dancing and swinging of earlier days. With head wedged tight close to bone and the tenuous muscle walls shivering, it senses or perhaps knows that a change is occurring, although the possibilities are a mysterious blank. With very little room for high jinks, it twiddles the thick cord erupting from its round belly, strokes the bumpy braided surface, and hiccups at the pulsations that cause the cord to move up and down within its palm. It stares wide-eyed at the thick purple walls, kicking out as far as it can, which at this point is not very far.

Then the tastes arrive, infusing the atmosphere with colors and something else—emotions. Green, green, fresh green, bitter and pungent. Red, sweet, and greedy, curls the tongue. Yellow, thick, and glowing, warms and comforts. Orange sparks puckered tangy excitement. White flows serenely. Tan, beige, rust, black, sage, brown, gray sprinkle and spice the atmosphere with intrigue. The sounds and images of the womb are forgotten by the born, unknowingly kept in a tiny receptacle deep within the gray tissue of the head, and tucked neatly within a pink valve of the heart. Some are tinged more strongly with images, or tastes, or spirit, but all are divine.

Second Chances

Gus followed his nose, absentmindedly carrying Manny, who was getting tired by now of all the commotion, music, and crowds. He hung limply on Gus's shoulder falling into sleep. Gus could see Penny up ahead talking to her children, kneeling before them and reflexively fixing their clothes and hair, and then pulling them in close to her body. They clung to her with arms around her neck and shoulders, draped on her with abandon and surrender. Gus hugged Manolaki a little closer to him, feeling a warmth in his heart that spread to his cheeks and erupted into a spontaneous smile. He didn't know what was coming next in life, but he knew he loved his son. Everything will work out fine, he told himself, not sure why he was feeling so confident.

A look back over his shoulder revealed Callie and Xeni sitting close together, framed by the entryway of the Koimisis Chapel, Xeni leaning against Callie, and Callie tenderly placing her open palm on Xeni's belly. Xeni looked up at the sky through the chapel dome as if waiting for a sign, and receiving none she placed her hand on top of Callie's, and moved it a little farther to the left, where both hands jumped at the kick of the unborn child. This made Gus smile wider, and he knew that he was finally free. Xeni really did hold his fate, he thought. He both hated and loved how his mother was always right.

"What's with the big smile, Constantino? We've got to get Xeni to the hospital," Penny teased Gus, surprising him out of his reverie.

"I was just thinking about my mother. You ought to meet her sometime. She's really feisty." Gus laughed.

"Of course she is. Aren't all Greek mothers? You ought to see me in action."

"I'd like that," Gus murmured. "What about your kids? If we go to the hospital . . . will their father come to take them home?"

"Look, Gus. When I was young, I made some mistakes, trying to run away from the old-country ways, you know? The best thing that came out of it was my kids. Their dad is no longer in the picture. So you can stop asking about him."

Gus beamed. "Well that's too bad, I guess."

"Not really. It's all for the best, I think." Penny paused, "Everyone deserves a second chance at happiness, no matter what their past, right?"

"Right." Gus was warmed by this thought and he felt excitement rise within him at the chance for a new beginning.

"Okay. So, my parents will take the kids home. What about your little guy and your wife?"

"She's not my wife." Gus felt a bit sheepish. "I was never sure it was the right thing, but I was trying to make it work for my son's sake."

"And now? She seems . . . involved?"

"Yeah. I guess so. I guess that makes me free." Gus smiled.

"Well, you know what they say, Constantino."

"What's that, Panayiota?

"If you see a penny, pick it up, and all the day you'll have good luck."

"Oh man, you've totally used that line before." Gus laughed.

"Actually, no. I haven't," Penny said quietly, pushing her black hair behind her ear.

Gus's heart lifted a second time that day. It isn't often that a man is caught and released all in one day. "How about tomorrow night? Mediterranean Soul is performing! Dinner and dancing?"

"Depending on how late we're up with Xeni tonight, but that sounds perfect."

"Well, let's get moving then! No time to waste. Let's get her to the hospital."

The Brilliant Host

I never thought I'd find myself here, sitting in a car with Callie and Gus and a strange woman who insists on taking me to the hospital. Manny is sleeping in the car seat between Callie and Penny while Gus drives. Gus is nervous that I'll get his seat wet, so he's spread a large black garbage bag under my bottom. I can't see it. I can't see anything right now except the road and the cars ahead of us, blocking the way. Manny's babysitter will meet us there and take him back to their house on stilts.

I don't know why Callie says she loves me. Can't she see that I am troubled? From when I was a little girl, and my *nouno* . . . I never wanted anyone to come too close to me after that. Not my mother, not my father. They never saw me anyway. I was a ghost who cleaned and cooked, silent and brooding. As long as I kept to myself, they were happy fighting. They never protected me because they were too busy tearing each other apart.

If I am not crazy. If I am not fat. If I am. If I am carrying a child in my womb at this moment, I will always protect it. I will always look into its eyes and make sure its spirit is vibrant and not dull. I will teach it to say "yes," and I will teach it to say "no." I will teach it to say "NO!" with a righteous thunder, and I will run to its side when it needs me. I will be its home, its mother-land, its protector, and savior. My child will answer proudly when someone asks where they come from, who their people are. My child won't lie, like I do. My child will be pure and brilliant as the sun, free from the darkness of shame.

343

At the Hospital

Callie sat behind Xeni in the car as they drove to Berkeley and reached forward to touch her arm, to feel closer to her. That morning she didn't know if she'd ever see Xeni again, and now she was helping her breathe deeply through contractions. Xeni was about to birth a baby, a baby that Callie might have helped bring to life. She squeezed her eyes shut and said a prayer of thanks to the universe for all of her blessings. As Gus pulled the car into the driveway of Alta Bates Hospital, Penny directed him to park in the temporary parking up front. The row of parking slots was nearly full, with only one space left near the entrance. The other cars represented laboring women upstairs on the third floor of the hospital in various states of dilation, somewhere on the painful road to motherhood.

"We've got to get Xeni up to triage and have them take a look at her. With no prenatal treatment at all, we should take a thorough look at what's going on. Make sure Mama and baby are okay. Is that all right with you, Xeni?" Penny asked.

Xeni paused before answering, "I'm afraid to go up there. What if they tell me I'm crazy?"

"Well, it won't be the first time," Gus joked. Callie kicked the back of Gus's seat, "Gus! That's not funny."

"Okay, I know. I know. I'm sorry!"

"Hey, you two. Let's focus on Xeni right now," Penny intoned with authority, then changed to a soft and reassuring approach as she addressed Xeni.

"It's going to be all right. I promise you. They won't say you're crazy. I won't let them. And it isn't true. You are pregnant. I can see that with certainty, and I am a nurse. You can trust my medical opinion, okay?" Penny reached forward and placed her right hand on Xeni's shoulder. Callie was grateful for Penny's reassuring words, and imagined love and courage flowing from her heart into Xeni's core.

Callie touched Xeni's arm. "She's right, Xeni. You are pregnant. In just a number of hours you'll be holding your sweet baby in your arms. It's the most wonderful feeling in the world. I promise you when you look into your baby's eyes the first time that everything else will just fade away. It will all be worth it."

There was a pause, and then Gus added, "It's true, Xeni. When you have a child, you try so hard to become the person you want to be, for them. Sure, sometimes they drive you nuts, but overridingly they give you the greatest gift a person can receive, unconditional love." Gus paused, and reached his open palm toward Xeni. "We're your family now. No matter what happens, we'll back you up."

Callie found herself tearing up at Gus's words. *It's true. We tried so hard to be the people we thought we should be for Manny. But no matter what our flaws, or family configuration, Manny loves us all the same.* Callie watched as Xeni took Gus's hand and, finding herself crying happy tears, suggested they go up to the maternity ward.

No More Secrets

Callie and Gus sat in the waiting room on the third floor of Alta Bates Hospital while Penny took Xeni to triage to get checked by the hospital staff. The room was packed with expectant parents and grandparents. Some stood wearily against walls or draped onto padded seats, while another group sat huddled praying in a circle while their loved one labored. All carried a look of utter exhaustion and excitement, as if they too were laboring under the promise of a life on the brink of transformation.

"Did you really mean what you said down there?" Callie asked Gus.

"What?"

"About us all being family now?"

"Yeah, I guess. I mean, Xeni is Manny's godmother. That makes her family."

Callie hesitated. "Are we still family?"

"What? You mean because you told Xeni you were in love with her in front of me, God, and everyone at the Greek Church?" Gus said crossing his arms and snorting.

"Look, Gus, I'm sorry. I should have talked to you. I've been trying so hard to make it work with you. I wanted Manny to have a stable home and a dad, all the things I didn't have. And I wanted to give you what you wanted. And what your mother wanted. I tried my best to be a good Greek wife, but in the end—

I'm just me, Callie, child of a hippie, lover of world culture, kind of a dork with weird boundaries, but someone that always tries hard to do the right thing."

Gus put his arm around Callie. "Look, Cal. We both tried. I love you. You gave me a beautiful son. But we never really fit together. I think it's all right to say that now."

Callie nodded. "Do you regret it?"

Gus paused for a moment and said, "Nah, it's been great," and gave Callie's shoulders a squeeze. "But I will admit, since we're coming clean—I have a secret that I should have told you about."

"You do?" Callie asked. "I have one, too," she said as she looked down at her palms.

"Another one?" Gus smiled. "I don't know if I can take another one."

"Well . . . you go first then." Callie smiled weakly.

"Don't get mad, okay?"

"Uh . . . okay, I guess," Callie agreed.

"After you got pregnant with Manny, I kind of freaked out. I wasn't ready to be a father. I mean, you know, it was a one-night stand that turned into some fun dates that turned into being an expectant Dad all within a month."

"Yeah. It was really, really fast." Callie nodded.

"Well, like I said. I kind of freaked out and I did something and I didn't tell you."

"What did you do?" Callie asked.

"I was scared and definitely not ready to have any more kids, but I didn't know how to tell you."

"And . . ."

"I got a vasectomy."

"Huh?"

"A vasectomy."

"You got a vasectomy?" Callie stood up and stared at Gus.

"Uh yeah. You mad? I mean. It doesn't really matter anymore. To you. Does it? We just broke up, right?"

"Yeah. We just broke up." Callie paused. "What do you mean,

a vasectomy? That's when they 'snip snip' and you can't make babies anymore, right?"

"That's it. I'm sorry. I freaked out. I wasn't ready to have an instant brood of kids."

"When did you do that? The vasectomy? When did you do it?" Callie's voice was rising in volume, and the other people in the maternity waiting room stopped their vigils to turn and look their way.

"It was a long time ago. Right after you got pregnant. Forever ago," Gus said.

"You freaked out and so you went and got a vasectomy? Who does that?" Callie asked. "Most guys are terrified of getting snipped."

"Yeah, well. I guess I was terrified of being a father." Gus looked down.

"Are you sure it worked?"

"Vasectomies are about ninety-nine percent effective. So yeah. I'm sure."

Callie's mind was swirling. If Gus had had a vasectomy, then how had Xeni gotten pregnant? Did vasectomies ever fail? Could it be a miracle? Callie felt all the confusion and guilt of the last nine months fall away, and felt new emotions rise—awe and elation. Xeni was pregnant. Callie had tried her best to bring it about, and whether through the power of good intention or the ultimate power of love, a miracle had occurred. Xeni's wish had come true.

"Gus, when you asked Xeni at the church how she got pregnant, what did she say?"

"How'd we get back to Xeni?"

"Do you remember? What did she say?" Callie asked again.

Gus shrugged. "She didn't say anything."

Callie rushed out of the waiting room and out into the hall, looking up and down the wide corridor to see if she could catch a glimpse of Xeni. *It was meant to be. This was all meant to be. From that first moment when we met in the grocery store.*

"Hey! Callie! Where are you going? You didn't tell me! What's your secret?" Gus called out at her retreating back.

"I don't have any more secrets, Gus!" Callie cried as she started running down the halls searching for Xeni. She wanted nothing more than to find Xeni and to be with her as their miracle baby emerged into the world.

Birth

The new self, filled with ideas to forget, and wisdom to relearn, tries unsuccessfully to turn, to readjust, to get comfortable, and finally enters a phase of willingness. As this moment forms, so does a new thought: *What else?* As the connections are made between desire and impulse, the corporeal form starts to secrete a whirling substance that rises and floats from its body, coloring the amniotic fluid with an unexpected directive. The substance triggers another substance in the body of its host, which in turn triggers another substance, and it is as if a key has turned in some ancient lock allowing the possibility of release. Release from the comforting embrace of the womb and out into the unknown. As the bloody key falls out of the lock, and into the outside world, the process of emergence begins. The liquid drains from the cramped chamber, and a pinprick of light begins to slowly enlarge as the mighty cervix begins its process of opening the gates to the world, with all of its imperfections and adventures. The self, about to become a human child, with all of its accompanying labels and legends, begins its slow descent through the bony passageway of the pelvis, head first, with chin tucked down into its chest. The womb, no longer a place of rest, becomes active, contracting and expanding to create waves of movement that help push the self along. No longer padded by the cushion of watery membranes and sensing that there is no turning back on this road, it willingly follows the compulsion to immigrate by pressing its pliable head against the cervix, dilating it further with each push until the passage is fully open. The self, pressing on the portal to the world, turns its head toward the opening and, unable to catch a glimpse, cranes its head backward. On the precipice between two worlds, it rests for a moment with the cervix hugging its crown, until the next big wave hits, and it pushes against the walls of the womb with its feet, cranes its head back again, and feels a pop as its head emerges into a waterless and blindingly bright place. It turns its head away from the light and toward the thigh of the woman who is home—and in a fast-forward flash the child emerges all at once; a shoulder pops out, another wriggle, another shoulder, and it suddenly catapults outward, chest, heart, back, legs, and feet at last out into the new world. Taking its first breath, with lungs freshly wrung dry by the journey, it inflates and hovers, exhales. It rests with the knowledge that it has forever left the body, its homeland, and is filled with a hunger so intense that it screams with the desire to return to what is known, what is familiar, and weeps with the sudden knowledge that what once was, is lost, and what is, is unknown. With that thought, the child is lifted onto the belly of its mother. It nests into her deflated womb, closes its wailing mouth onto her nipple, and finds divine comfort in suckling the tiny drops of honey that emerge.

Marina

My daughter. I am holding my daughter in my arms. My sweet, amazingly new, perfect child. She has my eyes and mouth. Her hands are strong. One day she'll hold a knife in her hands and slice ripe watermelon into thick slices and we'll eat it in our sunny garden, juices running down our arms.

My daughter. She is real after all. This first year has gone by so quickly. I remember when I first brought her home. She cried and pooped and screamed all night. She clamped down on my nipples and sucked until I bled. She was so hungry, and I could never give her enough. Now while she nurses I can see words floating through the quiet air of our bedroom, "*Manoula, tha se faw.*" She will eat me alive, and I will willingly give her my flesh, milk, blood, heart, whatever she needs to grow strong and feel loved. She will always feel loved.

So many people love her. My world used to be so small, just me and my desires, bitter and hopeful. They used to fill my mouth with a cottony numbing regret, like when you eat a persimmon before it's ripe. But now, the world is expansive. I have a family. They have all gathered round in our home to love her, and celebrate her first birthday. They love her so much that they forget to fight with each other. They sing her songs and rhymes in Greek. We gather together in the dining room and eat and eat. We pass her around from one pair of loving arms to another, Penny, Gus, even Mrs. Horiatis has come to visit. Manolaki is just big enough

353

to carefully hold her in his lap. He and Penny's kids all stand in a circle around me and gently touch her toes and fingers. They call her little sister, *athelfoula*. But she always comes back to me to rest, to find comfort, to eat.

And Callie. After everything, Callie did learn how to be a good Greek wife. And she taught me a lot about how to be a good mother. I see God in her eyes, an unshakable faith and infinite love. She can make miracles happen.

What is God?

God is in the kitchen.

It is the same as when you put water, yeast, olive oil, and flour in a bowl. You don't know how it happens, but it does. The separate ingredients join and rise into something wondrous. The scent of it makes your heart happy and open, the warmth of it in your hands is reassuring and safe. God gave us bread to remind us of what humans can do on this Earth.

Put together the ingredients, say a little prayer, and watch as the miracles rise.

Acknowledgments

This book was sparked out of a deep need to heal and process my grief after miscarrying my first baby at ten and a half weeks, when I thought I was almost out of my first trimester and safe. There is silence around miscarriage and loss, and I needed a place to express all of my sadness, anger, unacceptable thoughts, and unending longing for a baby. When my baby's heart stopped, Xeni was born, and my thirst for a miracle began. After years of infertility, I truly never thought I'd have a baby, and endured a second miscarriage along the way. So first I'd like to acknowledge all the women who have lost a baby and continued on despite carrying that huge hole in their heart. I see you and your strength and loss.

Thankfully, life has shown me that miracles do happen, and that they come in threes. Somehow through the miracles of science and God, and perhaps my persistent nature, I now have three brilliant, kind, funny, smart, and amazing children who are my sun and moon and reason for living. I love you with all my heart Skyler, Theoni, and Apollo. Thank you for choosing me to be your mother.

Around the time of my first miscarriage, I had just started an MFA program in Creative Writing at San

Francisco State University. What interesting timing that I would experience such a significant life experience within a laboratory to write. During that time I was lucky enough to work with Toni Mirosevich who taught me to leap fearlessly, Nina Schuyler who introduced me to the art and craft of writing a novel, Maxine Chernoff who encouraged me to trust my instincts, and Robert Gluck who made me feel I could never be too weird. Also during that time I met my writing group partners, The Quintet, who over the years read so many versions of this novel it would make your head spin. Thank you, Patti Wang Cross for always getting me and my work in the deepest of ways, Maggie Harrison, Dan Johnson, and Eva Guralnik.

I'd also like to thank both Martha Klironomos and the Modern Greek Studies department at San Francisco State University for giving me an important grounding in my culture and Greek American literature within an academic setting and honoring me with the Thanasis Maskaleris Scholarship.

I have such gratitude for all the writers I have met in my travels. You have become my virtual writing community who have inspired me, shown me the way, and given me hope. Seeing your books on my shelf keeps me going.

Thank you, Brooke Warner for seeing the promise in this book and pushing me to reach ever higher than I imagined I could. You are a true writer's advocate and a dazzling guiding light.

Hilary Zaid you are the kindest, most generous writer friend I could have ever dreamed up. You stood by me and opened paths, held my hand and put up with me. You are an amazing editor. Thank you.

There are no words to describe the gratitude I feel toward the brilliant Salem West, who surprised me on April Fool's day with an offer of publication with

Bywater Books. She urged me to apply for the GCLS Writing Academy and the Sandra Moran Scholarship, and I was awarded both to my great honor. Salem, your encouragement kept me on this writer's path when I was about to give up. While I can be prone to exaggeration, this is one time that I can sincerely say you have made my dream come true and I will always, always be grateful. Thank you to Ann McMan for your kind words, good humor, and gorgeous cover design.

Eternal thanks to the Golden Crown Literary Society and their wonderful Writing Academy. I am actively creating new writing community and it feels like coming home.

Thank you to Willy Wilkinson for your support, belief, and feedback over time.

Over the years I searched for a place to feel comfortable as a first-generation Greek American femme lesbian. Until my thirties, I literally thought I was the only Greek lesbian, and that is also a huge part of why I wrote this book. I needed to write us into existence. I have collected as many Greek LGBTQ+ friends as possible and as this book is released out into the world, please know that I wrote it for all of us, with great love.

Thank you to Alexandra Kostoulas for inviting me into a Greek American writing community and letting me read and write alongside you. Thank you to Patricia V. Davis for your Italian magic, you'll always be Greek to me. Also, I cannot forget my time spent with the Moms and Tots group of the Greek Orthodox Cathedral of the Ascension. It was my first attempt to enter a Greek church community as my full self, and I am grateful to those moms who welcomed me in. The Ascension Cathedral holds a special place in this book. It is both a symbol of home and of exile for me, and it brings me to tears each time I enter those cool, serene walls.

As most of my relatives are in Greece, I'll raise a glass to them, the faraway family I always long for and love. Thank you to my sister, Athens Kolias, who enthusiastically cheers me on and whose creativity and intelligence I sincerely respect. Big love to my sister from another mother, Alexandra Threadgill-Inouye. Your steady presence in my life has brought me so much comfort. And to the woman who taught me to love with my whole heart, my mother, Christina Kolias, the original Fierce Greek Mama. No matter what we went through growing up I knew one thing for sure—my mother loves me with the power of a thousand shining stars and I have always rested easy in that knowledge.

Alex Delgado, you caught me by surprise. I wasn't expecting you to come into my life like a force of nature. You are larger than life, my sweet ferocious brute. I love every day by your side and live for your laughter. Thank you for loving me, and giving me your gifts of humor, intelligence, passion, loyalty, and honor. I love you enough for a thousand lifetimes.

I can't possibly name every name or kindness, but I want to thank every generous soul who has walked alongside me on this journey. Your love, belief, and support kept me going.

And a special thanks to the angel who sparked this story, and whispered it into my ear.

About the Author

Georgia Kolias grew up in a traditional working-class Greek immigrant family in San Francisco during a time of queer liberation. She was deeply influenced by both the unchanging ritual and interdependence of Greek culture, and the American values of freedom and individuality, and always seeks to embody both. She holds an MFA in Creative Writing and an MA in English from San Francisco State University. Her first person essays have appeared in *The Huffington Post*, *Advocate.com*, *The Manifest-Station*, *Role Reboot*, *Everyday Feminism*, *When Women Waken*, and various anthologies.

Georgia has spent her professional life chasing the written word, and has worked as an acquisitions editor, a teacher of creative writing, a bookseller, at the public library, and in literary management. Georgia lives in Oakland, California with her three beautiful children. *The Feasting Virgin* is her first novel.

You can find her at www.georgiakolias.com, on Facebook at Georgia Kolias, Author and on Twitter @georgiakolias.

Bywater
BOOKS

At Bywater Books we love good books about lesbians just like you do, and we're committed to bringing the best of contemporary lesbian writing to our avid readers. Our editorial team is dedicated to finding and developing outstanding writers who create books you won't want to put down.

We sponsor the Bywater Prize for Fiction to help with this quest. Each prizewinner receives $1,000 and publication of their novel. We have already discovered amazing writers like Jill Malone, Sally Bellerose, and Hilary Sloin through the Bywater Prize. Which exciting new writer will we find next?

For more information about Bywater Books and the annual Bywater Prize for Fiction, please visit our website.

www.bywaterbooks.com